The Incident in the Orchard

Cecilie H Ralph

First published in 2022
Copyright 2022 © Cecilie H Ralph

The right of Cecilie H Ralph to be identified as the author of this work has been asserted in accordance with the Copyright, Designs and Patents Act of 1988.
All rights reserved. No part of this book may be used or reproduced by any means, electronic or mechanical, including photocopying, without the publisher's written permission.

The Incident in the Orchard is work of fiction. All names, characters, organisations, places, and events are either products of the author's imagination or used fictitiously. Any resemblance to actual persons, living or dead, or real events is entirely coincidental.

First e-book edition June 2022

Cover design and formatting by www.ebookdesigner.co.uk

Prologue

Thinking themselves unseen, Isabella and her friends shook the ripe apples from the tree and gathered them up from the ground. She bit into one. It tasted juicy and sweet. It was well worth the trek from the town to the orchard, where they were guaranteed a good crop.

As Isabella bent down to pick up another apple, a man's irate voice rang out through the trees ordering them off his land. It was the gentleman from Aldwen Hall, to whom the orchard belonged. Furious at the theft of his fruit, he looked menacing as he advanced towards them.

In terror, the young thieves took to their heels.

The Hall's cape-coated owner knew it would be impossible to catch them all. Even if he were to march a couple of them the two miles to the local constabulary, they would likely be let off with a warning and a quick clip around the ear; only to return the following year. Satisfied they were on their way, he turned back to the house.

Believing herself to be at a safe distance, Isabella, in a moment of peevish impetuosity, grabbed the largest apple she could see and lobbed it at the landowner's retreating back. The projectile hit its target squarely between the shoulder blades, winding him in the process. A weaker man might have buckled, but not this one. Toughened by years of military service and training, he made a rapid recovery from the assault. Then with a sudden burst of anger-fuelled energy, he set off in pursuit of his prey.

Isabella, having realised she had badly miscalculated the distance between herself and the man, instantly regretted her action. In a heart-pounding panic she ran like a gazelle from a hungry lion, hoping he would lose interest and abort the chase. Unfortunately, the rough, tortuous path served to hinder her progress. Alas, her nemesis was precipitated by a protruding tree root which clipped the toecap of her scuffed boot. In ignominious fashion she tripped, stumbled forward and landed with a painful thud on the compacted ground.

Upon her in seconds, the aggrieved victim of her aggression hoisted her up by the scruff and smartly dispensed her come-uppance.

Chapter 1

Three years later…

Isabella Acton stood with her friends on the freshly cut grass verge of Oakwich town's main thoroughfare under a dazzling sun perched high in a delphinium-blue sky. She was among a crowd of onlookers watching the rushbearing procession march by. The procession was led by a booming brass band and accompanied by a colourful troupe of Morris dancers with bright ribbons and jingling bells strapped to their legs. The annual event was an ancient tradition in which a group of parishioners paraded through the town bearing new rushes for the church floor. Although the church floor was no longer covered in rushes the custom endured.

Like a whoop of chimpanzees at a tea party, Isabella and her friends laughed, joked and clowned around. The fun of the festival provided a welcome diversion from the daily difficulties plaguing her personal life. Each time the crowd cheered, clapped and whistled, she joined in, bobbing up and down with unashamed bonhomie.

That same afternoon, Major Hereward Aldwen was also in town on a matter of business at the bank. As he thrust his way through the riotous throng, his attention settled on the form of a young female on the footpath opposite. With her chalky curls, subtly contoured cheekbones, nubile figure, and smile revealing the kind of dentition seldom seen outside the pages of fancy magazines, she stood out like a beacon on a hill.

The Major was well acquainted with the quintessence of beautiful womanhood; however, there was something singularly compelling about this particular young bloom that he found difficult to define. She wasn't the typical English rose held up by society as the epitome of prettiness; her mouth was a little too large, her lips a touch too generous, her whorled hair a tad too wild and unwieldy. Set against the light-golden tone of her complexion, her pelagic-green eyes bore a commanding brilliance. And although her worn clothes and weathered boots indicated a distinct dearth of resources, they in no way diminished her loveliness.

Scratching the top of his head, the Major stared at the mesmeric young woman with an intensity contrary to his connate self-containment. There was something vaguely familiar about her face that he couldn't quite place. Then, after studying her for several more moments, a light switched on in the vault of his memory. Good gracious me! he said to himself. It was the feisty young thief he had chased from his orchard, now almost full grown and on the cusp of womanhood.

As the procession rounded a bend and disappeared from sight, most of the crowd dispersed and the road reopened to traffic. However, the subject of the Major's fascination and her playful pack continued their tomfoolery as they headed towards the town's square, still laughing, joking and teasing one another.

Tracking their movements with an eagle-eyed absorption, the Major noticed a juvenile chap clinging to the seraphic blonde like a heel dog awaiting its next command. He begrudged the young buck's liberties, especially the flirtatious manner in which he nudged, pushed and prodded her. And he pondered on whether the lad's behaviour indicated a budding romance between the teenage two. Much as he would have liked to continue observing them, he was obliged to honour his appointment, so with reluctance went on his way.

The following day the Major was afflicted by a severe case of lovesickness. The man was besotted. His nascent preoccupation with his prepossessing discovery upset both his physical and mental equilibrium: sleep evaded him, concentration proved impossible, work was out of the question. Night and day her image haunted his consciousness and refused to leave. Yet he knew nothing about her, not even her name.

Desperate to locate her, he cut a sombre figure clad in dark clothing, topped with an equally dark hat, wandering the streets of Oakwich in search of a young lady with whom he was largely unacquainted yet powerless to purge from his mind; no matter how hard he tried.

A week later, fearing her forever gone, the Major spotted his infatuation entering a second-hand bookshop on a cobbled lane just off the high street. After following her into the gloomy interior, he stole to the back of the overstocked store. And there amongst stacks of dust-coated books crowding the floor, he listened to her negotiating with the bookseller over some leather-bound novels she seemed desperate to sell.

The Major wondered why anyone would wish to part with such fine volumes. They brought his own comprehensive collection to mind. In his view, books were treasures to be preserved regardless of age, condition or contents. He could never dispose of a book, not even when he felt certain it would never be opened again.

As he continued to listen in to the young woman's plaintive petitions, the comparison between her genteel linguistic refinement and apparent poverty struck him as somewhat curious and he knew not what to make of the incongruity.

After agreeing a price with the bookseller, she left the books behind on the counter, thanked him for the money he placed in her hand, and departed the shop.

The moment the door closed behind her, the Major strode over to the counter, lifted the front cover on the book at the top of the pile and read the short dedication: *To Isabella on the occasion of your birthday. With love Mama and Papa xxx.*

The discovery of her name was the Major's first sign of progress. Such a romantic name too; it rolled off the tongue in a smooth euphonic undulation. Like a man on a mission, he hurried out of the bookshop, noted her direction and set off in eager pursuit. To enable him to make discreet enquiries about her background and personal circumstances, he thought her address might prove useful.

It soon became apparent that the young woman was as nimble, as agile and as floaty as a ballerina. Her footfalls barely registered on the ancient cobbles as she made her way along a thoroughfare in the town's centuries-old quarter which led to a plexus of passages and alleyways.

To avoid alerting her to his presence, the Major tried to tread soundlessly on the echoey footways. Not an easy feat by any means. Concerned his loping footsteps might soon overtake her dainty ones, he shortened his stride and synchronised his footwork with hers in order to maintain an exact measure of distance between them. Still, he felt like a gryphon following a fawn, and a couple of times he even questioned the wisdom of his quest.

Midway down a crumbling brick-lined corridor with a flagstone floor and a sour whiff of urine, vomit and who knew what else, the girl came to an abrupt halt and bent down to fasten her bootlaces.

To avoid running into her protuberant rear, the Major came to an abrupt halt too, held his breath and hoped she wouldn't turn around.

Satisfied her battered black boots were secure, she straightened back up again, smoothed down her old gingham skirt and resumed walking at a steady pace. When she reached the end of the corridor, she turned into a paved passageway too narrow for vehicles and carts. The ease with which she navigated the network of walkways suggested she was local to the area and must therefore be close to her place of residence. Finally sensing there was someone behind her, but without glancing back, she broke into a rapid run and disappeared from sight.

Deflated but not discouraged, the Major returned to the bookshop.

Chapter 2

According to the bespectacled bookseller, the girl's full name was Miss Isabella Acton. Unfortunately for the Major, the man suffered from a severe case of verbosity; however, since it suited his purpose, he wasn't complaining on this occasion.

"She's one of my regulars," said the bookseller, peering over his metal half-moon spectacles. "Comes here quite often as it happens. The pawnbrokers too, or so I'm told." He paused and pulled on the point of his grey goatee. "Fine-looking young lady, if I might be permitted to say so. Archibald and Agatha Acton, they're her parents by the way, were once very wealthy, but fell on bad times a while back. Rumour has it, it had something to do with risky investments. What with that and the father's libertine lifestyle. Not that I'm one to gossip you understand." He paused again; this time to dislodge a food particle stuck between his tea-stained teeth with a ridged fingernail. "They had to let go most of their staff, including the family retainer. A most unfortunate state of affairs." He shook his head. "I doubt they've got anything left to…"

The Major was forced to interrupt. "You don't happen to know where Miss Acton lives by any chance do you?"

"As a matter of fact, Sir, I do. It's not too far from here as it happens."

The Major left the bookshop with Isabella's address written on a small slip of paper and her relinquished books in a brown-paper package secured with string.

One must assume, he reasoned to himself as he strode back to his motorcar, there was sure to be a legion of admirers competing for the adorable Miss Acton's affections. Such uncommon beauty would without doubt attract a rush of romantic interest.

The premise left him contemplating desperate action. He was a fiercely competitive man with a reputation for ruthlessness when circumstances demanded. The numerous awards, trophies and prizes on show in his library testified to his physical and academic excellence. He believed he possessed the power to influence outcomes and he would use any means at his disposal to achieve his aims.

Returning to his house that instant, the Major went straight to his desk and penned a letter to Miss Acton's father. The letter, addressed to: *Archibald Acton Esquire*, was written on watermarked vellum paper and signed with a flourish. Its contents included his personal details, educational, sporting and military achievements, excellent prospects, his marriage proposal, and a request for a meeting at Mr Acton's earliest convenience.

Major Hereward Henry George Aldwen, to furnish him with his full title, was a thirty-two-year-old former army officer who had served the bulk of his distinguished career in India, before growing tired of military life; especially military life in India. Although there was much to be admired about the subcontinent and its people, Hereward found the commotion and chaos there exhausting. The citizens' *go-with-God* fatalistic attitude to life often drove him to distraction. Nonetheless, he observed a peculiar kind of paradox: that beneath the disorder prevailed a strange kind of order that, given time, one ultimately got to grips with. But on the whole, India was far too populous for a man of Hereward's temperament and disposition. Even in small villages a crowd could collect at a couple of hand claps or finger clicks. He found crowds, wherever they were in the world, confining and claustrophobic; especially hot-climate crowds with their overpowering miasma of body odour and medley of competing, discordant sounds.

Following years of boarding school and cantonment life, Hereward nursed a deep desire to be alone. However, he found it impossible to shake off the habits of a lifetime of institutionalisation imposed on him from an early age. Being of an obsessive bent, he found routines reassuring. Any deviation from his orderly lifestyle made him grumpy, impatient and ill-humoured.

After resigning his commission, Hereward returned home to his English country residence, Aldwen Hall, set in acres of ancient woodland and pleasant pasture. Boyle, his faithful butler, who also doubled as his valet, ensured the household ran as smooth as a tram on a track. Both men were formal, old-fashioned and conservative to a fault. Henceforth, Hereward devoted his daily life to recording military history, his contribution to which was already significant. He spent the greater part of his day undisturbed at his desk in the library, where he adhered strictly to his chosen hours of academic enquiry and writing. By nature, restrained and reclusive, he was content in his own company and never felt lonely. He left the Hall only when necessary and seldom travelled beyond Oakwich, except to visit the theatre occasionally and his London publisher. Unlike most of his class and generation, Hereward loathed large social gatherings, parties, balls, and any event with more than a handful of people in attendance. Dinner parties in particular were anathema to him and he avoided them like the plague.

Sad to say, he suffered from late-onset asthma precipitated

by an equine allergy and no longer rode. Exposure to most, if not all, animals left him wheezing and gasping for breath. The stables at Aldwen Hall lay empty; a great misfortune for a man who loved being in the saddle and playing polo. However, he accepted his condition with equanimity and remained well provided he avoided his triggers.

In line with ancient tradition, the Aldwen family practised primogeniture, whereby property passes from father to firstborn son, thereby putting pressure on Hereward to produce the requisite heir. This presented him with a dilemma: in the interests of his bloodline's prolongation should he marry the human equivalent of a brood mare? If he were to die childless, then the estate would pass automatically to his younger brother. Except his younger brother was also unmarried and in no hurry to quit the bachelorhood.

The thought of a woman disrupting his precious peace and quiet on a permanent basis filled Hereward with horror. All those foolish frills, tiresome tassels and pointless bric-à-brac he associated with the female sex were a burden he refused to bear. In India he found most of his unmarried female compatriots insular, snooty and shallow. Husband hunters he called them. They bored him to death. Back in Britain he felt the same. Once a woman served her purpose, he was glad to see the back of her. Even after he rebuffed them, some hopefuls were slow to take the hint and lounged about smoothing their skirts and powdering their expectant faces until, with a lordly tact, he offered to telephone a taxicab to take them home.

There was, however, one hard-nosed huntress who remained under the erroneous impression that he and she shared a future. The idea of marriage to that marbleise mare made Hereward's blood run cold. In wifely terms she was his worst nightmare. But since he wasn't a sadhu, he continued to partake of her exceptional favours. He considered her, on the rare occasions he could be bothered to consider her, to be a pushy woman whose abiding passions pivoted on her matrimonial ambitions and physical appearance. She painted her long visage with painstaking attention to detail. Never once had he seen her without her 'face' on, although he had seen her as often as not without her clothes on.

Hereward suspected there was a degree of sophistry in the way some women brazenly exposed their bare bodies to him, but never their bare faces. Of all his lovers Rosalyn was the most amenable. He enjoyed making love to her, as did she. And he couldn't help but admire her confidence, her chutzpah, her disregard for convention; when it suited her to disregard convention. In India she had been one of the infamous 'fishing fleet' in search of a husband owing to the reduced numbers of young marriageable men in Britain after the Great War. Some women looked for a mate beyond their own male-unpopulated pools and a fair few sailed for the colonies. In Bombay there were prostitutes aplenty, but man-chasing spinsters like his lady friend made sure the officers' needs were well met. She had even followed him home to England and relocated to Oakwich town to be close to Aldwen Hall. Hence, they continued where they left off, and in much the same vein. But he could never have married her, never in a million years.

Chapter 3

As Archibald Acton perused Major Aldwen's correspondence, he dared to hope that the submerging tide of financial misfortune had finally begun to subside. After twice reading the letter, he endeavoured to acquaint himself with the character and repute of its author. Via the grapevine he was delighted to discover the Major was a man of refinement, erudition and, most important of all, considerable means. Despite not knowing the fellow on a personal level, Mr Acton persuaded himself it was prudent to give full consideration to such an unusual yet promising proposal. Having Isabella married off prematurely would be a blessing, since it would mean one less problem to worry about. She would be another man's headache. As things stood, she needed to be taken in hand by someone capable of controlling her excesses; his chief concern being the company she kept, specifically the company of those from the lower classes. One never knew where such liaisons might lead. Plus, the Major's maturity in age was additionally advantageous, since a gentleman wise in the ways of the world would exert a greater influence over his wayward daughter than some soppy callow boy.

A week later Hereward arrived at the Acton's residence. Located in the most-select and salubrious district of Oakwich, it stood in a semi-circle of similar properties behind tall iron railings topped with spikes overlooking the public park. From where he stood, Hereward could see a group of young people milling around the Victorian bandstand on the newly mown grass. The herbaceous aroma prickled his nose, but not unpleasantly. With a critical eye, he surveyed the façade of the family's once-splendid property and noted a chronic lack of maintenance and repair. The edges of the grimy stone steps showed signs of crumbling, while the paint was slowly peeling from the neo-classical front door.

With a slight sneer, Hereward raised the tarnished brass knocker, which protested with a painful creak, and rapped it thrice in rapid succession. An absence of response made him wonder if he had the right address until footsteps could be heard dragging behind the front door. Drawing back a little, he waited for what he assumed would be the butler to open up.

Instead, the door was opened by a hoary, sour-faced old maid in a faded grey uniform. After he identified himself, she invited him in. He then tagged her shuffling steps down the dull chequerboard hallway floor and into the study, where she mumbled his name and shuffled back out again.

The moment Hereward appeared in the doorway, Isabella's father sprang to his feet, extended his arm and gave his visitor's hand a vigorous shake.

"Major Aldwen, welcome. This is indeed an honour. Pray, be seated," he said gesturing to the chair opposite his.

Taking care, Archibald Acton lowered himself into his seat and rubbed his swollen kneecaps, sorely regretting the alacrity with which he had risen to greet his guest. Don't appear too desperate, he warned himself, as he leaned back and steepled his fingers over his bloated belly. It was plain to see the years had not spared him: his shoulders drooped, his cheeks sagged and his face furrowed deep. One could be forgiven for thinking he was a decade older at least.

Before speaking, Archibald Acton cast a cursory eye over the cursive of Hereward's letter, which lay unfolded on the desk. "Major," he began, "I have read your letter with the greatest interest, and have considered your request with the utmost seriousness. It's not every day one receives such an ardent proposition. Although, as I'm sure you'll appreciate, Isabella is not short of admirers, many of whom are top-drawer. Still, I'm delighted to tell you that I'm fully satisfied your intentions towards my dear daughter are honourable and sincere. I therefore accept your marriage proposal on her behalf. There is, however, one condition that is not negotiable." He paused, crossed one leg over the other and compressed his insipid lips.

Hereward remained motionless as he waited with baited breath.

Archibald Acton uncrossed his legs, leaned forward, cleared his throat, and presented his case: "That upon marriage a sum of fifty-thousand pounds be settled on Isabella's name."

Hereward's cheeks inflated a little as he exhaled with relief. However, not wishing to appear too amenable, nor trusting the reprobate before him, he consented to the proposition provided his own terms of agreement be cited in the contract: first, that the money be placed in trust with himself as sole trustee; second, that Isabella should not be permitted to access the fund until she came of age on her twenty-first birthday. In the meantime, she would be afforded a small monthly income from part of the interest accrued on the balance.

Since Hereward wished to avoid a long engagement, he insisted the wedding arrangements be expedited without delay. Such hare-brained hastiness was antithetical to his usual level-headedness, more especially since he lacked experience in matrimonial matters. Notwithstanding, he was wise to men like his future father-in-law. He found it difficult to believe the creature seated opposite him had fathered Miss Acton. It was patently obvious that Archibald Acton *Esquire* was more interested in the generous loan he had wheedled out of his soon-to-be son-in-law than he was in his daughter's happiness and wellbeing.

Both satisfied with the outcome of their negotiations, the two men shook hands firmly. After which Archibald Acton called his wife into the study to meet their daughter's fiancé. Placing a fatherly hand on Hereward's back, he invited him to return the following afternoon to meet Isabella; who was yet to discover her destiny had been decided in her absence.

The moment Hereward took his leave, Archibald Acton smiled at his wife, placed his palms together and looked heavenward in a gesture of gratitude. At last, their prayers had been answered.

Chapter 4

Isabella felt baffled by her father's summons. Archibald Acton had shown little interest in her since the day she was born. He and her mother had made no secret of the fact that they would have preferred a son. As things stood, she was just another expense they could ill afford. That morning the maid had happened to mention in passing that Mr Acton had received a visitor the previous day whose name she couldn't recall. But Isabella, who happened to be out at the time, attached no significance to the intelligence.

The air in her father's study was sullied by a damp musty odour as the fire was never lit and the windows kept closed even in summer. Against a backdrop of bare bookcases, Archibald Acton was seated at an old rosewood desk that had journeyed down generations of his progenitors. With no consideration for his daughter's feelings, he cleared his throat and came straight to the point.

"My dear child, I have received a proposal," he informed her with a bullish smile before glancing at the back of the room. "An excellent proposal, I might add, for your hand in marriage to an honourable and upstanding gentleman by the name of Major Aldwen. Which you'll be pleased to hear I have accepted on your behalf."

"What!?" For a second, Isabella half assumed she had misunderstood or misheard her father. Then as soon as the veracity of his statement hit home, the blood drained from her face. She had never heard of a Major Aldwen. The name belonged to a stranger. Although she did wonder whether he was in any way connected to the Aldwen estate on the edge of Oakwich. But then she knew few people from her own social milieu. After they lost their fortune, the Actons soon became society outcasts and nowadays they received few visitors and even fewer invitations.

"What marriage proposal? Which gentleman? Who is this person, Papa?" she asked with mounting consternation.

Expecting her to be biddable, Archibald Acton smiled, rose from his chair and gestured to the back of the room.

As Isabella turned, her eyes grew enormous, her mouth dropped open and her hands gripped her face. In the shadows stood a tall figure she had failed to notice upon her arrival in the room. Nevertheless, she recognised him in an instant. There was no mistaking him. It was the man from whose orchard she had pilfered a huge pile of apples and whose back she had struck with the plumpest, heaviest one.

Major Aldwen looked imposing in a dark custom-made suit worn over a crisp white shirt and blue-silk necktie. The fine quality of his attire contrasted sharply with Isabella's wrinkled old skirt and washed-out blouse.

Smiling, he made towards her.

In alarm, Isabella stepped back in order to reinstate the distance between them.

Undeterred by his daughter's adverse reaction, Archibald Acton made the introductions: "Isabella, please allow me to present to you Major Aldwen. Major Hereward Aldwen, the gentleman to whom you are now betrothed."

The Major smiled again, bowed a little and said: "Miss Acton, we meet anew. I trust you are well."

His voice was rich, deep and dynamic with vivid undertones. His reference to their brief but significant encounter three years previous made its mark and the slight smirk around his mouth caused her blanched cheeks to flush crimson. Then to her dismay, his probing eyes, suffused with excitement, swept over her form with the intensity of a searchlight beam.

Transfixed, Isabella stared at her black-bearded suitor with a mixture of eye-popping horror and fascination. Strong, powerful and athletic, he stood erect, possessed of a bold and confident carriage. He was a tad less tall than she recalled, most probably because she herself had grown a few inches since their first encounter. Notwithstanding, this made him appear no less forbidding. His short sable-black hair, high forehead, light-brown complexion, dark-grey eyes, and angular jaw gave him something of an Iberian flavour. Isabella also observed a barely perceptible scar below the Cupid's bow of his upper lip and wondered what had caused it.

Something undefinable in the Major's expression made Isabella want to fade into the wall like an apparition. Trembling all over with a combination of trepidation and internal rage, her chest rising and falling in a rapid rhythmical motion, she shrank from his penetrant gaze. As the walls of the airless room bore down on her like a megalith, she began to sway. Convinced she was about to collapse, panic engulfing her petite frame, she grabbed the back of the nearest chair for support. Placing her hand on her breast, she tried to stay calm, but calm proved elusive.

As she stood in a state of sheer inexpressible shock, Isabella attempted to weigh up her options. What options? She had no options. Not a single one. Being fully conversant with the certitude of her father's rulings, she knew he would disown her should she choose to defy him. Then what would she do and where would she go? Her aspirations, her ambitions, her dreams of academic achievement, had been dashed in one single blow. Without bothering to excuse herself, Isabella fled the room and the confounded faces of both her father and unforeseen fiancé.

Mrs Agatha Acton was sitting beside the hearth in the cheerless sitting room perusing a well-thumbed periodical when her daughter burst through the door looking visibly shaken.

"Mama, is it really true that I'm betrothed to that frightful fellow in Papa's study, and have you had anything to do with this cruel decision to marry me off to a man who must surely be almost old enough to be my father?"

Mrs Acton remained unmoved. She admitted to being informed of the Major's proposal some days previous and was wholly in favour of the union, since she believed it to be an excellent match. She also held the view that Isabella should be grateful her future life, all being well, would be a comfortable and prosperous one; even more so in view of their straitened circumstances.

"Really, my dear child," she advised, "I do hope you haven't been filling your pretty little head with silly notions of love and romance. I can assure you such things exist only between the covers of cheap novels and trashy magazines."

Isabella disagreed: "Nowadays no-one marries for the sake of convenience. Not even those of noble birth. Everyone marries for love. It's what makes us human. Otherwise, how do we differ from beasts?"

Agatha Acton, a hard-hearted and unemotional woman remained resolute. In her restricted view of the world, well-chosen marital alliances were essential to the survival of long-established customs and traditions peculiar to their class. She conceded that modern-day relations between the sexes were less formal and constrained than in previous eras, but insisted that, for the most part, people still preferred to stick to their own sort.

To support her contention, Isabella's mother, whose upper lip was normally as stiff as a stanchion, resorted to the use of a little emotional manipulation. Disregarding her daughter's obvious distress, in a contrived trembly voice she said: "My dear child, we can no longer afford to keep you. Your being married means we will have one less burden to bear. Knowing you are well taken care of will be a huge weight off our shoulders. Should you decide to renege on our agreement with Major Aldwen, which will be nigh impossible since we have already given him our word, and the terrible stress causes your dear Papa to suffer a heart attack and die, then I shall hold you personally responsible. And I shall never forgive you. The opportunity is one that will not be repeated, so we cannot afford to refuse the Major."

As Isabella stood listening to her mother's justifications, it occurred to her how little her parents cared for her future happiness.

Chapter 5

Despite her vehement protestations, Isabella was to be married once the banns had been posted on the church door and read out during Mass on three consecutive Sundays. Every night before climbing into bed she knelt and prayed that an impediment to the marriage would be revealed in good time to prevent it going ahead.

During his negotiations with her father, Hereward had insisted on a short engagement. To his mind, the sooner he and Isabella were welded in wedlock the better. A view Archibald Acton fully endorsed in anticipation of the pecuniary and societal advantages he hoped the union would confer on him.

Isabella was more than mystified by the Major's proposal. Except for the brief but memorable incident in the orchard three years previous, they were complete strangers. Why a rich gentleman of obvious good standing should wish to marry a destitute girl he had once chased from his land was beyond her comprehension. But then she knew little of men and even less of men's lust. She was too young and unseasoned to know the Major's compulsive craving for her was driven by a primitive libidinous impulse that sent normally sane men mad with desire.

In the interim Archibald and Agatha Acton decided it would benefit the prospective bride and groom to become better acquainted before the wedding, both convinced that once Isabella spent an afternoon in the company of her betrothed, all her doubts would be dispelled.

A few days later Hereward arrived at the Acton's house, excited at the prospect of spending the afternoon in the company of his heart's desire. The thought of her exquisite face and figure thrilled him to his core. He likened the sensation to taking a sneak peek at a present days before being granted permission to remove the entire wrapping and partake of the wonderful contents within. Having to wait almost a month to get married was an agony and the day of the wedding could not come soon enough.

To impress Miss Acton Hereward wore an elegant linen suit over a lawn-cotton shirt and burgundy-silk bow tie. A straw boater in an appetising shade of cream completed the outfit. His feet, not to be outshone by the ensemble, were clad in fine tan-leather oxford brogues. In his right hand he carried a single red rose, while under his left arm he held a box of chocolate-coated candies.

The shuffling old maid showed him into the drab drawing room redolent of soot and a decade's dust on the drapes. Dressed in their faded fineries, Archibald and Agatha Acton stood ready to receive him. They greeted him warmly and invited him to be seated on an old horsehair sofa opposite the hearth. To Hereward's dismay, there was neither sight nor sound of his intended.

"We're expecting her shortly," said her affectedly cheerful father with false assurance. "She had some errands to run and appears to have been unavoidably delayed."

Hereward frowned to himself at the dubiety of Archibald Acton's explanation. However, for the sake of politeness, he accepted the couple's invitation to take tea with them. And while he supped from a scuffed china cup, dined on flat crumpets and exchanged polite pleasantries with his future in-laws, he covertly consulted his wristwatch at regular intervals as the clock had been pawned along with everything else of value.

At the end of a two-hour period, by which time it was indisputably obvious Miss Acton had declined to join them, Hereward stood up with abrupt haste and told his fiancée's embarrassed, apologetic parents there must be no repeat of their daughter's discourtesy on the day of the wedding. With that, he donned his hat, bid them a curt farewell and took his leave. But before climbing into his motorcar, he took a final look at the street. Sadly, for him, there was still no sign of Isabella.

At the mere mention of Major Aldwen's name, Isabella felt a lump form at the back of her throat. For days she had been dreading the obligatory date with him under her father's strict supervisory gaze. It was too much, too soon, and her strained nerves were tenser than a tightrope.

Since she would soon be losing her precious freedom, Isabella resolved to make the most of the time remaining. Instead of subjecting herself to a travesty of courtship in the drawing room at home in the presence of her parents, she arranged to meet up with her friends by the park's bandstand. Ironically, at least for Isabella, they spent the afternoon amusing themselves on and around the Aldwen estate; a thirty-minute walk from the town via the woodland route. However, she made sure to keep her distance from the Hall. The closer she came to the Major's residence, the more the thought of marriage to him unnerved her, especially when she recalled the incident in the orchard. Nora, the friend Isabella was closest to, had once claimed that gone sunset the Hall's reclusive resident turned into a vampire, then abducted young ladies in order to drink their blood. Safe in the knowledge that vampires were no more than creatures of myth, Isabella had dismissed the monstrous defamation with a loud guffaw. But the assertion, stored deep in her subconscious mind, resurfaced at the most inopportune time.

Isabella agonised over her forthcoming marriage and meditated for hours on ways to avoid going through with it. To begin with, she considered seeking employment. Despite the economic downturn, new opportunities were opening up for women in the world of work, with increasing numbers employed in the expanding retail, commercial and recreational sectors. But even if she could secure a position, considering she had no qualifications, training or experience, she would still need to find lodgings should her tyrannous father turn her out of the house. Which is what he was threatening to do if she declined the Major's suit. With her plummy vowels and clarified consonants, Isabella was unlikely to find a job as a lady's maid in a middle-class or upperclass household, or as a scullery maid, come to that. Moreover, compared to men, women were paid a pittance, and even if her father relented and allowed her to stay, whatever she earned he would appropriate for himself.

Thus, with a heavy heart and as much courage as she could muster, Isabella agreed to do what generations of oppressed young women and gullible girls the world over had done before her: marry a man of her father's choosing on a date designated by him; a man about whom she knew nothing except his name, address, class, and occupation, and a man she neither loved nor liked. And in common with the aforesaid females, she would perform her conjugal duty on the night of the wedding and thereafter with quiet acquiescence. While in well-to-do houses throughout the land, battalions of well-to-do women were celebrating the ongoing gains of women's emancipation.

There were, of course, those who thought Isabella simply deranged to consider for even one moment refusing the Major's well-heeled hand; especially Nora who, despite the vampiric slander, said she would gladly take her place. Which made Isabella realise how fickle her friend was, not to mention how unprincipled.

"You mustn't throw away this chance," advised Nora when Isabella confided her serious reservations regarding her imminent marriage. "You'll be making a huge mistake if you reject the gentleman's offer. Choice is a luxury we poor can't afford," she added, forgetting her friend's parents were also struggling to keep the roof over their heads. Live on this street for a month the way we live, and you'll be begging to marry the Major. Give a girl the chance to escape these terrible conditions and she'd marry a monkey I can promise you that. Year in, year out, we live hand to mouth. Every day's the same old struggle. It grinds you down. Many of the women on this street lost their men in the war and their kids are now fatherless and the family without its main breadwinner. And if they're lucky enough to find a job, they're paid in pennies, far less than men get and barely enough to live on. Open your eyes and look around you. Do you seriously think any of these women would turn up their noses at a good-looking, wealthy man?"

Following their candid conversation, the girls went their own separate ways: Isabella to a life of leisure and Nora to a lifetime of labour.

Chapter 6

A month after the banns were posted, the wedding of Miss Isabella Elizabeth Acton and Major Hereward Henry George Aldwen took place before the altar of an ancient stone chapel on the outskirts of Oakwich. Since the ceremony had been arranged at short notice, the guest list was strictly limited.

Walking down the aisle on the arm of Archibald Acton, Isabella felt like the condemned being led to the scaffold. Marriage meant the loss of her freedom as a single girl, her individuality, and her precious dreams and ambitions. Nevertheless, she looked stunning in a full-length, long-sleeved gown fashioned from plain white satin and accessorised with an organza veil. In her white-gloved hands she held a small bouquet of white roses; a well-known symbol of purity. Unable to conceal her sorrow, she wept throughout the entire ceremony and spluttered her vows.

Hereward, looking magnificent in his military uniform, came close to despairing. On what should have been a joyous occasion, at least for him, the bride was clearly distraught.

As soon as the priest pronounced them man and wife, Hereward raised his bride's veil to kiss her for the very first time.

To avoid having his lips touch hers, Isabella averted her head so that they brushed her cheek instead.

Hereward felt saddened by the sight of his beloved's

unveiled face moist with tears and her gorgeous green eyes puffy and red. Still, he remained hopeful that once she settled into her new life all would be well.

Among those watching the wedding party from outside the chapel that day, was a woman who was also weeping, albeit discreetly. The woman's name was Miss Rosalyn Dumbarton and the groom was her former beau. Despite being dumped like a dissevered ragdoll, she had a perverse and pressing need to see her replacement.

Rosalyn Dumbarton was an imposing and commanding figure whose confidence and self-assurance were typical of her class. As a rule, she achieved her goals with single-minded, unwavering and ruthless resolve. In the strictest sense of the word, she could not be called beautiful, although she could rightly be called handsome, and a few even considered her to be stunning.

Like Hereward, Rosalyn was tall, lean and long-legged. She wore her lustrous black bob curved like scimitars around her jawline, embellished her dark-amber eyes with multiple coats of mascara, and stained her broad thin lips claret red. Unconventional in many respects, but conventional with respect to marriage, she craved a shiny gold band with which to gild her stark-naked ring finger. But in a cruel twist of fate a mere slip of a girl had beaten her to it.

It was only a fortnight since Hereward had broken the news of his forthcoming marriage; smashing her hopeful heart to smithereens in the process. She was still struggling to come to terms with his betrayal, and she doubted she would ever recover from the shock of losing the only man she had ever truly loved.

Rosalyn had first met Hereward in India, to where she had sailed in search of a suitable husband. The moment she got her claws into him, or so she thought, she assumed he was hers for life. Trusting that they would one day marry, she had been more than happy to oblige whenever he condescended to avail himself of her favours.

"How could you do this to me?" she wailed when he announced their relationship was over. "How could you do this to us? I thought we were serious. That's why I gave myself to you. Hell, we were lovers."

Standing rigid in Rosalyn's regal drawing room, her life-size portrait at his back, Hereward denied proposing marriage to her, denied misleading her and denied seducing her. He reminded her that as a modern woman she had given herself to him freely and they had been equals in that respect. And since there had been no engagement, formal or otherwise, there was no breach of contract.

"I'm sorry, Rosalyn, but that's that," he said in his typical blunt fashion. "I've always been fond of you, but I've never loved you. Surely you must have known that all along?"

Isabella, on the other hand, he loved with an all-consuming passion, despite barely knowing her. The whole situation was a complete mystery to him. The second he set eyes on her at the summer festival, he fell madly and passionately in love and he would move heaven and earth to be with her.

"How can you profess to love someone you barely know?" shrieked Rosalyn with exasperation.

Although Hereward doubted it would make one jot of difference, he attempted to explain. "Look, Rosalyn, I don't expect you to understand. I'm not even sure I understand it myself. In India I heard people speak of karma and such things, of our destiny being written in the stars. To be honest, at first, I thought it was all a load of mumbo jumbo, but now I'm not so sure." He paused, looked askance and sighed. "I suppose what I'm trying to say in my own convoluted way is that I believe Isabella and I are destined to be together."

Having realised the pointlessness of prolonging the discussion, Rosalyn narrowed her eyes, tensed her cheeks and made bitter, sarcastic reference to Isabella's maidenhood: "And would it be correct to assume the chosen one's a virgin?"

"That's none of your damned business," he snarled. There was no point in telling her the woman worthy of being his wife must be pure and chaste. Not once had it occurred to Hereward that his wife might be entitled to demand the same moral standard from him.

Too grief stricken to show him out, Rosalyn wept at the front window as she stood and watched the love of her life stride down the flower-bordered garden path to his motorcar and forever out of her life.

Chapter 7

As soon as the wedding luncheon concluded, the guests gave their good wishes and waved their goodbyes, the unaccustomed couple set off for Aldwen Hall in Hereward's shiny black motorcar.

Through swollen red eyes Isabella stole a glance at her new husband as he dropped smoothly into the driver's seat. Having changed out of his uniform, he looked dapper dressed in a double-breasted light-wool suit and fedora trimmed with pheasant feathers. As he hitched up his trousers and placed his feet on the pedals, her attention was unaccountably drawn to his socks. They were dress socks woven from the finest quality silk. Socks like those were usually stored wrapped in tissue paper inside cedarwood boxes to protect them from moth damage. Come wintertime, she wondered what her well-groomed spouse would make of her own humble hosiery full of snags, darns and pills.

"Excuse me," said Hereward, reaching across her to retrieve his grey chamois gloves from the dashboard compartment, inadvertently brushing her breast with his arm. The contact gave him a sudden frisson of excitement between his thighs. After sliding his hands into his gloves, he inserted his long lean fingers into their corresponding sheaths. Unlike the coarse calloused hands of a labourer, his hands were smooth and supple.

With her own small hands clenched tight in her lap, Isabella shivered involuntarily, turned aside her head and peered out of the passenger window without looking at anything specific.

The couple sat in silent suspense as the motorcar advanced along a lonely tarmac road bridged by interlocked overhead branches. Isabella looked sullen and withdrawn as she stared at the timber columns lining both sides of the road like soundless sentinels on watch. In a steadily shifting perspective, the blended trees on the hazy horizon parted, increasing in magnitude until they came to tower over the vehicle, then disappeared from sight. For the very first time in her young life, Isabella experienced a strange sense of detachment from reality that seemed almost surreal. And as their destination drew nearer, she tried not to dwell on what lay ahead.

When Aldwen Hall came into view, it looked the same as always: formal, solid and stable, but not lacking in elegance and grace; similar to its master in many respects. The house stood isolated in a woodland clearing at the end of the road, which terminated at a set of tall wrought-iron gates hung on two lion-topped pillars. The gates stood open in anticipation of the newlyweds' arrival. On a small patch of grass to one side a confirmatory signboard reassured rare visitors that this was indeed their destination. Originally built as an antidote to city life, the Hall was also considered an ideal venue for hosting weekend shooting parties. However, the shooting parties no longer took place.

The substantial red-brick dwelling was topped with a steep-pitched roof accommodating several tall chimneys. Save for the façade's dark-stained double doors, the woodwork was painted white. All the bay sash windows were large by design to admit maximum light during the long winter months' short dismal days, but were partly obscured by thick, heavy drapes to combat the draughts. Come nightfall, Isabella imagined the place would look gothic and ghostly and the gargoyles more grotesque than they did during daytime.

The location suited Hereward's hermitic nature. It provided the perfect situation for a person who preferred spending life in tranquil seclusion, and wished to avoid bumping into neighbours or being invited to their social events. He loved the house, he loved the surroundings, and he felt sure Isabella would grow to love it there too. After all, as he well knew, she wasn't exactly a stranger to the estate.

After Hereward brought the motorcar to a halt on the gravel driveway in front of the house, he turned to his reticent wife and gave her an encouraging smile.

"Welcome to Aldwen Hall, my darling," he said.

It was the first time he had used the endearment. To Isabella it sounded uncomfortably overfamiliar, and she offered no reply.

Then to her mortification, after helping her out of her seat, Hereward insisted on carrying her over the threshold. Shrinking from his proximity, Isabella breathed a sigh of relief when he placed her back on her feet. After which she smoothed down her hair and clothing in preparation to meet the staff, who were waiting to greet them in a large wood-panelled hall containing a huge open fireplace overlooking a well-polished parquet floor.

Isabella struggled to speak as Hereward made the introductions. She took an instant dislike to the butler and suspected the feeling was mutual. Quite simply, the sight of him made her blench. His broad, flat face on its own might have looked bland and inoffensive had it not been for his round rubicund nose, which bore a bulb of fat aside each nostril, and his eyes, one of which wandered while the other remained focussed. Boyle, as was his name, had worked at the Hall for decades, and, with cunning astuteness, had acquired a significant measure of power over the household, behaving as if were his own personal fiefdom.

Standing each side of Boyle but two steps behind him, two grey-garbed maids, whose names were Barbara and Tilly, tried not to fidget while they waited to greet their new mistress. Isabella observed the girls were scarcely older than herself. And although they smelled of sweat, grease and carbolic soap, she still envied them their unmarried status.

After that, Hereward took her below stairs to meet the cook, Mrs Jenkins, who remained in the kitchen because her arthritic knees prevented her from climbing the steep narrow steps to the hall. Isabella warmed instantly to the motherly woman. Given the choice, she would have preferred to remain in the kitchen with its comforting aromas of homemade bread, roast potatoes and suet pastry. So, with reluctance she returned upstairs with her new husband.

At four o'clock sharp the couple took tea in the library, which also served as Hereward's study. The expansive room possessed a calmative odour of vintage books, beeswax and old leather. French doors opened onto a paved terrace leading to a lawned garden containing several flowerbeds. The garden looked a little overgrown and neglected, which mattered little to Isabella right then. At the far end of the room beneath the window a large square desk as traditional as its owner made its presence felt. The long walls were lined from floor to ceiling with orderly, well-stocked bookcases. The focal point of the room was a grandiose fireplace carved from dark oak with a big brass carriage clock on its shelf. Opposite that sat an old chesterfield sofa whose dints and depressions hinted at the hosting of bottoms in an assortment of shapes and sizes over the years.

Hereward invited Isabella to sit in one of the oxblood

leather armchairs flanking the hearth, then took the other one for himself. In the grate a small crackling log fire removed the chill from the early autumn air. Despite the warmth radiating from the flames, she felt chilled to the bone and wondered whether she might be developing a cold.

The butler entered with the tea tray, unfolded a small gateleg table between the couple, draped it in a well-laundered white Irish-linen cloth and laid out the tea things on top.

"Will that be all, Sir?" he said in an ingratiating tone after pouring the tea into two gold-rimmed bone-china cups.

"Yes, thank you, Boyle," replied Hereward in a genial manner.

Without acknowledging Isabella, the butler vacated the room.

The couple ate without speaking.

As soon as they finished their tea, Hereward took Isabella outdoors to show her the garden. Since she made clear she wasn't in the mood for small talk, he gave up trying to engage her in conversation, returned inside and left her to her own devices.

Since they had consumed more than enough food that day, they ate only a light supper in lieu of dinner, after which they repaired to the sitting room. There they sat opposite each other in armchairs in front of another small fire. Then at nine o'clock sharp, Hereward tuned into a recital on a wireless housed within a gothic-grilled wooden case. Isabella, her mind elsewhere, was oblivious to the music. In spite of the warm fire, she shivered like a nervous puppy suddenly removed from its dam to an unfamiliar new home.

The moment the concert concluded, Hereward, eager to acquaint himself with his young bride's body, announced it was time to retire. After which he rang for Barbara and told her to show Isabella to her bedroom.

Chapter 8

Isabella cast her sore, red-rimmed eyes around her allocated bedroom. The room, situated at the front of the house, overlooked the drive, beyond which grew a line of laurels before a belt of broadleaved trees. It was meant to be a temporary arrangement, since the room adjoining her husband's bedroom was scheduled to undergo refurbishment in the near future.

The bedroom's walls were papered in grandiose shades of gold and red, its windows dressed with stage-style drapes, and its floor covered with a large rug handwoven with threads of peacock blue, tropical green and Rajput red. Unfortunately, the décor's heavy and dramatic affectations served to further compound her anguish and distress.

Isabella's old leather suitcase containing her meagre trousseau had been unpacked by hands unknown and put away inside the closet. Her white nightdress lay draped across the mahogany bed's carmine-red coverlet. Isabella shuddered as she looked at the modest garment, chosen specifically to avoid arousing her husband's ardour.

After removing her travelling suit, Isabella hung it up inside the wardrobe, the interior of which smelled of patchouli and lavender, plus a hint of something piquant and spicy. She slipped the thin straps of her satin undergarment over her arms, let it drop to her feet, stepped out of it, and folded it away inside a drawer. Crossing the floor, she was arrested by the pitiful sight of a sad-eyed, pale-faced girl in the cheval glass whom she failed to recognise at first. She picked up her nightdress, a foot-skimming, full-sleeve, thick-cotton affair adorned with pintucks, tiny bows and rosebud buttons, and put it on over her head. Then with timorous fingers she fastened it all the way up to her throat. After which she went straight to the bathroom, filled the sink with cold water and splashed her face several times.

As soon as she returned to her bedroom, Isabella climbed into the bridal bed. The bedsheets smelled fresh from the laundry. She lay supine and contemplated the plaster ceiling's matrix of custom-made medallions. The decorative Victorian vestige reminded her of the once-grand ceilings of her parents' house. Overcome by a sudden and intense attack of homesickness, she rolled onto her side, curled up like a little dormouse and wished she could hibernate for a hundred years.

Presently, the bedroom door slowly opened, heralding her new husband's arrival. All at once the room possessed the anticipatory air of a stage set up for an opening performance. However, in this instance, the female part lacked the advantage of a single rehearsal.

"I hope you are comfortable and everything is to your liking." said Hereward in a cordial manner as if addressing an honoured guest.

Isabella bristled but said nothing, quite simply because nothing was to her liking. She wanted to weep, she wanted to be alone, but more than anything else in the world she wanted to be back in her own bed. Except this was her bed now, she reminded herself with sad regret.

In complete silence, Hereward untied his long plaid robe, removed it and laid it over the ottoman at the foot of the bed. Beneath the robe he had on blue-silk pyjamas purchased specially for the wedding night. Their newness emanated a mildly metallic, loamy aroma which blended with the subtle scent of male arousal. Using his fingers, he raked his hair back from his brow and joined his innocent bride in her bed. To his pleasure, she smelled of rose petals and sweet perspiration.

As the bedframe creaked with her groom's movements, Isabella cringed inside. Hot tears pricked her eyes and her mouth felt drier than a summer drought. She had only a vague idea of what would happen to her on her wedding night, which alone filled her with dread. Agatha Acton had made no reference to marital intimacy and Isabella had felt unable to ask, since it would have been acutely embarrassing for them both. What little she knew about the sexual act came from overheard genteel euphemisms expressed in unguarded moments; inconceivable to a girl as green as her eyes.

Hereward, on the other hand, was grateful the wedding formalities were done with and his wife would shortly submit to him. Fully conversant with the arts of sexual congress, he had complete faith in himself to make Isabella's initiation a pleasurable experience. Not for one moment did he consider a woman might not share his penchant for this peculiarity of human relations. Moving aside her curls, he kissed the back of her neck and in an assured tone told her to turn over and face him.

In the heavily oppressive atmosphere of the nuptial chamber, resentment combined with revulsion rendered Isabella rigid and unyielding. Tight knots formed in her stomach, chest and throat. And without a word, or a look, or a movement, she rebuffed him.

Her mute defiance, however, did nothing to subdue the tumidity of Hereward's ardour. Undeterred by her rejection, which he attributed to a combination of innocence and wedding-night nerves, he lifted up her nightdress, hooked his fingers in the waistband of her homely white drawers, pulled them down and ran his eager hands all over her irresistibly soft flesh.

Expecting physical relations to be more perfunctory in practice, Isabella felt shocked by the manner in which the stranger in her bed ran his hands over her body without first seeking her consent.

Undeterred by her passive resistance, with hands as capable as they were commanding, Hereward rolled his recalcitrant bride onto her back. Unable to contain himself any longer, he loosened the drawstring of his pyjama trousers, parted her thighs and consummated the marriage.

Chapter 9

Upon awakening to her new surroundings, Isabella yawned and rubbed the sleep from her eyes. Glancing around the room, she felt grateful to be alone. The Major, as she still thought of him, having satisfied himself at her expense the previous night, had returned to his own suite to sleep. She felt soiled and sore; a deep-aching, saddle-like soreness right through to her core. Despite the discomfort, she was relieved the dreaded deed was done and the anticipatory fear forever extinguished.

The pillow beside hers retained a hint of her unfamiliar husband's musky scent. With a look of loathing and disgust, Isabella sat up and tossed it out onto the floor. Then she lay back on her tear-stained pillow, swamped by a profound sense of sorrow such as she had never known. But resigned to her fate, to what could not be undone, she resolved to weep no more. Weeping solved nothing. It only drained her of energy and weakened her spirit.

No-one had bothered to enlighten her as to what would happen on her first full day at the Hall. Being unacquainted with the customs and conventions of the household, Isabella knew neither what to expect nor what was expected of her. As a wave of weariness washed over her, she closed her eyes and debated whether to remain in bed for the rest of the morning. At that moment she could only envisage a lifetime of unending ennui. Then she reopened her eyes and, focussing on the medallions above the bed, imagined ways of abnegating her marital obligations.

A sudden knock at the bedroom door interrupted Isabella's ruminations. "Come," she said. Following which a figure in uniform entered and waddled across the carpet with the breakfast tray. Suddenly the air was filled with the thick smoky smells of dried-up kedgeree, burnt toast and over-boiled egg.

"Good morning," said the grey figure in a flat tone; its cheerless voice the perfect match for its cheerless face.

All the same, Isabella felt relieved it wasn't Major Aldwen come to wish her good morning. Her face reddened at the recollection of his wedding-night wantonness. She wondered how she was ever going to face him again. There was something to be said for separate bedrooms, she decided, repulsed by the thought of lying next to him all night long. Her mama, a strict advocate of separate spheres, once said that a wife should never appear before her husband without first making herself presentable. Momentarily, Isabella considered making herself unpresentable to her new spouse in order to discourage him from seeking intimate relations with her. But doubting the strategy's success, she soon abandoned the idea.

After switching the light on and placing the tray on her new mistress's lap, the maid left her alone to eat breakfast. Frowning in surprise, Isabella regarded the pitiful portion of kedgeree, hard egg and one thin slice of toast scraped with butter. Despite the meal's unappetising appearance, feeling ravenous, she wolfed it down. Her throat parched with thirst, she also gulped down the lukewarm tea as she reflected on her newfound prosperity with a sense of irony.

Presently, the young misery came back to collect the breakfast things. She informed Isabella that once she disposed of the tray, she would return to assist her with her dress and toilette. There was something about the maid, other than her inanimate face, which Isabella took exception to. Preferring not to be trussed up like an old chicken destined for the pot, and being of a generation that had never suffered the agony of boned foundation garments or multiple layers of clothing over corsets and stays, she declined her assistance. Times had changed for the better with respect to women's fashions and she resented the girl's presumption, not to mention her dictatorial manner.

"It's Barbara, I believe," said Isabella in her iciest tone.

Barbara merely nodded her confirmation.

"Well, Barbara, I'll thank you to remember that since my sartorial requirements are somewhat simple and straightforward, I am perfectly capable of dressing myself; therefore, I shall not require your assistance, either now or in the future."

"As you wish, Ma'am," Barbara replied. Following which she departed the room with a scowl an owl could be proud of. It was not an auspicious start.

With an almighty effort Isabella flung back the bedclothes and hauled herself out of bed. Going straight to the mahogany wardrobe, she opened the double doors and peered inside. Her principal garments were already hanging on the rail. They included a couple of day dresses, two dinner gowns, one old, one new, a smart wool suit and an ivory blouse. A handful of underclothes lay folded inside a drawer, while a second nightdress identical to the one she had on occupied a separate drawer. The small trousseau was all her parents could afford from borrowed funds.

Isabella chose to wear one of the dresses, a pink-cotton affair with square-cut shoulders, three-quarter sleeves and a matching belt that accentuated her slim waist. She slipped the garment off the hanger and laid it out on the bed. Under different circumstances she would have been delighted to wear a new dress, but the previous day's traumas had curbed her enthusiasm.

After completing her toilette, Isabella dressed, brushed her hair and checked herself in the mirror to make sure she looked tidy. Twisting her body this way and that, she had to admit the dress looked attractive and suited her figure.

On her very first morning at the Hall Isabella's foremost consideration was how to occupy herself until luncheon. After giving the matter some thought, she decided to familiarise herself with the layout of the house. However, she excluded the library from her plan because that was where she assumed the Major would be; like all men hunkered down at his desk. And she intended to avoid him as much as was humanly possible.

Drifting from room to room, Isabella noted the house was furnished in a style typical of large period houses at the time, with a congestion of antique, handcrafted pieces, careworn rugs and saggy sofas that sighed when sat upon. Everything was muted in colour and faded in pattern. In the sitting room Isabella perched on an armchair atop a hand-knotted carpet frayed at one corner. The carpet looked Indian in origin, with a quintessential opus of clashing and complimentary colours that only subcontinental designers managed to harmonise. The dated wallpaper was awash with motifs of flora and fauna on a dull beige background. Isabella wondered who must have chosen it, for the house had a distinctly monastic aura at variance with the integrated miscellany of appointments, textures and colours. There were no fresh flowers in any of the rooms, no silver-framed family photographs and no ornaments; only oil-painted ancestral portraits, log baskets, companion sets, and some tragic-looking stuffed animals in a glass cabinet. Every room featured a fireplace and every fireplace housed a clock on its shelf. In the dark sombre hall, which mirrored her mood, a tall grandfather clock oversaw arrivals and departures. Above the hall's fireplace the mounted head of a stag cast a mortified stare over the room.

From the hall Isabella moved onto the morning room, where Boyle served his master breakfast at the exact same time every day. The room gave onto the unused, unkempt conservatory. The vaulted triple-aspect glass structure, which spanned one full side of the house, was flooded with natural light and commanded a broad view of the Hall's immediate surroundings; providing a welcome contrast to the rest of the interior.

Isabella exited through the double doors that opened onto the garden, then crossed the lawn to take a closer look at the flowerbeds. In some places the lawn was blighted with patches of moss at its outer rim where trees predating the house cast it in permanent shade. Fortunately, a number of vivid-blue delphiniums and raspberry-red sedums gave the garden a colourful late-summer boost; as did the rose garden's bumper crop of voluptuous blooms in vibrant shades of red.

While admiring the roses Isabella pricked her finger on a thorn. She rubbed her thumb over the minute puncture mark and observed a tiny bead of blood seep out from the wound. After inserting the tip of her digit between her lips, she licked the dark-red fluid. It tasted salty and metallic on her tongue. Then with eyes downcast she continued her perambulations.

From behind the library's heavy brocade curtains, Hereward watched his young wife as she wandered the garden deep in contemplation. Although he was disappointed with her unenthusiastic response to their first intimacy, he was nonetheless satisfied with the acute cry that had validated her virtue. He wondered how many men discovered on their wedding night that they weren't the first. He hoped she would be quick to settle, he prayed she would be compliant, and he dared to dream she would welcome him into her inner world. The graceful way she moved her willowy limbs looked to him utterly enchanting. And as she floated around the flowerbeds, pretty in pastel pink, her ice-blonde curls hanging over her neat shoulders and down her back, she put him in mind of fairies and other unearthly beings. However, the moment she turned and began making her way back towards the house, Hereward moved away from the window, lest she catch him discreetly observing her. Although why it should matter, he didn't quite know.

Chapter 10

Every day at Aldwen Hall included a fixed programme of meals and refreshments served strictly in order and strictly adhered to. The long-case clock in the hall chimed every quarter, half and full hour, providing an audible reminder of the regulatory routines of the house. Barbara, her face an overcast sky promising rain, rolled in at the same time every morning with the breakfast tray containing the self-same rations and the same tepid tea. Throughout the day the hands on the clocks moved with a slow and steady insouciance. With little to do in her new role, Isabella found herself consulting them at regular intervals. She spent most of her time in the sitting room, where she read, listened to the wireless and practised the pianoforte for short periods. Despite the room's generous proportions, oftentimes she felt as though the walls were closing in on her, making her want to outstretch her hands and hold them back. Living in isolation with a stranger she was forced to marry, and no longer in contact with her old friends, Isabella felt hollow inside, lonely and lost. Moreover, she feared her life of idleness and poverty of purpose would drop her down a deep well of irreversible depression. And while the clocks continued their ceaseless ticking, she pondered on ways to alleviate the tedium of her existence.

In accordance with household protocol, Isabella had a bath at the same time every evening before changing into a gown for dinner. Dinner was a formal occasion served in the large dining room, where she and Hereward sat at opposite ends of a long mahogany table covered in a white-damask cloth. Ordinarily, she found the practice somewhat formal and outdated, but was now grateful for the distance it afforded between her husband and herself. A fine wine always accompanied the meal. Isabella, however, cared little for alcohol, being so young she had still to acquire the taste. To occupy herself and ease her discomfort while waiting to be served, she spent an age unfolding and smoothing her napkin over her lap, then took several slow sips of water in between fidgeting with her hair and clothing.

The meal was invariably served by the butler with one of the maids in attendance. However, before the couple tucked in, a pious-looking Hereward intoned grace. Despite her low mood, Isabella found the observance strangely amusing and struggled to keep a straight face when she murmured *Amen*. Since it obviated the need for conversation, it was a relief to start eating. Throughout the meal, or ordeal, as she secretly called it, Isabella felt her husband's eyes on her as she chewed her food. Still, she ate heartily and cleared each course of the stodgy fare; about which she had no complaints as she relished the satisfying sensation of a full stomach.

After dinner they repaired to the sitting room for a nightcap and to listen to the wireless. At that time of evening the standard listing usually included a concert or a play. Isabella, however, struggled to concentrate on the performance, being too busy brooding on the business that followed it as a rule. The entertainment's conclusion always coincided with the arrival of the maid to collect the empty cups, which was also the cue to start making their way upstairs.

During the first few weeks of married life, uprooted from the town, Isabella could see only an unfillable void in front of her.

The days seemed interminable yet the nights came around too soon. To her husband, she felt she was no more than an amatory amusement, for which he had an insatiable appetite. How she wished she had been born a boy. For a boy would not have been given in connubial bondage. And although there was little love lost between her parents and herself, she still missed her old house, the elderly maid, and her boisterous friends. But what she missed more than anything else was her former freedom, such as it had been. A freedom she had taken for granted not knowing she would lose it so soon.

Isabella's profound sense of alienation weighed her down. Many times, she wanted to fall sleep and not wake up. But as before, she resolved not to cry; crying proved pointless and provided only temporary relief. Moreover, it offered nothing in the way of solutions for her lonely predicament.

One unremarkable night a few weeks into her marriage, Isabella went up to her bedroom, changed into her nightdress and sat on the vanity stool to brush her hair. Her late grandmother's silver vanity set sat on top of the dressing-table. Since it had great sentimental value, Isabella treasured it. Unlike most of her possessions, it had escaped the pawnshop by a whisker.

As she beheld herself in the mirror, she considered her uncompromising mop, remembering how her mother had often denigrated her curls during her childhood years, describing them as untidy, unruly and unmanageable. Isabella, however, disagreed. She loved her curls, she loved their wildness, their vitality, their resistance to the punitive strokes of the hairbrush. Neither her mother nor the nanny had ever succeeded in taming them, nor for that matter her. In her nursery days she had called them curly curls because of their exceptional curliness. Inclining her head, Isabella took hold of a helix of hair, unfurled it, watched it recoil, and became lost in thought.

Behind her the bedroom door swung open and Hereward swept into the room, bringing with him a draught of cool air from the galleried landing. He had on a plaid dressing gown, plain blue pyjamas and black-leather slippers. The instant he caught sight of her reflection in the mirror, he halted and stared at her for a time.

In the heightened tension of the room, Isabella, hairbrush in hand, refrained from looking at him as one might avoid the eyes of a dog with raised hackles. Still, she remained acutely conscious of his scrutinising presence in her peripheral vision.

Seemingly impervious to her aloofness, Hereward strode over and stood at her back. Then with his eyes fixed to her reflection, he bunched her hair in his hands and yanked it backwards, thus obliging her to meet his gaze in the mirror.

"I must insist that in future you wear your hair tied up," he said in a peremptory tone. "Except, of course, in the privacy of your own bedroom. Or at my specific request," he added with a presumptuous smile after a short pause. "It's most improper for a married lady to wear her hair in the style of a young girl." Then he released it and let it fall.

Eyes wide with incredulity, Isabella stared at her husband for several seconds. Following which, she rose erect from the stool and climbed into bed. Then in a further snub, she picked up her book from the bedside cabinet, opened it at the marked page and began to read. However, she kept returning to the same sentence as the words failed to register on her brain.

In the meantime, Hereward removed his robe, folded it in half over the ottoman and joined her in bed. Impatient to explore the pale-golden dunes of her delectable body, and brooking no dissent, he promptly removed the book from her hands and put it aside.

"Lie down please," he said with a distinct note of authority in his voice.

After sucking in a sharp breath, Isabella slid under the bedclothes, closed her eyes and, in the manner of a recumbent sculpture atop a sarcophagus, waited with resignation for the act to finish.

Chapter 11

The following morning Isabella met Boyle at the foot of the staircase, looking buffed, stuffed and starched in his black-and-white livery. Thus dressed, his barrel-shaped chest gave him the appearance of a pigeon impersonating a penguin. In common with many other bald-headed men the world over, he had adopted the universal practice of spanning his bare scalp with wisps of waxed hair to hide his failed follicles; but the feint fooled no-one.

"Good morning, Ma'am. I trust you are well and everything is to your satisfaction?" he said in a monotone.

"Yes, thank you, Boyle," Isabella replied. Something in his manner made her feel like a guest in the type of hotel where patrons are considered an inconvenience. Her childhood butler had been a warm, respectful and benevolent man, but Boyle was altogether a different species. His mode of speech, purporting politeness, was wooden and stilted, as if every word were carefully scanned before selection.

"If there is anything you require, Ma'am, you have only to inform me and I shall do my best to provide it," he stated as his uncoordinated eye went awry.

"Thank you, Boyle. That's most kind of you," she replied with a rigid smile, wishing he would go away and leave her in peace.

"If I am unavailable or otherwise engaged," he went on,

"Barbara is there to assist you."

His pointed reference to the deposed personal maid Isabella duly noted. She presumed it was his way of reminding her that he ruled over the household.

"I shall bear that in mind," she responded with cool composure.

"Well, Ma'am, if you'll kindly excuse me," he said as if she were the one detaining him, "since I've much to be getting on with, I must return to my duties forthwith."

If Hereward's puffed-up sycophant thinks he's going to lord it over me indefinitely then he's in for a rude awakening, said Isabella to herself as soon as he left. After which, she went straight to the sitting room, settled herself down on one of the fireside chairs and pondered what to do next. Never in her life had she experienced such boredom. When she had lived in town and hadn't felt like reading, she had at least been able to look out of the window and watch people pass by on the street, or take a walk in the nearby park, or a peek in the shop windows.

Later that same day, Isabella, having grown tired of her limited pastimes, decided to explore the unused conservatory. Unlike the gloom-ridden house, which stifled her spirits and fed her melancholy, the conservatory's spacious glass structure spread light and air. Light and air was what she needed; light and air was what she craved.

Her hands clasped behind her back, Isabella entered the room and wandered around. Her footsteps echoed on the glaze-tiled floor disfigured by multiple leaf-veined cracks. Sadly, several cadaverous plants lay abandoned about the room, silver cobwebs swagged the windows, timeworn wicker chairs sat cracked and split, while a hint of stale tobacco hung about the air. Isabella imagined the place filled with miniature citrus trees, lush tropical plants and a potpourri of bright-coloured blooms.

After first mulling over the merits of her plan, the young wife determined to take action, aided and abetted by the ever-willing Tilly, whom she got on with rather well. The following afternoon she and the maid donned their aprons, rolled up their sleeves and, with some old cloths and a pail of hot water apiece, set out to transform the glasshouse into a gleaming oasis.

Elsewhere in the house, Barbara, motivated by malice, was busy briefing the bumptious Boyle on the latest developments on the domestic front. Such was the butler's hubris, he totally disregarded Isabella's status as mistress. With a bordering-on-delusional sense of his own supremacy, he considered her actions a direct challenge to his hitherto unchallenged authority. Damnable insolence, he said to himself. How dare that impudent little parvenu not consult him. Then without further ado he alerted the Major to her endeavours.

Unfortunately, Hereward reacted to the butler's report with undue haste. Upon entering the conservatory, he came upon Isabella with her sleeves bunched above her elbows and a wet cloth in her hand, looking to all the world like a common skivvy. And to add insult to injury, she was happily chatting with Tilly as if the maid were her friend and equal.

"What the devil d'you think you're doing? Stop that at once!" he bellowed, his face purple with lividity, his hands on his hips and his voice reverberating throughout the cavernous space.

Isabella's frustration and resentment at the situation in which she found herself at the Hall began to build, culminating in a moment of sheer madness. With no thought for the consequences, she picked up the pail of dirty water and chucked it all over him. However, the instant her brain registered her folly, her eyes grew wide, her hand flew to her mouth and regret set in.

To say Hereward was thunderstruck would be an understatement. With his wet fringe affixed to his forehead and his hands clenched in white-knuckled ferocity, he stood drenched and dripping in his smart Norfolk tweeds and fine derby shoes. In slow motion he closed his eyes and drew in a long deep breath through his nose to recover his composure. Then he removed his damp handkerchief from his jacket's wet pocket, unfolded it and mopped his face with a deceptive calmness that surprised even himself. After which he stared at his wife for several seconds in silent fury before raising his hand and slapping her smartly across the cheek.

Isabella's cheek smarted where it sported a bright pink handprint and she rubbed the spot where it hurt. Horror-struck by her loss of control, she ran from the room, dashed upstairs to her bedroom and threw herself on the bed. What on earth had come over her? She could barely believe what she had just done, and in the presence of a servant too. Clearly the stress of her situation was having an adverse effect on her conduct.

Soon after, Isabella heard the front door slam, followed by the hum of the motorcar as the wheels crunched over the gravel and rolled onto the road. Hereward must have taken himself off to cool his ire, she rightly assumed. Seeking to soothe herself, she went down to the library to browse the bookshelves undisturbed. It was normally impossible to have the place to herself during the daytime and she decided to take advantage of the sudden opportunity.

The library at Aldwen Hall was impressive. It housed an extensive collection of books, many of them first editions. There were also several collections of rare catalogues, periodicals and gentlemen's magazines on the shelves. Beside the chimneypiece, cups, trophies and prizes for this and that were displayed in a satinwood case. Her husband was evidently a talented and capable man. What she couldn't understand, however, was what made him so reclusive and unsociable.

After choosing a novel at random, Isabella sat in one of the winged armchairs to read. The chair's wings gave her a sense of enveloping comfort. The log fire flickering and crackling in the grate made the room feel warm and cosy. The pumpkin-orange flames had a strong soporific effect, so that her eyelids grew heavy. Then after making herself more comfortable, she closed her eyes for what she assumed would be only a moment and drifted off to sleep.

Isabella awoke to find a dry-clothed, dry-shoed, dry-haired Hereward watching her closely from the armchair opposite.

"I'm sorry, I must have dozed off," she said sheepishly. Feeling like an interloper, she got up to leave.

"Sit down, Isabella," Hereward said firmly, his piercing eyes pinned to her penitent face. "There is something I must say to you."

Isabella was aware of the gravity of the situation and desperate to avoid another argument; the last thing she needed. Not trusting herself to speak, she sat in silent surrender, clasped her hands childlike in her lap and waited to be berated.

Hereward straightened his back, cleared his throat and said in a low but assertive voice: "What happened today in the conservatory must never, do you hear, ever be repeated. Not only was your behaviour extremely unladylike, it also set a bad example in front of a servant. I will not under any circumstances tolerate such uncouth and outrageous conduct. Should you in future have more bright ideas then I expect to be consulted first. I am the head of this household and you will do well to remember it. I hope I have made myself clear."

There was no point in pouring oil on troubled waters, so Isabella gave her husband a placatory smile and her sincerest-sounding apology. Although she considered him equally culpable and deserving of condemnation, mounting a defence of her actions right then would have been futile.

Hereward's manner softened and he visibly relaxed. "Don't make things more difficult than they need be, Isabella," he advised. "Whatever you require you need only ask Boyle or the maids. That's what they're there for. They're not paid to sit idle. There's no need for you to do anything they can do."

Isabella thanked him and excused herself from the room. However, she had been careful not to say she had no intention whatsoever of deferring to that Machiavelli and his mischief-making minion, and if Hereward didn't like it, he could jolly well lump it.

Chapter 12

Weather permitting, for the sake of her sanity, Isabella began roaming the Aldwen estate every afternoon straight after luncheon. The tranquil trees and grassy meadows around the Hall provided a much-needed counterpoint to the immurement of married life. As she treaded the unmade nodulous tracks and trails, many of them overshadowed by leafy canopies, Isabella marvelled at the untamed verdant terrain and the sweet silvery sounds of birdsong. Walking for lengthy periods not only lifted her spirits, it also enabled her to evade the snooping attentions of the sebaceous Boyle and the venomous maid. Since the incident in the conservatory, she felt a pressing need to escape the house as often as possible.

Although she loved the countryside, Isabella missed the town's hustle and bustle, the citizens' comings and goings, the busy shops, the miscellaneous market stalls under striped awnings, and the loud-mouthed hawkers with their cheap, tacky wares in the square. How she wished the Hall wasn't so remote from the main community.

Bending down to pick up an old penny from the path, Isabella felt a tight band of pressure around her head, which she attributed to tension and stress. Since she got married laughter and fun had flown from her life like a summer bird in search of warmer climes, and it seemed like they might never return. As she closed her eyes and rubbed her temples, sweet memories streamed into her mind. Memories of her teenage friends whose loss she felt with lachrymose mournfulness.

The said friends were a mad and motley lot in whose company there was never a dull moment. Isabella first came across them in the public park where she was sitting on a wooden bench with only a book for companionship. To begin with, she had incurred their displeasure for no other reason than her social rank. One of the girls, a tough-looking type, had called her a toff in a confrontational tone. A boy named Jack, who was also a member of the gang of rag-tags, told them to leave her alone. Isabella had a natural humility and they soon started talking in a typical teenage way. Other than on a master-servant basis, the group had never associated with anyone outside their own class. With unashamed glee they lampooned her precise pronunciation, ridiculed her rounded vowels and mocked her smooth modulation. And they sniggered not unkindly at her use of the word luncheon to describe what they called dinner, and her exclamations of golly gosh! It was impossible to remove Isabella's veneer of refinement. She was too well versed in upperclass parlance to express herself in any other way. Yet she never once took their parodies to heart, but recognised them for what they were: just simple, light-hearted fun. Soon she began meeting up with the group on a regular basis and acquired some very useful new skills. Now she was married and restored to her own social stratum, she was unlikely to associate with any of them ever again; except perhaps on a master-servant-type basis.

Sometimes Isabella tried to think of ways to escape her empty existence. But fantasy, she deduced, was a poor substitute for reality and would only deepen her discontents. Wifehood was her life now, for better or worse. Despite the limitations imposed on her, she recognised the wisdom of adapting to her new circumstances and making the best of a bad situation. All things considered, easier said than done. In most respects she and her husband stood on opposite sides of a gargantuan gulf. His attempts to engage with her were thwarted by her resentment of his rigid paternalistic attitudes. She was forever yoked to a man for whom she felt neither love nor affection, and to whose near-nightly demands she must willingly submit.

As a coping strategy, Isabella consoled herself with the thought that her husband was at least handsome, handsome and smart. Not that pretty-boy handsomeness that appealed to silly young girls. Hereward's handsomeness was more of a robust, red-bloodied and grave sort of handsomeness. But what would she have done, she mused, had her father insisted she marry an obese, bald, bumbling oaf with a face like a puffed-up toad? The thought of being stroked by some saurian monster made her flesh crawl.

"Gosh, perish the thought!" she cried out loud in frank disgust. She would have been forced to enter a convent or, worse than that, drown herself in the lake. Then the pitiful figure of John Everett Millais' *Ophelia* muscled in on Isabella's musings and she pictured her own perished form afloat on the water's surface. Pull yourself together, Isabella, she counselled herself before giving her head a vigorous shake to dislodge the dead girl's image.

From the outset Hereward let it be known that he disapproved of unpunctuality. Conversely, Isabella saw no reason to turn up on time every single day for the tedious ritual of late-afternoon tea. She resented having her husband's fixed schedule imposed on her redundant existence. Each time she went out she forgot about food. In her new life of plenty she need not worry where her next meal was coming from. Every lunchtime she devoured a three-course meal, every evening a five-course feast, with tea and light refreshments served in between; which made her wonder why the breakfast portions were always so paltry. Sometimes she considered going down to the morning room to help herself from the breakfast buffet on the sideboard, but she wasn't sure how well her actions would be received. Hereward was strict in his habits and he disliked being disturbed for whatever reason. So, she said and did nothing for now.

Oftentimes Isabella arrived back from her forays to find the tea things had been promptly cleared away. Once she overheard Boyle reminding her husband in a tactful and circuitous way that the tea things must be removed on time to avoid the consequential delay with the dinner preparations. The look on Hereward's humourless face conveyed his annoyance, not with Boyle but with her. And she soon surmised that what her husband wanted was a biddable child in the domestic realm and a willing woman in the bedroom.

Ultimately, Isabella decided that forgoing food for a measure of freedom was a price worth paying. Henceforth, no matter how often Hereward scolded her, most of the time she continued to be late. To some degree, doing so appealed to her rebellious nature. He seemed determined to mould her into a model of conformity and she was equally determined to resist him.

Chapter 13

"I wasn't expecting to see you in town today," drawled Rosalyn Dumbarton, bumping into Barbara on the high street. "Doesn't Tilly normally run the errands on Fridays?"

"Yes, Miss Dumbarton," replied Barbara with almost a curtsy. "She used to, but not anymore."

Barbara moved to the inside edge of the pavement to allow a group of pedestrians to pass by. It was market day and Oakwich town centre was heaving with people from all over the district dashing about like diligent ants.

Rosalyn, however, remained where she stood, forcing people to skirt around her or step into the road. She looked conspicuous in a long green wrap coat with a fox-fur collar and coordinating hat. When one man gave her a dirty look and another made a disparaging remark about her height, she appeared not to notice.

"Whatever do you mean? Has Tilly been dismissed?" enquired Rosalyn, nonplussed.

"No, Miss. She's still at the Hall. But she's sort of Mrs Aldwen's own maid now. Not officially you understand. The mistress just calls her and not me whenever she needs assistance."

"Really. How odd. But surely Tilly isn't of the right calibre to be a lady's maid. And what does Boyle have to say about the situation?"

"Well to be honest, Miss, I get the impression he's none too pleased about it." Barbara paused as she began to question the wisdom of discussing the mistress's domestic arrangements outside of the Hall. After all, as a maid she was hardly Miss Dumbarton's equal. However, the opportunity to unburden herself proved far too tempting and so she continued to disclose her dissatisfactions. "The mistress doesn't actually need much help because she does so little with herself."

Rosalyn looked puzzled as she waited for Barbara to expound.

"With her appearance that is," explained Barbara, getting into her stride. "For a start, she does hardly anything with her hair, except to tie it up in a sort of a bun with only a comb and a couple of clips to keep it in place. So, by the afternoon, some of it hangs loose and she appears not to notice or even care. She never wears makeup, not like you, Miss Dumbarton. Nor the sort of clothing that requires help with the fastenings, you know like at the back."

Rosalyn, who was under the distinct impression corsets were making a comeback, looked astounded. "What exactly do you mean? No girdle, and no brassiere? Surely not. Goodness me, whatever is the world coming to. If you ask me, I think it's a most unsatisfactory way for the wife of a gentleman to comport herself."

With a knowing look, Barbara nodded in agreement.

"And what does Major Aldwen have to say about all this?" enquired Rosalyn.

"The Major says a lot, Miss. Him and her disagree all the time. And he's always telling her off. You can hear him because the sound of his voice always carries when he's cross." Barbara omitted to mention she had been listening at doors and spying through keyholes. "But most of the time she just ignores him. She's quite stubborn you know. And most days she takes herself off on her own for long walks in the woods and stays out for hours at a time."

"Goodness me," exclaimed Rosalyn once more. She considered Isabella's behaviour most peculiar. Hereward must be perfectly mad to tolerate such nonsense from his immature wife, she thought.

"And more often than not she's late for tea," revealed Barbara. "Or she turns up just in time to start getting ready for dinner. You know how the Major's a stickler for good timekeeping."

"Quite so," agreed Rosalyn in a grave voice, recalling the way Hereward repeatedly consulted his watch.

Having realised she had allowed her words to run out into the open and it was too late to pull them back, Barbara began to sweat, excreting a bitter whiff of odour from her unwashed armpits. Had she revealed too much? she wondered. What if the Major came to hear of her remarks? She might lose her job. Despite disliking Isabella, Boyle always behaved with constraint and was careful not to openly criticise her. He was far too canny and astute to be caught commenting on matters that weren't meant to concern him.

Although desperate to know more, Rosalyn didn't entirely trust Barbara to be discreet. Nonetheless, their impromptu chat had been most enlightening. Her mood lifted and she smiled for the first time in weeks. The prospect of there being serious strife between Hereward and his new wife was a bandage around her wounded heart. At this rate the couple could soon separate or, better still, file for divorce. Rosalyn knew the grounds for divorce were less stringent than in previous times. And even if the Aldwens were to remain married, she saw no reason why she and the Major shouldn't rekindle their romance.

The instant she took leave of Barbara, Rosalyn returned to

her tall three-storey townhouse, threw off her hat and coat, then poured herself a large cognac in the drawing room. Glass in hand, she drifted upstairs to her dressing room, dropped onto the daybed and cogitated on Barbara's news. The maid's information was most revealing, not to mention enormously encouraging. Every morning since that dreadful day when Hereward had ditched her in such a casual manner, she had had to rouse herself from a drunken stupor. Unable to contemplate the future, she spent most of her time palliating her emotional pain with alcohol and tobacco, while occupying her mind with sadistic fantasies featuring a blood-soaked Isabella Aldwen spreadeagled on an ice-cold mortuary slab, having been slain by Rosalyn's own manicured hand.

After giving the matter some serious thought, she decided she must reopen the channel of communication between Hereward and herself as soon as possible; the best way being, at least to begin with, via friendly correspondence. Then as soon as he needed a shoulder to cry on, hers would be primped and primed in eager anticipation.

Rosalyn drained the remains of her drink, rose from the daybed and sat at the dressing table. Peering into her handheld mirror with the decorative forget-me-nots on the back panel, she licked her forefinger and smoothed down her thin eyebrows. Aghast, she realised she had clean forgotten to retouch her makeup while she was out.

Most of the time now, Rosalyn confined herself to the house. In mixed company an unmarried woman was a conspicuous woman, even when everyone mixed; either pitied or considered a siren. In reality, she was the proverbial spinster pinned to the proverbial shelf. She thought of Hereward's sister, the doughty Miss Maud Aldwen, one of a new generation of women who managed commendably well without a husband. But Rosalyn didn't want to be husbandless; she wanted to be a wife with Hereward as her husband.

On that fateful day when he fell under Isabella Acton's spell, Rosalyn's dreams of marriage to him had been forever destroyed. And she was still reeling from the shock. Her head advised her to move on, but her heart dug its heels in. Wisdom promised the heart would mend, wisdom insisted the pain would pass, but wisdom, thought she, was clearly misinformed.

More recently it had begun to dawn on Rosalyn that the man she once considered her destiny had always been distant towards her. Admittedly, he could charm the tail off a tiger when it suited him; but coldly so. The alarm bells had long rung out in her head but she chose to ignore them. She was in love and nothing else mattered. Having spent a decade searching for a suitable man, her efforts were finally rewarded when she stumbled upon Hereward. In Rosalyn's immodest mind they made an admirable pair: two stylish figures with flamboyance and flair hobnobbing in high society. A factor which enabled her to shrug off his numerous foibles and idiosyncrasies. She longed for romance and old-fashioned courtship. Hereward offered neither. While on military manoeuvres he seldom bothered to write. When he did write, it was little more than a scribbled message on a scrap of paper or whatever else was to hand, and he always signed with regards or best wishes and never with love. Even during furlough, he took his own good time to get in touch. Rosalyn dismissed her doubts and convinced herself that in a relationship with an active soldier she must be prepared to tolerate the vagaries of his profession.

She recalled the very first time she set eyes on him. It was at a cocktail party. He was the last to arrive and the first to leave. The moment he entered the room she was smitten. His handsomeness, erect military carriage and quiet air of confidence made him a sight to behold. He was quickly surrounded by a knot of annoying women. Putting her sharp-edged elbows to excellent use, Rosalyn nudged her way through the group in order to introduce herself. And it was plain to see he wasn't strictly a party wallah.

Later, when he was about to leave, she invited him back to her flat for a nightcap. Not wishing to appear too fast, she affected the mode of a modest young lady. Hereward, however, was quick to detect the deceit. A man like him could always tell when a woman was experienced in the bedroom, and Rosalyn was experienced in the bedroom more than most. Blinded by her own ambivalence, she swiftly succumbed to his advances; after all, she was a modern woman and modern women enjoyed pre-marital indulgences. Thereafter, each time they met, after first downing multiple shots of Bombay Gin, she ended up in bed with him for the rest of the evening, but never for the rest of the night.

It was by pure chance that Rosalyn learned of Isabella's former friendships with a group of lower-class louts, having overheard her maids speaking in loud whispers while they worked. Rosalyn was content for her staff to chat provided they completed their chores on time. She enjoyed listening to tittle-tattle. One heard all sorts of tasty titbits about the conduct, or rather misconduct, of friends, neighbours and acquaintances. Most of her servants came from large extended families with relatives and friends employed in other big houses; hence there existed a well-grown grapevine of gossip, rumour and hearsay. One soon came to know what everyone was up to and who was fornicating with whom.

Rosalyn was fortified to discover her newest employee, a girl named Nora, was once a friend of Isabella's. Nora's untethered tongue reported that a chap called Jack was once head-over-heels in love with Hereward's wife and had followed her around like a little lapdog. Everyone assumed their friendship had ended on the eve of Isabella's wedding. Rosalyn, however, wondered if that were true and decided to investigate. There was nothing to lose and everything to be gained should her suspicion prove right. Without a doubt a scandal would ensue and she would set her machinations in motion to make sure of it. Despite Hereward's cold-hearted rejection, she was determined to reclaim him, whatever it took.

On the day he broke the news to her of his forthcoming marriage, Rosalyn had asked him to name the lucky lady. But he outright refused. Thereafter, she consulted every church door in the district until she located the relevant banns. For some unfathomable reason she needed to discover the identity of the female responsible for wrecking her life. And when she finally came upon Hereward's name alongside that of his fiancée's, she felt as though her heart had been torn in two.

As Rosalyn sat brooding over her loss, her rage rose to the surface like milk bubbling up in a saucepan. No longer able to control her emotions, she pounded her thighs with her fists, wailed like a toddler in the grip of a tantrum, then sobbed into her hands until her tears were spent.

To soothe herself, she poured a large cognac from a sparkling cut-glass decanter. Cupping her glass in her hand, she swirled the liquid around to release its sweet, woody aroma. After gulping it down, she followed it up with a second one, then a third, and continued until she lost count. To think, she had sold her Kensington house to be close to Hereward and was now living in some inconsequential, unsophisticated satellite town. She wanted to kill him; correction: she wanted to kill his wife.

Chapter 14

Gingerly, Rosalyn handed Aldwen Hall's former gardener a brown envelope containing several clean, crisp pound notes withdrawn from the bank that morning.

Parker smiled to himself and shoved the envelope into the inside pocket of his second-hand jacket. The man who sold him the faded green garment boasted it came from the London Army and Navy Stores. Parker gave two hoots where it came from provided it had deep pockets and kept him warm.

Rosalyn had used the envelope not out of politeness or common courtesy, but to avoid touching Parker's ghastly spatulate hands in case he had scabies or some other contagion. It paid to be careful. Many poor people suffered from all kinds of infectious diseases, some of which were incurable. Otherwise, the condition of his hands was of no concern to her. He was there because he served her purpose; which made it just about possible to tolerate his malodorous shortcomings. He smelled horrid: essence of rotting tissue on a maggoty carcass came to Rosalyn's mind. She endeavoured to keep her distance and tried to avoid inhaling too deep. Why, she couldn't remember, but Barbara had once mentioned that he lived in one of those rodent-overrun crumbling cottages without bathrooms or lavatories in one of the hamlets near the river. No surprise there. The information had, however, proved useful, making him easy to track down.

After removing her lace-edged silk handkerchief, Rosalyn held it close to her nose. Each time he exhaled she noticed his halitosis had a peculiar pungency to it, similar to rotting vegetation. And when he spoke, she could see a black edentulous cavity between his discoloured canines.

"You're to follow Mrs Aldwen in secret. You know the way a hunter stalks an animal, without being seen or heard," Rosalyn instructed her temporary agent.

Parker knew only too well how a hunter stalks an animal, but he kept quiet. Throughout the years he had poached animals for food, fur and fun on a regular basis. Tender young rabbit meat provided the bulk of his diet. Rabbits not only cost nothing, their numbers also ran into thousands on the estate. The arable farmers waged a never-ending war on them. And although he required the landowner's permission to kill them, he never bothered to ask since he doubted Major Aldwen would mind.

"Proceed with caution," she continued. "She must not under any circumstances see you. I must be absolutely clear about that."

"Understood," said Parker, who relieved his annoyance by scratching the inside of his right nostril with a chunky forefinger. Her patronising posh voice grated on him like a badly played violin. However, he froze out her tone and focussed solely on her words. After all, she was paying him and she paid well. At the end of the day, money was money no matter its source. Parker wasn't one to moralise. His personal philosophy was plain and simple — rectitude was an extravagance for those on the breadline. The whys and wherefores of Rosalyn's motives mattered not to him.

"I must also advise you to first visit the Hall on some pretext or other," Rosalyn went on. "That way you can get a proper look at her before you begin, so that you know exactly who she is. I've only ever seen her briefly. She's a touch Nordic in appearance with pale-blonde curly hair. High forehead. Small and slim. Quite striking I suppose if one likes that sort of thing."

Which the Major obviously does, said Parker to himself, suppressing a wry smile.

"You mustn't go too near her now. I don't want her getting spooked. There's this lad, Jack. I believe that's his name. I've been told he's a tall, good-looking sort of chap. A bit on the thin side. Hair dirty blond and sometimes covered with a cloth cap. I have it on excellent authority that they were once involved on an intimate basis. I need to know whether they're still seeing each other and, if so, what they get up to."

Parker rather enjoyed observing what courting couples 'get up to'. He had done so plenty of times in the past. In fact, he considered himself rather an authority on the subject. The woods on the outskirts of Oakwich town centre provided excellent opportunities for peeping Toms. However, this was the first time he was being paid for the privilege. And although the Aldwen estate was further than he preferred to walk, the money more than compensated for the inconvenience and discomfort.

"Very well then," said Parker, wondering what the Major had ever seen in her equine face with its prominent square teeth, long nose and flared nostrils, made even less attractive by a constituent sneer.

"Get in touch with me as soon as you've something to report," she ordered.

Parker lifted the peak of his cap a fraction and exited the garden by the back gate. Time to celebrate, he thought, trotting off to the nearest slum ale house, where there were plenty of men who smelled just like him. Payment for pleasure, that's what it is. Bloody brilliant, he said to himself. Secretly watching a woman, or spying on her to use a more apt term, was surprisingly simple. Parker sometimes fancied himself as a spy. He only hoped the weather was favourable to his new endeavour.

After Parker departed, Rosalyn returned inside to the drawing room and went to the window. Outside, a dark-coloured motor-car slowed. For one fleeting moment her spirits rose when she thought she saw Hereward at the wheel and assumed he was coming to see her. But then, to her disappointment, the vehicle speeded up again and disappeared from sight.

The more Rosalyn thought about it, the more she became convinced that Hereward's wife was seeing someone. The girl just had to be. There was no other explanation for her aberrant behaviour. In Rosalyn's opinion, no normal woman spent all afternoon, every afternoon, wandering the woods alone. Well not without good reason. Then her lips curved into a sly smile. And that good reason was almost certainly Jack.

Rosalyn went upstairs to her dressing room, lighted a Sobranie and took an extended drag. Then she began to examine her face in the mirror. A green-headed pustule stood proud of the surface of her uppity chin. Spots were a curse: a collection of nasty red nodules she was convinced made her resemble the victim of some disastrous dermatological disease. It took only one spot to spoil the faultless finish of her foundation.

After resting the Sobranie in the groove of a black-marble ashtray, she flipped open her compact and patted a little extra powder on her chin with the puff pad. Achieving the desired result took patience and practice. It must look natural. Too heavy an application might give the wrong impression and attract unwanted attention.

As she took another suck on the cigarette, Rosalyn's mouth

puckered like a purse-string bag. She had to admit it looked unattractive. She recalled Hereward had been less than impressed by her smoking habit. He complained the odour of nicotine made him feel nauseous. Not only that, he also loathed the all-pervasive pong of stale tobacco that lingered in the air for days. Whenever she stayed at the Hall and needed to assuage her craving, she was banished to the grimy conservatory, even on cold winter days. And since there was no longer a room there reserved for smoking, she was obliged to comply.

Tapping the cigarette's ash trail into the ashtray, Rosalyn returned her attention to her face. Although the movie-star makeup was meant to conceal any defects on the skin, it couldn't perform miracles. With an audible sigh, Rosalyn slumped her shoulders. I should be married by now, she said to herself, not single and unattached. Married to Hereward that is. He must have once found her attractive. After all, he had bedded her, hadn't he? Bedded but not wedded, unfortunately. Without exception, she always made the most of her physical attributes. But even she had to concede she was no match for his beautiful young wife.

Rosalyn put down the cigarette, added more lipstick to her painted lips, pressed them together and moved them from side to side to ensure the product was evenly applied. Finally, she scraped off any smudges with the edge of a fingernail. Satisfied, she took one last look in the mirror before transferring the cosmetics to her handbag in case she might need to touch up her face while she was out. Then she re-stretched her stockings to remove the wrinkles and reattached them to her corset. The undergarment felt tighter than usual. Either the maid had fastened it on the wrong hooks or she had gained weight. Knowing Hereward abhorred fat ladies, she prayed it wasn't the latter.

Chapter 15

The early weeks of Isabella's marriage coincided with blackberry season. She adored blackberries: those round, purplish-black juicy jewels growing wild and abundant on prickly thickets throughout the estate. As a child she had once feasted on them before they had ripened and had suffered a most-painful colic. Fortunately, the experience had done nothing to spoil her love of the late-summer treat and she was keen to collect as many berries as she could.

The best time to pick them was when they reached full maturity, without so much as a hint of pink or green on their tiny drupelets. Since the weather was still clement, after luncheon Isabella spent hours outdoors with her basket gathering the fruit to give to Mrs Jenkins to make jam, puddings and a plethora of other sweet indulgences. And, to her delight, there was no shortage of sugar at the Hall.

Isabella was blissfully ignorant of her appearance when she joined Hereward for tea in the library later that afternoon. Without bothering to protect her clothes, she had been popping the plumpest, choicest, juiciest berries into her mouth to savour their sour sweetness. After seating herself in the chair opposite him, she debated whether to begin with a cheese sandwich, buttered crumpet or scone topped with strawberry jam.

Meantime, Hereward clinked down his china teacup on its matching saucer and cast a censorious eye over his wife's face and clothing.

"What the devil have you been doing?" he said, scowling at her with obvious displeasure. "You've stained a perfectly decent dress and your fingers and lips are purple."

"That's blackberry juice," she chuckled, unruffled by his sharp rebuke. "I've been gathering blackberries. They're awfully good. Would you like to try some?"

"No thank you," replied Hereward tersely. "A slovenly appearance denotes a slovenly attitude, my dear. For heaven's sake, girl, go and clean yourself up. I'll ask the maid to put aside some tea for you."

Gosh, what a curmudgeon, said Isabella to herself. She detested the way he put a damper on everything she did. Did he seriously expect her to sit on the sofa all day long like a porcelain doll? Why should a few small stains on her dress matter to him? Picking blackberries had at least provided a welcome diversion from her usual humdrum existence at the Hall.

That evening, feeling downcast by the perpetual dullness of much of her daily life, Isabella decided to retire early. Hereward remained in the sitting room listening to the wireless. He appeared to be back to his normal self and was no longer vexed with her, although she remained vexed with him. After excusing herself, she mounted the stairs, mooched into her bedroom and changed into her nightclothes. Then she went to the window, parted the curtains and looked out. And as she gazed up at the bright creature constellations in the night sky her eyes glistened with tears. Wiping them with the back of her hand, she walked away, fell into bed like a big brass bell-weight and curled up into a tight ball. There was no point in going to sleep as Hereward's arrival was virtually guaranteed. And she prayed that in time she would become immune to his moods and accustomed to his nocturnal ministrations.

Upon entering the room, Hereward observed Isabella facing the wall, as was her habit. The pig-headed posture not only tried his patience, it also spoiled his mood. So much so, that he felt sorely tempted to slap her.

"I see you insist on presenting your rear bumper to me again, my dear wife," he said coarsely. "Where are your manners, young lady?"

After removing his robe and tossing it over the ottoman, he climbed into bed, rolled onto his side and took a long hard look at the bulwark of Isabella's back.

Although she bristled at his chiding tone, Isabella tamed her tongue. Ice-cold silence was her weapon of choice in the bedroom; silence and stillness.

Without another word, Hereward took hold of the hem of her nightdress, drew it up to her waist and yanked down her drawers. Then he kissed the nape of her slender neck and fondled the dips and domes of her delectable body.

Isabella stiffened as his fingers explored her most-intimate zones. And as he continued undeterred by her cold response, she wondered what might happen if she were to deny his intrusions with a polite but firm *No, not tonight, thank you, if you don't mind.* Would he overrule her? Storm off in a huff? Or never return to her bed and take a mistress instead?

Despite the intense pleasure Hereward derived from making love to his wife, he nonetheless resented her repudiation of what he deemed to be his marital right to loving intimacy and mutual affection. Isabella's antipathy towards his ardent advances confounded him like nothing else. No other woman had ever responded to him with such callous indifference. No other woman had ever spurned him. It bruised his ego. It angered him. And when he was angry, he was unsparing of his antagonist.

There and then, Hereward decided the time had come to

teach his disobliging wife a lesson. A lesson on espousal etiquette that would serve to broaden her sexual horizons simultaneously. She would be given to understand that her passive non-cooperation in the marital bed had unforeseen but not perforce unpleasant consequences. So instead of rolling her onto her back, as she no doubt expected, he allowed her to remain in situ.

Isabella gasped when without warning Hereward drove himself deep inside her in the style of an animal. Practically impaled on his galloping manhood, she compressed her lips, squeezed tight her eyelids, braced her body, and waited with silent resignation for his appetency to be appeased.

Once satiated, Hereward withdrew triumphant, gave Isabella's uppermost buttock a resounding slap and, with a smirk to match his self-congratulatory manner, wished her an excellent night's sleep.

Isabella sighed with relief. Relief it was over. Over that is until next time, and the time after that. In fact, if her husband's current appetite served as an indicator, she knew to expect countless next times in the coming years.

Just as Hereward was about to exit the bedroom, he halted, half turned and told Isabella in an arbitrary tone that in future she must remove her undergarments before he joined her in bed.

Chapter 16

Wandering the estate, tucked into her cosy coat, passing the hours in peaceful contemplation, breathing gently through her nose, Isabella felt more relaxed and less constrained than she ever did inside the house. For the benefit of her mental well-being, she realised the importance of putting some distance between herself and the Hall's inhabitants. Whatever she wished to do, obstacles were put in her way. She would have liked to help Mrs Jenkins preserve the blackberries, but she knew for certain Boyle would raise some bogus objection to her presence in the kitchen. And there was no point in soliciting Hereward's support, as he was too aggrieved by her aversion to his romantic affection. Furthermore, she knew full well his objections to her performing menial labour, even when the choice was hers; evidenced by the unforgettable fracas in the conservatory. And when she remembered the water dripping from his fringe into his eyes and rolling down his cheeks, she couldn't help but smirk.

Back at the Hall, Mrs Jenkins, having decided to make jam, ordered Barbara to stir a batch of blackberries in a copper pan on top of the cast-iron range. Ordinarily, the maid would have been happy to assist the cook. After all, stirring fruit was easy. But since Isabella had supplied the berries, Barbara felt a perverse reluctance to lend a hand. Not that she was free to express her resentment. Old Jenkins and Tilly had only praise for the new mistress and, for the most part, Boyle kept his opinions to himself; although his face sometimes betrayed his true sentiments. Thus, Barbara had no choice but to keep her opinions to herself too; which frustrated her at the best of times, as there was no-one with whom to share her spite. Her wise mother, who had herself been in service as a single girl, advised her daughter with a wide-eyed nod on the day she started at Aldwen Hall that all walls have ears.

In the passage outside the kitchen Boyle could be heard ticking off Tilly for some minor misdeed. Lately, he seemed to have it in for the guileless girl. Most probably because the mistress favoured her, which went down like a sack of cement with the bullying butler. Such was a poor girl's lot, Tilly had to put up with his persecutions.

Barbara, however, being cannier than Tilly, quickly discerned that the best way to stay in Boyle's good books was to do his bidding. He had so much power, so much clout, he presumed he was accountable to no-one. Nevertheless, since the Major got married a subtle current of discontent had begun to flow through the Hall, slowly chipping away at his authority.

What the maid would have given to be married to a man like Major Aldwen. Or better still, the man himself. For the life of her she couldn't comprehend what made the mistress seem so morose. The ungrateful girl had everything a woman could wish for: beauty, leisure and comfort along with a wealthy and incredibly handsome husband.

With her usual sharp abruptness, Mrs Jenkins intruded on Barbara's musings to enquire how the mixture was coming along, making her jump like a jack in the box.

"Still stirring, Mrs Jenkins," said Barbara. Her back to the cook, she sucked in her insolent cheeks, half-rolled her mutinous eyeballs and expressed an expletive in her head before returning to her considerations. If not the Major, then she would like to marry a man from the middle-classes. One with his own business, a motorcar and pots of money. One who would buy her a fur coat and a suitcase-full of fancy frocks. One who would take her out dancing every Saturday night, and to Blackpool every year for a fortnight's holiday. Then she would tell that rat-bag Jenkins what to do with her stinking jam.

"Well make sure it doesn't stick to the bottom of the pan and burn," the cook said shortly. "You're looking a bit dreamy standing there and I've seen that spoon come to a standstill several times."

"Yes, Mrs Jenkins," said Barbara, followed by "Three bags full, Mrs Jenkins," under her breath. And while she stood stirring the sticky substance, she imagined herself to be a witch in a pointy black hat brewing potions in a gigantic cauldron with flames licking the sides. The first potion, she decided, would be given to Major Aldwen to make him fall madly in love with her. Barbara smiled to herself at the thought of his fine hands on her body. The second potion would be given to Isabella to make her disappear. Pouf! she would go in a cloud of smoke, never to be seen again. And the final potion she would take herself to transform her into a great beauty. Even more beautiful than Isabella. Three wishes, she decided, would suffice for now.

Meantime, out on the estate, a couple of stray curls dangling from under her cloche hat, Isabella roamed around, alternating between spells of aimless inattention and studied interest in the environment. Hereward had once said that some of the land had been in the Aldwen family for centuries, hence she felt a strong sense of his ancestors as she walked.

She liked to wander for a couple of hours at minimum, wherever the mood took her, each time either venturing a little further or following some unfamiliar trail. She preferred to be outdoors. It was better than moping about inside and struggling to keep boredom at bay. Only recently, as she recalled, Virginia Woolf had published a book titled *A Room of One's Own*. The book was about the importance of a woman having her own space in which to write fiction. Maud's bookcase boasted a copy. Isabella decided she would like to have a kitchen of her own in which to bake cakes, make fudge and whatever else she fancied concocting. Her imaginary kitchen contained a large dresser with a collection of recipe books along one complete shelf. During childhood, out from under her mama's unmotherly feet, she had spent many happy hours in the kitchen with the kindly servants, who would pet and spoil her no end. Perhaps I should write a book, she suggested to herself in a moment of lightsome contemplation. And I could call it: A Kitchen of One's Own.

After looping the lake, above which clouds traversed the sky, Isabella watched the wild ducks paddle back and forth across the water. The not-unpleasant aromas of pine, leaf mould and green sludge mingled in the air. Close by, a colony of rabbits hopped around, feasting on fibrous grasses, leafy weeds and whatever else was available to fill their herbivorous stomachs. One rabbit hobbled about and she felt desperately sorry for it, thinking it must have suffered an injury.

By the time she left the lakeside, Isabella felt more buoyant and less leaden than when she set out. Watching the wildlife on and around the water always lightened her mood and lifted her spirits. Everywhere the sounds of birds shrilling, twilling and tweeting filled the air with cheer. Birds were plentiful on the estate and she was attempting to teach herself to identify the various types from a book in the library. Still, the different bird calls continued to confuse her. She knew it was going to take time to recognise them all. However, to her delight, a conspicuously bright-plumed bird, which she now knew was a yellowhammer, sang a merry song in a nearby hedge.

Whenever Isabella got stuck in the house, for whatever reason, she felt like banging her head against the wall. More especially when Boyle or Barbara, or both together, entered the sitting room on some pretext or other. Given half a chance, they would probably watch her in the woods too, like they kept an eye on her in the house: slyly, silently, surreptitiously, waiting for her to make one wrong move so they could inform their master. In her mind's eye she pictured Boyle, stiff as a yard brush, standing behind a bush; Barbara behind a hedge, her face harder than a week-old scone left out in the open. Sometimes, to avoid them completely, Isabella remained in her bedroom, wrapped in a shawl, feet tucked under her thighs, nose buried in a novel.

As she watched a nuthatch scramble up the trunk of a tree, Isabella realised that although she was tired from rambling all afternoon, not to mention feeling peckish, she was reluctant to return to the confining atmosphere of the house. Her disagreeable relationship with Hereward weighed heavy on her mind. Back when the hasty marriage arrangements were taking place, she had given little thought to what her future life would be like as his wife. She was too distressed by the process of being passed from one despotic patriarch to another, like her mother before her. Except that her mother had considered marriage to Archibald Acton preferable to the unenviable state of spinsterhood.

Had Isabella been permitted to choose her own husband, she felt sure she would have chosen an entirely different man. A man who treated her as an equal, believed in female advancement and education, and was liberal, open-minded and outgoing. Although she preferred not to be poor, she cared little if her ideal man were rich, upper class and influential.

During the daytime, living the estranged life foisted on her, Isabella often felt lonely, especially for want of female companionship. In the evenings, thankfully time was taken up with soaking in a hot bathtub, dressing for dinner, eating a substantial meal, and being entertained either by the wireless or Hereward on the piano while she sat looking pretty in a long gown. Which reminded her, she needed to ask Tilly to launder her good gown.

Chapter 17

Sipping his aperitif, Hereward looked Isabella over with an appraising eye. "I see you're wearing your dear mama's old hand-me-down again. Where is your other gown?" he asked.

Colouring under his close scrutiny, Isabella folded her arms across her breasts. "Tilly has taken it to be laundered and it won't be ready for a day or two," she explained.

"You have only one decent gown, is that correct?" he enquired with a slight frown.

"Yes," she admitted. Although she accepted his interest was well-meaning, Isabella nonetheless bristled at his lack of diplomacy and inadvertent reference to her financial deficiencies. More specifically, she resented the inference, even if it were unintentional, that without a dowry she was wholly dependent on him to fund her wardrobe. And since pride prevented her from requesting more money, she made do with what little she had.

"For heaven's sake, my darling girl, must you behave like a pauper? Visit your dressmaker at the first opportunity," urged Hereward with impatience. "Or else pop into town and stock up on a few wardrobe essentials, and whatever else you require. It beats me why you wear that same outfit to dinner almost every evening."

Isabella threw her husband a questioning look. "I'm afraid my allowance doesn't stretch to haute couture," she said in a tone honed with sarcasm. "I thought you would have realised that."

Hereward looked at her as if she were a foolish child and shook his head in slow motion. "Then open an account," he said in his slowest, most-patient voice. "You can tell the dressmaker, or department store, or whatever you decide on, to send the bill here. Boyle can take care of it. If there's any problem they can ring and speak to him directly."

Isabella baulked at the idea of the butler settling her clothing bills. It was far too intrusive, and she suspected he would rather enjoy the process.

"I'll ask him to drop you in town whenever you decide to go," Hereward volunteered to be helpful. Even though no-one except himself and the servants saw his wife's gowns, her meagre wardrobe nevertheless reflected badly on him and he felt duty bound to rectify the problem.

Isabella found the notion of being chauffeured by the beastly Boyle repellent, and she declined her husband's offer with cold politeness.

"Thank you all the same, but I'm perfectly capable of making my own way into town." A while back she had noticed a couple of bicycles in the outhouse and had made a mental note of their future usefulness.

Hereward scowled at her over his glass. "I don't know why you insist on being so damned self-reliant," he said in an irritated tone. "And what if it rains. You'll get soaked."

Having already made up her mind, Isabella made no further comment to signal the subject was closed.

The day after that, Isabella rolled out the lady's silver-framed bicycle and checked the tyres were fully inflated. Then, without informing anyone of her intentions, she set off on her shopping expedition. Many years had gone by since she last rode a bicycle, but she was mobile in no time at all. Although Hereward's remarks from the night before regarding her gown still rankled, the ride revived happy memories of her own two-wheeled companion long since sold; an early casualty of the Acton's financial misfortunes.

Cruising down the deserted road improved Isabella's mood and, in an unseen act of rebellion, she released her topknot. And while the emancipating wheels whizzed forward on the road's smooth surface, her liberated locks flew backwards on the wind. Autumn had definitely dropped anchor, and although the chilly air chafed her cheeks, the activity warmed her up rather well. And to her relief, the weather was still dry when she coasted into Oakwich town centre.

The eponymous ladieswear shop, Martha's, was one of the more-select businesses on the high street. Sandwiched between the haberdashery and the hat shop, it was a place where women lingered to check out the latest fashions in the window display before those with sufficient funds ventured inside. Isabella looked up at the large gold letters on the big black signboard, dismounted and left the bicycle leaning on the lamppost opposite the entrance.

As she entered the shop, the brass doorbell pinged to alert the proprietor to her presence. It was quiet inside, quiet and peaceful; a place for women and women only. The décor's delicate palette of pinks, creams and greens gave the interior a reassuring ambience of relaxed intimacy. Beside the window, a button-back chaise was draped in a selection of chiffon-silk scarves. While along one wall a couple of salon chairs provided a place for clients to take the weight off their feet while Martha showed them a variety of gowns endowed with movie-star style and glamour.

Isabella adored the smell of brand-new cloth, more especially wool, which had its own distinct but indescribable aroma. She cast her eyes over rails of Hollywood-inspired gowns and dresses made from contemporary fabrics in that season's colours. Lingerie and stockings were stored in gleaming-glass cabinets both beneath and behind the counter.

Owing to her dislike of them, Isabella seldom wore stockings. Not silk ones at any rate. Only woollen ones in winter, and only then when the weather was bitterly cold. She considered all things restrictive a hindrance, especially the garters worn to prevent the stockings from sliding down one's legs. Or worse still, those silly suspender belts with long dangling attachments whose clasps left small indentations at the tops of the thighs. Not that Isabella had ever worn a suspender belt. She felt sure it would inhibit her ability to move about in freedom and comfort. To date, Hereward had passed no comment on her bare legs. She presumed he must not have noticed them. Should he do so, she expected he would without doubt impose another one of his strict dictates to correct her sartorial offence. A slightly rebellious smirk lifted her lips and cheeks a little as she imagined his authoritative voice proclaiming the unseemliness of naked legs on a married lady. Oh, the horror!

Suddenly an assured voice called out: "I'll be with you shortly." Thereafter a woman emerged from a room at the back of the shop. She was a smartly dressed, attractive brunette in her early thirties with bright baby-blue eyes and the kind of face one instantly warms to.

"Good afternoon. How may I be of assistance?" asked the brunette with a professional smile.

Isabella said she was looking for a gown. Although what sort of gown she was looking for she hadn't a clue. Having never dressed for a season of debutante balls and high-society events, she was thus uninformed about the latest fashions.

Discreetly, Martha considered her new client up close. She

appeared to be about sixteen. However, because the girl was precocious in figure but not in face, she found it impossible to gauge her age precisely. The shop's owner was also surprised to see the young woman, or girl, for she straddled the adult-adolescent divide, was wearing a 22-carat-gold wedding ring. Whatever her age, her polite, polished and genteel manner indicated she was high-born, but lacking the usual crest of condescension those of her class display to people they consider beneath them.

"Would it be possible to open an account?" Isabella asked with an almost-apologetic smile. "I live at Aldwen Hall. It's only a couple of miles from here."

Martha had heard of the Hall. She estimated Isabella's dress size with an expert eye, then, with an efficient hand, removed several fancy gowns from the racks.

"Let's see what we have here," she said, holding them up in turn for Isabella's appraisal. "I think these will all suit you very nicely and the colours will enhance your skin tone and complement your hair."

Isabella, who viewed clothes purely in terms of comfort, quality and practicality, had never considered the tone of her skin and shade of her hair in relation to what she wore. Hereward had never mentioned them either, although he did sometimes tell her she was beautiful when he came to her bed. He also looked at her rather a lot, especially during mealtimes.

How to address her young customer placed Martha in a quandary. To refer to her as *madam* felt inappropriate in view of the girl's youth, and *young lady* seemed too patronising.

"If you prefer, I can have them tailored to fit you?" she offered. "Alterations usually take about a week at no extra cost unless they're extensive."

With Martha's able assistance, Isabella tried on several garments and was pleased with her appearance in most of them.

After much humming and hawing, she purchased the two dresses she considered the most modest and demure.

"As soon as the alterations are completed, I'll arrange to have them delivered to the Hall," said Martha. "Payment is expected at the end of the month where clothes are purchased on account."

In addition, Isabella bought gloves, handkerchiefs and two sets of soft-cotton, lace-edged underwear. However, she politely declined Martha's offer to show her a selection of brassieres. Or what her mother's generation called bust bodices. Isabella had never worn a brassiere. Nor did she intend to. Why must a woman swaddle her breasts? she asked herself. It's unnatural. A foolish invention. She considered the brassiere, like the suspender belt, an unnecessary encumbrance, not to mention a waste of good money.

Speaking of which, Isabella feared she had overspent. Years of mending and making do had made her cautious with cash and she counted every single penny in her purse. Unfortunately, on this occasion, she had succumbed to Martha's persuasive sales techniques and spent more than she originally intended to. She tried not to think of what Hereward might say when he saw the bill.

Martha accompanied Isabella to the door. "Goodbye, Mrs Aldwen, and thank you," she said warmly. She always felt gratified when she gained a new customer, and she hoped to see the young lady again. After all, one could never have too many wealthy customers, and this one she actually liked.

A woman in black high heels tottered past the shop as Isabella stepped down onto the pavement. Having recognised Hereward's memorable wife, she came to an abrupt halt and, swaying a little, stared at her replacement with undisguised contempt.

"It's you, you little strumpet!" she spat, spraying tiny droplets of saliva in Isabella's shocked face.

"Excuse me!" said Isabella, thinking there must be some mistake.

The woman was tall, lean and straight, with the amber eyes of a territorial tiger. Her blunt-cut ebony hair was styled precisely, her angular face embalmed in Max Factor foundation cream, and her thin lips painted dark crimson to make them look sultry, but the effect was more savage than sultry.

"Hereward and I were practically engaged until you came along and stole him from me," she fumed. Her hot breath emitted a flatus of brandy and tobacco into the immediate air which competed with the zest of her expensive French cologne. "Are you pregnant? Is that it? I shouldn't be at all surprised. You must have trapped him you little trollop."

The irony of the epithet wasn't lost on Isabella, who concluded in light of the raging evidence before her that the harridan harassing her must be Miss Rosalyn Dumbarton, her husband's former lover; the details about whom Tilly had let slip inadvertently. And before the man-eater could harangue her any further, Isabella mounted her bicycle and pedalled back to the Hall as fast as her size-four feet would permit.

Chapter 18

On her return to the Hall Isabella observed Hereward standing at the front door while checking his wristwatch. She sensed his mood as she propelled herself forward onto the gravel. Halting at the front steps, she dismounted, leaned the bicycle against the wall and, with her chin set firm, stared up at him.

He looked unimpressed. But then looking unimpressed was one of Hereward's distinguishing features that made him look less than distinguished. His mouth was grim, his eyes were flinty and his left hand was planted on his hip.

"You and I are in need of a frank discussion," he said without the customary greeting. "Please go upstairs to your room and wait for me there. I'll be along shortly."

Anxious to avoid another ugly scene in front of the servants, Isabella duly obliged. The memory of the sodden episode in the conservatory remained fresh in her mind. I wonder what heinous crime I've committed this time? she said to herself after slumping in one of the hearth chairs. Well, she would soon find out.

Five minutes later Hereward entered the bedroom. He leaned on the chimneypiece and shoved one hand inside his trouser pocket. As usual, Isabella's behaviour galled him. He tried not to let it, still it did, and he decided it was time to raise the issue with her. Nevertheless, he was determined not to sound cross. Sounding cross was a bad habit of his which he accepted more often than not inflamed the situation. Before speaking he tugged at his earlobe, a mannerism peculiar to him whenever he was about to make an important point; important to him that is.

"Darling," he began, "I must insist you inform me whenever you leave the estate. At teatime when I asked Barbara to call you, she said you weren't back yet. She also said she'd heard you go out, but that you hadn't gone in your usual direction. Then Boyle came in to say one of the bicycles was missing from the outhouse. Well, since both maids were still here in the house, naturally I assumed you must have taken it, especially since we rarely see thieves this far from town."

Speaking of thieves, Isabella suspected Hereward of making an ironic reference to the incident in the orchard. Owing to their ambiguity, she often struggled to interpret his remarks correctly, especially when his facial expression gave no indication of whether he was serious or simply joking.

"I didn't tell you I was going into town because I wished to avoid disturbing you at your desk," she said quickly in her defence. Which wasn't strictly true and she touched her nose in a subliminal nod to Pinocchio.

"Then may I suggest that in future either you tell one of the servants where you are going or leave a note stating your destination and when I should expect you back?"

Hereward grew pensive, paused, then took a deep breath. "Look here," he said, "if you were to meet with an accident, or for that matter any misfortune, I would have no idea. If I have no idea that you're in any sort of trouble, then I cannot come to your rescue. Do you understand me?" Fixing his eyes on hers in the manner of an adult dealing with a child, he awaited her response.

With quizzical eyes Isabella stared up at him. *Rescue*? An intriguing choice of word thought she with mild amusement.

In her imagination the word *rescue* evoked dramatic scenes of distressed damsels and immured maidens commonly featured in fairy tales and romantic fiction. It sounded frightfully old-fashioned, not to mention awfully far-fetched. She suspected his impressing upon her the notion of female fragility was a subtle means of undermining her confidence in order to exert greater control over her. However, on this occasion, she agreed that writing a note was sensible and, tired of the constant enmity between them, promised to leave one on the hall table whenever she left the estate.

Hereward released a long sigh of relief at Isabella's untypical compliance. For how long her compliance would last, however, was anyone's guess. Regarding his headstrong wife, he was under no illusions. The little minx was a law until herself, and he wondered if he would ever manage to contain her or bend her to his will. She tried his patience and raised his passions in a way her predecessors had never done.

The day after that, when they were having their tea beside a crackling log fire, Isabella became aware of an unfamiliar face looking askew at her through the library window.

"Who's that odd-looking chap out there?" she asked Hereward, motioning her head in the man's direction. "I must say he looks rather creepy." Then her upper body convulsed with a sudden cold sensation and she whispered: "Gosh, I think someone just walked over my grave."

With a resonant clink Hereward set down his teacup on its saucer and twisted around to face the window. As he did so he saw a man make off quickly into the murkiness of the late afternoon.

"It's only Parker," said Hereward, turning back to face her.

Isabella was convinced the oddball had been peering in specifically at her. "Who is Parker, and what's he doing in the garden?" she enquired.

"He might have come to chop some logs," explained Hereward. "He's the gardener, or rather he was. We don't see him nowadays except on the odd occasion when he needs extra money. Presumably for beer or cigarettes. He lives in one of the outlying small villages over near the river and prefers to work closer to home now. I suppose one can hardly blame him. Boyle will of course need to find his replacement shortly if we're to have the garden shipshape in time for summer."

"Since the gardener rarely comes now, who chops the logs the rest of the time?" asked Isabella before biting into a small crustless sandwich cut in the shape of a thin rectangle.

"I do."

"What!" A crumb caught in her throat and she coughed into the side of her curled hand.

"I do," Hereward reiterated with a straight face.

"You do?" she replied with a doubtful smirk before dabbing her mouth with her napkin.

"Well, the logs can hardly chop themselves, can they?"

"Sarcasm doesn't become you, Hereward."

Since it wasn't entirely undeserved, he ignored the admonishment, picked up his teacup and sipped his Darjeeling.

"I assumed it was Boyle's job," said Isabella, "since there appeared to be no-one else around here to do it."

Hereward laughed with derision. "He doesn't have the physique I'm afraid. At least not to chop the big tough hardwoods. Shoulders too narrow, hips too wide and arms too flabby," he said in a clipped voice. Then he whispered: "Built more like a middle-aged woman than a man."

Isabella laughed a little too loudly. Hereward can be awfully amusing at times, she thought. "I've never seen you do it," she said. "Are you serious or just pulling my leg?"

He paused, clanked down his teacup and sighed with mild

exasperation. "I can assure you I'm not pulling your leg. I do it first thing, between my walk and breakfast."

"You take a walk?" said a goggle-eyed Isabella in a high-pitched voice.

"Yes, I most certainly do. I'm not sure why that should surprise you. I usually set out very early while you're still fast asleep, my little kitten."

Isabella wished Hereward would stop calling her patronising pet names, but she couldn't quite decide how to tell him.

"Then I return here and chop the wood whenever the pile starts to shrink," he continued. "I must say I enjoy the exercise. I need something to keep me fit now I'm no longer in the military. Writing is such a sedentary occupation."

"Yes, I can imagine it is. Anyway, I'd like to watch you do it," she said. "You know, swing the axe."

"Why are you hoping to see me fall on my blade?" he said dryly with a forced smile.

"Of course not. Don't be silly," she chuckled.

There then followed a momentary silence. Isabella wasn't sure whether to take him at his word. She thought he might be hoodwinking her, amusing himself at her expense by playing her for a fool.

"Well perhaps you could chop a few extra logs for my bedroom," she said, then immediately regretted it.

Hereward looked puzzled but made no response.

Chapter 19

Desperate to escape the house, Isabella put on her walking boots, threw an old shawl around her shoulders and exited by the boot-room door. The sky was its usual gruel grey, but the weather was otherwise dry and the air sedate. After closing the rusty side gate, she cut through the orchard and followed the path to the right. Then she continued on past the farm field where the cows grazed in a haze of contentment. The odours of fresh manure, wheat straw and graniferous grasses tickled Isabella's sensitive nasal passages and she absently rubbed her nose with the side of her forefinger.

On arriving at the lakeside, humming a lilting tune to herself, Isabella stopped for a rest and watched the water gently lap the shoreline. All around her, birds called, frogs croaked, ducks quacked, and squirrels chittered. The moist air smelled of mud, pondweed and moss. And although it intensified her longing for times sealed in the past, the lake remained her favourite place on the estate.

After lowering herself onto a large log on the littoral, soothed by the dewy tranquillity, Isabella soon fell into a nostalgic trance. The water's reflections aroused recollections that made her sigh with sentimental bliss. A collapsed tree bridging the south side of the lake was still undergoing the slow process of decomposition. On the hottest days of her fourteenth summer, it had served as a platform from which she and her foolhardy friends had flung themselves into the water, laughing and screaming with glee. How she missed those comparatively carefree days spent climbing trees, playing childish pranks and exploring the countryside.

Even now, Isabella fancied she could still scale a tree trunk and swing from a bough. Alas, her smart new clothes were unsuited to such active pursuits. Her eyes moist with emotion, she thought of the verbal thrashing Hereward would most likely mete out should she return to the Hall with her coat in less than immaculate condition. He can be such a tyrant at times, she told herself. Also recalling his warnings about potential hazards and mishaps, plus his emphasis on her female weakness and vulnerability, she pondered on why he tried to make her feel unsafe. It was impossible to say what lay behind his thinking and she preferred not to misinterpret his motives or cast doubt on his sincerity.

After abandoning her improvised seat, Isabella walked into the woods directly opposite the lake. Although they were dark and dense, and impassable even in many places, still they drew her into their bowered seclusion. Everywhere the odours of damp black bark, leaf mould and wild fungi perfused the air. Poison ivy crept unchecked across the cold earth, coiling itself around trees and wherever else its demonic tendrils could take hold. The ground was a damp mossy carpet covered in matted leaves, many of them more crinkled than a centennial crone; while clusters of mushrooms cropped up in random arrangements around the bases and stumps of trees.

Mushroom hunting after a rain shower was one of Isabella's favourite pastimes. A pastime she refused to forgo despite being married to a man of means. She searched for the rare lion's mane mushroom, a delicious delicacy that would shortly be out of season. Weaving in and out of the towering trees in a quasi-zigzag configuration, she harvested as many of the mildly aromatic fungi as would fit into her basket without getting crushed.

Feeling the first fall of raindrops on her face, Isabella held out her palm for confirmation while looking up through the thinning tree canopy at the fast-changing sky, more granite than gruel now in colour. The accumulation of rain clouds made the forest feel cooler and look darker than when she first entered it. Conscious that a few droplets could soon become a deluge, she decided to call it a day.

However, as Isabella started to retrace her steps to the main pathway, she was assailed by the strangest sensation. A sensation hitherto unexperienced. There also existed an unsettling vibration in the atmosphere, similar to when a distant storm is brewing. It made her distinctly uneasy. And as she continued walking, the sensation grew stronger and more concentrated. Then all of a sudden, she felt she was being watched. That someone or something was observing her from somewhere within the trees.

Half expecting to see some dark shadowy figure, Isabella stopped, slowly rotated a complete circle on the spot and scanned the surroundings. As she did so, her spine and shoulders shook involuntarily. But all she could see was a rich collage of autumnal colours in the dense woody backdrop.

Isabella knew from experience that no-one ever ventured deep into the Aldwen woods. In fact, after moving to the Hall she had seen not a single soul walking or hanging around in them. Now and again, itinerants and pedlars passed through the estate on their way to the town, but they always stuck to the central path. As did those who frequented the farm as casual labourers and journeymen in search of an honest day's work. On the odd occasion, the farmer or his son could be seen returning a runaway cow to the field. Not one of them had ever posed a threat to her, nor had anyone else for that matter, so she couldn't comprehend her unusual disquietude.

Setting off again, at faster pace than before, Isabella kept a lookout for signs of movement. Since her mild myopia made everything in the distance appeared blurred, she wondered whether she should purchase a pair of spectacles to wear on her walks. However, as soon as she emerged from the trees back into the open, the strange aberration faded. Feeling settled once more, she slowed down and made her way back to the Hall thinking only of fresh-brewed tea, buttered crumpets and toasted teacakes.

Hereward happened to be in the boot-room when Isabella returned. He frowned, first at the mushrooms, then at her. It was plain to see she had been caught out by a spell of drizzle: her clothes were damp, her boots were dewy, and her curls were frizzy around her hairline. His dark brows abutted in a heavy scowl and he barked: "Look at the state of you. Good heavens, girl, you'll catch your death going out without a mackintosh."

Since Isabella understood her husband's outburst was his own peculiar way of expressing concern, she tried her best not to take umbrage.

"I've been for a walk," she said with cool constraint. "There's little by way of occupation in the house. I far prefer to be outdoors. And besides, as you can see, I'm wearing a warm woollen shawl. Plus, a little light rain never hurt anyone," she said with a dismissive wave at the wet window.

All of a sudden Hereward's mood altered and he smiled sardonically. "Ah yes, the great outdoors," he quipped, one eyebrow arched above a puckish eye. "The perfect place to pilfer a barrowload of apples."

Isabella could see it pleased him to taunt her. However, on this occasion his playful provocation fell flat. She stared at him boldly, unamused by his amusement.

"I shouldn't think it possible to *pilfer* what is now also my property by virtue of our marriage," she replied with a scornful smile.

"Touché!" conceded Hereward with a devilish grin.

Incensed by his teasing, Isabella turned her back to him and started to walk away.

"I can see I'm going to have my work cut out with you, my good lady," he called after her.

Isabella stopped dead. "Lady!" she echoed with feigned bemusement. "I ceased to be a lady the day I married you."

Hereward, however, refused to bite the bait. "My dearest darling you are very much mistaken if you think your spurs will wound me. On the contrary, your propensity for sparring with me serves only to heighten my fervour, and I look forward, by virtue of our marriage, as you so rightly say, to our regular night-time rendezvous with even greater anticipation."

Isabella, her face crimson, winced and quickly walked away.

Come bedtime, Hereward was true to his word. His eyes gleamed like black sapphires as he held back the bedclothes and playfully patted the capacious bed.

"Come along now, look sharp, and don't keep me waiting," he said with a teasing smile.

Recollecting his risqué remarks in the boot-room early that afternoon, Isabella winced internally with embarrassment. Her cheeks blighted by big red blotches, she climbed into bed but refused to look at him.

Hereward strode around to the opposite side of the bed and slid in beside her. Despite his slight swagger, his wife's cold response to his romantic endeavours continued to irk him. She could not be more distant if she tried. She reminded him of a magnificent Ming vase: stunning without, empty within, and he wondered if her attitude towards him would ever soften or grow warm.

Isabella knew full well her indifference to his lovemaking wounded him, but she cared not a jot for his masculine pride. After all, she had been forced to marry him, and he had arrogated her girlhood without a grain of regret or guilt. According to her understanding, a wife's duty to her husband was simple submission; she owed him nothing beyond that.

Hereward switched off the night lamp, lay back and interlocked his fingers behind his head. The fading fire cast the room in a soft, warm glow, which would have felt romantic had Isabella been so inclined. And while he loved to savour her sweet scent and fondle her honeyed flesh, he felt sorely tempted to tear off the shapeless shift she always wore to bed like a suit of armour. He considered buying her a slinky nightdress or a pair of fancy satin pyjamas. Something soft and silky that clung to her fine calligraphic curves. Still, whatever she wore to bed, even an old hopsack, could not make him want her less.

Moreover, Hereward's concupiscence wasn't solely confined to the bedroom. Wherever he was, one look at his wife's alluring loveliness was all it took to set his loins alight. Throughout the day he confined himself to the library, where he focused his mind on his work. However, he always made one important concession: that no matter how onerous his workload, he and Isabella must convene for luncheon every day without fail.

Unhappily for Hereward, her mood during the midday meal was not in any way conducive to making casual and cordial conversation. She said little at the table quite simply because she had little to say. Nor did she look at her husband. Once in a while, she looked out of the window when a bird flew past, the sky changed shade or rainclouds appeared. Her primary focus was the food on her porcelain plate and she applied herself to the dishes with a diligence verging on the devotional.

Her taciturnity did not, however, stop Hereward from looking at her. The sight of his wife across the table enjoying her food was a feast for the eyes. Nonetheless, following a morning of eye-straining scholastic enquiry, he would have welcomed the relief of a little light-hearted, inconsequential chitchat with his beautiful spouse.

Without exception, a soup course was always served at luncheon. The dish, however, was never a consommé. Hereward preferred something more substantial with a consistency that dissolved smoothly on the tongue. He loved to watch Isabella dip her spoon sideways into the soup plate, skim it over the soup's surface, raise it to her mouth, and consume the semi-viscous liquid. There was something about the way her lips latched onto the spoon, their semi-softness against the hard silverware, that he found intoxicating. What he would have given to be placed between those lips.

Isabella reserved her greatest affection for what she considered the pinnacle of the meal — the scrumptious plump pudding. With a tooth sweeter than a butterscotch biscuit, she savoured every sensational mouthful of syrup sponge or sticky tart or fruit crumble. Although she was dainty, she was never dainty with her food. Not a morsel went wasted, and she scraped her plate clean until it squeaked. To Isabella food was pleasure, comfort and consolation.

Hereward envied the attention his wife paid to her food and wondered if he could ever compete. Nevertheless, now and again he made the effort to communicate with her on a companionable basis. There came a time when, in an attempt to relieve the tension at the noontime table, he decided to indulge in a little light banter.

"The fodder certainly seems to be to your taste today," he said with a tentative smile as he considered her cleared plate with an amused eye.

Displeased by his teasing, Isabella half raised her eyebrows, narrowed her eyes and stiffened her cheeks. Although she considered his comment a thinly veiled criticism, she had yet to decide whether he was mocking her man-size appetite or calling her greedy. Whichever it was, she had no intention of curbing her food consumption.

"I'm taking a long walk this afternoon," she replied curtly after a lengthy pause. "So, as I'm sure you'll agree, I must have sufficient food inside me to maintain my energy levels. After all, you wouldn't drive your precious motorcar on an empty fuel tank and expect to reach your destination, would you?"

"Quite so," he concurred with a suggestive smile. "Sustenance of *every* kind is essential for the maintenance of mind, body and soul."

"And gluttony of *every* kind is a deadly sin," she replied in pointed reproof.

Since Boyle was hovering in the doorway, Isabella rose from the table before Hereward could fire off another ribald riposte in his hearing. She thought it unwise to allow the butler to eavesdrop on their marital combats, which he no doubt enjoyed.

Tired of the scrutiny to which she was subjected at the Hall on a regular basis, Isabella declined the post-luncheon coffee and went straight to the boot room. There she changed her footwear, donned her coat and pulled her hat down over her topknot. After exiting the Hall and stepping through the side gate, she walked at a steady pace along the hedged path and cut through the orchard. And as she inhaled the crisp country air, her mood began to improve and she gave no further thought to her husband's irrepressible insinuations.

Chapter 20

As a light breeze licked the leaves and the birds tweeted in the trees, Isabella, a bounce in her step, decided there was no better tonic than a country walk, especially a woodland walk. Out there on the estate no clocks ticked, clicked or chimed to remind her of the rigid routines of the Hall, whose every room felt like a cell no matter its size. Away from the house she could escape Boyle and Barbara's assiduous observations. A bonus if ever there was one.

At the point at which the path left the orchard, it broadened and ran south between farmland to the left and open pasture and forest to the right. After sweeping past the lake, it continued onwards, terminating at a stretch of arable fields, each one bigger than a rugby pitch. Beyond the fields meandered a long lane bordered by the grass bank of a mighty river, which functioned as a conduit for the movement of cargo. The habitat was home to a large variety of wildlife including deer, foxes, squirrels badgers, and birds, not to mention lots of greedy rabbits that, given free rein, ravaged the crops with their tough teeth.

Despite the dissatisfactions in her young life, Isabella felt privileged to reside in such an idyllic and picturesque place. Especially when she remembered the slums of Oakwich, where her former friends lived in tiny back-to-back terraced houses tenanted by innumerable deprived families who could only dream of the kind of life she now led.

On passing by the farm field, Isabella noticed a hardy herd of dairy cows nibbling the grass and swishing their stringy tails with their typical air of detachment. Not that she minded, but they seemed blithely unaware of her presence. On the days when she felt inclined, she would call them over to the gate where she stood waiting. Led by the bell cow, they would plod over to her with a swaying motion, as though trying to balance their bulk on their thin knock-kneed legs. After which they would stare at her with their soulful, treacle-brown eyes as they continued chewing the cud. She found pleasure in the simplest things, often stopping to observe a bird, pick a wildflower, or study some unfamiliar botanical feature. There was so much to see, so much to learn, she never grew bored.

After two hours spent exploring the estate's many paths and trails, Isabella typically lost track of the time. In such a marvellous unspoiled setting it happened so easily. That afternoon the forest air smelled like the greengrocer's shop with a whiff of the fishmonger's thrown in for good measure. Once, during dinner, Hereward had explained that several areas of the Aldwen woods were still recovering from their wartime decimation. Legions of trees had been sacrificed to the war effort, which was why woodsmen were no longer seen wielding their axes around the estate. However, he also said that because reforestation was going so well, he was thinking of employing an estate manager in the near future.

As she continued to reflect while she walked, Isabella became conscious of an unaccountable atmospheric change and a frisson of disturbance in the general air. It had a similar presentiment to when things go bump in the night, generating an unnerving uncertainty about what might happen next. Then as goosepimples surfaced on her skin, she encountered the same perturbing sensation as before: that eyes were watching her;

cold, cruel, ruthless eyes, the eyes of a fiend subjecting her every move to intense scrutiny. The sensation was incredibly strong; so strong, she felt as if the eyes were physically touching her back.

Thereafter, Isabella heard a creature's distress call. Then from the corner of her eye she caught sight of a momentary movement in the tight-packed trees. Half swinging around, she stood still and stared stiffly at the spot where the movement had occurred. Unfortunately, her short-sighted vision made some objects in the distance difficult to decipher. Prone to engaging in flights of fancy, Isabella found her fears and insecurities soon multiplied. Something about the dark shadows and their indeterminate outlines made her feel doubly afraid. Yet wherever she looked there was nothing to explain her puzzling perceptions.

Giving way to an intuitive impulse, Isabella thought it best to begin making her way back to the Hall. At the same time, she tried to banish her forebodings from her troubled mind by attributing them to her over-vivid imagination; which proved impossible when her fear began to acquire a more sinister aspect. From the depths of her extravagant psyche a menagerie of monstrous beings floated to the surface: werewolves in the woods, murderers in the meads, man-eating beasts in the bushes.

Only recently, after viewing a collection of sepia photographs in a medical textbook she came across while exploring the attic rooms, Isabella had developed a phobia of mental asylums. The absence of colour made the images appear additionally disturbing. She feared that if she failed to conquer her neuroticism, she might easily suffer the same fate as those poor sequestered souls in the textbook. On the outskirts of Oakwich stood an old redbrick institution where it was rumoured that once a woman went in, she never came out. Not only that, but also detainees were subjected to cruel and barbaric treatments that destroyed their essential selves. Isabella imagined the redoubtable Boyle would undoubtedly be delighted to hear of her incarceration in some kind of custodial compound. If the butler had his way, the entire female population would be locked up.

Since darkness was beginning to descend, more rapidly than usual it seemed to her, Isabella decided to hurry. Having spent much of the afternoon immersed in thought, and impervious to the passage of time, she had again strayed too far. Even if she ran all the way back at full speed, she doubted she could reach the house in time for tea. The maids would shortly be clearing away the tea things under Boyle's strict instructions. In fact, she suspected Barbara took pleasure in depriving her of food. And she imagined the mean-spirited maid dashing downstairs on her milk-bottle legs with the tray of uneaten tea in her squarish hands, while kind-hearted Tilly did her best to delay her.

Added to which, Hereward would almost certainly be wearing his reproachful face, ready to rebuke her for the umpteenth time for her rude disregard of his monolithic rules. Rules that suited his convenience and took no account of hers. However, since she was now accustomed to his tempestuous castigations, not to mention that all-too-familiar angry flush on his forehead and cheeks, they had next-to-no effect on her. As a married woman and, indeed, mistress of Aldwen Hall, she could hardly be banished to her bedroom like a naughty child, could she?

Owing to her growing nervousness, Isabella picked up her pace. Her back, now damp with perspiration, began to prickle and itch. Unfortunately, it was impossible to scratch it through the thick fabric of her coat. Inexplicably, the woods seemed denser and more shadowy than usual. Then she got wind of a weird presence moving through the trees. Its vibrations disrupted the atmosphere. The phenomenon was similar to knowing when an intruder was inside the house without being able to see them.

A couple of minutes later, Isabella almost jumped out of her skin when she heard a cracking sound. Turning rapidly in the sound's direction, she surveyed the scene. Not a single disturbing detail stood out. All the same, she remained rooted to the spot for several seconds listening attentively. But she heard nothing more. Nothing except a distinct hush. The kind of hush that foreshadows a fateful event. She wondered whether a stag could be wandering through the nearby trees. Not long since, Hereward had warned her to stay clear of stags, especially during the rutting season, when they were known to be aggressive and unpredictable.

As the sky continued to grow dimmer and the landscape began to lose depth of colour, Isabella's anxiety increased tenfold. In the morbid gloom of the late afternoon the twisted, tuberous trunks and their distorted limbs took on an eerily supernatural appearance. Dwarfed by ancestral trees, terrified of what might happen next, scary images swirling inside her head like winged beasts, she struggled to maintain her composure. Never before had she had felt so vulnerable, so defenceless, so unprotected. Right then she wished the entire estate was illuminated by gaslight like in the town's streets at twilight.

Upon finally reaching the path that led back to the house, although there was still some way to go, Isabella breathed a cautious sigh of relief. But since something told her to beware of whatever might still be out there, she remained vigilant. Wouldn't do to fall at the final hurdle, she said to herself. And soon enough, a significant sound penetrated her ears; the unmistakable sound of boots on rough ground. Being unable to see to whom the boots belonged felt especially unnerving.

Presently, the thumping vibrations grew louder and more emphatic. Automatically, Isabella's senses switched to their highest level of alert. With her wide-open, white-ringed eyes darting in every direction, she attempted to pinpoint the sound's location. But the thickening twilight restricted her vision, forcing her to place greater reliance on her hearing.

As dusk continued creeping up on the land, the vibrations strengthened and intensified. They seemed almost to shake the ground. On they came like a marching army: relentless, dogged, determined; sending her pulse into an unstoppable gallop. Then from around a bend in the path, silhouetted against the sepulchral surround, a tall, dark figure stormed into view and advanced in her direction.

Besieged by an almighty panic, red-hot terror rushing through her veins, her heart drumming dementedly in her chest, Isabella stood petrified. Then a voice in her head shouted run! Run for your life! But to where? she asked herself. To where should she run? Should she turn tail and run in the opposite direction? Would that be wise when night was imminent? Plus, whatever was wending its way towards her gave the impression it would keep on coming regardless.

Hysterical inside, thinking it might be best to hide, Isabella looked frantically in every direction. She had never felt so afraid in her entire life; more afraid than she ever thought possible. The fear consumed her, smothered her, choked her. How she wished her old friends were there alongside her. Fearless and brave, every one of them tougher than teakwood, they would have lent her courage.

As the figure continued closing in on her with a pounding momentum, it loomed larger and larger. Taking a desperate split-second decision, Isabella fled the path, retreated into the shadow of a giant sycamore, and stumbled backwards over a log concealed in the grass. Feeling more vulnerable on the ground than when standing up, she scrambled to her feet and hid behind the sycamore's trunk.

And as the pounding went on climbing the scale notch by notch, Isabella's heart clambered into her throat. Although shielded by the giant tree, she still felt exposed and extremely vulnerable. Moreover, the tension and suspense were pure torture. Like an infant afraid of the dark, she placed her palms over her eyes. Delirious with fear, she tried telling herself the situation was simply a dream, a nightmare, her imagination gone haywire, and that reality would shortly return. But as her ears continued to relay the soundwaves to her brain, she feared there was no escaping whatever fate had in store for her.

Feeling powerless, trembling behind the tree trunk, every last vestige of her courage depleted, Isabella prayed in silent anguish: Please help me, God, in the hope that whatever was pounding the path would charge past and not see her.

But to her hag-ridden horror, she heard the silhouette come to a sudden halt a few feet from where she stood with her body pressed hard against the bark. There followed a brief minacious silence. Then the steps stole towards the sycamore.

Hunched like a spoonbill, her hands gripping her face, her heart rapping inside her ribcage, her voice on the verge of screaming, Isabella felt like a snared creature hearing the trapper approach. Unable to bear the uncertainty any longer, she steeled herself and opened her eyes.

Chapter 21

"What the devil do you think you're doing? Do you know what time it is? Yet again you failed to turn up for tea. It beats me why you can't confine yourself to strolling around the garden like a normal person instead of roaming half the district. Has it never occurred to you that I worry about your welfare when it's getting dark and there's no sign of you? Why I've a jolly good mind to..."

Isabella interrupted her husband before he could tell her. "I'm sorry, I didn't mean to be so late — truly. I had every intention of returning before dusk, but I lost track of the time."

"Evidently," he said dryly.

"Please, Hereward, don't be cross. And anyway, how did you know I was behind that tree?"

Hereward shook his head at her. "Because, you stupid girl, believe it or not, I could actually hear you. For one thing, you were panting like a pie dog in the summer heat of an Indian plain."

Rendered speechless by surprise, Isabella stared at him.

"And look at the state of your clothes, for heaven's sake," he barked before grabbing hold of her and brushing the detritus off her coat, front, back and sides. He could have cheerfully shaken her. But as he began to remove a few blades of grass caught in her curls, she looked so ingenuous that affectionate frustration soon overrode his fury.

Isabella wished Hereward would stop treating her like a small child. In her opinion, he behaved more like a custodian than a husband. Even so, she accepted his concern was born out of love; a love expressed in pipe-hot impatience and fervent vexation.

Unaware that another dark form was creeping away in the opposite direction, Hereward took hold of his wayward wife and marched her back to the Hall.

Once inside the safety of the house, Isabella freed herself from her husband's grasp and rushed upstairs to have her bath. She was determined to arrive on time for dinner, since she didn't think she could cope with another one of his red-cap roastings. One a day was plenty.

As soon as she submerged herself in the soothing warmth of the bathwater, Isabella began to relax and unwind. After dunking her hair, she washed it with green soft soap, gently massaging her scalp with her fingers while she reflected on her state of mind. Feeling fearful in the forest was a new sensation, and she again wondered if her imaginings were manifestations of some kind of mental disorder.

Presently, Tilly knocked at the bathroom door to remind her it was time to start dressing. Isabella climbed out of the bath, wrapped herself in a thick fluffy robe and went to her bedroom. There the maid helped her towel dry her hair while they chatted about all kinds of trivial things. Since getting married she no longer had friends her own age and she felt the loss keenly, so she was glad to have sweet-tempered Tilly to talk to. Still, they were careful not to let Boyle overhear them in case he accused the poor girl of forgetting her place. Isabella suspected he was looking for an excuse to sack her so as to restore Barbara to what he believed was her rightful position.

"Feeling fresh and clean again?" asked Hereward, the ghost of a smile gracing his lips, as Isabella entered the room looking revived and smelling fragrant. "You must be famished," he added, "having missed out on your tea this afternoon. I daresay you'll have an even bigger appetite to satisfy than your usual one. Or did you find some of those wild herbs you're so fond of nibbling during your manic meanderings? I'm beginning to think I might have inadvertently married a rabbit."

Isabella simulated a moue. She preferred her husband when he was playful and light-hearted instead of bossy and brusque. Sometimes he amused her in spite of herself. However, she also knew it took only the smallest incident to alter his mood.

Hereward handed her a drink from a silver tray on top of the sideboard. "Not too fast now," he advised as she raised the glass to her lips. "We don't want it going straight to your head on an empty stomach."

As Isabella compressed her lips to muffle her mirth, he gave her a mock look of disapproval.

At that point, Boyle entered to announce dinner with his customary formality, followed by an emulous Barbara.

Hereward escorted Isabella to the table and pulled out her chair. Then as soon as she was seated, he planted a tender kiss on top of her head, grateful she was safe and sound.

Later, however, in the sitting room he grew grouchy again. The wireless wouldn't stop crackling and, despite twiddling the knobs repeatedly, he couldn't find the programme he was looking for.

So, while Hereward cursed the entire British Broadcasting Corporation in a booming voice, Isabella escaped the room and went to the library to choose a new novel. At that time of day, she felt more relaxed as Boyle was busy below stairs supervising the staff as they cleared up after dinner and prepared to eat their own supper.

That same night, Hereward was late coming to Isabella's

bedroom. By which time she had ceased to expect him and was absorbed in her book. However, as soon as he entered, from habit she placed it back on the bedside cabinet, switched off the lamp and slid beneath the bedclothes.

Hereward climbed into bed, but remained sitting up. With a nasal sigh, he folded his arms and stared at the fire without speaking.

Isabella soon realised he was in a sulk. And she wondered why he had bothered to join her. It was impossible to gauge his moods. They were as changeable as the weather and equally unpredictable.

After unfolding his arms, Hereward turned to look at her and said: "I was worried about you, you know, when you failed to turn up for tea and it was getting dark. Isabella, my dear girl, your behaviour frustrates the life out of me. It's enough to make a blasted warrior weep."

As he chastised her, Isabella stayed silent and focused her full attention on the glass light fitting above the bed. Getting embroiled in yet another tiresome contretemps with Hereward seemed pointless. He'll burn himself out shortly, she told herself.

"You should have stopped that nonsense after we were married," he went on, running his hands through his hair. "Gallivanting all over the place like a wild child. It's time you grew up, young lady, and started to behave like a responsible adult." Then he lay down and turned on his side to face her.

For the sake of peace, Isabella apologised. Sometimes she felt as though she was forever saying sorry.

Hereward's expression softened. After which he rolled over, turned out the lamp and rolled back again. In the fading firelight he studied his delinquent adolescent wife. Whatever she said, did, or failed to do, he still adored her; however, he had no idea how to deal with her juvenile ways. He knew he should have given proper consideration to her young age and lack of maturity when he made the decision to marry her. Maud had advised him to wait at least a year before taking the plunge. "Marry in haste, repent at leisure," she had said after stressing the importance of getting to know Isabella first. But he was having none of it. For the very first time in his life, he was in love, and he was leaving nothing to chance. It never occurred to him for even a second that a new wife would require a period of adjustment after relocating to the Hall, or that her role as mistress would need to be defined, or that Boyle's role would need to be redrawn. Not for one single moment did he imagine his faithful manservant might feel resentful. He somehow expected things to continue in the same old way and everyone to be satisfied with their lot.

Chapter 22

Back home, slumped in a shabby chair spewing its innards, his elbows resting on its arms, his thick legs fully extended, Parker warmed himself up before a roaring log fire. Unfortunately, his feet were taking their own good time to thaw out after his afternoon foray around the forest. Thinking he must be getting old, he considered treating himself to a pair of socks. Socks were a luxury now his dear mother was no longer there to knit them from odd scraps of old wool, or darn them when they developed a hole. Living as a single bloke, he often felt lonely and miserable. After all, he remarked to himself, every man needs a woman to mend his clothes, feed the fire and keep him satisfied in bed.

For the second time that week, camouflaged in the appropriate seasonal colours and wearing an old olive-green cap, Parker had trailed the Major's wife around the estate, hoping to see her in cahoots with Jack. He had to admit, it was more fun than rabbiting, even if the rabbits did taste excellent.

As he absently rubbed his face, Parker realised he needed to shave; until he remembered the beard had a purpose. Having never worn one before Miss Dumbarton hired him, he was still struggling to get used to it. If anything, he thought it made him resemble a scarecrow. In terms of comparison, it was the complete opposite of the Major's well-groomed facial growth that never varied in appearance. And he wondered what the little lady thought of her husband's clipped bristles and whether they prickled her delicate skin.

In response to a sudden intense itch, Parker scratched the back of his neck with a ragged fingernail, accidentally slicing the head off a boil. Without flinching at the pain, he cursed his carelessness. The last thing he needed was another bloody carbuncle. His previous one, as he recalled, was almost the size of a billiard ball and took months to heal. Be careful, he warned himself, you can't afford to be laid up now your old lady's no longer here to look after you. Still, he couldn't help but scratch his scabby head, from which solid lumps and cysts poked through his scalp like marbles on a solitaire board. With his penknife, he scraped the bloodstained pus from his fingernail then wiped the blade back and forth on his trouser leg.

Suddenly, Parker became pensive and sighed sorrily. To begin with, he had assumed tracking the Major's wife would be a doddle. Far easier than hunting game. For one thing, he knew animals' senses, including their sixth sense, were superior to those of humans. Yet that afternoon there had been something about the lady's behaviour, the way she adopted a listening stance and looked about her every so often, that bothered him not unduly.

To unstiffen his fingers, Parker cracked his knuckles a couple of times, then decided he needed a smoke. After removing a fag, he tapped it a couple of times on the packet to compact the tobacco and placed it between his lips. The tapping habit came from his grandfather. His grandfather, the greatest ferreter that had ever lived, and about whom it was often said loved his ferrets more than he did his missus. Yet despite the small creature's ability to flush out rabbits, Parker preferred to use snares and traps. Ferrets needed to be cared for and he couldn't be fussed with all that.

As he continued to gaze into the fire, the burning fag

dangling from his lips, Parker experienced a rare pang of guilt. But it just as soon passed when he remembered the pounds in his pocket. Then he smiled and said to himself: who would have thought a particular pastime could prove profitable? Secretly watching people felt different somehow when it was waged. It gave it a sense of responsibility. The responsibility not to get caught, for one thing, he sniggered.

In an unconscious connection, Parker's thoughts switched to the town's flasher who used to follow teenage girls around the park to show them his wares. The man's name was Malcolm, Malcolm something or other. Malcolm always wore a long beige mackintosh in desperate need of a wash, had stringy, greasy grey hair, also long, and once worked as a photographer. Every so often, after a teacher or parent reported him, the police carted him off to the cells. One time, a judge jailed him, but he reoffended shortly after release. Then one day he simply vanished, never to be seen again.

Parker chortled to himself when he recalled the one occasion from his own adolescence when he had flashed some schoolgirls to test their reaction. But since they either laughed or sneered, he never repeated the performance. Flashing's harmless, he said to himself, and certainly nothing to get all worked up about. No woman was ever injured by it. That way, he reasoned, there was nothing wrong with the job he was doing for Miss Dumbarton. If anything, it was no different from working as a private detective; which, he decided, gave it a measure of respectability. As far as he knew, there was no law banning a man from looking at a woman or, for that matter, a girl. Out in the open, he was committing no crime. Plus, peering through a hedge or a bush or a clump of trees wasn't the same as peeping through the window of a private house. The Aldwen estate was a public place. Well sort of. And he convinced himself he was doing the little lady no harm by simply watching her.

Nonetheless, Parker failed to understand why Major Aldwen allowed his young wife to go out alone and then went looking for her. In his opinion, a girl like that required a close chaperone. Recalling his reaction upon seeing her for the very first time, an unpleasant smile warped his face. For not only was she beautiful, still in her teens and tender as a young green shoot, she also looked tasty; so tasty, he grew hot, sweaty and swollen just thinking about her.

Chapter 23

In the manner of a pupil at a strict boarding school after lights out, Isabella sneaked out of her bedroom. Since she always ate her full at dinner, it was unusual for her to feel famished late at night. She was hoping to find a few leftovers in the kitchen. Failing that, a slice of bread topped with cheese and a dollop of chutney would do nicely, thank you.

After her unnerving encounter with Hereward on the path a few days previous, Isabella had yet to learn her lesson. It was as though she had some sort of mental block when it came to behaving as an adult. Life at the Hall continued to challenge her in a number of ways and she was still finding her feet. In fact, she was beginning to wonder if she ever would. In spite of her familiarity with the well-established mode of running a household from observing her mother's example, she nevertheless struggled to put her impressions into practice. But then her mother hadn't had to contend with the likes of the insufferable brace that was Boyle and Barbara.

Afraid of being rumbled, Isabella crept downstairs in her pink slippers as quietly as possible. She didn't switch on the landing light in case Hereward noticed the bar of buttery brightness under his bedroom door and came out to investigate. Wisely, she wished to avoid receiving another pyretic rollicking so close on the heels of the last one.

So as not to take a tumble on the staircase, Isabella tackled the dark descent by gripping the handrail and feeling her way one step at a time. With tentative toes, she tapped the edge of each tread in order to locate where the rises and falls coincided before dropping a level. However, as she landed on the lowest step, the long-case clock in the hall struck midnight with a resounding gong. Flinching in alarm, she closed her eyes, placed her palm on her chest and blew out a *phew!*

Once she recovered her composure, Isabella tiptoed across the hall, groped her way along the connecting passage and down a steep flight of narrow steps to the kitchen. Behind one of the doors could be heard long-drawn-out snores. That's bound to be Boyle, she said to herself. Trusting the rest of the servants were also sound asleep, she fumbled for the light switch, flicked it down and opened the pantry door an inch at a time to prevent it creaking.

The small room smelled like a grocer's shop. All it required to resemble one was a counter with a cash till on top. The shelves were piled high with provisions; some of them fresh, some of them canned and some of them pickled in jars. Gosh! Isabella exclaimed to herself, who knew a secret cave of comestibles existed at Aldwen Hall? With relish, she devoured some chicken left over from dinner, a thick chunk of cheddar cheese and a wide wedge of fruitcake. Then, fully satisfied with her sinful supper, she stole back to bed and slept like a glutted log.

Isabella gave no further thought to her late furtive feast until Hereward appeared unexpectedly in the sitting room the following morning. He stood on the hearth rug warming his well-toned rear with the clock ticking away behind him like a time bomb. His well-fitted Norfolk jacket drew attention to his broad shoulders, strong chest and long, lean torso.

"May I have a word?" he said crisply after extending his neck and loosening the knot on his tie.

In silence, Isabella raised her enquiring eyes to his and wondered what heinous crime she had committed this time. Boarding school must feel less constraining than this, she thought.

With typical aplomb, Hereward apprised his wife. When he spoke, it was with preciseness.

"This morning, Boyle, having discovered certain items of food had disappeared from the pantry overnight, questioned the staff. Since they have all denied helping themselves, he approached me to see if I could throw any light on the mystery."

Isabella resisted the temptation to offer an instant reply. She needed to think. Boyle's reporting of the midnight raid on the pantry directly to his master seemed to her an odd thing. Why, she asked herself, was the butler bothering her husband with such a trifle when he could have come straight to her? After all, she was the mistress, or she was meant to be. Nor could she understand what all the fuss was about anyway. There was enough food in the house to feed an infantry for a month at the very least.

Had Isabella been a woman of majority, property and independent means when she married Hereward, she would in all probability have dealt with the situation in a markedly different way. However, her immaturity, inexperience and sense of powerlessness at the Hall led her to conduct herself in a manner incommensurate with her actual station. Biting her lower lip, she hunched her shoulders and cuddled her ribcage for comfort.

"I took the food, I was hungry," she confessed, feeling like a criminal and no doubt looking like one too.

For several mesmerising moments, Hereward stared at Isabella's mouth as he imagined her plump lips moist with the pleasure of mastication. Outside, during the hiatus, a pheasant cackled as if to mock the absurdity of the situation.

Isabella felt the sudden urge to laugh; however, she managed to control the impulse. What a lot of fuss over a little leftover food, she thought with a smirk.

"Where were we? Ah yes, the missing food," said Hereward bringing himself back to the present. "In case you feel peckish after the servants have retired, my sweet, there are always biscuits in the morning-room sideboard. There's no need for you to visit the kitchen."

An unexpected change came over Isabella, a defiance in her face never seen before, and she snapped: "Since I am not psychic, please be good enough to point out all the rooms in this house to which I am forbidden entry. Oh, and as for the biscuits," she said after a brief pause, "I shan't be touching them, thank you all the same. I bet Boyle counts them every night, notes their numbers and produces a report, which he then presents to you at your desk the next morning."

Hereward winced as his wife sprang up from the sofa, flounced from the room and slammed the door with enough force to shake the walls.

Later at luncheon, Isabella's mood showed no signs of improvement. Despite Hereward's best efforts to humour her, her huff persisted and she parted her petulant lips for no other purpose than to consume her food.

After some reflection, he regretted getting involved in what was essentially a minor domestic matter. Boyle, he now realised, should have spoken to Isabella directly. After luncheon he rang for the butler, handed him the motorcar keys, and sent him to the town's most-exclusive confectioners to purchase the most-expensive box of chocolates; cautiously confident of Isabella's complete forgiveness the moment he presented her with his irresistible olive branch.

Unfortunately, for Isabella that day it was raining in sheets. The prospect of remaining indoors all afternoon compounded her maudlin mood. After banging out a few notes on the piano, she settled herself in a chair beside the hearth and picked up her novel. Then, as she was about to apply herself to the page, Tilly skipped in on the pretext of checking the log basket. With the trace of a smile, the maid mentioned the butler's sudden, unexplained absence.

"Mr Boyle's been sent into town on an important errand, Ma'am. Although he didn't say what it was," she added, a hint of mischief behind her eyes.

Isabella questioned the urgency in her head. Boyle left the Hall only when he was obliged to. And when he did, the mood in the house always lightened in much the same way as when a strict teacher is called out of the classroom, leaving the pupils unattended.

Later that afternoon, the shrill sound of the telephone rang out in the hall. Isabella, however, paid it no heed, since it was never for her. She shifted in her chair, chewed her thumbnail and continued scaring herself half to death with another horror story from the Hall's considerable collection.

A reluctant rap on the sitting-room door made Isabella look up from the page. To her surprise, Boyle entered, obviously back from his errand. In addition to hair wax, he smelled of coal tar soap and Epsom salts. Tempted though she was, Isabella made no mention of the pantry palaver. As soon as the right opportunity presented itself, she intended to handle the conniving snake in her own special way. Revenge tastes sweeter when it's served chilled, she reminded herself.

"The telephone, Ma'am. It's for you. Miss Aldwen wishes to have a word," he said with his usual air of solemnity.

It was Maud on the line, Hereward's sister, inviting Isabella to tea the following afternoon. "Telephones are so awfully convenient, my dear, don't you think?" she enthused. "One can simply pick up the receiver and invite a person over, just like that," she said with a click of her stout fingers. "It's strange really. Rather like two people are engaged in a conversation in the same house but speaking from separate rooms. The trouble is, they make one so dreadfully lazy at keeping up with one's correspondence and so on, but a great deal more sociable, since a group of friends can be gathered together at short notice." She paused for a much-needed breath. "Anyhow, my dear, I was sitting here and it suddenly occurred to me to invite you over. So here I am. Well, not in person of course." Maud laughed her infectious laugh.

"I'd love to, yes. Thank you so much for inviting me. It's awfully good of you."

"Don't mention it, dear girl. I'll see you tomorrow then. Goodbye."

Isabella returned the receiver to its mount. She was always glad of an opportunity to escape the house. Then as she turned to go back to the sitting room, she noticed Boyle at the far end of the hall pretending to search a drawer in order to eavesdrop on her call.

Rather than allowing Isabella to use a taxicab or the bicycle, Hereward insisted on dropping her himself at Maud's place for the afternoon tête-à-tête. He and Isabella were on speaking terms again, but only just. The bumper box of fancy chocolates along with his most-abject apology had done the trick. Hence peace was restored to the household, at least for the present.

"This really isn't necessary," she told him as he held open the passenger door. "I'm perfectly capable of making my own way to Maud's on the bicycle, or I can walk even. How d'you think I managed to get around before we were married? And what about your work? I know how strict you are about your schedule."

Hereward withheld comment as he climbed into the driver's seat, adjusted the rear-view mirror and slipped his hands inside his gloves. However, as the motorcar moved forward, a slight smile appeared on his lips.

"From what I recall, you got around surprisingly well before we were married," he stated. "Rather too well, if my memory serves me correctly."

Isabella said nothing. She knew Hereward revelled in making reference to her early teenage transgressions and she refused to give him the satisfaction of knowing it irked her.

"This will make a change from your afternoon walk," he said turning to look at her when he should have been watching the road. As he studied her face, he thought she had the most-perfect profile with a nose that curved gently upwards, and a finely contoured chin that was cute when it wasn't contrary.

"Yes, I expect it will," she said looking at the road instead of him.

"I regret to say my sister's something of a rebel, so I'm not sure it's advisable for you two girls to be left alone together for too long. I don't want her filling that pretty little head of yours with all that women's emancipation rubbish. Damnable woman has the vote and she's still not satisfied. You're at an impressionable age, and believe me she'll do her damnedest to indoctrinate you with all that *New Woman* nonsense. I have enough trouble controlling you as it is."

"Why d'you think it's necessary to control me?" she replied, turning to glare at him. "Anyone would think I was a dog and not your wife. Next thing you'll be chaining me up outside the outhouse," she added with a scowl.

"Don't tempt me," he said, and he gave her a pretend warning look.

Isabella turned back to the windscreen and an emphatic silence came over them.

Upon arrival at Maud's house, Hereward decided to make an immediate return to the Hall to get on with his writing.

"I'll be back at six sharp to collect you, so be ready to leave on the dot," he said, tapping his wristwatch.

As he was about to climb back into the motorcar, Isabella called out his name.

"Yes, what is it?" he said with impatience.

Wagging a slim gloved finger in his direction, she said with a sassy smirk, "Don't be late now."

"You, impudent little madam," he said. "I'll deal with you later."

As she watched him drive off, Isabella regretted her provocation, since she knew that *deal with her later*, he most definitely would.

"How're you getting on at the Hall, my dear? Have you settled in now?" asked Maud kindly as she passed Isabella her tea in a hand-painted art-deco teacup and saucer. The design went well with the furnishings and general style of the room. Clearly, Maud favoured a more-modern approach to home décor. Since taking possession of her tall, elegant villa, she had introduced a number of changes to bring the interior up to date. In addition, the air in the room was heady with the scent of blue hyacinths in colourful glass bowls.

"I'm slowly adjusting, thank you. It's kind of you to ask," said Isabella moving the spoon back and forth in the teacup. Tears were never far from the surface and she struggled for a moment to compose herself. After removing a clean handkerchief from her pocket, she gently dabbed her eyes.

"There's so little to do at the Hall except read all day long. I'm not accustomed to such extreme inactivity. Boyle keeps an iron grip on the household management and one can't seem to do anything without his say so."

"You mustn't mind him," advised Maud. "He's terribly loyal to my brother. Efficient too, but he does sometimes forget his place, I'm sorry to say. Hereward promised father he would keep him on, so I think you're rather stuck with the old blighter."

"I'm sorry to be so blunt," said Isabella, "but I don't much care for him. He has far too much power, far too much influence over your brother."

"I expect that's true to some degree, but I can assure you Hereward's no pushover. Boyle can only go so far with him. Remember, my dear, you're the Hall's mistress, so don't be afraid to speak up. And if old bossy boots objects, then that's his problem."

"I'm sorry to burden you with my troubles, especially when you've been so kind as to invite me here," said Isabella.

"It's no problem at all, my dear," Maud assured her. "So please don't concern yourself on my account. I'm sure it can't be easy for you, especially being so young. Besides, I'm always happy to lend a sympathetic ear. Where would we ladies be without our supportive sisterhood?" she beamed. "Now more to the point, what to do about that brother of mine and Boyle."

As Isabella inhaled the room's floriferous air she was reminded of the absence of flowers at the Hall. According to Tilly, it was because Boyle believed flowers belonged in the garden and not in the house. Too feminine for his tastes. Well, we'll see about that, she said to herself. Maud was right. It was time to start making her mark.

Chapter 24

Isabella wasn't the only one incensed by Boyle. It was the first time Martha had had dealings with the butler and she hoped it would be the last.

"How may I help you?" she asked after he introduced himself over the telephone.

"I'm in the process of writing the cheque in settlement of Major Aldwen's account, which he has asked me to take care of, and I have a query regarding the amount stated on the invoice."

There followed a sharp intake of breath. "If you're referring to *Mrs* Aldwen's account, which I assume you are because I've no gentleman clients on my books, I can assure you, Mr Boyle, that the amount stated is correct down to the very last penny." It was turning out to be one of those days. She had burnt the breakfast, laddered a new silk stocking, and now she had this brass-neck lackey on the line to make it a hat-trick.

"The final figure seems to be a little on the excessive side," said Boyle with a sibilant hiss.

How would you know the price of ladies' particulars? she said to herself. The sliminess in his manner made Martha want to scratch her skin.

"I should be very much obliged if you would be good enough to provide me with a little more information which, as I'm sure you'll appreciate, I require for my records," he persisted. He was like a dog with a bone, but Martha's teeth were equally tenacious.

"Information? Exactly what sort of information do you want, Mr Boyle?" she said consulting the ledger in front of her.

"To be specific, Madam, I require an itemised bill. By that I mean a breakdown of costs; a list of individual purchases with the price placed against each one."

Martha could not help raise her voice. "I may be a woman, Mr Boyle, but for your information I do understand what an itemised bill is. Let me get this right. Do you seriously expect me to divulge the details of a young lady's purchases, some of which may be of a more personal nature, to a member of her staff who also happens to be of the opposite sex?" Martha wasn't about to dignify him with the title of gentleman. "Tell me something else, Mr Boyle, since you have a peculiar interest in, shall we say, the more intimate details of a young woman's wardrobe, exactly how much detail would you like me to divulge?"

The insinuation proved effective and Boyle was put on the back foot, albeit temporarily. There was no way on earth Martha would agree to reveal the price of a lady's unmentionables to a manservant.

"Madam, I really must insist…"

"I'll expect the cheque in the next post, Mr Boyle. Goodbye."

To his surprise Boyle heard a click. He was still holding the receiver to his ear and his mouth was ajar in mid-sentence. Well really! He intended to speak with the Major at the first opportunity. He wasn't putting up with some bolshie shopkeeper getting above her station with him.

Isabella could hardly believe her ears when Martha informed her what Boyle had been up to. The barefaced cheek of the man, she thought. He was far too big for his butler's boots and on this occasion he had well and truly overstepped the mark. Well, she intended to speak with her husband about the situation as soon as the time was right.

That night Hereward was removing his robe when Isabella broached the subject of Boyle's behaviour. She had chosen the most-opportune moment to maximise her chance of success. Only recently at Martha's she had been privy to a low-voiced conversation in which a client had revealed with a knowing smile that a little guile in the bustle of the boudoir paid handsome dividends. Another customer confided less coyly that whenever she fancied a new frock, she made sure to ask her husband for the money when he was in the mood. It took Isabella a few moments to interpret what in the mood actually meant and, after recovering from her initial shock, she was curious to discover if the strategy had merit.

"I need a cheque to settle my bill at Martha's," she said keeping her voice light and casual.

"Isn't that Boyle's department? And anyway, I've already instructed him to send the cheque," Hereward murmured with a slight frown.

"He's been awfully rude to Martha, questioning her integrity, and I'm incredibly cross about it," said Isabella. "And the account has still to be settled. In fact, Boyle appears to be holding out as long as he can. And in the meantime, I'm left looking like a debtor."

There followed a brief silence as he settled himself in beside her. Then he said: "Darling, this is neither the time nor the place for a discussion about such matters. I'm sure it can wait until tomorrow."

"He's demanded a breakdown of costs on my account at Martha's," she ploughed on undeterred.

"Why's that a problem?" he asked. "After all, the man has

a meticulous eye for detail. And he does have full responsibility for the Hall's finances. Every year he carries out a complete audit on the household expenses. Which I must admit saves me the time and trouble. I daresay he enjoys it. Plus, to be fair, he can't be expected to do a proper job without the relevant information. And most important, I can trust him." He began playing with her hair as a prelude to what was to come, twining a curl around his finger.

Isabella regretted unclipping her hair. Knowing how much Hereward loved to see it hanging loose in the bedroom, she should have kept it tied up just to spite him. But then it would only have made her feel uncomfortable and head sore in bed.

"Because I object to having my wardrobe included in the household accounts," she explained. "For one thing, my purchases are none of that interfering old busybody's business," she added in high dudgeon. She was too embarrassed to spell out the real problem and, by all accounts, Hereward was never going to catch on.

"Isabella, my dearest darling, I do think we should discuss the matter tomorrow," he reiterated with a heavy sigh, impatience now apparent in his tone.

Isabella, however, pressed on regardless. She was determined to have her own way. "I'm sorry, but I must disagree," she asserted. "The issue must be discussed now, quite simply because this is the only time when we're unlikely to be overheard. Boyle and that poisonous puppet of his are both devils for eavesdropping and I dread to think how much those two already know about our personal affairs from listening in to our conversations."

Hereward knew when he was browbeaten. It was clear his wife had no intention of dropping her demand until he consented and he had a more pressing need to attend to.

"Very well then," he grumbled, "I'll write a cheque first

thing in the morning and you can go and give it to Martha in person if you prefer. Happy now?"

"Yes, thank you," said Isabella turning her head aside to hide her victorious grin.

In his basement bedroom, Boyle returned the heavy ledger to the cupboard and turned the key in the lock. He put the key back in his waistcoat pocket and gave it a light pat. No other person had a duplicate to his private cupboard, not even Major Aldwen.

Placing his palm on top of his head, he checked his hoax hairdo was still secure. His pate gave the appearance of a dry riverbed between two banks bridged by strings streaked with grey. Unfortunately, his hair loss showed no signs of slowing. If it carried on at its present rate, his entire scalp would soon be hairless. Realising the impossibility of keeping up the pretence indefinitely, he planned to purchase a good quality toupee with some of his savings.

Before returning upstairs, Boyle checked himself in the mirror. A place he preferred not to linger as it reflected with cruel honesty his physiognomic failings. He felt grateful Major Aldwen seemed oblivious to his repugnant face and always treated him like a human being. Which was one of the reasons he held him in such high esteem. Unlike the mistress. He detested the Major's wife with an intensity bordering on derangement. And since he was well aware of the strains in the couple's marriage, he made sure to exploit their differences whenever an opportunity presented itself. Whatever it took, he was determined to hang onto power at the Hall. He was also determined to reinstate the tardy but mouldable tell-tale Barbara to her designated place. It was time to remind the mistress that he allocated the staff their roles and they were answerable to him.

Chapter 25

While lounging on the sofa, Isabella heard an emphatic knock on the sitting-room door. But before being invited to enter, Barbara skulked in, her face set in a mount of pure impudence and her eyes gleaming with malice.

"I've been sent to say the master requires your presence in the library as soon as you like, Ma'am," she stated.

Isabella wondered what was amiss. If the maid's expression offered an insight, there must be some sort of trouble afoot. But in what respect the assumed trouble was connected to herself she could barely conceive. Furthermore, she failed to understand why Hereward hadn't approached her directly. Still, who knew how his mind worked? Whatever the case, the situation evoked memories of the numerous times she had been summoned to her father's study to be scolded for some minor misdeed.

After tapping lightly on the library door, Isabella entered without waiting to be admitted. Well-fed flames roared up the chimney like a dragon breathing fire in the face of a medieval knight. They gave off an acrid odour redolent of smoked mutton and charred earth. Yet despite the heat, the room's atmosphere felt cool and uninviting.

Hereward was sitting at his desk surrounded by a mountain of paperwork, manuscripts and handwritten notes. His tweed jacket hung in perfect symmetry across the back of his chair, while the knot on his necktie looked neat and natty. Yet to her surprise there was a weariness in his eyes and an untypical slump to his shoulders not normally apparent.

After walking straight up to the desk, Isabella stood waiting for him to finish his task.

He appeared to be taking his own good time.

She put her hands behind her back, rocked back and forth on her heels and chewed her lip.

Presently, he looked up at her without smiling and placed his editing pencil down on top of his notes.

She spoke first, her eyebrows half-raised in query. "Barbara informs me you wish to have a word?"

"Yes, that's correct, he confirmed in a formal tone. His fringe had flopped down, hiding his forehead and he ran his fingers through it and swept it aside.

"You look serious, is there a problem?" she asked with a slight frown.

Hereward sat up straight in his seat, rubbed the back of his neck and stifled a yawn. It was one of those times when the tension between them felt draining. After stroking his chin for a few seconds, he began to speak.

"Not exactly a problem," he said guardedly. Then, as if in preparation for what was to follow, he paused and cleared his throat. "It has not gone unnoticed that you've been making increasing use of Tilly's assistance. Unfortunately, when you do so Tilly is removed from her regular duties." He took a deep breath and swallowed. "Upon your arrival at the Hall, Barbara was assigned to assist you in her capacity as personal maid and I'm given to understand you've not been adhering to the arrangement."

Throughout the entire time Hereward spoke, Isabella fought an internal battle to keep her temper in check. Since getting married, she found containing her temper an ongoing challenge.

"Assigned by whom, may I ask?" she said curtly.

"By Boyle of course," he replied as if she should know. He then picked up the pencil, twirled it between his thumbs and index fingers and stared at it for a moment before continuing. "It's his job to manage the household and ensure the place runs smoothly. He employs the staff, assigns them their duties, manages the accounts and whatever else needs doing around the place. It has been necessary to give him complete authority with respect to that in order to allow me to get on with my work without constant interruptions. He's been here a very long time, my dear, since my childhood in actual fact, and has always done a sterling job."

Even though she had enquired, in her mind the identity of the complainant had never been in doubt. It was simply a matter of confirmation. Isabella knew full well she was involved in a power struggle with Boyle and he was trying his best to create conflict between Hereward and herself. After all, their mutual antagonisms were hardly a secret, since their raised voices undoubtedly breached the Hall's walls on a regular basis.

"That's all well and good," she stated, her voice rising an octave, "but, with respect, I think I should be the one to appoint my own lady's maid. There's no way I will permit a manservant to do so on my behalf. So let me make myself abundantly clear. I'm sorry but I will not, I trust you understand, accept Barbara as my maid. Should you decide to oppose me, then I shall have no option but to manage without a maid entirely. Since, unlike some people, I am perfectly capable of dressing myself."

Hereward's face darkened, but Isabella continued regardless. "I should also be grateful if you would kindly remind your vindictive vassal not to consult you about domestic matters behind my back. You appear to have forgotten that by virtue of our marriage I am mistress here. When a servant is permitted to have too much power, as is the case with Boyle, it serves only to undermine my position and authority over the household."

Thinking Isabella might possibly have a point, Hereward became conciliatory. "Darling, please try to understand…"

Isabella cut across him like a cutlass and pinned her hands to her hips. "I understand perfectly well,' she asserted. "There's a simple solution to this manufactured complication; so simple I can't think why anyone hasn't thought of it before."

"What solution is that, my dear?"

"The maids can simply swap duties."

Despite a valiant attempt to control her emotions, Isabella felt her calm composure begin to slide and she thought it wise to curtail the discussion. However, the temptation to throw one last spear proved irresistible.

"Would that be all, *Sir*?" she said in a tone laced with sarcasm.

Stung by the inference, Hereward's eyes grazed her face. Then banging his fist on the desk like a gavel, he sprang from his chair.

"How dare you speak to me with such blatant disrespect," he bellowed. "I am your husband, Isabella, not some schoolmaster."

With dazzling defiance Isabella fired back in an instant: "I regret to say, dearest *husband*, it is often nigh impossible to tell the difference." Then with the carriage of a queen turning her back on her courtiers, she exited the room, leaving the door ajar.

Hereward sank back in his chair, chewed the end of his pencil and stared at the door through which his dissenting wife had only just departed. Things were going from bad to worse and he hadn't a clue what to do about it.

Chapter 26

In dire need of solitude and a dose of fresh air, Isabella set out for an extended walk. However, beforehand, she had given herself a good talking to, insisting she must learn to control her outlandish thoughts before she became literally insane. There's nothing to fear in the friendly fields and forest, she assured herself repeatedly. Your troubled mind is simply inventing far-fetched scenarios and you must stop falling for its deceptions.

With the Hall behind her silent as a mausoleum, Isabella went down the garden path and entered the orchard. Eager to explore the estate's numerous tracks and trails, from there she cut across the meadow and plunged into the woods. Blown about by the wind, the autumn leaves were starting to pile up all over the place. Those still attached to the trees fluttered as she threaded her way through row upon row of towering timbers, between which virescent shafts of light imbued the forest with an awesome, heavenly aura. The estate was salve for her soul and, despite being town-raised, Isabella felt blessed to live on its threshold. Inside the house, save for the library and the conservatory, there was little to stimulate her interest. Too many things were out of bounds or beyond her ambit. Away from its confining atmosphere, she felt free to do as she pleased, and free from the restraints of the decorative, idle role Hereward wished to impose on her.

While returning to the Hall after an uneventful and

pleasant roam, Isabella took a short sojourn at the lakeside. Although her mood was much improved, her jaunt had left her feeling a touch jaded, so she convalesced on a log that once belonged to a horse chestnut. As she closed her eyes and listened to the whispering breeze and the sweet, mellow birdsong wafting through the trees, a wave of serenity washed over her, and she delayed her return a little longer.

Upon reopening her eyes, Isabella stretched her legs and caught sight of her new walking boots. The toecaps were already scuffed and she wondered what Hereward would say when he saw them. Quickly dismissing thoughts of her cantankerous spouse from her mind, she tore out a few tufts from a colony of creeping grasses. On the ground near her feet a brown-spotted, olive-green frog hopped by on its way to the water. Concerned for its safety, Isabella tickled its tail end with the tip of a stem to hurry it along in case predators lurked in the long grass. Recalling a story about a frog that turned into a prince, she thought of her hapless father and concluded that princes could also become frogs. Yet at the same time, she couldn't imagine Hereward being anything other than handsome.

Although she knew she needed to get a move on, Isabella couldn't resist lingering at the lakeside to observe the ducks and bald-headed coots glide over the water. The air had begun to feel heavy; however, it wasn't the sort of heaviness that heralded a storm. After several more minutes she forced herself up from her seat and set off walking. In a nearby meadow a rabbit sat upright, wrinkled its nose and disappeared down a warren. Further along the way, she caught a whiff of manure and saw the big red bull in the cow field. Fascinated, she climbed up on the five-bar gate to get a better look at the formidable bovine. Over a ton of powerful lean muscle stood chained to a stake in the ground by a metal ring through its nose, presumably to prevent it running amok among the cows. Poor thing, thought Isabella, naively forgetting the danger posed by a huge, unpredictable beast when permitted to run free.

Jumping down from the gate, Isabella got going again. Upon reaching the point on the path where it began curving back to the house, she paused and took a short detour to the tree on which she had carved her name many moons ago. It felt like a lifetime. She must have done it around the time of the incident in the orchard. With a bittersweet smile on her lips, she traced her soft pink fingertips over the dark indentations in the rough bark. The letters spelled Isabella Acton. Except she was no longer Isabella Acton. Isabella Acton was no more; reduced to a mere inscription, such as on a plaque or a headstone.

As Isabella shivered at the thought, the harsh sound of a twig snapping nearby tore through the air, sending several sparrows into flight. With her head held high, she stood to attention and attuned her ears. Her hearing was sharp, not as sharp as a canine's, but sharp nonetheless. Quickly, she directed her eyes towards the locus of the sound, but saw nothing of note in the composite landscape. Intrigued still, with slow deliberation she twirled an entire circle on the spot while she listened for any disharmonies in the familiar harmonies of a late afternoon. A stretch of long grass adjacent to the path gave the impression of having been flattened only recently. But Isabella couldn't recall whether it was already like that. It was impossible to keep a mental record of every change and variation in the constantly evolving landscape.

Shortly after that, something made her wrinkle her nose like the rabbit. A strong pungent smell spoored the air; so pungent she could almost taste it on her tongue. It made her feel queasy. After giving the matter some thought, she reckoned there must be an animal in the vicinity of the hedge. Perhaps a small timid deer grazing in the undergrowth. They were seldom seen during daytime hours. On the rare occasions she spotted them trotting through stubbled fields on the far edge of the estate, she initially mistook them for dun-coloured dogs. Once during dinner when she mentioned seeing deer, Hereward told her he had to keep a permanent lookout for them as they sometimes charged across the road without warning in front of the motorcar.

"If I were to hit one of those blasted things," he moaned, "it might cause a heap of damage."

"Is it damage to the vehicle you're concerned about or the animals?" she asked in an affectedly sweet voice.

For a moment he looked at her wryly, then replied snappily: "Both."

As Isabella resumed walking, she felt icy cold all of a sudden. It was an uncanny kind of coldness, like that of a haunted house. As winter was well underway now, she was glad to be wearing the warm woollen coat Hereward, in one of his solicitous moods, had bought for her. There was a certain solace to being well off, well fed and well clothed, she concluded. To want for nothing in the material sense, even though she lacked direct access to the well of beneficence. She attempted to pull her cloche hat over her ears, but it refused to stay put because of the topknot. The blessed topknot, she thought. I must remember to pick up a hatpin next time I'm in town.

Self-absorbed, her head full of mindless chatter, Isabella at first failed to notice the slight scrunching sound similar to that of a knife scraping across burnt toast. But when she did, the sensation of being watched also returned. In an attempt to ignore her nagging perception, she told herself to show some mettle and stop being such a mouse. It's just a silly old deer, you ninny, she said to herself with feigned reassurance as her nervous eyes trawled the terrain. Still, her doubts continued to mount as her courage diminished. It seemed to her unlikely the noise came from a deer. For one thing, she reasoned, deer consider humans to be dangerous predators. They keep their distance from them with good reason; as a means of ensuring their survival. Yet despite her misgivings, Isabella continued trying to convince herself that the Aldwen estate was a harmless place. Unlike the well-populated town, its isolation made it safe. However, when a deathly hush settled upon the land, an internal hand tugged at her innards, the hairs on her nape rose up as if in warning, and her guardian angel of instinct screamed at her to get away from there as fast as she could.

Chapter 27

Standing on tiptoes, Parker stretched his short taurine neck as best he could above the hedge. His eyeballs bulged like golf balls as he watched the Major's lady belt back to the Hall like a pony spooked. What a sight!

With a gurning grimace, the gardener exclaimed in a gravelly voice: "Well, bugger me!" Her speed astonished him. For all the girl's womanly proportions, she was surprisingly fleet on her small slender feet. It seemed to him that something had alarmed her. She must have heard him, and he hoped it hadn't put her off visiting the estate permanently. Especially since he had still to report to Miss Dumbarton, who might demand her money back if she suspected he had messed things up.

It had taken Parker no time at all to begin enjoying trailing the charming creature, wrapped up warm in her plush coat, around the estate. He thought her a rare thing. A rare thing indeed around those parts. So completely different from every female he had ever known, or seen. A sentimental, urban-bred girl lately resident in the countryside with a rich landowner husband, and a lover to boot if the rumour were to be believed.

Tramping homeward, feeling far removed from the world at large, Parker spat a flob of green sputum on the ground, then lit up a cigarette. As he puffed away like an old steam engine, he reviewed his stalking techniques. Something had definitely gone wrong, again. And there was little doubt the fault was his. She must have heard him. Of that he felt sure. Heard his large plodding feet creeping, or attempting to creep, behind the hedge. He could think of no other explanation for her shooting off like that. Foolishly, he had forgotten the extent to which even the softest sounds are amplified in the relative silence of the fields and forest. It stood to reason that if he could hear her, then she could also hear him.

Oblivious to the odours he brought with him everywhere, Parker had no idea he smelled thoroughly mouldy and sulphuric. More sulphuric than a stink bomb. His most-recent bath, always a memorable occasion, was several months since. It took only a brisk breeze in the right direction to alert others to his presence. And there was no-one to tell him he reeked because he lived alone and worked outdoors unassisted.

Evening time, from the orchard the trek to his cottage usually took Parker about an hour, provided he kept up a steady pace, and the moon was available to guide him. He quite liked the walk when there was sufficient light. In the dark it was all too easy to stumble down a rabbit hole and sprain an ankle, or worse. Out on the estate in unfavourable conditions an injured lower limb placed a person at significant risk of freezing to death.

Parker was in the habit of dividing the day into two distinct periods: before dark and after dark. Despite the added risks, he preferred after dark. Night-time had its own special magic when the sky was sprinkled with a trillion stars twinkling like miniature lightbulbs. He loved the nocturnal forest, the ear-piercing calls, cries and screams as night predators hunted and consumed their weaker neighbours. As always, he was eager to reach home, light the fire with the wood and bark he usually gathered along the way, and roast the tender young rabbits he had trapped that day.

Right then a significant question occurred to Parker. Why would a wealthy wife risk her privileged life for a bit of hanky-panky on the side with some poor lad like Jack? Perhaps the little Aldwen woman isn't as innocent as she looks, he said to himself with a note of disapproval. Whatever the case, he cautioned himself against doing anything that might jeopardise her meeting her alleged lover in the woods; of whom to date there had been neither sight nor sound. Still, it was early days yet, he said to himself, and he had patience in bundles when it came to tracking his prey.

When he reached the crop fields on the outer edge of the estate, Parker turned east and trudged alongside the riverbank to his hamlet home. There the unpleasant stench of raw fish from the docks downstream offended his nose. Although he would eat virtually anything if he were starving, he had never been fond of fish. To his mind, fish was convalescent food and no match for meat. Too light and flaky for his tastes, with tiny needle-sharp bones that became lodged in the throat. He was strictly a brawn, game and fowl man who preferred his food immediately post-mortem. Meat consumption, he believed, was the only means for a real man to maintain his strength and muscle mass. Nothing except animal flesh and offal truly satisfied his stomach and tickled his tastebuds.

Upon arriving at his thatched home, Parker entered through the rickety unlocked front door and lit a candle. A loaf of home-baked bread from his elderly next-door neighbour lay on an old butcher's block in exchange for the rabbits he supplied her with once a week. The place smelled of woodsmoke, mildew and yeast. Wearily, he emptied his sack on the cracked concrete floor, crushing and scattering insects, spiders and other mini beasts. After which he got the fire started, skinned and dismembered the rabbits, skewered their parts, and roasted them over the flames. And as the air grew thick with the distinctive stench of charred wood, sizzling muscle tissue and burnt blood, Parker stared at the fire and immersed himself in thoughts of the Major's tasty wife and her magnificent bosom.

Chapter 28

Bored with reading, Isabella yawned, rubbed her eyes and got up from the sofa to stretch her limbs. She was still feeling a little on edge and unsettled from the previous day's unnerving experience. You're becoming hysterical, she told herself. For pity's sake, pull yourself together, you gutless girl. All the same, she decided a few days indoors would do no harm and might even prove beneficial. Hereward would naturally be pleased to see her sitting opposite him at the teatime table, thinking she had turned over a new leaf. As if.

After adding a couple of logs to the flagging fire, Isabella idled over to the angled box bay, pulled aside one of the heavy drapes and watched the wildlife going about its business. How free it seemed despite the dangers it faced on a daily basis. Still, she preferred not to dwell on the remorseless reality of rural existence. The perpetual struggle to eat and avoid being eaten. She delighted in seeing animal life, not animal strife. And she shrank from the bloody brutality of animal mortality. Which proved difficult when in that very same room behind panels of polished glass sat the wood-mounted, marble-eyed, furred and feathered trophies, testaments to the talents of the taxidermist.

As she continued to look through the window, Isabella soon became captivated by the sight of a puffed-up ringdove engaged in a charming but comical courtship display to an ostensibly oblivious female. Like a fawning footman, the bird bowed, scraped and turned circles while splaying its feathered tail. Thoroughly engrossed in the creature's romantic endeavours, Isabella failed to register her husband's arrival in the room.

Hereward was likewise captivated. Not by the ringdoves, but by his other half. With her hands resting on her waist and her fingers fanning her fertile hips, she looked like a decorative hourglass. Her pert posterior was balanced to perfection by her shapely thighs and slim middle, while her tethered tresses exposed the nape of her long slender neck.

Unable to control himself in her presence, an amorous smile playing on his lips, Hereward approached his winsome wife from behind, cupped her ample breasts in his manly palms and pressed himself hard against the body he believed belonged to him.

Simultaneously startled and shocked, Isabella recoiled in prudish horror. She was incensed; incensed by what she considered a gross infringement of her personal space outside the private sphere of the bedroom. Removing her husband's hands with an extraordinary force, she spun around like a vortex and slapped his audacious cheek.

"Shameless rake. How dare you touch me in such a disgusting manner!" she half-shouted, her eyes ablaze as she stared at his stupefied face.

The harsh immediacy of Isabella's rejection stung him. The epithet stung him. Never before had Hereward been called a rake. Seizing hold of her in his powerful grip, he made plain he was not a man to play the devil with.

The moment she managed to escape his clutches, Isabella flew from the room, through the front door and down the stone steps. The gravel grunted beneath her feet as she bolted across the driveway and into the neighbouring woodland situated between the Hall and the town. Then, after pausing to catch her breath, she took a quick look behind her. Thankfully, there was no sign of Hereward in angry pursuit.

Since her husband had chosen not to chase her, Isabella soon calmed down and started walking towards the town. Her arm felt sore from the steely pressure of his subduing fingers and she rubbed her skin to ease the discomfort. Right then it seemed to her ironic that on the day she had decided to stay out of the woods, she had ended up in them after all.

The woodland to the west of the Hall was a terrain of interconnected tracks and trails laid down by a diverse collection of countless creatures. The minor pathways branched off in multiple directions, with some looping back on themselves, and others disappearing altogether under a mass of mulch and other organic material whose earthy odours tickled her nose.

Isabella hiked the main path, which cut a broad diagonal line through the trees straight to Oakwich town. The route was a long-established cross-country highway hammered by an endless succession of hooves, pads and feet, not to mention the tyres of bicycles ridden by time-pressed delivery boys. Compared with the Hall's echoey and unforgiving hardwood floors, the ground had a sympathetic surface that felt comfortable underfoot.

In her heightened emotional state, Isabella's wits were soon whetted by the dim-lit woodland. The further she walked, the greater her awareness of the breathy breezes, rustling vegetation and creature vocalisations that possessed the air. But instead of being scared, she felt soothed like a baby rocked in its cradle.

Once the trees began to thin out and a cacophony of loud, strident voices supplanted the forest's charming musical notes, Isabella knew she was near to her destination. At that point in her impetuous flight, she could only hope her parents would be sympathetic to her plight and agree to her return. Then it occurred to her that in her desperation to escape from

Hereward, she had given little thought to their possible reaction.

By the time Isabella arrived at her destination, daylight was fading fast and the lamplighters were out in force lighting the gas lamps. As she climbed the steps to the front door, her feet felt like cast-iron weights. The old maid let her in and was delighted to see her, but Agatha Acton was confounded by the look on her daughter's face, which informed her the visit was anything but a social one.

Isabella wiped her wet eyes and described as best she could, employing polite euphemisms, Hereward's improper performance in the sitting room earlier that afternoon, its stormy aftermath and her subsequent flight.

Mrs Acton, however, an old-school relic of the late-Victorian age, believed the institution of marriage to be immutable and must therefore be upheld whatever the circumstances. Unmoved by her daughter's woes, she asserted that striking one's husband, no matter how uncivil or boorish his behaviour, was guaranteed to incite a reprisal. Whatever the provocation, violence could never be justified. Moreover, she would not be party to her daughter's preposterous plan to abandon an affluent and socially advantageous marriage.

"My dear child, you must learn to tolerate your spouse's affectionate advances with good grace," she advised. "He is well within his rights and you are not at liberty to refuse him. You must remember your vows dear. Now we'll speak no more of separation and divorce. Divorce is for the disreputable, and I will not have this family's good name dragged through the courts, not to mention the local newspapers. I'm sorry, but that is the end of the matter. You will return to your husband at the earliest opportunity."

Chapter 29

Behind at the Hall, rubbing his face in mindful consideration, Hereward bitterly regretted his loss of control earlier that afternoon and the harsh manner in which he had manhandled Isabella. Such behaviour was not only ungentlemanly, he decided, but also unlikely to endear him to her. He had to admit her rejection of his affection brought out the worst in him. For one thing, he couldn't comprehend why she reacted to his loving embraces with such icy frigidity. Had it been Rosalyn in her place, she would have responded to his touch with pure, unashamed rapture.

Boyle plodded in with the tea tray and gave his master a sympathetic look. To his mind, the Major's hassles were overwhelmingly of his own making. The vainglorious Miss Rosalyn Dumbarton would not have presented him with anywhere near the same problems. For one thing, she too concerned with preening her unruffled feathers. If the butler had his way, the only women allowed in the house would be the maids. And only then to do the housework. With their petulant pouts and acrid tongues women were more trouble than they were worth. As a proud and unapologetic misogynist, Boyle preferred to exist in a world without women; a world without women was his perfect world.

Even though Hereward tried to convince himself that Isabella had simply lost track of the time, as usual, her ongoing absence worried him. After all, she had run from the Hall in a distressed state and without her winter coat when the weather was cold. Despite searching for her in the most-obvious places, he could see no sign of her. He had even checked with the farmer, but the farmer said she no longer visited the farm. Which meant there was only one place remaining.

Donning his hat and coat, Hereward hurried out to the motorcar. As time passed by his guilt increased exponentially. He feared something bad had befallen Isabella as a number of worrisome scenarios played out in his mind. She might be in danger and unable to call for help; she might be injured and unconscious; she might be seriously hurt and in urgent need of medical attention. She might be… No, it didn't bear thinking about. Whatever had happened to her, he blamed himself. To his eternal shame, he had again lost control. With distressing images swirling around inside his head, Hereward raced towards the town, scanning the road's margins in case she was already making her way back to the Hall.

By the time he arrived at his in-laws it was dark and the temperature had dropped even further. There were few people outside and no moving vehicles on the cobbles. The gas lamps cast the quiet street in a ghoulish-green glow, while in every house the heavy drapes were drawn to conserve heat and ensure privacy.

Lithe as a leopard, Hereward mounted the steps to the front door two at a time and rapped hard with his trademark impatience on the dull brass knocker. Following what seemed like an age, the doddery old maid admitted him. He brushed past her, strode purposely down the hallway's lacklustre chequerboard floor and into the sitting room, where his rebellious wife was standing beside her mother.

Although he was greatly relieved to see Isabella safe and sound, Hereward decided not to show so much as a trace of weakness or remorse on the basis it would give her an advantage.

"Get in the car!" he commanded through clenched teeth.

"I will do no such thing," insisted Isabella.

"I said get in the car!" he repeated, this time with a hint of threat in his voice.

Agatha Acton placed a gentle hand on her daughter's arm and, with a guiding nod, directed her to do as she was told.

Devastated by what she considered a betrayal, Isabella sobbed quietly as she departed her childhood home and climbed into the motorcar's cold black-leather interior. Although she felt reluctant to return to the Hall, her mother's hard-hearted rejection had forced her to face the reality of her situation.

Hereward, meanwhile, remained behind to speak with his mother-in-law, whose fine cheekbones and slender neck Isabella had inherited without the hauteur.

Mrs Acton, however, had other ideas. As her son-in-law opened his mouth to speak, she raised an imperious hand in a silencing gesture, narrowed her ice-blue eyes, and gave him the most-withering look from her entire repertoire of withering looks.

"Should it so happen that at any time in the future Isabella has recourse to seek sanctuary at this house, then that is what she will be given," she stated. "Regarding your lascivious behaviour towards my daughter this afternoon, may I remind you there is a specific place for marital intimacy. It is commonly known as the bedroom."

A couple of minutes later an abashed Hereward put the motorcar in motion and the tempestuous two set off for the Hall. Looking gloomy and glum, as gloomy and glum as was possible to look, they travelled back in a resounding silence. The silence at least allowed them to reflect on their respective agonies. Hereward was forced to admit to himself that for a man not given to gambling he had perhaps been unwise to marry an adolescent girl on the basis of a potent sexual attraction. Such impulsivity was ordinarily antithetical to his essential circumspection, but his pathological need to possess Isabella had overridden his usual objectivity. The second he set eyes on her at the parade, the effect on him was so momentous, her image had remained in his head like a palinopsia.

Marriage to Isabella, however, was not what Hereward had envisaged. What Hereward had envisaged was an unrealistic romantic fantasy wherein his wife requited his passion whenever and wherever. Her dispassionate responses to his approaches, and the way she tensed up every time he touched her, made him less than sympathetic to her personal difficulties. For his own selfish reasons, he also refused to consider the effects marriage to him had on his unworldly and innocent young wife. Added to which, he had no idea how to resolve his marital problems. Having long enjoyed the benefits of a disciplined and orderly lifestyle, he found Isabella's dissenting behaviour vexatious and disruptive. Notwithstanding, he had few regrets. Unwise or not, given the chance to turn back the clock, he knew he would marry her all over again without a second thought.

Isabella, on the other hand, viewed the situation from an entirely different perspective. Since she got married her life had been governed by a monotonous set of domestic hymeneal commandments. Her husband was a creature of habit and firmly fixed in his ways. The house revolved around his needs and she was expected to adhere to the established order. The established order was run with regimental precision in strictly demarcated zones. Whatever she required she must ask of the maids, who in turn deferred her requests to the omnipotent butler. But what Isabella most resented was being treated as a child in the domestic realm and a mature woman in the bedroom. Her refusal to live up to the outmoded feminine ideal rooted in her husband's imagination set them on opposing paths. Until he began to see her as a discrete individual with desires, interests and passions of her own, instead of an extension of himself, then their discontents would continue.

Chapter 30

Out on the estate, secretive as a woodcock, smelling of brown sweat, grease and mud, Rosalyn's scout sat hidden behind the hedge just beyond the orchard. Since there had been neither sight nor sound of her for several days, he feared the Major's wife had given up walking altogether. Having learned a valuable lesson, he intended to keep a greater distance from her in future and make the least noise possible.

For want of something to do while he waited, Parker studied his huge hairy hands. Flipping them over, he splayed his fingers wide before inspecting his palms. There was no disputing his hands were horrors. They were typical plebeian hands, shovel-shaped, calloused, scaly, and gristly from years of gruelling graft. Tipping them back over, he studied his knuckles, gnarled as ginger knobs. Frowning, he tried to recall the number of times he had injured them in a fight. Too many times to be counted he chuckled as he made a fist first with his right hand, then with his left. His grandfather had once said that fists were made for fighting before knocking him out cold on the flagstone floor with a powerful uppercut to his jaw. Wincing at the memory, Parker half unfolded his fingers and inspected his nicotine-stained nails. They were jagged, ridged and split, with a lifetime's dirt ingrained below their free edges. He found it impossible to remove the greasy residue completely. A curved black line always remained no matter how often he scrubbed his hands. Not that he scrubbed them that often. There was little point when they only got filthy again. Working for long hours on posh properties for penny-pinching rates of pay had damaged them irreparably. Unless they were desperate, even ladies of the night turned up their noses at him when they noticed his hands. As for his beard, he thought it gave his acorn-coloured face the look of a long-forgotten, fluff-covered caramel languishing in the corner of a coat pocket.

From deep inside his throat Parker hawked a glutinous glob of mucus, spat it out and dried his mouth on the back of his sleeve. Then he lit up a Woodbine and exhaled the smoke through his nose. Woodbines were strong. One of the strongest. He could never understand why they shared a name with the fragrant plant. The brand was popular with soldiers, soldiers and the working class; working-class soldiers. Officers had different smokes. Even cigs are divided on class grounds, he mused with a shake of his shaggy head. Every morning the first thing he did was to light up. Invariably, it made him wheeze like an oil-starved metal hinge. The sticky mucosity of his phlegm convinced him he was clearing out his lungs, although he felt more like he was coughing them up. How he wished he could remove them and rinse them under the village pump.

To save the partly detached soles of his dilapidated boots, secured with nails to prevent them from flapping as he walked, Parker had slept in the barn the previous night. He kept forgetting he could now afford to replace them thanks to Miss La-di-dah's largesse. Having risen early, he had gone straight to the cowshed and helped himself to a munificent measure of calves' pleasure, making sure to scarper before the farmer arrived to milk the herd. Milking cows required a certain skill. Some girls were sensitive souls, tetchy and temperamental. Aggressive even on some occasions. Much as Parker would have liked to, the teat must never be suckled directly. Even the most-docile beast objected to having its udders guzzled by the likes of him. As a young lad he had been warned by his grandad that a corrective kick from the hind leg of an indignant cow could maim or kill the culprit. Even passing between two cows could be dangerous.

To protect himself as best he knew, Parker always rubbed his hands together to warm them up. Then kneeling down, he pulled the teat of the nearest animal and aimed a jet of milk straight into his mouth. The liquid tasted warm, sweet and ambrosial. Once satisfied, he filled his dented enamel bottle to the brim and hung it around his neck by its strap.

After swallowing a generous swig of the filched milk, Parker pushed himself up from the ground. To ease the stiffness in his joints he tramped the path back and forth for several yards. Attracted by his warmth and strong odour, a cloud of annoying gnats clung close. After wafting them away, he removed a matchstick from a box of Bryant and May, struck it down the sandpaper side and lit up another Woodbine. A couple of puffs later, his nose pointed skyward, Parker sniffed the air and observed the sky for signs of precipitation. It was overcast but the air smelled dry. So, he settled himself back down on his hessian sack to wait. Come noon, if there was still no sign of rain, she might come. He desperately hoped she would. And perhaps the elusive Jack might even make an appearance.

To his joyous relief she came at her regular time. Sniffing the air like a pig, Parker inhaled her perfume. Then through a hole in the hedge he fixed his eyes on her form as she ambled by on the path. He liked the way her hips moved in a slow, easy rhythmic roll. To better ogle her, to submit her curves to closer inspection, he moved in nearer, taking care to remain unnoticed.

His eyes gleaming like the glaze on an uncooked kidney, Parker imagined her in a bathing costume, like the ones young women wore to the beach. He had visited the seaside only once, a wonderful occasion as he recalled, where he had seen lots of lovely half-naked ladies paddling in the waves and playing ball games. Lying on the sand, he had observed them at leisure while performing an act of self-pleasure. That was until one of them spotted him and alerted her companions. Suddenly, they all started pointing and shouting at him, so he was forced to find a more-secretive spot. Hence for observational purposes, he decided the woods were better.

After trailing the little lady for a while with painstaking attention, Parker decided it made sense to change his position periodically. That way she was less likely to get wind of him. So, while maintaining a suitable distance, he started to circle her. Doing so allowed him to study her from every possible angle. Despite the cold, as he went on watching her, he grew hot, sticky and sweaty. Then his face turned purple, his pulse quickened and his body quivered. Whenever she stopped to observe something up close, he thought how easy it would be to grab hold of her. After all, she was perfect for picking: the perfect size, the perfect weight, the perfect age. Tender as a newborn lamb and there for the taking, should a bloke be thus inclined. In only a few long strides he knew he could take her from behind in an instant. The thought of his big hands on her juvenile flesh awakened his slumbering man-part like Lazarus rising, so that it rubbed the inside seam of his trousers. Facing a tree trunk, he sought active relief. And soon enough a jet of watery white slime issued forth as he tried his best to mute his moans.

Parker wiped his hand clean on the grass. However, as his breathing slowed, he realised his loss of control placed him at greater risk of discovery. Which, paradoxically, heightened the experience and increased the excitement. Excitement, he presumed, from the risk of getting caught. Caught by a boyfriend, or worse, a husband. Yes, a husband, he stressed to himself, remembering he must take extra care because the girl belonged to Major Aldwen.

Chapter 31

A few weeks after bringing Isabella back from her parents' place, Hereward arrived at his sister's house unannounced. He looked desperately down in the dumps after another heated dispute with his self-willed wife. Almost eight years his senior, Maud was unmarried and, except for her staff, lived alone in a stylish Victorian villa bequeathed to her by her father. She was especially fond of her little brother, as she still thought of him, and was someone on whom he could depend for emotional support.

Maud beheld Hereward's harrowed face as he unburdened himself in her sitting room, and decided the time had come to be frank. It wasn't that she lacked sympathy for his adversities; she had every sympathy and more. Intimate relations could be challenging at the best of times and, as it was, her brother's marriage had started out on shaky foundations, and had been shaking ever since. Moreover, she knew only too well that of all Hereward's qualities, insight came low on the list. As the esteemed firstborn son of landed gentry, he had been indulged throughout his childhood and was accustomed to having his own way.

"If, as you say, you love Isabella," Maud began, "then please acquaint me with the steps you have taken to help her adjust to her new circumstances?"

What could he say? So, he said nothing.

As someone who believed passionately in female independence, Maud understood the situation most women found themselves in after marriage. Men like her brother exasperated her. On a number of occasions, she had observed him speaking to Isabella as if she were a child, and she had to admit it riled her.

"My dear boy, you treat your wife like a small puppy. It's almost as if you've grabbed the pick of the litter, taken it straight home and dumped it in a basket in the corner. After which you expect the poor wee thing to come bounding up to you as soon as you call its name. Then after patting and playing with it for a few minutes, you send it back to its basket. I doubt you even bother to take it out for a walk. That's how you see marriage. That's how you see women. All on your own selfish terms. You may well be an erudite gentleman, my dear, but when it comes to male-female relations, if you'll pardon my saying, you behave like a condescending old coot."

Maud fully understood why her brother had fallen for Isabella. Without a doubt the girl's beauty was exceptional; but beauty alone wasn't enough to sustain a marriage. And Hereward more than most should know, that for the most part, success was achieved through effort.

"If your love for Isabella is the genuine thing and not still some mad infatuation, then you must show her it is so. Get to know her, her likes and dislikes, her interests and passions, and whatever else appeals to her and makes her feel happy and content."

Hereward remained silent. Which meant he was mulling over Maud's insightful observations and advice. Her blunt and unedited honesty had caught him off guard and he needed to give the subject some serious thought.

"Let me put it another way," said Maud to inculcate her point. "Isabella isn't your common everyday garden plant. She's a rare and exquisite flower. In order to grow and flourish, such flowers require an understanding of their individual needs, optimal care and attention, life-giving sustenance, and oodles of pure clean air. Otherwise, they fail to thrive and become limp and lifeless. That's not what you want is it? The qualities that first attracted you to your wife: her joie de vivre, her independent spirit, her vivacity and, dare I say, her feistiness, are what you most seek to suppress. If you don't change your ways and stop being so rigid in your attitudes, and so neglectful of her, then you will both end up more miserable than you already are. And that's the last thing I want to see happen, since I care deeply about you both."

On Hereward's return drive to the Hall, he reflected on his sister's sage advice. Maud was a wise woman. A wise woman indeed. There wasn't a single word she said with which he could disagree. For the first time since getting married he was forced to admit he had been most remiss in his treatment of his young wife. Time to start making amends.

Isabella was curled up on the sofa with a murder mystery when Hereward entered the sitting room. Barely raising her head, she returned his greeting with her customary aloofness and continued turning the novel's pages with nail-gnawing concentration. The story was gripping and compelling, thus she resented his intrusion at a point in the plot that anticipated a moment of heart-stopping terror.

Never one to be discouraged, Hereward sat himself down beside her on the sofa, cleared his throat and forced a smile.

"I have some business to attend to in town tomorrow," he said, crossing his arms, "which hopefully shouldn't take too long. I thought perhaps you might like to come with me. Once I've finished, we can drive over to the Botanical Gardens for a bit of a wander. And, if you like, we can take tea in the garden café afterwards. What do you say?"

Isabella looked up from the page. The prospect of escaping the house for a few hours certainly appealed. She felt sure she would enjoy strolling around the flowerbeds and shrubberies. Returning his smile, she replied: "Oh yes, that sounds super. I should very much like to. Thank you."

Hereward rubbed his hands together. "That's fixed then," he said. Except this time his smile was genuine.

After he left the room and the sound of his footsteps faded, Isabella placed her book on her lap and reflected on her new life. Oftentimes her husband's disappointment with her responses to him was palpable. Well, there was little she could do about that. She couldn't make herself love him. In fact, there were times when she found being married to Hereward intolerable. And she wondered if she would ever manage to reconcile herself to her loveless life. She recalled a recent conversation with her mother, who told her to grow up and make the most of her many privileges.

"You must count your blessings, dear child," Agatha Acton had advised. "You seem to have forgotten how impoverished we were before you married the Major, and how close the wolf was to our door. Your dear papa out of his mind with worry. Little left to sell or pawn. You have everything a woman could possibly wish for: a rich husband of repute; an impressive house in the country; domestic staff; excellent food and fine wine; clothing of the highest quality; furs if you prefer, and a dazzling social life, should you feel so inclined. And instead of being eternally grateful, you object to a little physical intimacy between yourself and your provider. Well intimacy is a small price to pay for so many material benefits. You really are a most-thankless girl, Isabella. And to think your dear papa, with only your best interests at heart, found you an excellent husband."

With a deep sigh, Isabella tucked a loose curl behind her ear and returned to her nerve-racking novel. At least now she had a little something to look forward to.

Chapter 32

They entered the Botanical Gardens through a set of imposing wrought-iron gates standing open for visitors. The weather was mild for the month and thankfully dry, dispensing with the need for an umbrella. They both wore light overcoats in similar shades, sensible brogues and stylish hats. Hereward preferred to visit the gardens in autumn because they were less crowded than in spring and summer.

He offered Isabella the crook of his elbow.

After a little hesitation, she reminded herself he was after all her husband and shyly linked her arm through his.

Hereward welcomed her touch. The physical contact that informed the world she was his. And only his. Other than when they attended church, they rarely went out as a couple. To savour her rose-scented nearness, he adopted a leisurely pace. And as they wandered the gardens, he observed the envy on other men's faces, the way their eyes passed from Isabella to him, then back again. It made his chest swell with pride. Yet beneath the pride lurked an uncanny sense of unease. Rather like a darkening sky warned bad weather was imminent. He observed female envy too; but female envy was different from male envy and had different connotations.

Even gone summer the gardens were gorgeous. A chaotic canvas of red, gold and green splashes boosted by dashes of purple. The striking sight of nature in transition, late blooms, and the rich aroma of autumn ripeness cheered Isabella and soothed her sorry heart. However, as they passed through a tunnel of trees, the scene triggered traumatic memories of her journey to Aldwen Hall on the day her heartless father gave her away. And she was still adjusting to her new circumstances. Biting her lower lip, she blinked back tears and gathered herself to avoid spoiling the lovely outing.

They strolled around the flowerbeds, herbaceous borders and arboretum. Isabella was charmed by the rock garden's alpines, crocuses and cyclamens dipped in delicate shades of pink, lilac and blue. In the centre of the gardens stood a spectacular stone fountain whose water spurts sprayed them with a fine mist when they ventured too close. Isabella blushed deeper than a daylily when she observed her husband staring at the caryatids' half-exposed breasts. Silently, she unhooked her arm and ran on ahead.

Hereward caught up with her outside the orangery, where the tropical plants and ornamental trees were housed. Arms relinked, they progressed inside. Thinking out loud, Isabella expressed a wish to include some exotic plants in their own conservatory. She imagined they would brighten the place up and make it look more inviting during the dull winter months.

"It seems such a shame not to show the room to its full advantage," she said.

Hereward gave her an indulgent smile and agreed without exception. Had she asked, he would have agreed to anything at that moment. Apart from the slight hiccough at the fountain, it was the first time there had been communion between them and he was determined to make it last.

When they reached the bougainvillea, Hereward came to a full stop as he recalled the plant's profundity throughout India.

"You know this thing grows virtually everywhere on the subcontinent," he informed her. "It helps to brighten up the buildings' sun-bleached and whitewashed walls." Then he paused for a moment as if to gather his thoughts. "Do you know that bougainvillea is in actual fact a vine?"

"I've heard the name, but this is the first time I've actually seen one," Isabella replied.

"Yes, a vine," he reiterated. "Beloved by bees, butterflies and hummingbirds. As you can see, it comes in a variety of colours. I seem to recall the most popular shades in India being reds, purples and pinks. It's unfortunate our British weather isn't warm enough for them to survive outdoors. At least not in winter."

Once Hereward could see he had Isabella's full attention, he continued. "See here," he said taking hold of a specimen and lightly brushing his thumb over a bract. "There's this cluster of tiny white flowers rising up through its centre." He paused, grinned and said: "Actually it reminds me of you."

Bemused, Isabella turned to him. "Why ever is that?"

"Well, to begin with, it's beautiful all year round. In actual fact, it's highly prized for its beauty. Not only that, it's also a vigorous plant and an accomplished climber. Finally, it's cute, compact and utterly enchanting."

Isabella blushed. "Methinks, you flatter me too much."

"Not at all," he said suavely. "Oh, and I forgot to mention, it has a voracious appetite."

"Really, Hereward, I don't know why you persist in making fun of me. There's nothing abnormal about a lady having a healthy appetite." Then she half smiled and said: "I had no idea you were so knowledgeable about plants."

"I'm not especially. Well, no more than the average person," he said, before inviting her to sit on one of the wooden benches punctuating the pathways.

Accepting his offer, Isabella sat down. But when he joined her, she moved aside to create a small gap between them.

Hereward turned to look at her. She had the longest, thickest eyelashes he had ever seen. They put him in mind of minute wings. Resting his arm across the bench top behind her, he gently played with a curl that had sprung loose from its clasp.

The touch of her husband's fingers gave Isabella a pleasant tingly sensation at the back of her neck and she allowed him to continue. Away from the Hall and out of earshot and eyeshot of Boyle and Barbara, she felt more relaxed, more communicative and less inhibited

"India sounds fascinating," she said.

"I have to say it's something of a mixed bag. Up north, for instance, where I was stationed for much of the time, it can be exceptionally hot and at other times exceedingly cold. But it's a fabulous country and I enjoyed my stint out there immensely."

Hereward stopped speaking as two nannies in uniform pushing prams passed by them on the path. As he observed them, he wondered when Isabella would provide him with an heir. Thus far, there had been multiple opportunities to put her in the family way, he thought with an inner smile. Perhaps she was still too young.

"I'd like to go there," she said, cutting into his thoughts. "And ride in a howdah on an elephant. Oh, and see the Taj Mahal at sunset. I read all about India in a library book. It looks truly amazing."

Hereward loved to listen to her speak. He adored her voice. It had a soft, silky, breathy resonance that was irresistibly seductive. Removed from their regular surroundings, she seemed to him more talkative, more inclined to chat; a rare but welcome occurrence. Then without knowing why, he felt suddenly protective of her. She was sometimes the sweetest thing. In spite of her irrepressible need for knowledge and her increasing maturity, there remained a childlike innocence and fragility about her that made him want to enfold her in his arms and hold her tight.

"Why did you leave India?" she enquired after a long pause.

"A number of reasons really. For one thing, I was homesick and tired of the peripatetic lifestyle. And I wanted to write. And for that there's no place better than Aldwen Hall."

"Do you miss the military?"

"Sometimes, but only very occasionally."

"It must have been awfully exciting," she ventured.

Hereward smiled. "Yes, and sometimes awfully dangerous too."

"Then you must be awfully brave," she said.

He smiled again, this time revealing teeth in almost perfect alignment.

As soon as they completed the tour they headed straight for the café; a charming and pleasant place in a large conservatory. To eat, it served cakes, scones and finger sandwiches. To drink, it offered a choice of teas, coffees, hot chocolate, and fresh lemonade. In the centre of the café a black-suited pianist played light orchestral pieces with unobtrusive panache.

While Hereward drank his coffee and ate only one scone and a sandwich, he watched with discreet amusement as Isabella worked her way through the fare. He loved to watch her eat. She had the most-endearing manner of chewing her food, as if she were meditating on every mouthful. But since time was getting on and the day showing the first signs of drawing to a close, with some reluctance Hereward announced it was time to head back to the Hall.

"Must we?" said Isabella with a dropped face. "It's still far too pleasant to be cooped up inside the house."

"I'm afraid we must, my love," he said with a sorry face. "Come along now my gorgeous little gourmand." And he offered her his arm again.

"I'm surprised at you," she said in a prickly voice as she took his arm. "Surely you must know it's unmannerly for a gentleman to comment on a lady's appetite."

"My sincere apologies," he replied with a light bow and a teasing smile that bordered on a laugh.

That night, when Hereward joined Isabella in her bed, she was lying on her back for a change, but was otherwise quiet. He settled himself down beside her, stretched out his long lean legs and linked his hands behind his head.

"I must say the gardens were splendid," he said. "I appreciated the diversion. As much as I enjoy my work, the outing made a pleasant change from tapping the hell out of the typewriter and overtaxing my poor brain."

Then in a small display of affection, he rolled onto his side and stroked Isabella's cheek with his hand. It was the same cheek he had smacked in the conservatory when she threw the water over him. And despite the extreme provocation, he felt thoroughly ashamed of himself for hitting her.

"Yes, the gardens were amazing," she agreed. And I'm super excited about introducing a few new plants to the conservatory. In fact, I'm going to visit the nursery at the first available opportunity."

While Isabella chatted about her plans, Hereward's thoughts drifted. Thoughts that recalled predacious male eyes on her in the Botanical Gardens; eyes that revealed their innermost thoughts and feelings. Had he been one of those men, he would have felt envious too. Other men's envy was an unenviable emotion; to be feared when one possessed something so special. Being a man himself, he knew Isabella's feminine beauty made her more vulnerable than the average woman.

Taking hold of the hem of her nightdress in the unlit room, Hereward raised it above her breasts, then kissed and caressed her all over. Unable to withstand the rising pressure within himself for a second longer, he eased apart her legs, guided himself inside her like a finger into a glove and flooded her with his love.

Chapter 33

The success of the visit to the Botanical Gardens was sadly short-lived. Communication between the couple regressed to exchanging mundane comments during meals. Still, it was at least an improvement on the oppressive silences that hung over them like a concrete blanket during the first weeks of their marriage.

Having said that, Isabella was gradually growing accustomed to Hereward's mercurial temperament and abrasive manner. However, it was his dictatorial behaviour that generated the maximum friction between them. Even if, as he believed, his need to control her was in the interests of her safety and wellbeing.

It so happened one day that Isabella entered the library wearing a pair of navy-blue trousers she had purchased from Martha's the previous week. The trousers were sassy, chic and popular with fashionable young women. Martha said they fitted her fabulous figure to perfection and told her she must be sure to wear them. Choosing to follow her friend's advice, as soon as she put them on Isabella felt elegant, stylish and sophisticated.

Hereward noticed the trousers at once. It was impossible not to. With a dark scowl clouding his face, he looked her up and down as if she were some sort of curious exhibit.

"What in heaven do you think you're doing gadding about

in those abominations?" he barked.

"I believe the correct sartorial term is trousers," Isabella replied with a deadpan face. "They're women's trousers, designed specifically for the female form and they're supremely comfortable."

"I don't give a damn what they're called or how comfortable they are," he said with a thunderous face. "Go upstairs this instant and change into a dress. A lady doesn't wear trousers, not if she wishes to be considered a lady, she doesn't. They're most unbecoming."

"What utter nonsense," said Isabella, squaring up to him and staring him full in the face. "According to Martha, all the young women are wearing them and no-one has yet called them unladylike, so I can't understand why you find them so objectionable."

"I'm beginning to think that Martha woman is a bad influence on you. Can't you find a friend your own age?" said Hereward.

"She's the exact same age as you, as it happens," replied Isabella with a sneaky grin.

"That's different. Husbands are customarily older than their wives," he asserted.

"Yes, but I'm only seventeen and you're a whopping thirty-two. That's nearly twice my age."

Hereward's neck stiffened, his eyes narrowed and his voice hardened. "I can count, thank you," he stated between stiff lips.

"What about jodhpurs," Isabella put in. "They're also trousers and no-one complains about women wearing them in the saddle. It's fortunate I don't ride, otherwise I'm sure you'd insist on my sitting side-saddle dressed in one of those ridiculous voluminous skirts from the Victorian era. I'm not surprised Maud calls you anachronistic."

Hereward's throat tensed, his mouth formed a hard line

and he tapped his foot on the floor several times. "That's quite enough," he said. "I don't wish to hear my sister's opinions, thank you. And you shouldn't be listening to them either. Now do as you're told and go and get changed."

Isabella remained seated.

"Well, what are you waiting for? Get a move on or I shall carry you upstairs myself and remove them on your behalf."

Isabella blushed beetroot red at the thought of Hereward pulling down her trousers. She knew only too well the measure of his strength. Should he decide to, he could easily throw her over his shoulder like a sack of feathers and transport her upstairs in an instant.

"I'll change them straight after tea, otherwise the crumpets will go cold," she promised.

"Very well then. And make sure you do," he said.

At first, Isabella found Hereward's grumpy face only mildly amusing. Then, out of the blue, a bolus of laughter began to bubble up from her belly into her throat. With a gallant effort, she tried to control herself, but in vain. It was like trying to hold back the contents of a champagne bottle after the cork has popped. She wanted to roll on the floor laughing. In desperation, she grabbed her napkin, pressed it to her mouth and faked a coughing fit.

Hereward affected not to notice.

Mrs Jenkins had sent up a jar of homemade blackberry jam with the tea things. Isabella added a generous dollop to her crumpet.

"This looks nice," she said sweetly. Then she persuaded Hereward to try some. It was plain to see he was rattled: rattled by the trousers, her childish conduct and her cutting remark about his age. As she poured his tea from the silver kettle, she asked him if he preferred lemon or milk.

"Milk please. Most definitely not lemon," he said in a sulky voice. "I've had more than enough acerbity for one day."

Isabella made no further comment and returned to her tea. However, as soon as she finished eating, she rose and went over to him. For some reason, his looking so upset pricked her conscience. On reflection, she decided her remark about his age was not only uncalled for but also rather unkind, and that personal attacks could never be justified.

"One moment," she said softly. Then she licked the corner of her napkin, bent over him and swabbed a small daub of jam that was stuck to his beard.

Since she so rarely touched him, the small ministration performed with the gentlest of fingers took Hereward by complete surprise. His eyes full of longing, he looked up at her and smiled.

But as they locked eyes, Isabella experienced the strangest emotion. An emotion alien to her. She felt something stir deep down inside herself that she struggled to articulate. And she found herself staring at him for longer than usual.

"Well off you go then," said Hereward, pinching her bottom.

Astonished by his brazenness, Isabella rapped his knuckles with her napkin. "Please behave yourself," she admonished in a strict voice. Following which, she left to remove the contentious trousers.

Hereward ogled his wife's derrière as she departed the room. It looked delicious; far tastier than anything he had ever eaten. He had to admit, stretched across her rear like the hair on a horse's rump, the trousers looked divine. Which, if he were honest with himself, was the actual problem. He presumed they weren't meant to be worn so tight, but Isabella's well-rounded cheeks filled them out to the full. It was because Hereward liked her in the trousers that he disliked her in the trousers. If that made sense. The thought of men other than himself savouring the sight of Isabella's sensuous seat was too much to stomach. He realised times were changing. One only had to look at photographs of Wimbledon ladies to see that. To his mind, female fashions were heading in the wrong direction, especially when it meant his wife might be wearing them.

Since the trousers were ideal wear for country walks, more so now the weather was growing evermore wintry and there was often a hint of frost in the air, Isabella found Hereward's outdated views on womenswear frustrating. However, there was nothing to be gained from arguing with him. His mind was clearly made up. In the meantime, she would store them at the back of her wardrobe and perhaps wear them when he went out. Except he rarely left the house, and when he did it was only for short periods.

Powerless to resist the pull of the land, in spite of her episodic spates of uneasiness, Isabella resumed her habit of roaming for hours at a time. The Aldwen estate provided her with a refuge. A refuge from her adversarial marriage, purposeless life, and Boyle and Barbara's prying eyes and ever-alert ears. It was a place to while away the hours in blessed solitude and deep contemplation, where she could wander at will through fields of wildflowers and wade through tall weeds and overgrown grasses, with the sounds of animals and birds in the background.

Moreover, in an environment left to its own devices and allowed to grow and develop in its own unique way, Isabella could escape the constant tick-tick-ticking of the household clocks. Ticking clocks and dripping taps have much in common, she once said to herself. After all, they both have a steady beat. It seemed odd to her how people complained about dripping taps but never about ticking clocks. During the dreaded days when the rain drummed for hours on the glass panes, trapping her indoors, Isabella felt a powerful urge to smash every clock in the house into a hundred pieces. Some weeks it rained without a break. At such times she would sit beside the window willing it to stop. The clocks went on ticking whatever the weather. It was Boyle's job to rewind them every night after locking up and he never forgot. Sometimes she wished he would.

How Isabella longed for fine-weather days. Days when the low winter sun winked through the trees as she walked; when she marvelled at its reflection in the lake's glossy surface and watched it hover on the horizon before dropping like a penny into a slot. After which she would hurry back to the Hall, back to the rigid regimen of her inactive domestic life.

Isabella always set out straight after luncheon. Walking in the open air revived her spirits and helped to slacken the tight band of pressure around her head. The second she left the house she felt like an animal released from captivity. Or, perhaps more aptly, a cute canary let out of its cage. Isabella recalled a tale about a canary that escaped through an open window, only to be killed by a host of sparrows jealous of its colourful plumage. The story saddened her since the bright little bird had no control over its appearance and she sighed at nature's cruel irrationality.

She found Hereward exact and exacting, punctilious to a fault. She both feared and fought him. He scolded her every time she turned up late, and she was habitually late. She would steal into the library looking like a naughty schoolgirl guilty of smoking behind the woodshed. Sitting stiffly in one of the armchairs, Hereward would be wearing his cross face; so cross, Isabella almost expected to be sent to bed without her tea. Oftentimes alas, she found his furious face funnier than frightening, causing her to burst into a fit of girlish giggles, making him even crosser than he already was. Laughter was meant to be infectious, but Hereward was never infected with laughter. Instead, he would graft his dark-grey eyes onto hers and fly into a temper hot enough to heat the bathwater.

But no matter what, Isabella refused to live in fear; refused to allow what she called her self-inflicted insanity to rule her life. After all, while out on the estate, as she reminded herself multiple times, she had suffered no tangible threats to her safety from either human or beast. In fact, the only hazards in her life, if they could be called hazards, were her husband's raging rants and Boyle and Barbara's artifice.

Nevertheless, as winter progressed, the periodic sense of being watched persisted. Isabella could never quite understand why the perception waxed and waned. Somehow it always seemed stronger in the forest, where she discerned a distinct but unaccountable presence. There in the green-scented ubiquitous trees, many of whose branches were entangled like lovers' limbs, she felt a cold, animalistic gaze on her back. Even in the garden, a couple of times she had experienced an attack of the heebie-jeebies: that convulsive shudder of the shoulders, cold clamminess on the skin and sharp tingling in all her limbs. And when a faint fetid breeze wafted towards her like a forewarning, she made the sign of the cross to counteract an imaginary curse and hurried back indoors.

Chapter 34

Waiting for the Major's wife to appear on the path, Parker stroked his beard and brooded on his laborious life. Even though he had once been described as having the underbite of a bull-breed, he was beyond being bothered by his appearance. A mean comment, he reflected, to make about a fellow in his formative years, as he was then. Such is life, he said to himself with a heavy sigh.

Unlike many of his comrades, Parker had returned from the Great War largely unscathed, and thankfully without the sort of facial disfigurement that no amount of surgical intervention could put right; which put his mandibular misfortune into perspective. He considered himself fortunate; fortunate except with regard to the fairer sex.

After being discharged from the army at the end of the war, Parker found himself with a broad range of skills, but without a decent occupation to apply them to. So, with a degree of reluctance, he returned to gardening work. Nevertheless, his conversance with ground-based military operations, combined with his deer-hunting proficiency, rusty though the latter was, came in handy in his temporary new role. Even in winter, Parker knew how best to fool the eye. Since the eye detected movement, all he needed to do was to keep to the shadows and stand stock still whenever his inquisitive quarry cast her eyes around. Clad in the appropriate camouflage, Parker felt confident even the sharpest eyes would fail to spot him. Humans, he knew, like rabbits, were creatures of habit and, as a rule, frequented the same routes every time; making his task must easier, provided that is he could manage to make no noise.

Lost in thought, Parker continued fiddling with his beard. He half regretted not growing one earlier. The beard had a bundle of benefits and saved him a heap of hassle. For one thing, he no longer needed to shave every morning. And, for another, the long, hairy mat concealed his prognathic jaw. He reckoned he made a better job of trimming the lawn than he did of shaving his face. The hirsute feature also shielded his tough leathery skin from the harsh winter climate. And, most important of all, it enabled him to blend in well with the Aldwen estate's bucolic backcloth.

Since it was the first dry day after nearly a week of incessant rain. Parker was burning to see the young beauty again. Assuming that is she came. He felt desperate to see her. Having an interest besides gardening and trapping game, made a welcome change to his humdrum existence. His wife was long gone, as was his poor mother: the woman he adored no matter what the vindictive villagers said about her. It still hurt him to think of her buried in a paupers' grave.

Finally, the girl arrived, preceded by her soft humming on the air like the gentle strumming of a harp. As she strolled past his hiding place, Parker's eyes narrowed and his muscles tensed in anticipation. Time to get going, he told himself. Then he eased himself up from the ground, quietly stuffed his hessian sack into a tree hole, and stole behind the overgrown hedge that ran parallel to the path.

Anxious not to alert her to his presence, Parker maintained a safe distance, but stayed close enough to keep her in sight. However, it soon became apparent that whenever he accidentally trod on a branch or dislodged a stone, or cleared his throat, it could be heard. Silently blasting himself, he hit his forehead with the heel of his hand in frustration and hoped she hadn't noticed the sounds. Beneath his elephantine feet too many things creaked, crackled and crunched on the ground. And while he damned Mother Nature's noisiness and cursed her capriciousness in his head, he was forced to admit he needed to brush up his skills.

As he went on stalking the little lady, pretty as a primrose in her princess coat, Parker wondered why she was always alone. Then he remembered she was meant to be meeting Jack. He considered Major Aldwen most remiss for permitting his wife to wander the estate unaccompanied. If she were Parker's missus, she would be safe at home tending to the house, making his meals and keeping the home fire burning.

But then wealthy women weren't required to do housework, Parker commented to himself. He detested the upper classes. Always had. In his view, they took everything for granted, employing servants, contracting services, and whatever else they required to oil the wheels of their palatine lives. The Dumbarton bitch was a case in point; a perfect example of a person with pots of money paying some poor peasant, such as himself, to perform her despicable deeds. Although to be fair, he reasoned, she could hardly be expected to sit for hours with only a hessian sack between her square flat buttocks and the cold ground. Added to which, being of a great height, ramrod rigid, inappropriately attired, and lacking the requisite skills, she would be spotted a mile off. Town or countryside, she stuck out like an attack of gout on a big toe. Too tall and masculine for his tastes, and all hard edges. He preferred soft, supple women with curvy hips, round breasts and shapely thighs, such as those on the Major's wife.

Suddenly, Parker grew aroused at the thought of the said lady lying spreadeagled beneath her husband, whose manhood he imagined was of impressive proportions. And as his eyes passed over her on the path, he licked his lips like a lizard on a leaf leering at a tasty butterfly.

Chapter 35

Unaware of a mole in her midst, Isabella bounded across the autumn meadow under a plutonium sky. Happening to look up, she spotted a sparrowhawk overhead, its wings fully outspread. Fascinated, she halted and ceased humming, while all around her the warning sounds of loud squawking and frenzied flapping filled the air. There then followed a momentary silence, during which time seemed to stand still. Horrified but unable to look away, her hand brimming her eyes, Isabella watched the flying fiend hover before cutting a near-vertical dive.

Pandemonium broke out as the raptor plucked its dish of the day with deadly accuracy out of the long grass, then bore it away in its talons to be torn apart and devoured. Sickened by the ghastly sight, Isabella closed her eyes for several seconds to gather herself. Mother Nature was monstrous, monstrous indeed, monstrous and cruel.

Isabella got going again and tried to forget the gruesome scene. As she walked, old memories streamed into her mind. Memories of illicit swimming in the lake with her former friends, whose shrill ghostly voices now echoed in her head. Who could forget the bracingly cold water on even the hottest days of summer? Back then the future was mostly irrelevant, being nothing more than unforeseen or imagined events.

As her mind returned to the present, Isabella scratched her

head. Only a minute since, a small bird had been hopping about with bland indifference, until in the blink of an eye it had been plucked from the present, having had little more than a peck at life. And she shuddered at the thought of the number of secret predators out there in search of their next repast.

With some degree of difficulty, Isabella again banished the sparrowhawk from her mind. There were other things to think about. Only that morning she had come across a jar of cold cream in one of the bathroom drawers. It wasn't hers. She never used cold cream. Had no need to. Her youthful skin was as smooth and as soft as caramel custard. After unscrewing the lid, she had peered inside, then held the container close to her nose. It smelled of beeswax and lanolin perfumed with rose-petals. After dipping an exploratory finger into the pot, she dabbed a tiny amount of cream on her skin.

Then with sudden repulsion, she rinsed it off as if it were a contaminant. Apart from her mother and Martha, there was only one woman she could think of who might use cold cream — the dreadful Rosalyn Dumbarton. But instead of returning the pot to the drawer, or dumping it in the wastebasket, which she would have preferred, Isabella placed it in the box containing her other finds, which she kept in her bedroom closet.

Her thoughts then turned to Hereward. Being a man of the world, he must have had lots of lovers, she assumed. Women on the hunt for a husband would consider him prime marriage material. She wondered how many women had passed through his masculine hands. Most likely dozens of them. And why had he remained a bachelor until he saw her? One day she would pluck up the courage to ask him about Rosalyn.

Although she was beginning to flag a little, Isabella continued to roam. Wandering about the estate improved her mood and helped her to clarify her thoughts. She welcomed the privacy too. Only the animals and birds can see me here, she said to herself with satisfaction. Out here I'm free to do as I wish. As free as a bird, she thought without irony.

Since relocating to the Hall, Isabella spent much of her time indoors reading novels. With alacrity, she was working her way through the library's substantial collection of adventure tales, horror stories and murder mysteries. As she walked it occurred to her that her chosen genres might be overfeeding her fanciful imagination an unwholesome diet of the gruesome, grisly and macabre. And she decided it would make sense to restrict herself to biographies, historical works and family sagas in future.

But when a new breeze began to agitate the foliage, Isabella felt eyes on her once more, making her feel fearful. She tried to dismiss the sensation by deriding it, but doing so did nothing to stop her pulse racing or subdue her rising panic. This must be how a wild animal feels much of the time, she remarked to herself, constantly on its guard. Taking a diaphragmatic breath, she tried to restore herself to a state of calm. After all, she wasn't a wild animal, she reminded herself. Moreover, getting wound up was an exercise in futility. She must stay strong. So, paying close attention, she checked the surround several times over. Apart from the sounds of the breeze and the birds, everywhere seemed quiet and still. Seeing no signs of unusual activity and reassured all was well, Isabella's pulse returned to its regular rhythm and she resumed walking.

However, as daylight began to dim, Isabella decided she must reach the Hall before darkness began making its final descent. Right then she recalled Hereward saying that in India night arrives without prior notice at six o'clock sharp, as though the gods had thrown a thick black blanket over the entire land. Imagine that! And she felt grateful that advance warning was given in the Western Hemisphere.

The moment she emerged from the woods Isabella slowed down a little. All the same, she kept a close eye on the ever-changing sky. Dusk continued to roll in by degrees like an ocean tide as an outfit of coral-edged caliginous clouds sailed by. Meanwhile the breeze strengthened into a bitter wolfish wind blowing in belligerent bursts, raising dust and debris from the path, worrying the trees and rattling the leaves.

As soon as she reached the lake area, the sensation of unseen eyes returned to haunt her. Unblinking eyes glinting with grievous intent. Disembodied eyes boring into her back. The feeling was stronger, more intense, more palpable than ever before. Repeatedly scanning the landscape as she walked, Isabella again reminded herself to remain calm, stay alert at all times and be ready to run should that prove necessary.

A few minutes on, hurrying between hedges of holly and hawthorn, Isabella heard an odd sound behind her. She stopped with a start, whipped around, peered into the distance, then looked left and right. Seeing nothing of note, she turned back in the direction of the house and went forward. In reality, she knew she had no other option, since there was no way on earth she could return to the deep dark woods. And she regretted roaming so far and wished she was back at the Hall. The Hall, a place she once considered a bridewell, now seemed more like a sanctuary.

A short time later the noise came again. Except now, and more worryingly, it was ahead of her. On the ground in the shade of a huge horse chestnut tree a couple of black-billed, black-clawed carrion crows kept a close eye on her. Anxiety began to well up inside Isabella like an underground lake rising to the surface. Queasy with fear, her stomach rolling, her muscles tight with tension, Isabella tried to decide on the best course of action, but her mind was muddled and disarrayed. Meanwhile, the carrion crows croaked and flew off with soundless wings. Caught in the grip of horror's hideous hand, cold moisture from her skin seeping into her clothes, her legs shaking, she collected her courage. Then like a winded doe springing back to life, she broke into a rapid run.

But the noise repeated. This time louder and more pronounced. Sensing danger ahead of her, Isabella came to a full stop. Head poised, she listened. A rapid current of ice-cold dread ran through her. In the draining daylight, dark shadows began to emerge. With watchful eyes she stared at the indistinct, hazy shapes all around her. Then her imagination went crazy. Suddenly, axe murderers, hungry cannibals and starving wolves crowded into her head like a procession entering a circus marquee.

In the nerve-fraying situation, Isabella at first failed to notice the resumption of silence, albeit an uneasy, oppressive, intimidating silence. Moreover, the air was perfused with a vaguely unpleasant odour reminiscent of composting potatoes. Then a sudden bitter-cold gust of wind struck her face and lifted her hat.

"What's that?" she whispered upon hearing another strange sonance. Turning this way and that, she listened some more, but the sound had ceased. All she could hear was the thumping rhythm of her own heartbeat.

In the semidarkness, as Isabella agonised over what to do for the best in the circumstances, the sound resumed, calling her attention to a point on her right. With slow, hesitant, apprehensive steps she drew closer to the sound's proximity. Then to her absolute horror two large black glassy orbs, bold as Beelzebub himself, regarded her with silent interest through a small gap in the hedge. Briefly, she held her breath.

Then, with a tremendous roar, Isabella's heart began to beat a rapid tattoo in her chest, her throat, her ears, her head, as she stared wild-eyed at the hedge. Weighed down with terror, her insides turned to slush, her feet pinned to the path, she stood immobile and helpless. But by sheer force of will, she ingested an enormous breath, gulped down her fear and regained the use of her legs. And with her soles spanking the path, she sprinted faster than at any time in her seventeen years on the planet.

Finally, the tops of the Hall's chimneys appeared above the trees, outlined against the murky sky like a ship's funnels in the mist. Isabella almost sobbed with relief when she saw them. Not far to go now, she told herself by way of encouragement. In reality, she wanted to scream, to cry, to yell at the top of her voice for assistance. How she wished Hereward would appear on the path. For only then would she feel safe from the thing she had seen through the hedge.

But as she began to flag from exhaustion, Isabella heard a thick snort, such as when air is sucked up through the nostrils. The snort was followed by the sound of footsteps trotting behind her. Possessed by a full-scale panic attack, she started to run. But in an attempt to regain her former speed, she tripped over her toes, stumbled forward, limbs flailing, and landed on all fours. After which an air-piercing primal scream burst forth from her throat as something cold, wet and slimy touched one of her hands. Desperately, she tried to scramble to her feet. But before she could do so, the obsidian-eyed beast was upon her.

Chapter 36

"Get off me!" she screamed. "Get off me you foul thing!" Isabella shouted, shoving it away with her elbows. Undeterred by her hysteria, the beast persisted. And when a long slobbering pink tongue licked her ear, it finally dawned on Isabella that her pursuer was nothing more deadly than a young friendly farm dog. Utterly relieved, she laughed out loud, laughed at length, laughed without inhibition. And while she petted the affectionate, playful pest, she laughed at her own stupidity. Pushing the large gangly puppy away, she felt grateful there had been no-one around to see her make a complete fool of herself; more especially Hereward.

"Go on Rover, Rex, Fido, or whatever you're called. Off you go," said Isabella to the affable hound as she got up from the ground, dusted the dirt off her coat and rubbed her sore knees.

The dog, as if detecting a threat, stiffened all of a sudden and sniffed the air. Then it raised its hackles, pointed its ears and growled at a specific spot in the hedge further back from where she stood. However, upon hearing the distant barking of its pack, it lost interest, turned tail, and scampered back to the farmyard.

Following which, Isabella hurried back to the Hall.

As he watched the little lady leave the area, Parker chewed his fist. Had he been holding a gun he would have happily shot the blasted cur for spoiling his fun. He realised he had come close to revealing himself when, with a touch of chivalrous obligation, he had almost dashed out from behind the hedge to rescue her from the dog. Had he broken cover, his mission would have been brought to a premature end. Still, the animal's unexpected appearance had been fortuitous, since it occurred at the same time one of his clumsy clodhoppers cracked a branch underfoot.

Thinking about the girl positioned on all fours, Parker felt an intense, intumescent tingling in his nether region as he was seized by a sudden incontrollable urge. With a salacious smile on his slimy lips, he leaned against a tree trunk and fumbled with his fly button. It was the same smile he always assumed whenever he ogled a slab of raw sirloin in the butcher's shop window. On the rare days when the butcher was willing, he exchanged a batch of despatched rabbits for a fat chunk of prime lean beef.

Shuttering his eyes, Parker emitted a deep moan as he slimed his hand and the insides of his soiled trousers. Then he wiped a drool string from his mouth with a mucky rag and heaved a heavy sigh. The ruttish pleasure of watching and fantasising about the girl prevailed over his hunger. He felt bewitched. Bewitched by the Major's young wife. The Major of all men. The only toff he had never despised.

He imagined she must be back home by now, sitting in front of a roaring log fire, supping her tea, and nibbling small finger sandwiches while telling her husband about the daft dog. And they would most likely be laughing their heads off. Parker then pictured them together before another bright fire, this time in the bedroom. He visualised the Major gorging himself on her most-succulent parts; his hard backside bobbing up and down as he beat the band in a rhythm of love.

By the time Parker entered his hamlet hovel it was almost

dark. Once again, he reflected, there had been no sign of the little lady's assumed lover. He realised the Dumbarton woman would be desperately disappointed if she knew nothing had happened on that score. Early days still, no need to tell her just yet, he said to himself. Then his thoughts turned to his tracking techniques. It was obvious they required a little fine tuning. Since he no longer owned a rifle, he was out of stalking practice. He remembered how his gruff grandfather had taught him the best way to stalk an animal without being heard. The grump had said anyone could do it, even a big lump of a lad like Parker. Well, he was glad the old man hadn't been there to see him that afternoon.

Chapter 37

The snow arrived early that year in the second week of November. Waking up to a freezing-cold bedroom, Isabella shivered between the bedsheets. She sat up, swung her legs out of bed, shoved her bare feet into her slippers and threw on her warm winter robe.

Although pretty to look at, the feather-patterned frost on the glass panes blocked the outside view. After rubbing a hole in the frost with her fingers, she peered out at the lustrous landscape. Overnight, the world had turned a startling white, resembling the lustrous crust on an iced Christmas cake.

Isabella fastened her robe tightly around her and checked the grate. The fire had gone out during the night and the log basket lay empty. Boyle always made sure there was a decent fire in the library because Hereward spent the best part of his day in there. If the fire wasn't blazing, her husband most certainly would be. She expected his bedroom would be the same.

After breakfast, excited by the surprise snowfall, Isabella was desperate to don her wellington boots and dash outside. However, when she realised there was no-one to share the fun with, her eager anticipation became dampened by disappointment. Hereward was too staid and reserved to romp outside. And as for Tilly and Barbara, the illiberal Boyle would no doubt ban them from frolicking in the snow.

In Isabella's opinion, the maids were allowed too little time for recreation. She was tempted to flout convention and call them outside. However, she soon had second thoughts. Going over the butler's bald head would be sure to cause a rumpus. She also expected Hereward would consider it unwise to socialise with the servants in case it made it more difficult to maintain discipline among them in future. Suffice to say, the master-servant dichotomy in the domestic realms of upperclass existence reigned supreme at the Hall. Hence, she was obliged to amuse herself.

From the window Isabella watched slews of snowflakes float silently down from the sky as if by magic and accumulate on the ground. A solitary pheasant pattered across the lawn, leaving spiky footprints in its wake; its copper-brown plumage, iridescent-green head and bright-red face in bold relief against the brilliant-white backdrop. Isabella checked to see if the bird's dull, mottled brown hen was nearby. She recalled Jack saying that pheasants pair for life. Let's hope they get on better than Hereward and I do, she said in her head with a wry smile.

Having decided to build a snowman, Isabella wrapped up warm and went outside. The snowfall triggered treasured memories of throwing snowballs, riding on improvised sledges and skating across the park's frozen pond. But on remembering the reclusions of her married life, she felt momentarily disheartened.

As Hereward watched his wife from the sitting-room window, he was reminded of one of those Viennese snow globes with tiny figures inside, and which threw up a snowstorm when shaken. Certain she would be pleased, he decided to buy her a musical version for Christmas. He loved the way her face lit up whenever he gave her a gift, no matter how small or inexpensive. For a change, he was looking forward to Christmas Day and seeing Isabella's reaction when she opened her presents. Then he made a mental note to have a couple of small fir trees cut down for the hall and sitting room.

Every so often the wind blew in sharp icy blasts, causing the snow to fly crossways. Isabella closed her eyes and tipped back her head so she could feel the flakes on her face. As they melted on her lips, their crystallised texture tasted of nothingness, like some insipid sorbet served to cleanse the palate between courses.

By the time she finished her snowman, Isabella's hat and mittens were sopping wet and the skin on her hands, face and feet tingled sharply with the biting cold. After returning inside, she hung her coat on a hook in the boot room and put her woollens on the fender to dry. Then from the sitting room window she inclined her head and admired her handiwork.

Come afternoon, the wind waned and the snow drifted down like flour from a sifter. A bunting of silvery icicles hanging from the roof gave the Hall an eerie, haunted appearance; while the deep snow rendered the road inaccessible. But being cut off from the town had little impact on the self-contained, delimited lives of the Hall's occupants.

Hereward rubbed his hands together as he strolled into the sitting room to join Isabella for coffee after luncheon. He sat on his haunches in front of the fire and held out his palms close to the flames. In a nod to the weather, he had on heavy tweed trousers, thick wool socks, and a chunky navy sweater with a roll-neck top and leather elbow patches. A minute later he got up, tossed a few extra logs onto the fire and turned to look at his wife.

It was the first time Isabella had seen him dressed down in the daytime. She thought the casual nautical-style knitwear rather suited him. In it he looked more plucky and less pedantic. She could almost see him standing on the bridge of an enormous ocean-going vessel scanning the horizon through a maritime telescope.

"Well now, my dedicated little snow sculptress," said Hereward, sitting down and picking up his coffee cup, "since you've had your hour of fun, I hope you're thoroughly warmed up. It wouldn't do for you to catch cold. Beats me why anyone would wish to go out in this abysmal weather. The air is so dastardly cold, one should venture outdoors only when one is forced to."

Not quite sure how to respond to what she perceived to be a mild rebuke, but feeling she should say something to defend herself, Isabella looked at Hereward and opened her mouth to speak. But on finding herself tongue-tied, she closed it again and looked away.

"There's a huge pile of logs in the woodshed and a mountain of food in the pantry," he went on, "so we needn't worry even if the road's closed for a week."

Other than a few minor concerns about the drawbacks of being snowbound, Hereward paid scant attention to climatic conditions, since they had little impact on his routine. Having nothing more to add to the one-sided conversation, he drained his coffee and returned to the library to get on with his work.

Left to her own devices, Isabella looked around the room and sighed.

Gone sundown, the snow luminesced the landscape, making night and day almost indistinguishable. Isabella found the stark beauty of the pink-tinted sky against the blue-tinted snow compelling. Earlier that day, when she shared her observations with Hereward, he explained how the snow's reflected light was disadvantageous to those predators which relied on the cover of darkness to hunt their prey. A factor she preferred not to think about.

Before turning in for the night, Isabella checked her frozen creation from the bedroom window with the expression of a contented child. And she couldn't help but smile at the old houndstooth scarf tied around the snowman's neck which Hereward had donated in a moment of doting indulgence.

Speak of the devil, she thought, as the door slid open and he swept into the room clad in a long cord-trimmed robe worn over blue-flannel pyjamas. No matter the time of day, he always looked pristine and well-groomed, even in his nautical knitwear. This the man who had captained her maiden voyage. And he had been sailing her ever since. She wondered what Hereward would do if she ceased to be seaworthy, as her predecessors clearly had. Would he scrap her and find himself a new vessel? Bah! she said to herself. Why should I worry about that?

None too pleased at finding his wife out of bed, Hereward frowned and shook his head thrice in disapproval. Even though she must have grown a good inch since he married her, to him she still appeared small, delicate and fragile.

"For heaven's sake, Isabella, you'll catch a chill standing there in that icy draught in your nightclothes," he said sharply as he removed his robe. "Draw the drapes and come away from the window you foolish girl. And that means now, not next week."

Lips pursed, Isabella dragged herself away from the window, hung her robe on the bedroom door and climbed into bed. Shivering slightly, she burrowed beneath the woollen blankets topped with a dense fluffy eiderdown. For once, she welcomed the warmth of her husband's body as he enveloped her in his arms. Marriage does have one advantage after all, she thought drily. And by the time Hereward had finished with her, she felt meltingly hot and deliciously sleepy.

The following morning Isabella peered out of the bedroom window and saw the ground remained covered with snow.

Automatically, her eyes drifted to the snowman. To her surprise its head was missing. As was Hereward's old scarf. She was convinced the damage was the work of a vandal. But unfortunately, a fresh batch of snow had fallen overnight, concealing any incriminating footprints.

"Curse you, you rascal, whoever you are," she cried out loud.

After luncheon, Hereward noticed Isabella studying the frozen one from the sitting-room window with close attention. He was still in the habit of sneaking up on her when she was least expecting, but he no longer took liberties outside of the bedroom, much as he would have liked to.

"Your esteemed snowman appears to have parted company with its head," he said in his typical laconic manner.

Isabella turned around to face him. "Indeed, it has, and I simply can't understand how it happened. Yesterday evening it was rock solid, so there's no way on earth it could have fallen off by itself. It's clearly the work of some mean-spirited saboteur," she said, pulling a face in disgust.

Hereward shoved his hands deep into his trouser pockets, shrugged, and gave her a sceptical look. "I expect something just crashed into it," he said. "Could be a large deer tried to jump it. Who knows? There could be a number of explanations." He then paused to catch his breath. "In any case, why are we discussing a large lump of compacted ice, for heaven's sake? Surely you can find something more engaging to occupy yourself."

"Yes, as it happens, I intend to take a walk this afternoon," she said brightly. "I enjoy trudging through the snow when it's all dry and crispy. I like the scrunching sound it makes underfoot. It reminds me of cornflakes. And, if I'm lucky, I might bump into some like-minded people. You know the sort who love having fun," she said pointedly.

"You'll catch your death out there," he cautioned. "Before you know it, you'll be as stiff as that frozen rival to Michelangelo's sculptures."

Isabella ignored the flippant parody. She thought he was being ridiculous as always. "I'll be fine provided I wrap up well," she assured him.

"Well remember to wear several layers, and don't forget your hat and mittens," he said as if she were a child. Fussing over Isabella's health and wellbeing was habitual to him. It was one of the ways he expressed his feelings for her. As her husband he felt duty bound to do his best to keep her out of harm's way. Especially since he considered her flimsy, dainty and delicate, rather like a snowflake. But more important, he couldn't bear the thought of anything bad befalling her.

Isabella rarely objected when Hereward fretted over her. Most of the time she took little notice, having come to accept his motives were mostly well-meaning and sincere. Despite his imposing and domineering manner, she sometimes even welcomed his kind-hearted considerations. Throughout her childhood her selfish and self-centred parents had shown little interest in her, relying on the nanny and governess to take care of her needs. Once the two women had departed, having been served their notice, she was left to fend for herself.

Before leaving the house, Isabella unclipped her topknot, otherwise her hat refused to stay put. In an instant her hair tumbled out of its curly compound, crowding her back and shoulders. After gathering it into a ponytail, she tied it tight with a blue ribbon before Hereward could complain about her loose locks. Then she put her outerwear over a woollen cardigan Barbara had shrunk in the wash, and covered her coat with a shawl to placate her husband.

As soon as Isabella opened the outer door, a large section of compacted snow collapsed inwards onto the boot-room floor.

It came accompanied by a bitter-cold draught of Arctic air almost cold enough to make breathing a chore. To avoid adding to the maids' burdensome workload, she grabbed the shovel, scooped up the mess and flung it out onto the terrace.

From the sitting-room window, Hereward watched his beautiful ice-maiden trudge through the snow like a little lost soul in the depths of a Siberian winter, venting clouds of translucent silvery vapour from her mouth into the crisp atmosphere. Snowflakes, similar in appearance to the wings of white satin moths, lay claim to her clothes as she ploughed through the snow towards the farm.

But after several minutes of breath-constricting, paralysing cold, of forcing her legs forward against their will to places they were disinclined to go, Isabella ultimately decided her endeavour required too much physical effort and abandoned her plan to see lake frozen over.

The second she reached the conservatory she saw it. Frozen solid and tied around a low branch of a young rowan tree — the snowman's missing houndstooth scarf.

Chapter 38

"Whoever would do such a thing, and why? It's beastly," complained Isabella. "I can't understand it. It makes no sense whatsoever."

Hereward bemoaned his wife's melodramatic response to all things seemingly inexplicable. "You're being overly suspicious, Miss Sherlock," he said dourly. "I must say you do have rather an overactive imagination. It's time you grew up, young lady. The wind probably blew the blasted thing there. That's the most plausible explanation. Wind and snow are not exclusive to one another, you know. You've been reading too many of those damned detective novels. Give that Agatha Christie woman a rest for heaven's sake. Try some romance for a change. You never know, you may even grow to like it."

"I doubt last night's wind was strong enough to tie a scarf around a branch in that sheltered spot. For one thing, I would have heard it blowing, quite simply because it always rattles my bedroom windows and gusts down the chimney," she explained, ignoring the double entendre. "It was tied I tell you and I doubt even the strongest wind has that degree of dexterity."

"Well, there aren't any footprints," he countered.

"That's because a fresh layer of snow fell overnight," she reminded him, frustration etched in her voice.

"Well, there's not a lot we can do about it," he said. "And

I'm not about to waste any more of my precious mental energy on your paranoid suspicions."

Smarting at the slur, Isabella stomped out of the room, went to her bedroom and lay on the bed fully clothed. Hereward had touched a nerve for sure. How dare he call her paranoid. Although she was forced to admit she had often wondered the same thing. Still, he was far too dismissive of much of what she said. Well, she would resort to doing what she always did when he refused to take her seriously — turn to Tilly. Tilly always listened, sympathised and commiserated. Furthermore, given the opportunity, the girl was a fountain of useful information, not to mention an invaluable source of sound advice.

Later on, Hereward was at his desk when Isabella entered the library to look for a new book. Eyeing her with keen interest, he noticed she was wearing stockings again. Black-woollen stockings, coarse-textured, pilled and darned in several places.

"You must be cold, my love," he said. "It's rare to see you in hosiery inside the house."

Isabella, seizing the opportunity, turned to him and said in appeal: "To be honest with you, I'd much prefer to wear my new trousers instead of stockings. They're warmer and far more practical. Perfect for these awful weather conditions. I think the temperature must have dropped even further today."

Hereward's expression changed and his tone sharpened. "I've already made clear my views on that subject," he said. "So please don't use the snow as an excuse to wear trousers. Trousers aren't meant to be worn by ladies. I'm sure woollen stockings under a skirt work just as well."

Isabella pulled her face. "I must say your attitude towards womenswear is awfully dated and square. And anyway, I dislike stockings. I find them dreadfully uncomfortable. Not nice at all. It's impossible to keep them up without the support of tight garters, which I've heard cause varicose veins. Then they have to be re-stretched and untwisted over and over again. It's such a bind. Not only that, but they also feel perfectly horrid against one's skin and the woollen ones are terribly itchy. And besides, I should be free to wear what I choose."

Hereward had stopped listening to his wife's grievances. His mind was focussed on stockings. Silk stockings to be specific. He recalled Rosalyn always wore stockings made from the finest silk whatever the weather, even in the sweltering heat of India. Most of the British women he met there wore them. The Lord only knows why. Whenever he and Rosalyn had convened in the bedroom, she always encouraged him to unclip hers, slide them down the full length of her legs and over her long feet. However, he hadn't much cared for them. For one thing, the suspender clasps were annoyingly fiddly; especially for a man with little enthusiasm for bedroom preliminaries with a woman he considered no more than a friend and casual lover. For despite her elitist attitude and air of respectability, he thought Rosalyn had something of the brothel about her. And he could hardly be blamed for her failure to realise she was nothing more to him than a vehicle for his sexual relief.

Hereward could hardly imagine Isabella fiddling with a suspender belt or corset clasps. They would definitely irk her too. At least they had that much in common. Then his thoughts turned to her legs: her slim ankles, her curved calves, her tender thighs. He relished every exquisite inch of her from the top of her head to the tips of her toes. And although he had never seen her tender thighs in the actual flesh, he had fondled them often enough to enable him to picture their appearance. He also adored her light golden skin, which radiated a delectable glow. Whenever her skirt rode up her legs, he was treated to a delicious glimpse of her esculent flesh; which was vastly superior to the sight of Rosalyn's pallid, pitted inner thighs overspilling her stocking tops.

Isabella clicked her fingers in the air. "You've gone into a trance," she said. "I can tell because you've got that funny faraway look in your eyes."

"I was just thinking," he replied wistfully, snapping out of his reverie.

"About what, might I ask?"

"Nothing that need concern you, my dear."

Based on his evasiveness, Isabella intuited her husband's thoughts must be too improper to share, and she gave him a fleeting look of distaste before grabbing a book and dashing from the room.

The novelty of the snow quickly wore thin and Isabella felt a strong desire to start roaming again. No matter what happened, the woods always drew her back in. Once the thaw began, the snow dissolved at a rapid rate. And on the day the road became accessible again she lay dozing in bed, curled up like a cosy cat, when a great thunderous roar rolled over the roof like a juggernaut, followed by a heavy metallic thud.

Anxious to discover the cause of the commotion, Isabella hurled herself out of bed, ran barefoot to the window and dragged aside the drapes. Directly below, Hereward's much-loved motorcar lay buried beneath a mass of snow that had avalanched off the roof in a single compact. Surveying the scene at length, Isabella wore the widest, wickedest, most-triumphal grin as she thought of Boyle, assisted by a foul-faced Barbara, clearing the snow from their master's pride and joy.

That afternoon, Isabella had some essential shopping to do in town and Hereward was insisting on driving her in.

"Please don't disrupt your work on my account," she said. "I'll go on the bicycle. After a week's worth of snowbound boredom, I'm quite looking forward to being mobile again."

"Shall I tell Boyle to drive you?" he suggested, even though he knew she was bound to refuse. Still, it was worth a try.

As expected, Isabella raised her hand and flicked up her wrist. "Gosh no! I do wish you would stop trying to impose a chauffeur on me. I will not under any circumstances be driven by Boyle. Although I suspect he would love to drive me from the Hall altogether. Can you imagine the awful atmosphere in the confined space of the motorcar? It would be pure torture. Plus, I prefer not to suffocate on the fumes of whatever it is he applies to that bizarre *coiffure* of his."

Suppressing a smile, Hereward remained silent.

"And since you know perfectly well my feelings about your butler," she went on, "why you continue trying to impress his services upon me frustrates the life out of me. And unless you're blind, or hard of hearing, or both, you must also have noticed he has been less than welcoming to me."

"Very well, my dear, point taken," said Hereward with a sigh of resignation. "The road has patches of snow on it in some places, so it might still be slippery. There's greater stability on four wheels than there is on two and I'm not prepared to take the risk of your getting injured, so I'll drive you."

For the sake of peace, Isabella ceased objecting and agreed.

Chapter 39

The wool shop on the high street had been in the same family for several generations. It seemed to stock every type and shade of wool in existence; all stored in cubed shelves behind the countertop and smelling of summer moorland. As Isabella studied the lattice of light, bright, dark, and dull skeins, she quickly concluded she was spoiled for choice. A novel experience for a girl accustomed to going without for so many years.

Isabella tried to recall the colours Hereward wore the most and those he most avoided. She could easily have sought Boyle's opinion. As her husband's valet, he was bound to know his preferences. However, since she distrusted the snivelling snake, she decided to dispense with the butler's assistance.

"I'm planning to knit a scarf for my husband," she informed the bored-looking counter assistant, "and I'm afraid I can't seem to make up my mind regarding the shade."

"What colour are his eyes?" asked the assistant, who was checking her chipped nail varnish while wishing it was payday.

"They're an unusual shade of grey. Rather a dark grey," said Isabella, calling to mind Hereward's piercing eyes fringed with long black lashes. Depending on his mood, eyes that could flash with passion or anger.

"Well, what about this one?" suggested the assistant, removing a skein from the shelf. "It's called granite grey. Very nice too. The wool's excellent quality, lovely and soft. Not scratchy like some of the cheaper stuff. Perfect colour for a gentleman. It won't need washing that often either, not like the paler shades." She passed Isabella the wool, hoping it would meet with her approval.

It did. "How much will that be?" asked Isabella, reaching for her purse.

"Will you be taking it all at once or would you like me to put some of it away?"

"I'll take it all now, thank you."

The girl looked impressed.

In view of her restricted budget, and the fact that she was saving up to buy him a Christmas gift, a scarf was the only thing Isabella could think of to give to Hereward for his birthday. Although he was generous, she preferred not to ask him for extra money in case he enquired why she needed it. And she didn't wish to tell a lie, even a white one. She had considered opening an account at the wool shop, assuming such an arrangement was possible, but then she thought better of it. Boyle might query the bill, like he had Martha's, and out of meanness decide to spill the beans. Still, at least I needn't worry about the fit," said Isabella within herself, "And should Hereward hate it, I can wear it myself instead, so it won't go wasted.

Every morning after the maids had finished making the bed and dusting the surfaces, Isabella remained in her room until noon, clicking away on her wooden knitting needles. She found it a pleasure to use new wool instead of the old rewound yarn she was used to. Her teenage friend Nora had taught her to knit. The girl could turn her hand to anything, showing Isabella how to unravel worn-out but salvageable knitwear and turn it into something passable. The downturn in the Acton's fortunes had meant finding new and novel ways to get by. Unlike her indolent parents, Isabella wasn't too proud to put her hands to good use. She could also sew and mend all manner of things, and even darned her own drawers. Thinking it just a phase, her mother had turned a blind eye to her daughter's lower-class friends, provided they came nowhere near the house.

On the day of Hereward's birthday Isabella rose early, dressed quickly and made her way down to the morning room. First, she poked her head around the half-open door to check if Boyle was hovering over her husband like a fruit fly attracted to a wine glass. Satisfied he was elsewhere, she quietly slipped into the room.

Hereward had just finished breakfast, but remained at the table reading the newspaper. Thoroughly absorbed in the editorial, he failed to notice her enter.

Isabella coughed politely to attract his attention.

Surprised, he looked up at her with enquiring eyes.

Hesitantly, she stepped forward, shyly wished him happy returns and placed her humble homemade offering on the table in front of him.

Patently puzzled, Hereward looked down at the parcel and then back up at her. Having already opened his presents from Maud, Cynthia, his brother, and a couple of old friends, he had handed them over to Boyle to be put away.

"What's this?" he said, nonplussed.

Isabella bit her bottom lip, stared at the parcel and stuttered a few words. "It's f-for you. For your b-birthday. I made it myself. I know it's not much. But all the same, I hope you like it," she said with a nervous smile as she picked her pearlescent pink fingernails.

Initially, Hereward neither spoke nor moved. For the very first time in his adult life, he seemed unsure of what to say or do. However, he soon gathered himself.

"I wasn't expecting anything, my dear. Just your good wishes."

"Aren't you going to open it then?" she said, sounding strained.

Hereward neatly folded the newspaper and put it aside. Then after turning over the package a couple of times, he untied the white string. He had no idea what to expect, since he knew Isabella's allowance was limited. After tearing off the silver gift wrap, he removed the scarf, held it up to the light, and looked at it closely. Then he laid it out on the table, ran his right hand over the cabled weave, and touched the hand-embroidered monogram, HA, with his index finger.

Still, he said nothing.

Isabella fixed her eyes on her husband's face, fully convinced the scarf was a huge mistake. "You don't like it," she said, crestfallen.

Hereward removed a clean handkerchief from his jacket pocket and lightly blew his nose. Then he said in a low voice: "On the contrary, my angel, I like it very much. In fact, it's the nicest, most-thoughtful gift I've ever received. You've clearly gone to a great deal of trouble. As a matter of fact, this is the first time in my entire life that someone has made something specially for me. Don't misunderstand me, I have received many fine gifts over the years, but their selection and purchase has required little thought and even less effort. Thank you, my darling, I shall treasure it." Then he took her hands in his, held them to his lips and kissed them.

Isabella almost jumped up and down with relief.

Later at luncheon, Boyle laid eyes on the birthday knit for the first time. It surprised him to see the master wearing a scarf indoors, especially one that was clearly handmade. Since the object was unfamiliar to him, he couldn't help but ponder its origins.

Hereward, having noticed the butler staring at the scarf

with perplexity, proudly proclaimed that the mistress had made it herself for his birthday.

To avoid giving offence, Boyle maintained a neutral face and mumbled a polite but noncommittal comment. To preserve his power at the Hall, he recognised the importance of keeping his master on side. It seemed to him the mistress had done something right for a change, making her an even greater threat than before; since his power depended to a large degree on the couple's disunity.

Delighted not only with the gift, but also because Isabella had made it specially for him, Hereward wore the scarf all day long, draped around his neck like a cobra. He wore it at his desk, he wore it at the luncheon table, he wore it at afternoon tea. In fact, wherever he happened to be that day, he wore the scarf. And because Isabella said the colour suited him and the style made him look boyish, it pleased him even more.

Back below stairs, Boyle curled his lip with contempt every time he thought of the scarf. He detested the homespun thing. He detested everything about it: the colour, the texture, the design. But above all else, he hated the scarf's creator and, given half a chance, he would have gladly strangled the coy little succubus with it. In fact, as soon as an opportunity presented itself, he planned to nick a couple of the scarf's stitches with the nail scissors to cause it to unravel, believing her substandard handiwork would be blamed. And since the master's attire was always impeccable, he would be certain to discard it.

Slyly, Boyle pictured himself flinging the scarf on the fire and, with malign pleasure, watching it sizzle and curl up in the flames. Until, that is, he remembered wool burns with difficulty and gives off a dreadful odour. What must the master be thinking donning a crude handmade muffler in place of his fine-quality scarves from Saville Row, or those sumptuous paisley silks from India, or the super-soft cashmere Miss Dumbarton gave him for his thirtieth birthday? he asked himself. There was no doubt about it, his standards were slipping. And all because that fatuous female he had married on a whim had made him a gift with her own crafty hands. The Major, it seemed, had become a silly romantic fool whose gonads now governed his brain.

Plus, to add insult to injury, Boyle observed the mistress, who was clearly delighted with her successful gift, girlishly smile at her husband when she saw him wearing the scarf. To see the couple on friendly terms instead of at loggerheads made the butler's blood boil. Had there been a cat within reach, he would have kicked it to kingdom come. The situation was exacting a terrible toll on his health, to the extent that he feared he might suffer a heart attack. And should that happen, then that teenage termagant, as he referred to her in his head, would be wholly to blame.

Isabella, pleased with herself for once, returned upstairs to visit the bathroom. As she opened the drawer containing the toiletries, her attention was drawn to a small shiny object. Intrigued, she picked it up and examined it closely. It was a lipstick. A lipstick within a fancy gilt case with the name of the shade printed on the top section. It wasn't hers. She had never worn lipstick, nor had she ever desired to. And even if she had, her father would never have allowed it, and his word was law. In Archibald Acton's view only whores and tarts embellished their lips. Isabella wondered what Hereward would say if she sat down to dinner with painted lips. She could guarantee, he being a conservative and old-fashioned sort of fellow, he would insist upon its immediate removal.

After separating the two parts of the outer case, Isabella twisted the lower one to raise the inner stick. With her fingertip she touched the oleaginous stump, then held it to her nose and sniffed it. The fragrance was reminiscent of the sugar-dusted jellies called Turkish Delight which were sold in balsa-wood boxes at Christmastime. What remained of the lipstick looked similar in shade to that worn by Rosalyn on the day they bumped into each other outside Martha's.

There was no question in Isabella's mind as to whom the lipstick belonged. What she struggled to understand, however, was what it was doing in the bathroom drawer and why she had never noticed it before. Concentrating all her mind power on the conundrum, she told herself it must have been at the back of the drawer all along and had simply rolled forward on this occasion. Whatever the reason, she decided to hang onto it.

Besides the cosmetic, Isabella had lately discovered other odd items amongst her things, one of which was a red-silk handkerchief in one of the dressing-table drawers. It was of too fine a quality to belong to any of the servants. She had questioned Tilly about it. But the maid couldn't recall putting it in the drawer herself and was at a loss to say how it came to be there. Then she suggested it must have been forgotten by a guest and got mixed up with the household wash. An easy mistake to make, she seemed to think. Obviously, someone assumed the handkerchief, being silk, must be Isabella's.

With a look of suspicion, Isabella had placed the handkerchief under her nose and inhaled gently. The fabric had a faint floral bouquet. Although of what, she couldn't quite say as most of the scent had been washed away during the laundering process. Without knowing why, Isabella decided to keep it. Then she told Tilly to make sure only her own handkerchiefs were put away in future and promised to embroider them with her initials to avoid any confusion. And she had given the matter no further thought, until now.

Chapter 40

That evening, to help celebrate his birthday, Hereward had invited Maud and Cynthia over to dinner. Isabella always looked forward to their cheerful chatter. The two women were lively and amusing, especially when they were together. And feeling lonely most of the time, she welcomed their company.

However, as she soaked in the bathtub, Isabella's thoughts turned to the random handkerchief and the other items she had found amongst her things. She couldn't help but suspect someone at the Hall was doing their best to torment her. And should that be true, she need look no further than Boyle and Barbara, since as individuals or together, they were the most-likely candidates.

But then the question also arose in Isabella's mind as to the possibility of Hereward having a mistress. Did Rosalyn sneak in every time she went out? As she was usually gone for hours, he had ample opportunity for a romantic assignation. However, since her husband visited her bed so often, Isabella doubted he had the energy to make love to another woman. And he nearly never looked tired, she told herself. But then he was comparatively young and fit, and at the height of his physical capacity. Moreover, she knew it was not uncommon for a gentleman to keep a mistress. Some philanderers kept more than one, or so it was claimed. Isabella recalled her mother's advice not to deny her husband his marital rights in order to reduce the risk of his straying. Likening men to tomcats, Agatha Acton had also asserted that when underfed they invariably visited other houses in search of sustenance.

As she rubbed the slippery scented soap between her palms, Isabella reasoned to herself that if Rosalyn were visiting the Hall in her absence, then Tilly would surely have mentioned it, even inadvertently. But then again, she postulated, the maid might fear getting into trouble or being dismissed. And anyway, wouldn't it be safer for Hereward to go to Rosalyn's place?

A sudden knock on the bathroom door made Isabella jump. The soap flew out of her hands, plopped into the water and sank to the bottom of the bathtub.

"It's me, Ma'am," squeaked a voice through the door, "you said to remind you of the time."

"Thank you, Tilly. I'll be there shortly," she said, fumbling for the soap before it began to dissolve.

After scolding herself for her jumpiness, Isabella went on with her internal dialogue. In addition to being more emotional than men, weren't women reputed to be more nervously excitable, making them more susceptible to mental illness? she asked herself with a sustained sigh. Or was that a common misconception? She considered discussing the matter with Maud, who was sound of mind, resilient and eminently sensible. However, she worried her level-headed sister-in-law might think her at best hysterical and at worst deranged. Which Isabella herself believed possible and the last thing she needed was for Maud to agree with her.

Feeling troubled still, she climbed out of the bathtub, dried herself with a thick fluffy towel and returned to the bedroom, where Tilly was waiting to help her dress and do her hair.

"Is everything alright, Ma'am? You're looking a bit peaky," said the mousy-haired maid, who had the disposition of a sweet, docile dog.

Lovely Tilly, thought Isabella. The motherly girl had such a caring nature, she sometimes wondered how she would cope without her.

"I'm a little tired, that's all. I haven't been sleeping too well of late. Actually, I think I might have a lie down. Come back after half an hour, by which time I should feel fully revived."

"Very well, Ma'am. Shall I bring you a nice cup of tea when I return?"

"No, thank you. But before you go, there is something I'd like to ask you."

"Yes, Ma'am?"

"Does the master ever receive visitors during the afternoons?"

"Not that I'm aware of. Although at that time of day I'm always busy downstairs. But I expect Mr Boyle will know for certain. Would you like me to ask him?"

"Absolutely not," exclaimed Isabella. "So please don't say a word."

"Very well, Ma'am."

Left alone to reflect, Isabella decided it would be selfish to ask Maud's advice when it was Hereward's birthday and they were meant to be celebrating and having fun. Plus, knowing Maud, she would more than likely advise her to discard the stuff and forget all about it. Chuck it in the dustbin, my dear, she would say in her usual pragmatic way. Yet Isabella felt a strong inclination to hold onto her uncanny collection. It intrigued her. And who knew its full significance?

Later, when they were all gathered around the dining table, Isabella felt the first throb of a headache. She rubbed her temples, squeezed her eyelids together and screwed up her face. Suddenly, normal noises boomed inside her head, soft voices sounded harsh and shrill, while bursts of laughter became unbearable. She wished she could leave the table and lie down in a dark, quiet room. Which was what her mother always did when she suffered a bad migraine. It was impossible to focus on, let alone contribute to the conversation when her head hurt and negative thoughts continued to torment her.

Fortunately, none of her companions seemed to notice her quiet demeanour or pained expression. Hereward and his sibling were too engrossed in a lively and good-humoured discussion, with Cynthia chipping in with a few salient remarks. At one point, before her headache took complete hold, Isabella had contributed a comment of her own, but since no-one seemed interested in her humble opinion, she retreated into herself. And after dinner when they all moved to the sitting room, Isabella slipped away to the conservatory for a few minutes, hoping a change of air and a spell of silence would cure her pain.

Later, when the ladies had left, Hereward asked Isabella if anything was wrong when he came to her room.

"Just a pounding headache," she said.

"Have you taken a painkiller?" he asked.

"Yes, of course I've taken a painkiller," she said irritably, "but it has still to take effect."

"A good night's sleep and you'll be as right as rain come morning," he said as he stroked her forehead. Then he cupped her face in his hands, planted a light kiss on her nose and bade her goodnight. Returning to his room, Hereward felt terribly disappointed, having been hoping to end his birthday on a high note.

Chapter 41

With sharp-eyed attention, Rosalyn checked her hair in the hand-mirror with the decorative forget-me-nots on the back panel. To her despair, several silver hairs glistened in the glass.

"Where the hell have those ghastly horrors come from?" she cried out loud in alarm.

To Rosalyn, grey hair was a disaster on a par with famine and floods. A ripple of panic rising in her chest, she picked up an ivory toothcomb and ran it through her hair, separating and lifting it in sections to see if more silver sinners lurked below the surface. Fuming at life's unfairness, she cursed Hereward's perfidious feet, convinced he was responsible for her hair's premature pigmental loss. Although the phenomenon of hair turning white overnight as an extreme stress reaction was well documented, she somehow never expected to suffer such a calamity herself.

Hitherto proud of her bob's black glossy sheen, Rosalyn was willing to do whatever was necessary to maintain it. Picking up her black-leather diary, she licked her forefinger and leafed through the volume's pages. Except for a few lunch and tennis dates with other unmarried ladies, the pages were glaringly blank. On the plus side, her paucity of social engagements gave her plenty of time to have her hair restored to its former glory. However, having seen one too many disasters in the home-dyeing department, she thought it unwise to do it herself. So, she rang for her maid, told her to contact the salon straight away and insist on a same-day appointment.

Meanwhile, Rosalyn flipped open her silver cigarette case and removed a Sobranie in a colour that matched her mood. She picked up her cigarette lighter, also silver, pressed its lever with her thumb, ignited a tiny flame, and lit up. A gift from Hereward on her last birthday, the lighter had sentimental value. Rather an odd choice, she had thought at the time, since he abhorred her smoking habit.

Pursing her lips to direct a plume of smoke towards the upper region of the room, Rosalyn recalled her terrible disappointment upon unpacking the lighter. Especially as Hereward hadn't taken the trouble to have it engraved with an affectionate message, or even her name. She had been hoping for something extra special. Something extravagant with great significance. Something personal, such as a piece of expensive jewellery; preferably diamonds or pearls. Truth be told, what she had really wanted was an engagement ring. She still did. But Hereward had never got round to popping the question and now he never would.

With an unsteady hand, Rosalyn removed the stopper from a decanter on top of the chinoiserie cabinet and poured herself a brandy. She looked into the glass as though peering down some bottomless pit, then downed its contents in one. Some of the liquid had spilled onto the cabinet top, so she summoned the maid to mop it up. Since the day Hereward had ditched her like a worn-out overcoat for a chit almost half his age, and hers, she had been self-medicating with alcohol and tobacco. It was the only way she could cope with the long lonely days and the aching emptiness inside herself. No matter how hard she tried, she couldn't understand what Hereward saw in his childish wife. From what she could ascertain, apart from some superficial beauty, the girl had little to recommend her. Rosalyn did at least derive some comfort from Barbara's divulgences that day on the high street. News of the Aldwen's adversarial marriage was music to her ears. However, events were moving too slowly for a woman accustomed to having her demands met as soon as she clicked her entitled fingers.

The thought of life without Hereward at the heart of it made Rosalyn feel desperately mournful. She pined for him with an incapacitating, painful intensity. To think, some well-born but impoverished immature minx had somehow managed to appropriate her lover without even fluttering her eyelashes at him. In a sudden fit of irascible rage, Rosalyn flung her diary across the room, knocked back another drink and prayed Parker would soon be the bearer of good tidings.

Chapter 42

In late November Hereward went alone to London to meet his publisher. He didn't disclose, at least not to Isabella, the duration of his stay, and she made it a point not to ask him. Having risen extra early a few days previous, he had driven away while she slept, so there was no awkward parting between them. From that time that onwards he had not been in contact. However, since she overheard Boyle talking on the library telephone in a muted tone late every evening, she suspected Hereward of checking up on her. The butler was no doubt supplying his master with a detailed account of her movements throughout the day, and a record of her terrible timekeeping. Even if her husband were to ring her directly, she had no idea what she would say to him. It would probably be something banal, such as a question about the London weather. Boyle, however, never mentioned the calls and she never enquired about them. She refused to give him the satisfaction.

Isabella used Hereward's absence as an opportunity to browse the library bookshelves undisturbed. She loved the library; that and the conservatory were her favourite rooms. But unlike the library, which also functioned as her husband's study, she considered the conservatory her own special space. A few weeks since, he had allowed her to choose a new brass lantern for the conservatory ceiling. During the fixture's installation, she had caught Boyle slyly sneering at it from the doorway, although the sneak had made sure not to let his master see him.

She was always reluctant to peruse the shelves in Hereward's presence, mindful not to disturb him in case he was concentrating on his work. There was no fire lit that day, which Isabella assumed was down to his absence. Cold rooms, however, didn't concern her unduly, since she was well accustomed to perennially empty grates at her parents' place. It simply meant having to wrap up more warmly, and there was a selection of old scarves and shawls in the boot room for that purpose.

Bored with browsing, Isabella surveyed the room. Her inquisitive eyes soon settled on Hereward's desk; a fine example of early Victorian master-craftsmanship. After running her hand over the desk's smooth, dust-free, unscratched surface, she sat in her husband's brown-leather swivel seat and swung from side to side. Feeling suddenly like *Goldilocks* in *Father Bear's* chair, she lifted her feet and spun around several times, allowing herself the levity on the basis that fun was strictly limited at the Hall.

Having quickly grown tired of the activity, Isabella leaned back in the chair while she contemplated her next move. Out in the morbid quietness of the hall a door softly opened and closed, then footsteps clopped across the hard floor. She listened closely. Based on their emphatic resonance, she soon deduced the footsteps belonged to Boyle. Then as soon as silence resumed, she refocused her attention on the desk.

There was nothing trivial or casual about Hereward's desk. It was a place of serious, sober and scholastic industry. The typewriter took centre stage, surrounded by papers, notebooks and manuscripts; besides which was a plethora of objects pertinent to the fields of publishing and authorship, all organised in a neat, orderly manner. Typical Hereward, she mused. Then out of simple curiosity, she pulled the chair up close and checked the desk's drawers. All except one were locked.

On impulse, Isabella leaned over, drew open the unlocked drawer and peered inside. It was deep and quite full. On top of the drawer's contents sat a pad of writing paper similar to that on which Hereward had written his proposal to her father and not her, beneath which lay a pale-blue envelope. The envelope, addressed to Major Hereward H G Aldwen, emitted a faint aroma of lavender. The neatness of the slit along its upper edge indicated it had been opened with a paper knife, presumably the silver one always placed perpendicular to the letter rack on the desk. Sitting for one whole minute in turmoil, Isabella gripped the envelope in her hand while she grappled with her conscience.

"Oh, dash it!" she exclaimed out loud. Then with the utmost care, she eased the letter out of its enclosure, unfolded it and began to read:

My dearest Hereward,

I feel it is my absolute duty to tell you that you are making a very serious mistake by marrying with such haste. You have virtually nothing in common with Miss Acton, who I might add is very young, lacking in maturity and has little experience of the world. I feel that your fixation with her is simply a phase and will surely pass, as all infatuations ultimately do. If you cannot live without her, then keep her as your mistress for now, but do not become yoked to her, for once you do it will be difficult to extricate yourself from the contract. As I'm sure you know, divorce is a messy business and the process can take years, especially if one party is not agreeable.

It is also incumbent on me to inform you that you are undoubtedly being duped. Miss Acton's parents are living in severely reduced circumstances due to the father's feckless financial dealings, so it is entirely in their interests for their daughter to make a good marriage in monetary terms. She is simply marrying you for your assets, nothing more, and does not love you as I do.

You may also be interested to learn that her father is no longer welcome in polite society because of his drinking and fondness for chorus girls. His long-suffering wife, an upright and respectable lady, has tolerated his reprehensible and boorish behaviour for years. You will do well to avoid having any further association with a man of such ill-repute.

Finally, it is no secret in the town that Miss Acton herself does not keep decent company and frequently associates with those from the lower classes.

It is still not too late to call off the wedding. I'm sure the Actons will be more than happy to accept some sort of financial compensation should you endeavour to do so. In the meantime, I shall wait for you.

Your ever-loving Rosalyn xxx

Isabella reread the letter several times before tucking it back inside the envelope with the same care with which she had removed it. Then she checked the postmark, which indicated it must have arrived shortly before the wedding. And judging by Rosalyn Dumbarton's remarks, the woman had clearly done some research. Returning the envelope to the desk drawer, she made sure to put it back in the exact same place she had found it, knowing Hereward would remember down to the very last detail the arrangement of the drawer's contents.

After leaving the library, Isabella went straight to her bedroom and lay on the chaise to review her impressions. She thought it most remiss of Hereward to leave the drawer unlocked, not to mention uncharacteristic, and she assumed he must have been distracted or rushed. She also wondered why he had kept the letter and who else might have read it. Boyle undoubtedly had a good rummage around the place whenever his master was out of town. Therefore, it seemed probable he was familiar with Miss Dumbarton's defamations.

Isabella, however, cared little for the butler's opinions of either herself or her parents. Right then she was too busy trying to comprehend her own visceral response to Rosalyn's declaration of undying love, as revealed in her letter. For some inexplicable reason, Isabella felt resentful. Resentful of Rosalyn. Rosalyn Dumbarton of all people.

That evening, rather than sit alone at the dining table, Isabella decided to have dinner served to her on a tray in the library. As expected, Boyle avoided her like a leper and instructed Tilly to serve her. The simple meal consisted of stewed mutton, boiled potatoes and canned carrots, followed by treacle sponge and custard. The pudding was one of Isabella's favourites and Mrs Jenkins had sent up a generous helping. Afterwards she retired to the sitting room, where she supped a mug of warm malted milk. However, instead of staying to listen to the wireless, she went straight up to bed with a book.

Habituated to Hereward's presence, Isabella found his absence oddly disconcerting. She felt lonely and abandoned, hurt and disappointed he hadn't invited her to accompany him on his trip. She would have loved to visit the Capital, see the sights, go window shopping, and wander around the large department stores. Imagine the excitement, she thought. It must be a million times better than Oakwich town centre. She kept expecting her bedroom door to open and Hereward to sweep into the room wearing his long dark robe and a look of dissolute anticipation on his face.

After an hour spent reading another gripping murder mystery, Isabella yawned, switched off the night lamp and snuggled beneath the bedclothes. The fire was beginning to fade, but the room still felt warm and cosy, and she soon slipped into a deep and satisfying slumber.

A minute gone midnight Isabella's eyes snapped open. Sitting bolt upright, she brushed the hair off her face and stared into the opaque blackness. It was like looking at black cream. The fire had breathed its last and the room felt charnel cold. For several seconds of unsettling silence, she listened as her sight adjusted to the nebulous night. It seemed to her that something out of the ordinary had disturbed her unconscious mind as she slept.

Isabella was about to sink back into the pillows when to her dismay the floorboards creaked outside her room, followed by more creaking on the staircase. Thinking an intruder had broken into the house, she found herself shaking. Had Boyle blundered and forgotten to lock all the doors? she wondered. Was she about to be bludgeoned to death in her bed? Should she scream to alert the servants? At that time of night, they were all deep asleep and unlikely to hear her. And even if they were to, Boyle would be sure to barricade himself in his own bedroom, leaving her to face the situation alone.

Aware of the possible danger and the lack of a suitable escape route, but unable to stay still any longer, Isabella switched on the lamp. Then summoning every last ounce of her courage, she leapt out of bed and rushed barefoot across the carpet. However, upon reaching the bedroom door, she came to a swift halt and listened again with close concentration. Fearful of what she might find lurking on the landing, she slowly opened the door a fraction and peered out into the cavernous void. Except for the slim beam of dim light let out from her room, everywhere was shrouded in darkness. Other than the sound of the hall clock, all was silent and still.

Thinking Hereward might have returned late from

London, Isabella called out his name. Her quivery voice vibrated throughout the viper-black vastness of the hall, stairs and landings as she waited with bated breath for his reply. But the only response was a hair-raising hush.

"Who's there?" she whispered in a weak voice. Seconds passed. The clock ticked. More seconds passed. The clock went on ticking. Still no reply. Nothing except a penetrating silence, like that inside a morgue at midnight. Then somewhere deep inside the bowels of the house a door softly opened and closed. A sinking sensation in the pit of her stomach, Isabella pressed her hand to her clavicle as her blood turned to ice.

To calm herself, Isabella tried to convince herself she must have been dreaming; caught in some semiconscious, stupefied state in which the real and unreal conflate, such as during the brief prolongation of a nightmare upon awakening. Still doubtful, however, she turned back to the bedroom, padded over to the window and parted the curtains. There was no sign of Hereward's motorcar anywhere within range of the Hall. In an attempt to see beyond the grounds, Isabella strained her eyes, but the moon was a waning one which yielded little light.

Outside, it was also quiet, deathly so, until a screech scored the silence. Right then, Isabella noticed how lonely and isolated the Hall was in its secluded sylvan setting. Unlike the town, there were no rooftops or chimneys in view, not even distance ones. The farm was their nearest neighbour, but out of sight it seemed not to exist. And since the servants' bedrooms were all in the basement, she was effectively alone in a large rambling house surrounded by acres of uninhabited woodland.

Still not convinced she had been dreaming, Isabella fought her fear and braved a return to the landing for one last look; this time with all the lights on.

Chapter 43

Even with the electric lights illuminating the stairways and landings there was nothing apparent. No sign of a presence, either solid or supernatural. Regardless, there existed a feeling of unease in the general atmosphere. There was also the faintest odour of something sour that Isabella's nose hadn't registered earlier. She had never felt so nervous. So nervous, she wanted to flick every switch and light up the entire house; not to mention every shadowy niche, recess, alcove, and corner, leaving no place to hide, should someone be so inclined.

Isabella noticed she was trembling and her teeth were chattering. Gosh, what's happening to me? she asked herself. Had marriage made her feeble? Afraid of her own shadow? Was fear no longer a foreigner? There and then, she knew she must find a way to overcome her anxieties before they made life intolerable.

Since her tongue felt thick and her mouth drier than a rusk biscuit, Isabella went to the bathroom to fetch herself a glass of water. Upon opening the tap, she caught sight of her face in the mirror. It looked pale and drawn, the eyes circled with dark rings, the mouth tight with uncertainty. It was so unlike her regular face. In fact, it looked like the face of another person. You're overwrought, she thought. Better get back to bed and try to get some sleep.

However, on leaving the room, Isabella's attention was

drawn to the linen basket in the corner, where a small piece of flesh-coloured fabric peeped out from under a white chemise. She strode over to the receptacle, fished out the fabric and was astonished to find a pair of stockings knotted together. After first separating them, she inspected them at close range. They were made of silk; silk as sheer and satiny as a lace-spider's web. They smelled clean too. And apart from clip marks on the double bands at their tops, they were in perfect condition: devoid of snags, ladders and holes. The stockings were definitely not hers. She had never worn silk stockings, not even on her wedding day. They were excluded from her trousseau on account of the expense. The only stockings she possessed she had knitted herself and she seldom wore them.

Disconcerted by her strange discovery, Isabella returned to the bedroom in a state of apprehensive restlessness, too nervous to switch off the lights. She expected Boyle would notice their glow first thing in the morning and report the matter to Hereward upon his return. But so, what if he did? she asked herself. And why should she care? He was nothing to her, neither her superior nor her master.

To ensure her safety, Isabella wedged a chair at an angle between the door handle and the floor. After which she paced the carpet back and forth until she was overcome by exhaustion. Then she collapsed into bed like a falling tree and pulled the bedclothes over her head. Desperate for sleep, but still fearful, she sought to soothe herself by visualising a calm blue sea beneath bright yellow sunshine. But despite trying her best to conquer her negative thoughts, scary images kept flying towards her like bats at twilight. Tenser than a stretched rubber band on a catapult, she tossed and turned repeatedly while wishing it was morning.

Although it was impossible to say with complete certainty that the creaking sounds and stockings were in any way related,

Isabella started to make connections in her mind. Ultimately, she contended that a chain of discrete incidents demanded some sort of explanation when viewed collectively. But then again, she deliberated, it was also possible she was simply imagining things. And if so, might that be symptomatic of some kind of mental disorder requiring medical intervention? However, when she thought of the stockings and the odd assortment of stuff squirrelled away in her closet, she decided she had every reason to be suspicious.

As she lay pondering her predicament, Isabella continued listening to the night. From time to time the old lead pipes beneath the floors banged, gurgled and whistled, further unnerving her. Then when a sudden gust of cold wind rattled the windows and rushed down the chimney, she ached for Hereward's strong masculine presence. How she longed to run to his room for reassurance, even if it meant being called a silly girl.

But in reality, Isabella knew it would be difficult to discuss the odd occurrences with her husband upon his return. For Hereward was a man who resided exclusively in the realm of the rational. And she didn't wish him to think her a lunatic. He would more than likely insist there was some simple explanation for whatever had disturbed her sleep, and advise her to stop being so absurd and irrational. And he would be right of course, she told herself. Nevertheless, she slept not a wink for the remainder of the night.

Chapter 44

Late morning, Isabella recognised the sound of Hereward's motorcar on the road. Despite her tiredness from lack of sleep, she rushed to the front door to receive him before Boyle could reach him first. She had to admit she derived a perverse satisfaction from thwarting the butler's attempt to assist her husband.

Riveted by the sight of Isabella's loveliness framed in the doorway, Hereward feasted his eyes on her face and form as he climbed the well-scrubbed steps to greet her. However, stooping to kiss her cheek, he thought she looked a touch peaky. Gosh, how he had missed her. More than he ever thought possible. And despite their habitual verbal battles, not for one single moment did he regret his decision to marry her.

Isabella thought Hereward looked shattered. But then he had driven all the way back from London, she reminded herself. She helped him out of his overcoat before Boyle could get his obsequious hands on it and, with a look of childish triumph, hung it on the coatrack beside the door.

To make a none-too-subtle point, the butler, determined not to be outdone by her devilry, removed his beloved master's coat from the hook, then with a muted tsk gave the garment the once-over with the clothes brush.

Wisely, Isabella showed no reaction to his combative impertinence. For one thing, she refused to give him the satisfaction of knowing he riled her. Hereward, however, seemed oblivious to Boyle's hovering presence. Delighted with her untypical facilitation, he took no account of the butler's bold-faced behaviour as they transferred to the sitting room, sat next to the fire and chatted congenially.

That evening, Isabella, still perturbed by the previous night's disturbance, burst into her husband's bedroom as he was dressing for dinner, then came to an abrupt halt.

Hereward was in the process of tying a silk paisley cravat, his preferred neckwear of an evening. Since Isabella nearly never entered his bedroom, he stopped what he was doing and stared at her in mute surprise.

Boyle, who was assisting his master, removed himself to the dressing room. He then loitered behind the door in an attempt to eavesdrop on the couple's conversation. Since he loved to hear the Major berating the mistress with his barbed tongue, the butler hoped they would shortly become embroiled in an argument. Undeniably music to his ears.

Isabella spoke in a compelling staccato. "I can hear a woman screaming. It sounds as though it's coming from somewhere over near the orchard. I can tell you now, it's the most-dreadful, high-pitched scream. Absolutely chilling. She's clearly being murdered by some madman. We must do something. Run to her rescue. Right away, before it's too late."

Confident of her husband's gallantry, Isabella paused for a vital breath and beheld him with excitement as she waited for him to leap into action.

Instead, Hereward planted his hands on his hips and looked at his ingenuous wife with a mixture of irritation and wry amusement.

"Fiddlesticks! It's foxes you can hear, my dear, foxes," he said with added emphasis on the last word. "Most likely a dog fox and a vixen. What you perceive to be a scream is in actual fact a mating cry. When foxes mate they produce ear-piercing love cries," he explained in a slow, patient voice, light in tone but heavy in innuendo. After which he raised his brow to its full height, beneath which his eyes twinkled with mischief.

Isabella stared at her husband with red-faced distaste and advised him to be less indelicate.

"You might also be interested to learn, my dear," he continued unabashed, "that foxes are territorial. Which means they object to having other males on their patch. As far as I'm aware, that's true of most male animals. They protect their females from rogue rivals as a matter of instinct, so we mustn't judge them too harshly."

"Why haven't I heard the screams before?" Isabella asked, seemingly unconvinced.

"Lots of reasons, I suppose," he said, fiddling with his cuffs. "For starters, it depends on the time of year and in which direction the wind's blowing."

Hereward then walked up to Isabella, put his arm around her shoulder and escorted her to the bedroom door. "Now be a good girl and go and finish dressing or you'll be late for dinner," he said, giving her an affectionate pat on the bottom before dismissing her from his room.

Following a cordial dinner, during which they discussed his London trip and his single social engagement with a few old friends, Hereward asked Isabella to excuse him and disappeared into the library. A short time later he re-joined her in the sitting room. Although she appeared pleasant enough on the surface, he intuited an undertone of grievance beneath her sweet affability.

"I'm sorry I didn't invite you to accompany me to London," he said. "But there would have been too little time for sightseeing and entertainment. Having a number of important matters to attend to, I would have been obliged to leave you alone in an unfamiliar city."

"I wouldn't have minded, honestly. I'm perfectly capable of taking care of myself," Isabella assured him.

"I dare say you are, my dear, but sightseeing is something we should do together, don't you agree?"

"I suppose so," she said grudgingly.

"Anyway, I did manage to squeeze some essential shopping into my itinerary," he said, reaching deep into his pocket and extracting a small package. "This is for you." And he offered her the gift he had purchased for her in London.

Isabella was taken aback by his gesture. It was so unexpected. She stared at the small item, smiled and steepled her fingers in front of her lips. A glow of excitement spread over her entire face, removing any residual resentment. Nothing could ever compete with a present, more especially a surprise one.

Hereward smiled at her indulgently.

Without speaking, Isabella took hold of the package. After which she untied the ribbon, removed the wrapping paper and cast them both aside. Then wide-eyed as an excited child, she picked up the small velvet box and stared at it as if mesmerised.

"Well, aren't you going to look inside?" asked Hereward.

"Yes, yes, of course."

"Well for heaven's sake girl get on with it or we'll be here all night."

Thinking it would contain a mere trifle or a small bauble, Isabella flipped open the box, then gasped audibly. The last thing she expected to see was a solid-gold wristwatch, especially since it wasn't her birthday or a special occasion.

"I had meant to give you a special gift on the day of our wedding," said Hereward, "but there was too little time beforehand to search for something worthy of you."

"Gosh! It's beautiful. It must have cost a fortune," she exclaimed as she removed the watch from its holding, unhooked the clasp and attempted to fasten it on her wrist.

"Here, let me help you," said Hereward as an excuse to touch her.

With a beaming smile lighting her face, Isabella held up her arm so she could admire the watch face. Unsurprisingly, he had chosen well. The diamond-ringed casing and bracelet were the perfect size for her slim wrist.

"Make sure you wear it," he said in a blunt, dictatorial manner. "No more guessing the time while you're out roaming the Aldwen wilds. And in future you'll have no excuse for being late," he said, wagging an admonitory finger in her direction.

Isabella couldn't help but wonder if Hereward had purchased the watch more for his benefit than for hers.

"I couldn't possibly wear this out there," she said, turning her head towards the drapes now drawn across the window. "It's far too valuable. I should be too afraid to lose it."

"You're unlikely to lose it provided you fasten the clasp securely," he advised.

"Thank you so much for the wonderful gift. It's perfectly splendid," she said before planting a chaste tepid kiss on his warm cheek and making a rapid return to her seat.

Even the softest, airiest, coolest touch of her luscious lips aroused him. At that precise moment he wanted to gather her up in his arms, carry her upstairs to bed and feast on her sumptuous flesh. Seeing her sup her cup of hot beverage in the chair opposite his, her fine features lit up by the pyretic flames, he was enthralled by her quiet ethereality. Despite their frequent disagreements, he felt his life would be a well of nothingness without her in it. Rosalyn had satisfied his physical needs in a pedestrian way, rather like a glass of cold water quenching the thirst on a scorching-hot day, but nothing beyond that. In comparison, making love to Isabella was unsurpassable. It was like climbing aboard the most-luxurious boat in the bay, sailing her out to sea, sailing her softly, sailing her wildly, then bringing her back to her mooring from the pinnacle of an almighty wave.

Chapter 45

Over at the nearby farm Parker bedded himself down on a haystack. The barn stank of straw mould, dried dung and mouse droppings. Those of a more-delicate constitution might have considered such odours repellent; but not he. If anything, the yucky country yokel found them acidulously pleasant. Nor did the scratching and scraping sounds of rodents scurrying around the place with impunity bother him much. However, he missed seeing the bats, now in hibernation, popping out from their roosts, whizzing through the air and catching insects on the wing.

While fornicating foxes barked, howled and screamed in the background, Parker pressed his lips together and sighed down his nose as his mind drifted to the Major's wife. Ah, the Major's wife: that endearing, delectable young doe. He felt smitten as never before. Yet as much as he admired her fetching form, he knew for certain she would consider him a coarse country bumpkin; someone from whom she would run a mile if she ever clapped eyes on him in the woods and meadows. He still found it hard to forget the look of distaste on her discomposed face the day she caught him peering in through the Hall's library window.

As he listened to the late-evening noises, the sounds of life and death, Parker coughed and lobbed a mass of mucus through the air. Then he wiped his mouth with the back of his hand before his mind turned to more fundamental matters. Matters pertaining to the animal kingdom's freedom from moral imperatives. Licking his sloughy lips, he thought about how dominant males were at liberty to help themselves to whichever females took their fancy. If mankind followed the same system, speculated Parker with a goatish grin, then the lovely lady would be his for the taking.

Parker also pondered why Jack hadn't made an appearance as yet. The young cock's ongoing absence made no sense. Surely, he should have shown up by now. If he were Jack, he said to himself, nothing except his own death would keep him from a dalliance with the barely ripe young lady. He also thought Miss Dumbarton must now be desperate for evidence of wrongdoing. It was obvious the scheming woman was burning to tell Major Aldwen what his pretty little petticoat got up to with the unskilled but good-looking scallion. And he wouldn't be in the blond lad's shoddy shoes for all the tea in China when the military man caught up with him.

Feeling restless, Parker sat upright and removed his old battered boots and a talon blade from his pocket. The farm's organic odours were no match for the miasma of his manky feet, redolent of dry rot dressed in rancid cheese. After running his thumb along the blade's edge to its extreme point, and satisfied with its sharpness, he set to work trimming his brown-tinged toenails, all of them thicker than a horse's hoof. Knowing the barn would soon be pitch black, Parker, his tongue jutting through the gap in his teeth, worked quickly and deftly. He preferred to avoid slicing his toes in case they got infected, especially since he had managed to return from the war fully intact.

Once he finished his toenails, Parker decided to do his fingernails too. But first he poked a porky finger in turn up the holes of his saddle-bridged nose; so shaped having been pummelled by multiple well-aimed punches as he spilled out of pubs and ale houses with other belligerent drunks in his youth. After scraping away the mucus trapped in his nasal hair, he wiped it down his front, and set to work on his hands.

And while he continued his personal grooming, Parker's thoughts remained focussed on the Major's wife. After weeks spent tracking her, he was beginning to think she must be a decent type after all; which based on her behaviour to date was the obvious conclusion. It seemed highly improbable, at least to him, that a privileged lady with a rich, handsome husband would dishonour herself with some lowly labourer without a penny to his name. Miss Dumbarton, it seemed, had been misinformed by some muck-stirring gossip.

After re-sheathing the blade and returning it to his inside pocket, Parker shoved his feet back into his boots, lay on his side and considered borrowing a pair of binoculars from an old army mate. They would enable him to watch the Major's wife from a greater distance and reduce the risk of her spotting him. Her apparent awareness was continuing to cause him concern. The way she stopped periodically to check the surround perturbed him not unduly. Instinct coupled with long experience told him she was behaving like a prey animal. Furthermore, tracking her presented a greater challenge in the winter months when the deciduous trees lacked their leaves. Without the noise-absorbing foliage, sound travelled faster in the forest. Fortunately, for him, the estate had several sections of fast-growing evergreens planted to replace the trees felled for the war effort. In those areas it looked to him like a section of Scandinavia had been transplanted on Aldwen soil.

Suddenly, Parker craved a cigarette. Contemplation often had that effect on him. Since his need must be assuaged, and soon, it meant leaving the comfort of the barn and standing outside in the chilly air. Feeling lazy, he was tempted to light up where he lay. However, in the end plain common sense prevailed, as the risk of setting the barn alight was too great. Plus, the farmer would probably shoot him. Justifiably. Hence, he jumped down from the haystack and stole out into the darkness.

Puffing away on his fag outside the barn like an old steam engine, Parker glanced over at the Hall's tall chimney stacks from which plumes of woodsmoke curled into the cold night air. He supposed, judging by their numbers, there must be a fireplace in every room. He reckoned the Aldwens must be eating their evening meal. He pictured them stuffing their prosperous faces with the finest fare and supping the priciest wines, followed by the customary nightcap as they listened to the wireless.

Parker's thoughts switched to matters of a more intimate nature. Matters pertaining to the Major's missus. He wanted to know how she lived her life inside the Hall, and what she got up to when she wasn't out walking. More important, he wished to know what her bed looked like, and the bathtub in which she bathed her bare body every evening. He felt certain the Major must be exercising his marital rights every single night. Well, rich or poor, which man wouldn't? Mrs Aldwen was unarguably irresistible. Abstaining from feasting on her fabulous flesh would be like chucking a fresh slab of steak in the rubbish.

Crushing his dog-end underfoot, Parker, his eyes still fixed on the Hall, sniggered. Thanks to the Dumbarton dame, he had something thrilling to occupy his mind during the long, lonely winter nights when he craved a woman's company. Then, he returned to the barn, climbed back on the haystack and slipped his hand inside his trousers.

Chapter 46

"Would you like another slice of cake?" drawled Rosalyn Dumbarton as she sipped her black coffee in the town's most-select tearooms. Still suffering from the after-effects of the previous night's brandy binge, the thought of cream churned her stomach. To add to her discomfort, every tinkle, rattle and clink of china and silverware sounded abnormally loud; as did several simultaneous conversations taking place in the open space, setting her teeth on edge and making her want to shout shut your mouths to the other diners.

Barbara declined Rosalyn's offer, having already eaten her fill that day, including a large breakfast of scrambled eggs, devilled kidneys and kedgeree, plus toast and jam to top it off. The Hall's staff enjoyed the same diet as the master, although Boyle kept a close eye on their consumption in case it became excessive. All the same, every week Barbara managed to sneak out a few items secreted on her person to pass on to her parents when she visited them on her day off. The swag included half-used soaps, small amounts of tea and sugar, and whatever else she could manage to get past Boyle. Mrs Jenkins did at least allow the maids to take home any stale cake, which would otherwise be thrown to the birds, and which Barbara's mother served up for afters moistened with Bird's bright-yellow custard.

"How about another drink?" suggested Rosalyn.

Barbara hesitated. Although the air in the tearoom was rich with delicious competing aromas, one particular smell stood out above the rest.

"I wouldn't mind a hot chocolate, if that's alright?" said the maid, not wishing to appear too forward as she brushed a few cake crumbs from her skirt onto the floor and hoped no-one would notice. Chocolate being her most-favourite treat, Barbara was disappointed by its lack of availability at the Hall. Unfortunately, Major Aldwen wasn't a fan of the toothsome, finger-licking confectionery, which meant Boyle never ordered it in.

Having said that, the Major had once bought a large box of chocolates for Isabella, who was thrilled to bits by his generous gesture. He liked to spoil her, that much was certain. Unable to resist the temptation, Barbara had helped herself to a chocolate when she was left unattended with the box. It tasted like heaven on her tongue. Alas, the sensation was transitory and she almost succumbed to her weakness a second time. Regret set in almost immediately and for several nail-biting days she lived in fear of her crime's discovery. To be on the safe side, she devised a plan whereby the finger of blame would be pointed at Tilly. Luckily for Tilly, the missing chocolate went unmentioned.

Unknown to Barbara, Isabella had actually noticed the vacant space in the inner tray of the chocolate box. However, she decided to forgive the miscreant provided the misdeed went unrepeated. Being no stranger to hardship herself, she understood the power of temptation. She recalled the time she had used her cut-glass accent to excellent effect to distract the sweetshop assistant while her poor peckish companions, one of whom was Jack, made off with a few lip-smacking spoils.

Upon spotting Isabella outside the tearooms' large bow window, Barbara gasped, then froze in fear. She had assumed the mistress would be home that day. To be seen in the company of Miss Dumbarton, whatever the reason, was bound to arouse suspicion. What if she fancied a coffee and came in? Even though they were seated at a corner table, they were still visible from the entrance. Quickly grabbing the menu, Barbara shielded her face and pretended to study the offerings on the list.

Rosalyn noticed Isabella too. "Ah, your mawkish little mistress has just walked past the window looking ever so quaint in a nice new coat. Obviously taking full advantage of her husband's affluence, I don't doubt. I have it on excellent authority she only married him for his money. Since she's not coming in, you can come out from behind the bill of fare now Barbara. Anyway, what's she doing in town?"

"I've no idea, Miss," said Barbara, replacing the menu and breathing a huge sigh of relief. "She might've been to Martha's for a new gown or something."

"You mean Martha's the dress shop?" enquired Rosalyn, lighting up a long, coloured cigarette. She took a deep drag and slowly exhaled into the room's upper reaches. Although she had never shopped at Martha's, she had heard positive comments about the establishment. Her own outfits were of course couture, made to suit her exceptional personal requirements. Still, she thought, that shouldn't preclude her from taking a closer look at the place from which Hereward's wife purchased her clothes and accoutrements.

"That's right, Miss," replied Barbara breaking into Rosalyn's ruminations. "She sometimes visits her parents too, but not that often as far as I know. They don't appear to be all that close."

"Now Barbara, speaking of Mrs Aldwen's parents, close or not, let's hope she's back in their bosom before too long. After which you may return to your role as my personal maid at the

Hall. All being well, on a more permanent footing, if you understand my meaning. Meanwhile, I expect you to keep me informed of all future developments at the Aldwen house. Since I'm better acquainted with your master than anyone else, I really can't see him tolerating that stupid girl's inane antics ad infinitum."

Barbara had no idea what ad infinitum meant, but she got the message loud and clear nonetheless.

Rosalyn stubbed out her half-smoked cigarette in the glass ashtray in the centre of the table and took one last sip of her half-consumed coffee.

"Now I really must be on my way," she lied. "Don't forget our little arrangement. Keep both your eyes and ears open and you'll be amply rewarded in good time." Then she settled the bill, added a gratuity to the plate and glided through the tearoom door, leaving Barbara to finish her hot chocolate alone.

After Rosalyn departed, the maid picked up the discarded cigarette and pressed the tip between her thumb and forefinger to ensure it was fully extinguished. Then she slipped it into her coat pocket to be given to her father next time she met him. She smiled to herself at the thought of the big, rough drayman with a pink cigarette dangling from one corner of his mouth. Clutching her cup in both hands, she swallowed the sweet, velvety liquid and reflected on how her life had changed for the worse since the Major married Miss Acton.

Chapter 47

Soon after returning from town Isabella went to the library to choose a new novel, slipping in after Hereward slipped out for a breath of fresh air. The library housed a plethora of published material on a broad range of subjects, so she was never short of something to read. If anything, she found the choice overwhelming and often took an age to make up her mind. Sliding a book back into its allotted slot, Isabella ran her forefinger down the spines of several volumes before removing one that stoked her interest. She then opened it at a random page and read a couple of paragraphs to see if the writer's style appealed to her.

Soon after, the french doors opened and Hereward strolled in from the garden with a casual catlike grace. However, his countenance gave the impression he expected to find the room unoccupied.

Isabella looked around at him, acknowledged his arrival with a cool smile and returned to her task.

Without a word, he walked straight up to her, pecked her on the cheek and said: "Back already, my dear."

"It was just a short errand," she explained without looking up.

Hereward, undeterred by her air of detachment, with a rascally smile quipped: "If you're looking for a guide on fox behaviour, my little bookworm, there's bound to be one here on the shelves. Father was an avid book collector. Rarely went a week without buying one. There must be more books in here than in the public library. And a far greater choice. When he ran out of space in here, he started storing them in the attic rooms. Anyhow, I digress. You'll obviously need to use the ladder in order to reach the higher shelves, for which I'm always happy to assist you."

I bet you are, thought Isabella.

"And ready to catch you should you lose your footing and come tumbling to the floor."

Isabella tried not to blush at the obvious tease. And regarding his veiled reference to the sexual conduct of foxes, she gave him a bluenose look. Plus, there was no way on earth she was going to climb the ladder in his presence. Husband or not, she was giving no man the opportunity to peer up her skirt.

Hereward, having realised his reference to fox behaviour was injudicious, steered the conversation to safer seas.

"What sort of books do you most enjoy reading?" he asked after an uncomfortable pause.

Appreciative of his interest, Isabella thought for a moment, then shared with him her best-loved books, favourite authors and preferred genres. She also confided she found the flowery and gushing prose in some female-authored fiction not to her taste.

"I do believe too much sentimentality, overly long descriptive passages and overworked metaphors can spoil an otherwise good story. Would you not agree?" she said after returning another rejected book to its vacated space.

Hereward stuck out his lower lip as he considered the notion. "I suppose so, but I always assumed flowery language was what most women liked. I must remember to buy you an adventure novel next time I visit the bookshop," he said with a good-humoured smile.

"That really won't be necessary," she replied as she continued to browse. "You already have a plentiful supply of adventure novels."

Isabella became silent for a moment, then lowered her brows. "But I've also noticed a number of English-female-authored contemporary novels written and set in India here on the shelves, which I presume aren't yours."

"Oh those," he said with a dismissive air, "they're Rosa…" His voice trailed off. "I didn't realise they were still here. Not to worry, I'll have Boyle forward them on to her."

Isabella turned to face him square on, half raised her brows and said: "Didn't you?"

"Didn't I what?" he replied. Clearly uncomfortable, Hereward rubbed the cleft between his cheek and nose with his thumb.

"Realise they were still here?" she reiterated with emphasis.

"Why do you seriously believe I should wish to keep them? I told you they were overlooked," he said more sharply than he intended to.

"Because they remind you of Miss Dumbarton. You know like a sort of memento of what she once meant to you."

Hereward scoffed at the suggestion. "No, my dear girl, most definitely not. My relationship with Rosalyn was no more than a friendship of convenience. One which ultimately became a cramping inconvenience. It was the typical kinship of compatriots abroad with little in common except a shared nationality. As far as I was concerned it was never a love affair in any sense of the word."

Isabella, who was no longer listening to his denials, continued speaking, as if to herself, to maintain her train of thought.

"I sometimes find her possessions here in the house. Well, I assume they're hers since I can think of no-one else to whom they might belong. They appear in my bedroom and the bathroom, and at odd times too."

Other than frowning, Hereward made no response. Instead, he picked up the glass paperweight on his desk and examined it in an absent-minded manner.

"I can't think why, unless Aldwen Hall has a resident ghost," she said flippantly. "I do sometimes wonder whether your old lady-love visits you here," she said, scratching the side of her throat.

There followed a protracted pause during which Hereward's facial expression appeared pained. "Absolutely not," he said with an inflection of forcefulness in his voice. "Why ever would she?" The accusatory tone in Isabella's voice was making him feel both uncomfortable and defensive. As was her pointed reference to Rosalyn's age. He struggled to understand why his former friendship with a woman he had never loved should bother his wife. The woman's history, he thought.

"Or perhaps someone is playing silly games?" she went on, giving expression to her suspicions.

"Not knowing how to respond to what had become an awkward conversation regarding Rosalyn, Hereward located the offending books and moved to throw them on the fire.

"Don't do that," cried Isabella. "It's a sin to burn a book."

"Very well then," he said, "I'll have Boyle send them on to her. Nothing like a clean sweep."

Isabella, forgetting what she was there for, turned to leave. She had wanted to ask him more questions about Rosalyn, who clearly loved him, but her courage failed her.

Hereward regretted mentioning Rosalyn's name. Doing so had marred a promising conversation.

"Isabella," he called after her, a touch of tenderness apparent in his tone.

"Yes?" she said, half turning to look at him.

"I never loved her you know," he said, his arms folded across his chest.

Silence resumed.

Why she couldn't say, but Isabella's heart felt suddenly as heavy as a headstone and she bitched: "Whether you did or did not love Miss Dumb Barton, fails to alter the fact that you both behaved shamefully in what is my current bedroom. Believe me, I can't wait to vacate that tainted space. That's if the work on my new bedroom is ever completed."

A corner of Hereward's mouth twitched in response to Isabella's childish skit delivered as a rebuke. Still, he kept quiet. Having no idea how she came to know about Rosalyn, and how much she knew, he thought it wise to make no further contribution to the conversation.

Chapter 48

The scented letter lay on the hall table awaiting transfer to the tall red pillar box at the end of the street. The missive was the opening gambit in Rosalyn's plan to re-establish contact with Hereward via a disingenuous gesture of goodwill. The idea of deploying delusory diplomacy had occurred to her in a sudden flash of inspiration after she took leave of loose-tongued Barbara in the tearooms. After all, no reasonable person could object to receiving sincere salutations, even if they had stuck in her craw as soon as she dipped her gold nib in black ink and put it to Clairefontaine paper.

Still, it was done now, thank heaven, and she was overall satisfied with her final effort. Having spent hours agonising over the language in her letter, Rosalyn had produced several drafts in her sloping spidery hand. All except the one cited below were now torn into multiple pieces and consigned to the wastepaper basket.

Dearest Hereward,

I hope you are well. First, allow me to apologise for my tardiness in not writing to you sooner. I've been meaning to congratulate you on your recent marriage to Miss Isabella Acton and wish you every happiness in your new life together.

I would be lying if I said your betrothal hadn't come as a colossal shock. As you know, I truly believed our relationship was for the duration, so I was understandably devastated when you told me you had found someone else. Notwithstanding, I hope we can remain friends and keep in touch for old times' sake, and perhaps catch up with each other once in a while.

Yours affectionately,
Rosalyn x

Rosalyn stared into space, her sallow face masked in a thick layer of makeup to conceal the dark circles and bags under her eyes. As she reflected on her false felicitations, experience reminded her to tread carefully when dealing with Hereward. The fellow was nobody's fool and must never be underestimated. One wrong move could undermine her plan for reconciliation with her one true love, she counselled herself. And she was convinced he had loved her too until that vile, voluptuous little virgin had turned his head.

Should the first stage of her initiative prove successful, then a cordial epistolary intercourse would be established between Hereward and herself. Or so Rosalyn hoped. Then, once a suitable period of time had elapsed, she could proceed to the next stage of their resurrected friendship — meeting face to face. Following a further and hopefully shorter interval, a platonic flirtation should, all being well, reinstate a degree of intimacy between them.

Moreover, once Hereward learned he was a cuckold, assuming Parker managed to catch Isabella and her low-class lover in the act, then the Aldwen's marriage would inevitably collapse. After which, Rosalyn prayed, he would turn to her for solace, leading to the much-desired denouement. However long it took and whatever it took, she intended to worm her way back into his affections.

As she thought of the lavender-coloured envelope containing her mealymouthed congratulations, Rosalyn almost lost her nerve. However, she quickly calmed her qualms by reminding herself that Hereward was once an intimate friend and what she had written was perfectly acceptable, not to mention magnanimous in the circumstances. Then she cautioned herself to be patient and not to rush things. Patience unfortunately didn't feature too highly on Rosalyn's limited list of virtues. Still, after hearing of Hereward's mismatched, moribund marriage from the embittered Barbara, she had good reason to be optimistic.

Speaking of whom, no-one was more surprised than Barbara to learn the Hall's new mistress was a similar age to herself. That, however, is where the similarity ended. Unlike Isabella Aldwen, Barbara Brown was an unremarkable young thing, average in every way, plain as a potato with a personality to match. She had fallen for Major Aldwen within a week of starting work at the Hall, becoming red-faced, tongue-tied and butterfingered in his presence. To her utmost relief, he appeared not to notice when she dropped a dish, bumped into the furniture or knocked over a glass.

The maid dreamed of a day when her love for the epitome of perfect manhood would be requited. But being solidly down to earth too, Barbara recognised her wool-gathering for what it was: a foolish fantasy serving as a distraction during the long dreary days of her unrewarding life. In reality the dour young domestic knew her prospects of marrying a moneyed, smart and handsome man were nought, reinforcing her hostility towards his enviable wife.

For despite the enviable wife's tender years, Barbara found her difficult, obdurate and disobliging. She might look like an angel, but she behaved more like a childish brat. The maid also begrudged serving the girl with whom the master was madly in love. Added to which, in the presence of the mistress Barbara felt decidedly dull; like bread without butter or scones without jam. Every time she set eyes on the object of her odium, the green-eyed devil sprang onto her shoulder and poked her with its five-pronged pitchfork. But what angered her above all else, was the abrupt manner in which the mistress had dispensed with her services the morning after the wedding; meaning she was obliged to perform more-disagreeable chores under Boyle's close supervision.

And there was always a multitude of disagreeable chores to complete and errands to run at the Hall. Nothing escaped Boyle's astute observations. Barbara was convinced the butler had 360-degree vision in his divergent eyeballs. Whenever she stopped for a breather, he appeared out of nowhere like a card in a conjuring trick. Plus, he seemed to possess some sort of magical power which enabled him to see through walls, floors and ceilings. Moreover, not a single stain, smudge or dust speck went undetected under his watch.

Barbara missed Rosalyn. Not because she was fond of Rosalyn. Rosalyn was incapable of inspiring fondness. She missed her because her presence was advantageous. Whenever the imperious paramour stayed overnight at the Hall, the Major denied her permission to bring her own maid, which he considered an intrusive imposition. Hence, Barbara was deployed to fill the temporary vacancy. And since the role required little physical expenditure, it suited the workshy scullion down to the ground.

Since it took Rosalyn most of the morning to make herself presentable, she rarely appeared downstairs before elevenses. While consuming a leisurely breakfast in bed in the iniquitous *badroom*, as the guest room was dubbed downstairs in the servants' quarters, Rosalyn trawled the newspaper announcements to check which of her contemporaries had got themselves hitched. Following which, she rose from the bed in the manner of a princess, which she fancied she was. And when Barbara came to make the bed, to her maidenly mortification the bedsheets were invariably wrinkled on both sides of the mattress.

Barbara assisted Rosalyn at every stage of her long-drawn-out routine, which included massaging oils into her feet's furfuraceous skin, manicuring her pointed fingernails, fastening the hooks on her corset and superfluous conical brassiere, and brushing her bob until it shone. All things considered, the maid was at least grateful the bitch of the bedchamber, as she referred to her temporary mistress behind her back, applied her own makeup and sprayed her own eau-de-cologne. And on the days when Rosalyn was in residence at the Hall, poor Tilly got lumbered with Barbara's chores. Except on Mondays, which was washday. And for some unknown reason, whenever Rosalyn visited at the weekend, the master insisted on dropping her home on his way to late-morning Sunday Mass.

Out of all the chores, Barbara found laundry work the most laborious. Not only did it take up much of Monday, there was also no escaping it. And while the mistress immersed herself in the ancient wooded landscape, Barbara's arms were immersed to the elbows in the old wooden washtubs. Every week without fail she worked her way through a mountain of soiled linen in the stodgy damp conditions of the laundry room. To add to her woes, the meticulous Major insisted on changing his clothing more often than Barbara thought strictly necessary. In most poor homes people changed their clothes once a week, if at all, and only then after taking a bath in an old tin tub on a Saturday. The Major had unfortunately imported his scrupulous habits from India, where the scorching heat made bathing and changing twice daily a must, where practicable.

Back on home ground, he continued in much the same vein.

The combination of hot water and harsh soap used for the tablecloths, napkins and bedsheets excoriated Barbara's chronically rough red hands. With an expression of martyrdom on her mulish face, she picked up Isabella's smart blue frock and inspected it closely. It looked reasonably clean still and, in the maid's opinion, could easily have gone another week without a wash. Having no other choice, she dunked it in the tub of soapy water and pounded it with the poss stick; while with her nastiest smile she recalled Major Aldwen rebuking his wife for staining her clothes with blackberries. After which she spread the frock out over the washboard and scoured it with the scrubbing brush to abrade the fabric.

As expected, Boyle lumbered in to check she wasn't slacking. Although Barbara abhorred the butler, she made sure to keep on his good side. Her father would have called a man like him a bastard. Not in front of the ladies, of course. Bastard Boyle, she said to herself with a sneer. She thought the soubriquet rather suited the blatant snob. In particular, she despised the way he hid his blue-collar background behind a false frontage of white-collar hypocrisy. She also hated the manner in which he modelled his behaviour on that of upperclass gentlemen by clasping his hands behind his back and extending his neck to project an air of superiority. Major Aldwen never adopted any such pose and he was a genuine gentleman. Strong and brave too, thought Barbara, gazing into the distance with dreamy eyes.

When she finished feeding the laundry through the mangle rollers, Barbara hung it on wooden racks to dry, or outside on the clothesline when it wasn't raining. Later, while it was still damp, she pressed it with the flat iron; another task she detested. Many big houses sent their linens outside to be laundered, but not Aldwen Hall. Boyle refused to even consider it. Said he wasn't having some germ-ridden skivvies mishandling his master's raiments.

Feeling more aggrieved than ever before at her situation, Barbara felt tempted to burn a hole in Isabella's nightdress, but then she knew the butler was bound to withhold her wages as recompense. So, she snapped a thread on the back hem of her day dress instead. That'll teach 'er, she said to herself, hoping the Major would notice the loose hem and lambast his wife for her slovenliness. And poor put-upon Tilly would be told to repair it, ha-ha.

Upon hearing the cook calling her name, Barbara rolled her eyes. That bloody Eliza Jenkins is the bane of my life, she said under her breath. The sooner that old nag is behind the rusty gates of the knacker's yard in the sky, the happier I'll be.

Chapter 49

To begin with, the bane of Barbara's life presumed the new mistress would be taking responsibility for approving the menus. The old cook was expecting to send them upstairs for the young wife's perusal. But from the first, Boyle objected to the idea and refused to relinquish a single one of his duties. He informed Mrs Jenkins they would be maintaining the status quo; even though he complained on a regular basis about his onerous workload. However, with Christmas fast approaching, the cook believed the mistress should be included in all discussions and decisions regarding the festive fare.

Mrs Jenkins considered Mrs Aldwen a rarity. An upperclass lady ferreting for food in field and forest. Every season provided something new: berries, nuts, herbs, and wild garlic to name a few. The cook's late mother had been an expert forager. Unfortunately, the once-common pursuit had waned after countryfolk began migrating to the towns to work in the new industries. It saddened Jenkins to see people evermore estranged from nature. With great affection, she recalled her mother's hot poultices and herbal fomentations, which alleviated a broad range of illnesses and ailments. Boyle's sneering contempt for the contents of Isabella's basket niggled the cook no end. However, she chose to ignore his sheer bloody-mindedness. She was in charge of the catering and woe betide anyone who dared cross her in the kitchen. The kitchen was her domain and she was determined it should remain so. Even Boyle exercised caution in the kitchen, although he tried to disguise his fear under a facade of false bravado.

With her plump fingers, Mrs Jenkins rubbed lard and flour together in a ceramic bowl to make the pastry for Isabella's favourite pie. She knew the mistress appreciated her culinary efforts and particularly enjoyed the curry she made once a month for Major Aldwen as a special treat. Having acquired the taste for the spicy stuff in India, he insisted on keeping a generous supply of curry powder in the pantry. And although Boyle was tasked with procuring the product, he never consumed it. For not only did he detest the taste and smell of the bitter yellow concoction, he also complained it made him bilious and upset his bowels. Hence on curry days he made do with a plain chicken sandwich and a cup of tea.

Strutting into the kitchen, Boyle espied the pastry and halted. "Is that pastry?" he asked, arms akimbo, as Jenkins rolled a fat lump of dough into a large round on a well-floured wooden board.

"What does it look like?" snapped the cook.

"I don't recall pastry being on today's menu, Jenkins," said the butler in a confrontational tone.

"No, it wasn't originally, but the mistress has asked me to make some changes, so now it is. Was there anything else?" she said glowering at him as she draped the pastry over the rolling pin and transferred it to the pie dish.

For his own sake, Boyle, whose boldness was beginning to ebb, made no further comment. The old battleship, nicknamed *HMS Dreadnought* by one of the Hall's former servants, was brandishing a heavy wooden rolling pin, and she was best avoided when she had a potential weapon in her hands. The butler had fallen foul of her temper once when Hereward's mother was alive. Everyone knew not to get on the wrong side of the rolling pin, and nobody complained when they did. It was an unwritten rule of domestic service: what happened below stairs remained there. Although Boyle had long cemented his position at the Hall, he still feared Jenkins and made sure to keep out of her way when she was cooking. Even if he were to complain to the Major about her behaviour, there was no chance of her being dismissed.

Like Jenkins, Boyle had been in service at Aldwen Hall for most of his adult life and, apart from a few odd jobs in his youth, had never worked anywhere else. And he had been most content with his situation until the mistress saw fit to sabotage his operations. For the life of him, he couldn't understand what made the Major marry a town-raised teenage girl and think she would be happy at the Hall. The Dumbarton woman had been bad enough, but at least she kept her sniffy snout out of the Hall's domestic matters. She was too concerned with painting her conceited face. Having said that, she did rather monopolise young Barbara.

To serve his own interests, Boyle ignored the fact that Isabella was conversant with the customs and conventions of a typical highborn household. Back in the days when the Actons could afford to employ a cook, Agatha Acton had overseen the menu choices as a matter of routine. In common with most wellborn wives, she considered it one of her principal duties. Thus, the menus were always presented to her at her escritoire, after which she would make recommendations or amendments as she saw fit.

Based on her own personal experience, Isabella had never heard of a butler choosing the bill of fare on behalf of a mistress. It seemed to her somewhat unorthodox. She presumed the arrangement must have suited Hereward's convenience when he lived alone at the Hall.

Boyle, however, continued to insist the menus were his

responsibility by way of established practice, and saw no reason for change. He believed the mistress need not concern herself with household affairs when he was there to take charge of everything. Moreover, he insisted he was better acquainted than anyone with the master's dietary preferences. It had never occurred to him that the mistress might have predilections of her own. As he saw things, she was nothing more than her husband's appendant. Furthermore, he was determined to keep her out of the kitchen. The kitchen was strictly servant territory. The Major's late mother had never entered the kitchen, not even once, although she had approved the menus; a detail Boyle conveniently chose to ignore. Occupying the vacuum left by her death, he had expanded his role to increase his influence over the household.

And so, it happened that one cold day in late November Isabella summoned Boyle to the sitting room.

"I understand you wish to speak with me, Ma'am?" he said in a solemn voice, his hands clasped tight in front of his lower abdomen.

"Yes, that's correct," she confirmed. "I've decided to introduce some changes here at the Hall. Henceforth, I shall be approving the menus myself. And since I'll be liaising with Mrs Jenkins directly, I shan't require your assistance."

Boyle emitted a gasp of horror as he grappled with the magnitude of her announcement. "But, Ma'am, with respect, since I am fully acquainted with the master's palate, I should think it wiser to stick to the existing arrangement."

Isabella felt her blood begin to boil. "And what about my palate, Boyle? You infer I'm not entitled to my own preferences."

The butler made no reply. Instead, he shifted his feet, removed his pocket watch and checked the time.

Isabella stared at him in utter disbelief. She had never before been confronted by such blatant insolence from a servant. Nevertheless, she remained resolute.

"Has it not occurred to you that I am now fully conversant with *my* husband's dietary preferences?"

Still Boyle said nothing. Her emphasis on the proprietorial possessive had robbed him of speech.

"The new arrangement begins Monday next," she stated. "I'll agree the time with Mrs Jenkins." Isabella then curled her lip and added in her curtest tone: "Since you have openly indicated that you are pressed for time, I suggest you return to your duties forthwith."

Boyle, still in a state of shock, hesitated for a moment.

"That will be all, thank you," she reminded him in a tone as cold and sharp as an icicle.

Thrown off balance by the mistress's new assertiveness, the butler skulked from the room, closed the door with a soft click, and slunk downstairs to ponder his next move in the privacy of his own room.

The second Boyle saw Isabella exit the library after tea, he went straight to the Major and requested a word.

Hereward, having never before seen the butler looking so wretched, asked with genuine concern: "Is there something wrong?"

His face puce with outrage and resentment, Boyle unfolded a large cotton handkerchief with a tremulous hand and blew his nose.

"Major, please forgive the intrusion," he said with a distinct sniff, his voice warbly with emotion. "As you are aware, Sir, I have been a loyal and devoted servant of this household for more years than I care to remember..." And so, he went on.

Hereward sat perfectly still and listened in complete silence as the butler unburdened himself. "Very well, Boyle," he said at length, "leave it with me. As I'm sure you understand, I must first speak with my wife."

"Yes, of course, Sir, he said. Then he bowed and backed away.

Chapter 50

The debacle over Boyle and the menu business began the moment Hereward summoned Isabella to the library and rebuked her in the strongest terms possible for failing to discuss the matter with him first.

"I make the rules in this house and I expect you to obey them," he said in a commanding voice. "Whatever were you thinking? You can't just take it upon yourself to introduce changes here without prior consultation. It's jolly bad form."

Sparked by the severity of Hereward's scolding and his lack of support, Isabella banged her small fist on the desktop and bawled: "Please don't speak to me in that manner. I'm neither a child nor a servant. Although I must say the latter most definitely befits my status here."

To her mind, her husband and his scheming henchman were two stick-in-the-muds totally resistant to change. Whatever she wished to do Boyle did his best to undermine her. Well, enough was enough. Unable to contain her fury any longer, Isabella grabbed the nearest object, which happened to be the ink bottle, and slammed it down hard on the desktop. Instantly, the vessel smashed and blew off its cap, splashing ink here, there and everywhere. Meanwhile, the warring duo stood dappled and dotted like two Dalmatian dogs as they surveyed the scene in shocked silence.

There was normally an element of control to Hereward's

anger, but not on this occasion. Except for the incident in the conservatory, Isabella had never seen him look so angry; so angry she feared he might slap her again.

"Pack your bags," he ordered through clenched teeth. "I suggest you tell Tilly to assist you. I'm returning you to your parents. They're more than welcome to you. It's clear you're never going to be happy here. You decided that the moment you arrived. You've made no attempt whatsoever to adjust to life here."

With as much dignity as she could gather, Isabella told him she was perfectly capable of doing her own packing and went straight up to her bedroom alone. But as she transferred the contents of her wardrobe and drawers into her suitcase, she wondered whether Hereward really meant her to go.

Once she finished packing, Isabella lugged her suitcase downstairs one step at a time before returning upstairs to collect her valise. There was no way on earth she was prepared to give Boyle the satisfaction of bringing them down on her behalf. She doubted she could cope with the sight of his smug, exultant face. The temptation to punch it might prove irresistible.

As she stood waiting out in the hall like a little lost waif, Hereward emerged from the library looking stone-faced. "You should have said you were ready," he said coldly. "I would have sent Boyle up to fetch your luggage."

Isabella replied in a voice equally formal and frigid: "I no longer require his assistance, or yours for that matter. Thank you all the same."

"Why must you insist on repeatedly proving the point?" he protested.

"I would have thought *proving the point* is what your flunkey has been doing all along," she retaliated.

Grabbing Isabella's bags himself, Hereward loped down to

the motorcar and hauled them onto the luggage rack at the back. Then he opened the passenger door and gestured for her to get in. Following which, he lowered himself into the driver's seat, started up the engine and moved off at moderate speed, his hands gripping the steering wheel.

Meanwhile, Boyle stood watching them from the sitting-room window, looking ecstatic.

After travelling a mile in suffocating silence, Isabella suddenly raised her hand and cried: "Stop!"

Hitting the brake pedal hard, Hereward brought the vehicle to a swift halt. "What is it now?" he said wearily, the worst of his anger having already subsided.

Conversely, Isabella's anger was beginning to reassert itself. "I insist you release me *right* now," she said in a high-pitched voice. "Let me out here. I'll walk. I'm perfectly capable of making my own way into town."

Hereward denied her demand with good reason. The woods bordering the road looked lampblack and forbidding; while the missing moon made the motorcar's interior pitch-dark.

"I've no intention of letting you out here," he said with conviction as his breath condensed on the glass. "It's not safe at this time for a lady to be out alone. And besides, your bags are far too heavy."

"You can send them on later," she asserted. "That's if you don't mind. I'm sure your blessed butler would be more than happy to oblige. I shouldn't wish to inconvenience you, of course," she added with a serving of sarcasm on the side.

Hereward began to get angry again. Angry and frustrated. "You just don't learn, do you?" he said.

"I'm no longer your responsibility," Isabella reminded him. "Now let me out!" And she grabbed hold of the door's cold metal handle to test his resolve.

To prevent her from going through with her reckless threat, Hereward reached over and wrapped his fingers firmly around her wrist. "No! Absolutely not," he reiterated. He didn't relish the idea of having to chase her down the dark road and drag her back kicking and screaming to the motorcar, should she decide to implement her preposterous plan.

"Once I've delivered you to your parents' place you can do as you jolly well like. Until then, you're my responsibility."

Affronted, Isabella scowled at him and replied: "Deliver! I'm not a parcel for pity's sake. I'm surprised you haven't tried to box me up, mark me as fragile and sent me via parcel post."

"Don't be ridiculous," snorted Hereward. "And if there's any boxing to do, young lady, it'll be to your ears."

Heavens above. The man's a mass of contradictions, she said within. Then in a spiritous act of rebellion, Isabella unclipped her hair with her free hand, gave her head a vigorous shake to ease the tightness in her scalp, and made another attempt to escape.

"Let me out!" she squealed. "I'm no longer your responsibility. What's more, I do not require a chaperone. The days of women requiring chaperones are over in case you missed the news bulletin."

Hereward was starting to get cold feet. Having reacted on impulse to Boyle's grievance, or rather, overreacted, his regret was growing exponentially. Regret matched in equal measure by Isabella's fierce determination to outmanoeuvre him.

"I insist you let me out right now," she said for the fourth time. "You've no right to keep me here against my will. You're nothing but a vicious bully and a vile brute, and I detest you," she screeched.

Hurtful though they were, Hereward paid no heed to his wife's brickbats. Instead, he lowered his voice and attempted to calm the situation. They were like a seesaw: as one went up the other came down.

Isabella duly noted the sudden change in her husband's demeanour. Although she wasn't quite sure what it was, something had definitely subdued him. And on recalling his one major weakness, she decided to employ a different strategy.

"Now you've thrown me out of the house on account of your beloved butler," she said, "it means I'll be free to find somebody else. Somebody nearer my own age. Somebody who knows how to have fun. Somebody understanding and supportive who treasures me for who I am, and doesn't expect me to conform to some ridiculous, outdated and idealistic version of a wife."

Isabella's impassioned tirade pierced Hereward to his core. The thought of his beautiful young wife lying with another man delivered a powerful punch to his solar plexus. He was forced to admit to himself that she had well and truly trumped him. And he could tell there was more to come.

"The trouble with you, Hereward, is your inability to distinguish between love and lust," she continued. "Do you seriously think I'm too stupid to know why you married me? Do you think that because I'm only seventeen you can treat me like a foolish child?"

"Confound it, Isabella, I married you for no other reason than I fell madly in love with you the second I set eyes on you," he countered.

But there was no holding her back, not even to draw breath, and she ignored Hereward's heartfelt declaration.

"You clearly don't know the meaning of love. That's to say genuine love. Genuine love is selfless not selfish. The only love you know is self-love. I needed your loyalty. I needed your support. I needed your understanding. You have given me none of those things. Every time your malignant manservant and his miserable acolyte undermine me, you almost never take my side. The man behaves with impunity. Tell me why he has so much power over you," she demanded.

"I don't believe he does," scoffed Hereward.

"You forget the Hall is meant to be my place of residence too, and not yours alone, or yours and Boyle's. Since the day I arrived as a distressed young bride that loathsome lackey of yours has treated me like an imposter."

"I hardly think that's true," replied Hereward.

"Of course, it's true. Boyle is determined to have complete control over the household and you absolutely refuse to see it."

"That's utter nonsense."

"No, it's not!"

"Yes, it is. I've never heard anything so ridiculous in my entire life."

The discussion, like all their discussions, was a nonstop carousel of accusations and recriminations which Hereward decided for sanity's sake must be brought to a swift halt. So, after wiping the windscreen, he placed his hands back on the steering wheel and his feet on the pedals.

"What are you doing? I've asked you several times now to let me out here," cried Isabella in a perplexed, petulant tone.

"Please bear with me, my dear," said Hereward. "I've decided to do something I should have done weeks ago. Let's see if we can behave like two mature adults and sort this thing out once and for all, preferably somewhere neutral and where the servants can't hear us." Then he restarted the engine and drove off.

They travelled for a couple of hours after that, but spoke little during the journey. Strange as it seemed, Isabella no longer wished to leave the Hall. For better or worse, she had fallen in love with the estate's rustic splendour, and the idea of being back with her parents no longer appealed. However, she had no intention of revealing her change of heart to Hereward, knowing it would give him an advantage over her.

By the time they pulled up in front of a small, old-fashioned hotel, they had both calmed down considerably. It wasn't the sort of place Hereward normally patronised, but he was too tired to search for something better appointed. He told Isabella to wait in the vehicle while he went inside to enquire about a room.

Once they checked in, a deferential porter came out to collect Isabella's luggage, then he showed them to their room up a steep, narrow staircase redolent of lard-fried bacon and overcooked cabbage.

"Well at least it looks clean," said Hereward, surveying the scratched furniture, faded wallpaper and careworn carpet.

Isabella had ceased caring. She just wanted to lie down and close her weary eyes. It had been a long and difficult day and she felt cold and exhausted.

Presently, a spindly maid brought them a plate of salmon-paste sandwiches and a pot of steaming-hot tea which Hereward had ordered after signing the register. Then she switched on a small heater to warm the room and bid them goodnight.

As soon as they finished eating, Isabella removed her nightclothes from the suitcase. Then she went to the unheated communal bathroom at the end of the corridor to get changed, brush her teeth, and wash her hands and face. Although she felt in desperate need of a bath, she was too tired to run one. Too tired even to brush her hair. Upon her return to the room, she removed her robe, flopped into bed and drew the covers up to her chin.

Following her example, Hereward stripped to his combinations, got into bed and switched off the light. Despite being married to Isabella for months, he had never seen her naked. Without exception, she always insisted on having the lights out every time he visited her bedroom. All the same, it didn't stop him wallowing in the sensuous warmth of her body beneath the bedcovers, and luxuriating in the thrill of contact with her bare skin when he raised her nightdress and ravished her with rhapsodic bliss.

Since he always slept alone, never before had Hereward spent an entire night lying beside a woman in bed. He recalled Rosalyn's disappointment upon learning they had separate hotel rooms when they visited London together. An arrangement ostensibly to protect her reputation, but in truth he preferred not to lie next to her all night long, or look at her makeup-smudged, marble-hard visage at first light. In the interests of propriety, whenever she had stayed at the Hall overnight, she was given the guest room, where he slipped in and out unnoticed. Or so he believed.

Feeling restless, Hereward climbed out of bed, went over to the window, parted the thin curtains, and looked out at the night. The moonless sky made the grounds behind the hotel almost impossible to make out.

"What are you looking at?" said Isabella softly, flicking on the bedside light. Her eyes passed over the backs of his muscular calves and thighs under the close-fitted fabric of his combinations. They put her in mind of the powerful lower limbs of heroic male figures she had observed in classical art.

"Nothing much really," came Hereward's equally soft reply after a deep sigh.

"It's awfully dark outside, so I doubt there's much to see," she said.

Still, he carried on standing there as if in a trance.

"Hereward," she said, more forcefully, "it's unwise to stand at the window in winter undressed. Please, come back to bed before you catch cold."

Her rare utterance of his name in her sweet imploring voice was all it took to persuade him and he returned to bed that instant.

"What are we to do my indomitable little darling?" he said, snuggling up to her, kissing her head and nuzzling her neck. She smelled of hotel soap and pink tooth powder. "However long it takes, we must resolve our differences, even if it means remaining here for an entire week."

Isabella's eyes closed as her mouth opened in a wide yawn. She was desperate for sleep but equally desperate to make him understand her difficulties and frustrations. Things could no longer continue as they were. Certainly not with the subversive Boyle's blatant mischiefs. She knew that as long as her husband's loyalties remained divided there could never be peace in their lives.

There followed a prolonged and at times heated discussion regarding their respective disputations. After much prodding from Isabella, Hereward conceded that he was too concerned with his own selfish interests, too-dyed-in the-wool, and too uncompromising. It had never occurred to him that once he was married some aspects of his life would automatically change. Furthermore, female rebellion from one so fresh-faced and unfledged as his wife had disrupted his hitherto sedate existence. He also acknowledged, albeit to himself, that beneath his anger existed a layer of hurt and frustration at her standoffishness, especially in the bedroom. Nonetheless, her contumacy secretly impressed him. Never before had a woman stood up to him the way she did.

For Isabella, her moment of triumph came when Hereward finally agreed that Boyle needed reining in. He also accepted that he was himself partly to blame for the butler's grandiosity. But since he was still a man to be reckoned with, he was unwilling to allow his wife to have all her own way. Hence, he made her promise not to implement any more changes without first consulting him. She also accepted with some reluctance that replacing the butler would be a problem. Since the war ended, recruiting and keeping staff had become especially difficult for owners of country houses, as the lower classes had more alternatives to working in service. Thus, peace prevailed — for the present.

Chapter 51

Meanwhile at the Hall, Boyle ran his liver-spotted fingers over the Major's folded shirt before placing it on a shelf in the dressing-room. He liked everything to be perfect; as perfect as was humanly possible. Taking care of his master's wardrobe and helping him to dress were the most-rewarding aspects of his role as butler-cum-valet, giving him a deep sense of connection to the man himself. A man whose appearance he prided himself on, a man he admired above anyone else, and a man whose style showcased his excellent taste.

In Boyle's view, good taste was intrinsic. It could never be taught. Picking up another shirt from a stack of fresh laundry, he held it close to his nose and inhaled as if he were smelling a summer bloom. Even after laundering, a hint of aromatic muskiness always remained on his master's clothes. Best of all, he loved the smooth, light, lawn-cotton shirts. He had to admit the sumptuous silk pyjamas were also superlative, although he couldn't bear the thought of Major Aldwen wearing them in the nuptial bed.

Taking hold of a silver-handled horsehair hat brush, Boyle set to work on the Major's favourite fedora, paying particular attention to its teardrop crown. Following which, he paired and folded a selection of socks, diverting those with holes to the mending basket. He also inspected several sets of white combinations for signs of wear and tear. Those that made the grade were stored in ruler-straight order in dedicated drawers, with winter woollens and summer cottons in separate sections. He used the same system for socks, except the silks, which were reserved for special occasions and stored in moth-repellent satin-lined boxes. Then after applying a dab of wax polish, plus a little spittle for extra shine, to a pair of hand-stitched shoes, he buffed them with a yellow duster and stored them on a shelf inside a bespoke shoe cabinet crafted from local oak.

And as he busied himself with his work, Boyle hummed and reflected; reflected on his life at Aldwen Hall before Isabella née Acton's arrival upset the apple cart. All the time she was there, he had longed for the return of the days when it was just the master and himself; both of them reserved, obsessive and organised, rubbing along in perfect peace and harmony.

Shaking his head in dismay, Boyle recalled the ruckus in the library. What a calamity was that, the likes of which had never before been seen at the Hall. It took the poor maids an age to remove every ink mark. Still, it came as no surprise to him to discover the little minx had at last revealed her true colours. Nevertheless, he was delighted by her failure to have her own way and her subsequent departure. Raising a smile at the thought of her final humiliation, the butler felt a new sense of lightness and esprit within himself.

For the life of him, the butler couldn't understand what the Major had ever seen in the mistress. For the pair were clearly incompatible, not only in age but also in temperament. Some days they exchanged few words, while on others they argued hammer and tongs. Without exception, he believed a wife should always obey and never backchat her husband, but then Isabella Aldwen hadn't a single obedient bone in her bold little body. Well, he hoped the master had learned his lesson. Women should be given a wide birth. Except for procreational purposes and domestic work, they were good for nothing. Boyle preferred the company of men. In his view, men were intellectually superior to women, not to mention less complicated, less emotional, and more reasoned.

Frowning with frustration, Boyle tutted upon returning a shirt to the linen basket that wasn't finished to his high standards. He told himself he would be needing to have a word with young Barbara first thing in the morning. Admittedly, the maid had her uses, but that didn't mean he was prepared to put up with her sloppy work, especially where it concerned the Major's clothing.

Before turning off the light, Boyle cast his eyes around the room and sighed with contentment. For him, the months since the Major got married had been a trial, during which he had witnessed the sullen bride become an imposing little madam determined to disempower him and undermine his authority. Watching his beloved master fawning over the femme fatale, indulging her every whim, and capitulating to her every demand had been an agony. But the worst thing he had endured on a near nightly basis, while rewinding the hall clock, was hearing his master's eager footsteps crossing the landing to the mistress's bedroom.

Absently, distracted by mental images of his master's marital intimacies, Boyle wiped tiny sweat bubbles from his brow with the duster. Then he reassured himself that the infernal neophyte was no longer there to torment him. She was gone, gone for good, thank God, having failed to topple him for sure. More than ever, he was looking forward to his master's return. He wondered whether he should offer him his commiserations. However, on reflection, he decided against it, thinking the Major might not appreciate the presumptuousness or insincerity.

Chapter 52

The next morning Hereward awoke to the early light seeping through the unlined curtains of the hotel room, and the unaccustomed hum of traffic on the nearby trunk road. He blinked, rubbed his eyes and scratched his chin. Hooked on a branch of a crab-apple tree outside the window, a yellow-beaked blackbird issued a sweet tune, reminding him of the Hall and making him feel homesick. After checking the time on his wristwatch, he yawned like a lazy lion and cupped his face in his hands. Having had little sleep, he wasn't exactly relishing the long drive back. Conversely, Isabella had slept like a log throughout what remained of the night after they both agreed to get some sleep. Unlike him, she had not tossed and turned and huffed and puffed in little fits of frustration.

Hereward stretched out his lengthy limbs and wrinkled his brow at the sight of his wife tangled up in the bedsheets. Waking up beside a woman felt strange, even when the woman was his wife. With her back to him and her curls commandeering the pillow, she looked delicate and diminutive, nothing like the feisty female of yesterday. He wondered whether he would ever manage to contain her or bend her to his will. And he was no longer sure if he wanted to, since he couldn't help but admire her strong spirit.

A sudden throb of desire roused Hereward's manhood and he considered making love to her. But then he remembered he was wearing yesterday's underwear and would need to bathe first. Since their stay at the hotel was unplanned, he lacked the clean clothes Boyle laid out for him every morning. Ordinarily, he would be dressed by now, enjoying breakfast and reading his daily newspaper.

Isabella rolled over in her sleep to face him and her cool breath caressed his face. Watching her chest rise and fall in a gentle rhythm, he looked at her with ravenous eyes. Fast asleep she looked as delicious as a bowl of fresh strawberries drenched in cream. The petulant pout, the insurgent ocular flashes and the churlish chin from the day before had all vanished. For several moments he studied her like an art lover marvelling at the finer details in a prodigious portrait painting. Hers was a face that could upstage the sun. Her lips were as glossy as a flamingo flower, the upper one shaped like a recurve bow, while a small bump on the side of an otherwise perfect nose attracted intrigue. Knowing his once-wayward wife, she probably banged it while she was up to no good with her nefarious friends.

"Good morning, Miss Sleepy," he said as her eyelids flickered in the unfamiliar room. Softly stroking her cheek, he looked at her with rapt appreciation. Unlike Rosalyn, who never had a hair out of place, Isabella seemed to care little about her appearance. He had never known anyone so lacking in vanity as she. But then he supposed a female with such natural beauty need not be too concerned about her looks. Except for a wash with soap and water, her lovely face required little upkeep.

Looking back on the previous day's shenanigans, Hereward realised his actions had been nothing but bluster and bluff. And it had backfired on him, spectacularly. He knew he could never let her go, which became apparent the moment his anger began to dissolve. His position had been a weak one from the start and she had routed him.

"Shouldn't that be Mrs Sleepy?" said Isabella groggily after a long reposeful pause. "I mean now we've agreed not to get divorced." Then a smirk slowly formed on her lips, followed by a cheeky grin.

"Still argumentative I see, little wench?" he said with mock sternness as his warm lips skimmed her cheek. "You'd still be Mrs Aldwen even if we were to go down that route. The title remains the same after a decree is made absolute. As far as I know, there's no separate title for a divorcee."

"I expect there isn't," she conceded. "Also, have you noticed a woman's title changes after marriage but a man's remains the same? Strange that."

Hereward arched an eyebrow as he wound his finger around one of her curls. "Has Maud been at it again?" he groaned. "Filling your innocent head with more feminist claptrap? The woman's a damned menace, an agitator, a threat to the very fabric of society."

"You don't mean that, surely?" said Isabella with a light laugh.

"I suppose not," he said half reluctantly.

"I'm glad. I mean it's impossible to disagree with some of her arguments on the situation of women in the industrial age."

"Yes, yes, yes," said Hereward with absent-minded dismissiveness as he checked his wristwatch. "Come along now. Look sharp. Time we were on parade, Mrs Aldwen," he winked. "Boyle's going to wonder where the devil we are."

We? thought Isabella as she looked at him from under her fringed eyelashes. Later today the abominable butler's in for a big surprise.

Boyle wasn't the only one in for a big surprise later. Likewise, Barbara wasn't expecting to see Isabella again. At least not inside the Hall. And the maid's offer to do the library was extraordinary, it being the most-arduous room in the house to dust and clean on account of the enormous number of books on display, not to mention all the additional items. To avoid disturbing him, Boyle always insisted on the work being finished before the master arrived at his desk. As a rule, Barbara left the library to Tilly, but on this occasion, she had a special task to perform.

As soon as she was certain the others were engaged elsewhere, Barbara went straight to the telephone and gingerly detached the receiver from its mount. Then, despite her shaking sweaty hands, she managed to dial the number recorded on a slip of paper stored in her uniform pocket. She knew she was taking a huge risk, so in case Boyle entered the room she had an excuse at the ready on her tongue; which was to say she was wiping the telephone, having noticed some stains were still remaining from the angry couple's inky altercation.

To Barbara's utmost relief, Rosalyn answered on the third ring. Speaking in a barely audible voice, the maid said: "Hello Miss, it's Barbara at the Hall. Mrs Aldwen's gone back to her parents."

"What?" mumbled Rosalyn woozily, hungover from another brandy binge.

"The mistress has gone, Miss," she whispered swiftly. "The master's chucked her out. Yesterday he took her back to her parents' place."

To her dismay, Barbara heard Boyle talking to Tilly outside the library door and in her panic almost dropped the receiver. However, by the time the butler scuttled in she was already wiping a fabricated stain on the telephone base. Fortunately for her, he failed to notice her shaking hands and the beads of sweat on her felonious forehead.

In fact, Boyle was too busy humming a happy tune to notice anything untoward that morning. He looked oddly cheerful, not his usual self at all. Barbara preferred him when he was austere and unapproachable. In his current incarnation he gave her the creeps.

"How are you getting on in here, young Barbara?" he asked, imitating the Major's patriciate tone.

"Very well, Mr Boyle. Just about to give the Major's desk a good going over with the polish."

"Very good. Now be sure to keep up the pace. There's still plenty to do and I want the place spick and span upon his return. I'm expecting him back any time now."

"Yes, Mr Boyle." One would think he was planning a celebration, thought Barbara. Next thing he'll be ordering old Jenkins to bake a celebration cake with coloured icing and decorations on the top.

"Did you manage to remove all the ink marks by the way?" enquired the butler.

"Yes, Sir. Although I don't mind saying it took some doing. It was a right old mess. The ink had gone everywhere. That girl's got quite a temper on her, I'll say."

"Yes, a most unfortunate state of affairs," he agreed. "Now it's time to move on for the Major's sake." Boyle shook his head before breaking into another tune and leaving Barbara to get on with her work.

Heaven, help us all, said the maid to herself. The butler's buzzing like a blasted bluebottle. Whatever next?

Upon receiving Barbara's wonderful news, Rosalyn felt ecstatic. She sat up in bed, closed her eyes, then opened them again, wide. Owing to her post-alcohol fugue, it had taken her mind a minute or two to assimilate the maid's whispered message. At first, she thought she was dreaming, until her head cleared and reality returned. The servant, she decided, was turning out to be a most-useful ally and she congratulated herself on her own ingenuity.

"Hurrah!" she whooped, throwing out her arms with joyful abandon. Hereward was free and back on the marriage market; or rather he would be once his divorce was granted, she reminded herself. She hoped Isabella had no plans to contest it. If so, it might be necessary to pay her off with a substantial sum. Which wasn't a problem. Even though tongues were bound to start wagging, Rosalyn cared little for societal condemnation. Why should she? Her sole objective was reclaiming her man and she felt quietly confident Hereward would now see she was his ideal woman.

In a tizzy, Rosalyn rang for her maid. She realised she needed to dress and apply her makeup in case Hereward arrived at her house unannounced. The whole situation, although terribly exciting, was an absolute torment, since she felt so utterly desperate to see him. In fact, she could barely wait to console him in her own special way. She even toyed with the idea of contacting him by telephone right away.

Unable to decide on her best course of action, Rosalyn lit a gold-tipped cigarette to settle her mind and lay back on a pile of fat feather pillows to ponder her dilemma. "Shall I? Shan't I?" she debated out loud. Then she remembered the importance of patience. Taking a deep drag on her cigarette, she blew a plume of smoke upwards, stared at the ceiling and imagined herself mistress of Aldwen Hall.

The moment he heard a set of wheels grind the gravel Boyle scurried straight to the front door. "Praise be, at last," he cried out loud. He wondered where the master had spent the night. Presumably at his in-laws agreeing the terms of separation and divorce from his wife. He hoped Hereward hadn't been too accommodating, otherwise it might turn out to be a costly dissolution. What with the insufferable Suffragettes and suchlike, women had become too vocal and demanding since being given the right to vote. Who knew what their next campaign might be? Still, no amount of money was too much to rid the Hall of that teenage terror. Naturally, Mr and Mrs Acton must be besides themselves, since the Major was such a great catch. And to be fair, he sympathised, their distress and disappointment were only to be expected. Anyhow, what was done was done. There's no point in crying over spilt milk, he mused, as he stood poised to greet his master and take his hat and coat.

Then with the look of someone who had just dropped a priceless vase on a flagstone floor, Boyle watched Major Aldwen climb out of the motorcar, stride around to the passenger side, open the door, and extend his arm. His tonsils almost exposed, the butler watched a slim, gloved hand slip into the Major's. After which outstepped the mistress. Like a queen, she mounted the steps and glided over the threshold, followed by her husband looking tired but undeniably pleased.

"Boyle be good enough to collect my wife's belongings from the rack and take them straight up to her room," prompted Hereward sharply, irritated by the butler's immobility.

"Yes of course, Sir," said Boyle in a flash, spurred on by the imperative inflection in his master's voice.

Isabella rushed straight upstairs with a delighted Tilly, who had been left bereft by the loss of her mistress. She felt glad she had insisted on having Tilly as her personal maid. After long deliberation, Hereward had yielded to her demand despite Boyle's vehement protestations. Although she tried not to gloat, the look on the butler's defeated face gave her a huge measure of satisfaction. Nevertheless, she expected more battles ahead before he backed down and accepted his place; assuming he ever would.

Chapter 53

After four months of marriage, most of them fraught with tension, Isabella began to feel a small measure of affection for Hereward, although why that was, she had no idea. He must be growing on me, she said to herself. She was also learning to handle him in her own sweet way with some small success. However, in spite of her best efforts, changing his brassbound views on women wearing trousers was proving to be a humongous mountain to climb.

Slipping a humbug into her mouth, Isabella began to suck it. The striped tablet tasted sensational. The moment it started to melt, turning all soft and gooey, she felt compelled to chew it.

"What if I restrict myself to wearing the trousers in the house and promise not to go out in them? Or if I do, I'll wear them under a long coat," she pleaded as the sweet treat stimulated her tastebuds. Still, she was nothing if not persistent in her efforts to persuade Hereward to agree a compromise. And as she awaited his response, she continued chewing with enthusiasm.

"No," he said from behind his desk with a firmness that indicated there was no room for negotiation. "You know full well my views on females in male apparel. It's not worthy of you, my dear."

Using her tongue, Isabella transferred the humbug, now

moist and sticky with saliva, to the pocket of her right cheek.

"I must say that's an awfully outdated attitude," she asserted before running her tongue over her teeth. Bits of humbug had become lodged in her dental crevices. She felt tempted to dislodge the sticky fragments with her fingernail, but the stern expression on Hereward's face soon dissuaded her.

The humbug was from her favourite high-street confectioners. A place she frequented on a regular basis, and where some weeks she spent a sizeable slice of her allowance. The colourful shop stocked an impressive selection of chocolates and candies, all of which she planned to sample over the coming months. She had even considered opening an account there for the sole purpose of having Boyle settle her bills. Since the shop sold only edibles, he was welcome to as many details of her purchases as he wished. In her mind's eye, Isabella pictured the butler with a pointed pencil trawling her bill a line at a time: bonbons, wine gums, barley sugars, pear drops, sherbet lemons, aniseed twists...

With the sobriety of a judge at the bench, Hereward ordered her to finish munching whatever was in her mouth before continuing the conversation.

Isabella stopped chewing and cast him a childish look. She felt sorely tempted to stick out her tongue at him. His stringency often had that effect on her. And although his bearing at that point in their interaction indicated it would be wise to withdraw, on impulse she removed a wrinkled white-paper bag from her cardigan pocket, untwisted the top and held it out to him.

"Would you like a humbug?" she asked with her cheekiest smile. "I must say they're awfully yummy. But I'm still to decide if this one's my favourite flavour."

To Isabella's amusement, Hereward beheld the bag as if it were a packet of mouse poison.

"Thank you, but no thank you," he said with a pronounced note of disapproval in his voice.

"All the more for me then," she replied, bright eyed, flashing him a simian smile, the last of the humbug dissolving on her tongue. She had to admit, she derived a certain satisfaction from getting up Hereward's obstinate nose. However, something in his demeanour: its strictness, its severity, its disparaging response to a humbug from a humble paper bag sent Isabella into a fit of hysterics. With her body shaking like a loose jelly, her hand compressing her mouth, her eyes streaming with tears, as she imagined her po-faced husband sucking a hard-boiled sweet, she ran to the sitting room, collapsed on the sofa and clutched her sides until the paroxysm passed.

With a long-suffering sigh and a slight shake of his head, Hereward ignored Isabella's silliness, picked up his pen and went back to his work. He realised his wife still had some growing up to do; a factor he had failed to take into account when he married her.

Henceforth, despite their best efforts to coexist in peace and harmony, the couple's discords continued on almost a daily basis. Aldwen Hall, once a bastion of soothing serenity, had become a battleground of grudges, grumbles and grievances. Their marital combats often cast the house in a cloud of enervating vitiation. And barely a week went by without some dispute or other about Isabella's conduct, or rather misconduct.

One particular contentious and intractable issue was her visits to the cinema with her new friend, Martha. Hereward, who was yet to embrace the modern age of entertainment, painted picture houses and public houses with the same tainted brush. As Isabella returned from town one Thursday afternoon another quarrel broke out between them.

Hereward had on a new smoking jacket in the latest style

which Isabella found rather fetching. He looked like a Hollywood star, but sounded like a schoolmaster.

"Isabella!" he said, emphasising her name as if he were chiding a child. "Why must you always insist on being such a rebel?"

Isabella glared at him, boldness engraved in her eyes, as he treated her to one of his routine rants.

"From what I gather there's been a paucity of parental control in your upbringing," he informed her with a condemnatory air. "You've been poorly supervised and allowed to run wild with a group of wasters and vagabonds who wouldn't look out of place in a Dickensian novel."

As Isabella sniggered at the description of her former friends, Hereward gave her a warning look that froze her face. It had never occurred to her that he was unaccustomed to having his orders flouted. Had the men once under his command defied him the way she did, he would have dealt with them so severely they would not have transgressed again a second time.

"I must also remind you that I'm not unacquainted with your feral ways," he went on. "I refer to the time you and that rabble you were so fond of running around with decimated my fruit trees."

Isabella's face turned a rubescent red. "Well why don't you hire me a strict governess?" she returned with irreverence. "You know one of those martinet types one hears about marching up and down the corridors at boarding school in case some poor famished child sneaks out of bed after lights out to visit the larder." After which she stretched her mouth into a tight-lipped smile guaranteed to nettle him.

Hereward's cheek twitched. "That's quite enough, young lady. Damned impertinence."

"Well, what do you expect?" she replied, looking at him

with cool contempt.

His nostrils flared in anger. "I expect respect, that's what I expect," he stated in a strained voice.

"I'm afraid you're very much mistaken if you think that respect is a prerogative. Respect must be earned. And it travels in both directions."

Snubbing her words, Hereward launched into a husbandly tirade in which he asserted: "As my wife I expect you to adhere to standards of behaviour and conduct befitting a lady of your class and marital status."

"Oh, I do wish you would stop being such a pompous prig, Hereward," she complained, disregarding the undertone of threat in his voice. "You object to whatever I do. I have to say it's getting terribly tiresome." Then she patted her open mouth and simulated a yawn.

Hereward glowered at her. Never in his life had he been subjected to such blatant disrespect. To be described as a pompous prig by his very own wife infuriated him. Yet despite her provocation, he managed to control his temper. But only just. Controlling his temper with Isabella was an ongoing battle which he sometimes lost.

"I must also advise you to be more judicious in your choice of language," he said stoutly.

Isabella stood for a moment in mindful suspension. Then without knowing what came over her, she treated him to an enactment of sarcastic mockery.

"Yes Major!" she half shouted, stamped her foot and hammed a salute. But the second she saw the *Major's* scalded face, her vocal cords jammed in her throat and she beat a rapid retreat from the room.

Isabella got as far as the foot of the staircase before two powerful hands grabbed hold of her and lifted her clean off her feet. To avoid alerting the servants to her pink-faced predicament, she offered up no resistance as she found herself conveyed to the sitting room as if she were a tailor's dummy.

Dumping her down hard on the sofa, Hereward stood over her with his legs apart and his hands on his hips. Despite being enraged by her simulated obeisance, his fury was in part mitigated by his inner amusement; making her behaviour doubly difficult to deal with. It was like trying to manage a deviant but adorable monkey. Short of locking her up, he didn't know what the devil to do with her.

Knowing there was no chance of escape, and fearing what he might do next, Isabella kept quiet, hunched her shoulders and focused her attention on her fidgety fingers in her lap.

Hereward stretched himself to his full height and stared down at his wife. While half of him wanted to throttle her, the other half wanted to hoot with laughter. Taking hold of her chin, he raised her face to his and forced her to look at him.

"You clearly derive some sort of perverse pleasure from your childish gibes. But be mindful my precious that your procacious conduct doesn't one day unleash the monster in me."

Nervous now, Isabella cast her eyes downwards and bit her thumbnail involuntarily.

"Isabella!" he bellowed.

Startled, her eyes shot back up and she looked at him like a frightened calf.

"Stop, chewing, your fingernail. It's a most unattractive habit." Then with the air of a military man, he turned swiftly on his heels, exited the room and left her huddled on the sofa.

Isabella groaned inwardly and wondered if she would ever grow accustomed to her husband's high-handedness.

The following day upon entering the library, Isabella found Hereward sitting beside the hearth smacking his palm with an old leather riding crop. She looked at it with dubious eyes, then at him.

"Haven't used one of these for ages," he said holding her gaze.

"Yes, I know you no longer ride and the stables lie empty. Maud once happened to mention you suffer from asthma."

"Allergic asthma to be precise. I developed a rare allergy to horses in adulthood. Exposure triggers an attack in my case. Not only horses, but also dogs and cats. Any animal dander I expect is an aggravating factor."

The issue of Hereward's health had not been raised prior to their marriage. Not that it would have made any difference to her selfish father.

"Do you miss riding?" she asked out of genuine interest as she settled herself in the seat opposite his.

A reflective expression came into Hereward's eyes. "Yes, at first I missed it terribly," he admitted. "But I've come to accept it. Well, I don't exactly have a choice. I had to sell the horses of course, which was a bit of a wrench."

While Isabella sat looking concerned about his health issue, Hereward's eyes travelled over her form and face. At least I have a lovely new filly with which to console myself, he thought. Not that she would have appreciated being described in equine terms had she known.

"Yes, I'm sure losing the horses must have been dreadful," she sympathised. "But you're well now, aren't you?"

"Yes, I'm fine," he assured her. "Eradicating the root cause appears to have been successful in my case. The clean country air helps of course, which is why being back on English soil is a blessing. Some parts of the subcontinent were incredibly dusty because of the hot arid climate, not to mention the choking sandstorms. We had to ride like the clappers to outrun them. Although fortunately not very often."

"That must have been terribly exciting?" said Isabella as she imagined how dashing he must have looked in his uniform bestride a stallion. Suddenly embarrassed by her runaway thoughts, she blushed inwardly, lowered her eyes and examined her nails.

Hereward laughed. "I'm not too sure about that. It didn't exactly feel exciting at the time. I'm grateful I don't have hay fever too, otherwise I'd have to relocate to the town in spring and summer. And I should hate that."

"I heard somewhere that asthma's a nervous condition," she said looking up.

"Yes, so have I, but I suspect that's just an old wives' tale. Recent research seems to suggest there's a genetic component involved in the disease's development. But as far as I'm aware, none of my forbears suffered from it."

The door opened and Boyle entered with the tea tray. With the solemnity of a priest laying out the sacred vessels, he set down the tea things on the table between them.

"Will that be all, Sir?" he said, ignoring Isabella.

"Yes, thank you, Boyle."

The couple remained silent until he vacated the room.

"Still, the most important thing is that I'm not allergic to my lovely new wife, although I strongly suspect she's allergic to me," Hereward said with a rueful ring to his voice.

Ignoring the remark, Isabella lifted the silver teapot. Her insistence on pouring her husband's tea had usurped one of Boyle's favourite duties. And the butler was powerless to object as Hereward was delighted with her small devotion.

Chapter 54

A few days after discussing Hereward's health issue, Isabella returned from her walk just in time for tea. Yet again, she had felt eyes on her intermittently while she wandered the estate. But as usual, determined and undeterred, she discounted the sensation and carried on regardless, having decided, as a matter of principle, she would not be discouraged from exploring her husband's ancestral property because of some strange unaccountable impression.

As she entered the library Isabella came upon Hereward and Boyle poring over a selection of chintz swatches. With his head bent forward, the butler was studying a selection of small squares of fabric spread out on the desk and proffering his opinions. She resented the way he stood close to her husband, as if they were colleagues, or friends even, rather than master and servant. For some reason, it made her feel uncomfortable and spoiled her mood. Indeed, she thought the lickspittle was taking a liberty.

Isabella coughed to signal her presence. "What's all this?" she asked in a querulous voice.

"Ah darling, there you are," said Hereward, sidestepping Boyle. "The swatches have at last arrived." Expecting her to be pleased, he slid them across the desktop towards her.

Paying them no heed, Isabella stood motionless and fixed her eyes on her husband's smiling face.

Meantime, Boyle coughed into his fist, excused himself and withdrew from the room, leaving in his wake a strong whiff of hair wax.

"Why wasn't I invited to look at the swatches first?" she complained. "Or is the blessed butler choosing the fabrics for my new room now? Is there a single thing that man doesn't have a hand in?"

"Do calm down, my sweet. If you'll permit me to explain."

Isabella placed a hand on her hip, raised her eyebrows, pursed her lips, and waited.

Hereward took this as a cue to continue. "When Boyle brought in the package containing the swatches with the rest of the mail, he happened to mention the overgrown garden. As you know, we desperately need a new gardener. One who's reliable and clean. Since I opened the swatches in his presence, we had a quick gander. It was all perfectly innocent, I promise. I was intending to show them to you as soon as you arrived back from your wander."

"Oh really. How magnanimous. I must say, you're far too kind," she said with sneering sarcasm.

"Must you misinterpret everything?" he replied in a tone more combative than conciliatory.

Isabella felt tempted to slap Hereward on both cheeks this time; however, she controlled herself, having learned her lesson in the past.

"You can forget the new fabrics," she said with roiling resentment. "And you can forget the new room. In fact, you can forget the entire refurbishment too, because I've no intention of sleeping there, ever. I shall continue with the current arrangement. That is to say, I shall continue to sleep in the guest room. Which I'm sure you'll agree better befits my status here."

Hereward looked at his wife with grave concern, sighed

heavily and said: "Isabella darling, don't say that. Come here, please."

"I most certainly will not," she asserted. Then she stomped upstairs to her room, threw herself on the bed and punched her pillow.

Throughout dinner that evening, Isabella's mouth remained tight-lipped with taciturnity and she resisted Hereward's attempts to engage her in conversation, no matter how hard he tried. As for the swatches, since she refused to look at them, they remained on his desk. She doubted her indomitable mother would have tolerated Boyle's audacity, so why should she?

Men can be such insensitive creatures, Isabella mused as she supped a cup of Ovaltine in the sitting room. But instead of listening to the wireless, which is what he generally did after dinner, Hereward was playing *The Threatened Cloud Had Passed Away* from *The Mikado* on the piano. Whether the song choice was a deliberate attempt on his part to inject a touch of humour into the situation she couldn't be sure, but she curtly declined his invitation to sit beside him on the stool.

That night when Hereward visited her bed, Isabella conveyed her continuing displeasure by lying at the extreme edge of the mattress with her back to him, having decided she was unwilling to roll over like an obedient dog and forgive his omissions. She was tired of his insensitivity, tired of being taken for granted, and tired of having her feelings ridden roughshod over. Moreover, she knew no better way to communicate her resentment than rebuffing him in the bedroom.

For his part, Hereward recognised that most marriages had their own unique set of problems and his was no different in that respect. There had been few issues with the staff before

Isabella moved to the Hall and he found it difficult to deal with her discontents.

"Look here, Isabella, if you must sulk, then at least wait until morning. Now is not the time," he said, desire burning deep inside him.

"I'm given no say in anything. After our heart-to-heart at the hotel, you promised things would be different, but I'm afraid to say little has changed. What's more, I'm sick of playing second fiddle to that slimy sycophant of yours," she protested as he switched off the light.

"Really, darling, this perpetual pettiness on your part is beginning to wear thin. You've made your point. I've already explained what happened and I don't intend to go on repeating myself. Now it's time you moved on."

"You treat me like a child."

"You behave like one," he countered.

"I most certainly do not."

"You most certainly do. Before we know it, you'll be stamping your infantile feet and having another one of your blessed tantrums."

Incensed, Isabella moved to get up from the mattress.

A powerful arm like a tentacle encircled her waist, pulled her down and onto her back.

Furious now, Isabella fought hard to free herself from Hereward's grasp, but he held onto her while he laughed at her scowling contortions.

"Remove your hands from my person right now," she insisted. She was careful not to slap him despite the extreme provocation.

"So, my sweet sparrow, you've decided to play hard to get, have you?" Hereward teased as his breath warmed her face and the subtle scent of testosterone infused her nostrils.

The silly endearment only served to further antagonise her

and, twisting this way and that, she doubled her efforts to extricate herself from his firm hold.

Under the spell of an uncontrollable passion, Hereward hoisted her nightdress by its hem and began to kiss her all over. Her silken-soft nakedness tasted ambrosial on his lips.

Isabella, in no mood for his lovemaking, blocked him with her elbow and yanked her nightdress back down.

"Get your hands off me you animal," she hissed.

With ease of effort, he raised it again, pinned her to the bed and straddled her.

Driven by anger, modesty, and a refusal to submit to his physical mastery, at least not without a struggle, she squeezed her thighs together as tightly as she was able.

However, instead of having a deterrent effect, Isabella's fierce resistance stoked Hereward's tumescence like a propellant thrown on a bonfire. Eager to luxuriate in her creamy comeliness, rising royally to the challenge, his superior strength assuring success, he manoeuvred himself into position and prepared to conquer his bodacious combatant. Then the moment he felt her parry begin to ebb, he raised his body and attempted to force his knee between her legs.

But without warning, a searing pain tore through his loins like a locomotive as something roundly solid rammed into his most-vulnerable region. In the throes of agony, fighting the urge to vomit, Hereward rolled off her, doubled up, cupped his belaboured love-bulbs in his hands, and swore an oath.

And while he coughed, groaned and spluttered, Isabella sprinted straight to the bathroom, banged shut the door and locked herself in. After which she raised her eyes to the ceiling and exhaled a colossal sigh of relief. Convinced she was safe, she padded across the floor and settled herself into the wicker chair in the corner. She had no idea how long Hereward would take to recover, or what he would do after that.

Glancing around the room, Isabella felt suddenly fatigued by her strenuous struggle. As her eyes settled on the bathtub, it occurred to her to grab several large towels from the linen cupboard and make herself a temporary bed. Once she felt sure Hereward was fast asleep in his own room, she could safely return to hers. But as she prepared to rise from the chair, something hard struck the bathroom door with such force she feared it would fly off its hinges. There followed the sounds of wood splitting and the bolt breaking free from the doorframe. Then with a tremendous bang, the door exploded into the bathroom and rebounded off the wall.

Her eyes the size of saucers, Isabella sprang to her feet like a firecracker. To her horror, Hereward stood framed in the doorway, his legs splayed, his palms on the doorposts and his face a furnace.

Terrified by what he might do to her in his rage, she dropped back into the seat, looked at her lap, and trembled like a distressed dog.

However, as Hereward beheld his wife's terror-stricken face and cowering form in the corner, he was overcome by a profound sense of shame and self-loathing. He felt like a brute. He was a brute. There was no better word to describe him. Kneeling in front of her, he proffered his profuse apologies and defended his action as a reflex reaction to the shock of sudden severe pain.

Refusing to look at him, Isabella sank deeper into the seat, crossed her arms over her breasts and tucked her hands under her armpits.

Hereward offered her his hand. "Please sweetheart, come back to bed. There's no way in the world I would ever harm you. You have my word," he promised in a penitent tone.

"If you don't mind, I'd prefer to be left alone," she said in a quivery, timorous voice.

"Very well, if that's what you wish. I'll say goodnight then."

After he left, Isabella sat motionless and stared into space for a substantial time. Once she recovered her calm, she got up and examined the broken lock on the door. The servants will have plenty to say about that in the morning, she remarked to herself.

Maud was furious with her brother, absolutely furious. Isabella had burst into tears on her last visit. One kind word from Maud was all it took for the whole sorry tale of the swatches to come tumbling out. She adored Hereward's wife, who was more like a younger sister to her than a sister-in-law. Maud felt very protective of her and couldn't bear to see her upset.

"Whatever were you thinking?" she asked Hereward later over the telephone.

"It was nothing intentional," he assured her. "I'm afraid Isabella's far too sensitive in many respects. Especially regarding the damned butler."

"And you, Hereward, are much too insensitive in many respects. Now you must make it up to her as soon as possible," she advised. "Otherwise, such incidents can become festering sores that weep for a lifetime."

"Very well," he said, rolling his eyes. "I'll take her somewhere fancy for afternoon tea. That should soon sort it. You know how she loves her food. Strange really," he added after a thoughtful pause.

"What is?" enquired Maud.

"How often she turns up late for afternoon tea."

"She's still young," returned Maud, hoping to appeal to his better nature. "You really must learn to make allowances for her age, and I'm sure a little extra patience and empathy on your part wouldn't go amiss. And anyhow, why afternoon tea? Why not dinner at a first-rate restaurant? Make the effort, my dear, and take her somewhere romantic for a change. Treat her like an adult instead of a child. And you never know, a romantic dinner may even pay dividends."

"Very well, dear sister, dinner it is," he said with resignation.

"Good. I'm sure a little fine dining will put a huge smile on her face, which is more than can be said for you at the moment. But seriously, Hereward, you really must make a greater effort with regards to your relationship. Stop taking the girl for granted. She gets bored at the Hall. Dreadfully bored. Just because you are content with the life of a recluse doesn't give you the right to impose the same lifestyle on your wife. What's more, you have your writing. Tell me, what does Isabella have?"

"I should think Isabella has everything a woman needs and no worries," he replied dismissively. "It beats me why she doesn't appreciate her many privileges. Most ladies would give their eye teeth to have her charmed life. Still, there's no pleasing some people."

As Maud listened to her clueless brother, she wanted to throw up her hands in despair. "Really my dear boy, you must be the only person on this entire planet who is capable of striking me dumb. I'm surprised Isabella hasn't tried to murder you in your sleep."

Chapter 55

As Isabella despaired of her stifling, stormy marriage, Hereward's behaviour began to improve. To make amends for the swatch debacle, he took her out to dinner at a top restaurant with no expense spared. He was not only grateful for his sister's sensible suggestion but also happy to take the credit. Isabella, however, was no fool and suspected Maud of playing peacemaker behind the scenes. So, all was forgiven and forgotten and peace restored to the Hall until, that is, Martha invited Isabella to see the latest release at Oakwich's new cinema.

Since visiting the cinema was Isabella's favourite pastime, she accepted her friend's invitation with avidity. Desperate to escape the repetitive routines of her pedestrian life, she welcomed the opportunity to immerse herself in one of the most, if not the most, popular amusements of the early twentieth century. However, before setting out, Isabella remembered she must inform Hereward of her plans, since he insisted on knowing her whereabouts whenever she went off the estate. It was only after getting married she came to realise the level of freedom she had enjoyed as a single girl.

At the end of the midday meal Isabella reminded herself she must make haste to avoid being late for her date with Martha. After swallowing a large measure of water and dabbing her mouth with her napkin, she glanced across the table at

Hereward to assess his mood. His posture appeared relaxed and his facial expression neutral, which she judged to be positive signs. Discarding her napkin, she beamed up her brightest smile and began to speak.

"Oh, by the way, I'm meeting Martha this afternoon…"

"Martha?" Hereward interjected.

"Yes, Martha," she confirmed. "You know, the lady who owns the dress shop. I've made mention of her before on a couple of occasions. Anyhow, Thursday's half-day closing, so we're planning to visit the new picture house. The one that overlooks the town square. You must have seen it under construction when you visited the bank. The day it opened they held a ceremony of sorts and some local dignitary or other unveiled a plaque. I must say the new cinemas are becoming enormously popular. I expect that's why they're springing up all over the place. Well anyway, we're hoping to catch the matinee as it's less crowded during the daytime and I can be back well before dinner."

Hereward stiffened and scrunched his napkin with slow deliberation. "I'm not sure you should be patronising such places, my dear."

"Why ever not?" asked Isabella with a brief but incredulous chuckle.

Pushing back his chair, Hereward stood up in preparation to leave the room. "For one thing you're too young, that's why. You appear to think you can do whatever you like whenever it suits you."

Although Isabella believed his attitude bordered on medieval, she persevered in the hope that a little education might prove more persuasive than a verbal joust.

"It's called the Palace," she said, hoping the name would lend the place a little gravitas and prestige.

"The Palace?" Hereward parroted as a question, a deep

crevice forming in the centre of his brow.

"Yes, the Palace," she confirmed with the flash of another blinding smile that revealed all but her very back teeth. Her face was beginning to ache with the sheer effort she felt forced to put in.

"Well, that's a misnomer if ever I heard one," said Hereward acidly.

"I'm afraid you're wrong," said Isabella bravely. "The Palace is really rather plush. It's carpeted, and has upholstered seats and curtains similar to those at the theatre. Oh, and there's a huge screen above a stage. The new cinemas are nothing like the old flea pits you must be thinking of. You know, those infamous firetraps in converted buildings with small screens, hard seats, concrete floors, and no balconies."

Hereward, however, remained mulishly unconvinced. "I don't give a fat fig how plush the appointments are. Picture houses, palaces, cinemas, film theatres, the flicks even, or whatever else the confounded things are called these days, are unseemly. What's more, they're not meant for people like us," he said with strong emphasis.

"Whatever do you mean by *unseemly* and *people like us*?" asked Isabella.

"I *mean* that the cinema's meant for the masses. It serves as a distraction. A distraction that enables them to escape the harsh reality of their miserable lives for a few hours a week. It gives them something to aspire to while rendering them insensate at the same time. In other words, it prevents them from rioting and organising against the Government. As long as France has its film industry, its rulers needn't fear another bloody revolution."

Isabella couldn't believe her ears. "You consider everything outside your cloistered world unseemly," she asserted.

"Excuse me?"

"I'm surprised you haven't taken holy orders," she said with a churlish chuckle. "You know you'd make the perfect priest."

Swiftly sidestepping the issue and apprising his wife's upper body with wolfish eyes, Hereward said in a voice soft as suede: "Come to think of it, I did once consider taking holy orders, but the obligatory vow of celibacy soon dissuaded me." Then after a significant pause, he added: "You see I enjoy bedtimes too much."

On cue, Isabella's cheeks glowed the deepest red on the spectrum. Despite having done nothing shameful, she shrivelled up with shame all the same. Hereward knew full well how to unseat her and he revelled in her predictable discomfort. How she wished she could stop squirming every time he voiced a vulgarity. But rather than argue, she pressed on in a final effort to convince him.

"They have talkies now and it's truly amazing to hear the dialogue coming straight from the actors' mouths instead of having to read subtitles on the screen. Plus, it makes the action appear all the more convincing and much less hammy. So, you see, the cinema has more in common with the theatre than you think."

Hereward felt a momentary twinge of guilt as he beheld Isabella's bright eyes brimming with enthusiasm. Until, that is, he pictured those same eyes ogling some handsome young heartthrob on the screen and a pang of jealousy pierced his heart.

"It's damned decadence," he said, still rankled. "I forbid you to go anywhere near that place. You're not spending decent money on indecent forms of entertainment." Realistically, he knew it would be impossible to confine her to the house, since she would simply sneak out as soon as he turned his back. And locking her in her room as an extreme measure might prove counterproductive, as she would more than likely climb out of the window and slide down the drainpipe. She might be agile but she could still injure herself should the brackets come loose. And as he continued his internal deliberations, he began to feel more like a parent than a spouse.

Isabella sniggered. Then with undisguised glee she delivered the blow Hereward least expected.

"Incidentally, Maud and Cynthia are joining Martha and me for next week's matinee. So, you see *people like us* do visit the cinema. In fact, Maud says it's a great social leveller. Oh, and she has offered to drive me back here. I may even ask her to pay for my ticket too, since as well as being a killjoy you are now also a pinchpenny. Plus, it's all arranged, so I suggest you discuss your objections with your dear sister."

Isabella then rose from her chair in triumph as Hereward sat down in defeat. Nevertheless, as she left the room, she made sure to give him a wide berth in case he grabbed her and held her on his knee to delay her deliberately.

Well, that's that, I suppose, he said in his head. What more can a chap say?

Left alone, Hereward drummed his fingers on the table. Then he smiled with secret satisfaction as he consoled himself with the thought that the matronly Maud made an excellent if unwitting chaperone. With his senior sibling in attendance, no man would dare go near his beautiful wife.

Following a few magical hours of viewing a musical extravaganza on the silver screen, with a large bag of liquorice sticks in her lap, supplemented by a vanilla ice cream in the interval, Isabella hurried back to the Hall. On this occasion she was determined not to be late. For one thing, she preferred to avoid putting Hereward in an even worse mood than the one he was in when she went out.

Upon entering the house, she threw off her coat and dashed

straight upstairs to begin getting ready for dinner. She always enjoyed the ritual of her evening bath and often steeped in the water until her skin wrinkled. Since the lock on the bathroom door was still awaiting repair, Isabella took the precaution of pushing the wicker chair up against the door to prevent access.

The steam-filled room felt as humid and as warm as a rainforest. After stripping off her clothes and climbing into the big enamel bathtub filled almost to the brim, Isabella picked up a virgin bar of ivory soap and sniffed it. The scents of aloe, clover and buttercup reminded her of summer meadows. After dipping it into the water and rubbing it with vigour between her hands, she lathered her wet skin from top to toe. Then she slid even lower into the bathtub, closed her eyes and slipped into a trance.

The sudden sound of chair legs scraping across the tiled floor wrenched Isabella from her reverie. Upon opening her eyes, she was astonished to see Hereward in the bathroom. As he stood staring at her, she felt thankful the bulk of her body lay submerged below the waterline in a light meringue of soap suds. But to be doubly sure, she grabbed the washcloth to shield the shell of her precious pink pearl. And knowing the suds would soon solvate, she crossed her arms over her breasts to conceal them as best she could.

"What in heaven's name do you think you're doing? How dare you!" she said, fixing him with a storm-force stare.

Hereward made no answer. Brazenly undeterred, his eyes dark and dazzling as two Tahitian pearls, he continued to gaze at her. Since the day of their betrothal, he had longed to see her naked. To his frustration, every time he made love to her, she insisted on wearing her Victorian-style nightdress and having the lights out. Despite countless attempts on his part, it had proved impossible to persuade her otherwise, which was why he decided to turn the damaged lock into an opportunity.

Outraged still, Isabella bawled: "Get out of here, you despicable creature. A true gentleman doesn't intrude on a lady's privacy."

Like a panther, Hereward inched forward and perched on the edge of the bathtub, intrigued to discover if the pelt of her luxuriant love-mound was as pale as the hair on her head. But unfortunately, the washcloth prevented further enquiry.

"Please Hereward," begged Isabella, "respect my privacy." She felt sure her hot face would shortly catch fire.

Hereward, however, refused to comply, so she pleaded with him a second time, and a third.

"We're married my alluring little lioness," he reminded her with a cheeky grin. "As your husband it's my right to see you without your clothes on."

"Indeed, it is not!" she retorted with righteous indignation. "Your behaviour is beyond the pale. Have you no decency?"

The longer he went on looking, the more Isabella felt tempted to throw the wet washcloth at him. But then she recognised that removing her hands would be playing right into his. Not knowing what else to do, she glowered at him and issued the only threat she could think of.

"If you don't leave this room this instant I shall scream. Then the servants will hear me, and you know what frightful gossips they can be, given half a chance."

With the most-maddening smirk imaginable, Hereward thrust his hand deep inside his trouser pocket, withdrew a large lawn handkerchief, then scrunched it into a tight ball.

"Blackmail is a nefarious crime my little water nymph," said he. "Open your lovely mouth to scream and I shall mute you with this makeshift gag."

The glint in his eyes assured her he was only joking and defused some of the tension in the room.

"Why hasn't the lock been replaced?" Isabella enquired

prosaically in an attempt to divert his attention and douse his ardour.

"You'll have to ask Boyle about that," he said briskly.

As if she would.

To Hereward his wife looked and smelled as lemony fresh as a moonflower. As his pulse quickened and he grew incandescent with desire, it took him a mountain of self-control not to strip off his clothes, dive into the water and ravish her there and then.

"Dinner's at eight," he said by way of reminder. Then he blew her a kiss and returned to his room. Having seen slightly more of his wife's adorable assets than before, he could barely wait until bedtime.

Chapter 56

In the cold evening air, crouched low, his face interposed between two leafy laurels, his mouth hanging open, hungry and desperate for a smoke, Parker's eyes remained trained on the Hall. Over at the farm the bull could be heard bellowing in the barn, while the leaves quivered in the breeze and the familiar diurnal sounds slowly diminished. Lost in concentration, he retracted his lips, scratched his armpit, then his groin, then his backside.

No matter how many times he saw her, it was never enough to satisfy him. He thought about her constantly, and to the near exclusion of all else. Had he still been a teenage boy, Parker would have called his obsession a crush. He knew she belonged to another and could never be his, so he had to be content with using his imagination. For hours on end, he imagined her face, her figure, her unconsciously slow, sexy walk. A walk with a marked difference from the consciously saucy saunter of those he called sluts, and whom he paid to service his needs whenever he could afford to.

Parker's disappointment at catching only a glimpse of his fiddle-footed donna that day was palpable. It was akin to losing a pound and finding a penny. Especially since he had been waiting since morning to see her. Apart from the cold temperature, the weather had been almost perfect for viewing purposes. But to his profound regret she had dashed off elsewhere, and he had seen her only briefly on her return when she placed her bicycle back in the outhouse.

As dusk continued to drop, the Hall's windows lit up one at a time. The yellow apertures in its dark edifice made the house look majestic until the heavy drapes were drawn. The glow of electric lighting fascinated Parker, reminding him of summer sunshine. At home he relied on oil lamps and candles moulded from animal fats. Not that he minded, but they made the place reek something rotten. Unlike the imposingly handsome Hall, by the time he returned home his cottage would look cold, dark and uninviting.

Parker regretted giving up his gardening job at the Hall for one nearer home. Had he known the young lady would be coming to live there, he would have stayed on. As his eyes travelled over the doors, walls and windows, it occurred to him that he had never been further inside the house than the kitchen. The lovely warm kitchen that smelled of wholesomeness, but where the corpulent cook always looked at him as if he were a maggot as soon as she caught sight of him. Parker sneered at the thought of the formidable female's fat gut, fat bosom and fat limbs. Eliza Jenkins, he decided, was the sort of bint a man would only take as a last resort.

Wiping his nose on his sleeve, Parker attempted to figure out which window belonged to the beauty's boudoir. He knew posh couples slept in separate suites. Why even their clothes had their own rooms, he mused with a sardonic smile. Over in the slums of Oakwich entire families shared one bedbug-infested bedroom where silverfish and other creepies crawled out from beneath the floorboards and skirting after dark. He told himself that if the little lady were his wife, he would have no truck with sleeping apart. Once he had finished bedding her, he would hold her tight in his tattooed arms all night long, then hump her again first thing in the morning.

In his mind's eye, Parker pictured her in the nightgown he sometimes saw attached to the clothesline with dolly pegs. It was usually hanging next to her lily-white drawers. How spotless her clothes looked as they flapped like sails in the wind. When possible, he planned to pilfer a pair of the cute little pretties to add to his keepsake collection. Ideally, he preferred a lady's intimates to be unlaundered. But that would mean sneaking into the laundry room on a washday and whipping them out from under the maid's morose nose. Too risky, he decided, after given the matter some thought.

Agitated all of a sudden, Parker stood up, stretched his neck, narrowed his eyes, and looked at each window in turn. After many weeks spent observing the house, he had noticed the bathroom light flicked on at almost the same time every evening. Since he understood the finest folk bathed before dressing for dinner, he assumed it must be the mistress's regular bath time. Had the windowpane been clear instead of frosted glass, he would have risked shinning his bulk up the drainpipe and sneaking a peek at the beauty in her bathtub. The thought of her naked body submerged in bubbly suds made his breathing fast and his face shine purple.

Regarding his own personal hygiene, Parker remained impervious to his own polluted pong, pungent as a polecat's. Rarely did he wash, or brush his disintegrating teeth. The last time he begrimed a bathtub was months since in the town's public bathhouse, where once in a while society's poorest and most downtrodden reacquainted themselves with soap and hot water. Sixpence paid for a soak in a stained, chipped-enamel bathtub, a sliver of lather-resistant carbolic soap and a tiny returnable towel, abrasive as tree bark. After he climbed out, he always left behind him a legacy of sheep-shit-grey scum around the vessel's rim.

Near to where Parker stood, a late party of plump-chested

pigeons pecked at a few crumbs of stale bread on the grass strip that bordered the gravel. At the same time, the surly maid appeared at the dining-room window to draw the drapes. Oh my, thought he, that dumpy sow's a sour one, with a face that could curdle cream in a second. The thought of food made Parker feel famished. Famished for a slice of tender roast pigeon; or pigeon pie made with shortcrust pastry, like the one his mother used to bake specially for him. Licking his lips, he decided to bait a few birds on the morrow.

Since the wind was getting up and the dusk thickening, Parker decided to head home. He liked to whistle while he walked. Usually, a soldier's trench song or something catchy he could march to. It helped to maintain his momentum. Thankfully, the air although damp and dewy showed no sign of rain at that moment.

When he reached the lakeside, Parker took a brief break and sat on the same log the little lady usually occupied whenever she watched the ducks and other wildlife on the water. He thought he detected a hint of her perfume impregnated in the black bark. Emitting an abrupt high-pitched whistle through puckered lips, he thought of his big hairy buttocks on the same surface graced by her perfect rear on a regular basis. He felt reluctant to leave until his belly gurgled to remind him it was hours since he had eaten. Getting up with a geriatric groan, he continued on his way.

After plodding the path for ten minutes or so, Parker crossed over to the less-travelled track that marked a diagonal route to his cottage. At that time of day, the nocturnal creatures were slowly clocking on for the nightshift, and would shortly be busy devouring their weaker neighbours with relish. Oh, to be a predator, he thought, sucking in a breath with an intense shudder of pleasure.

As he went on walking, Parker's thoughts returned to the

Major's wife. The little goddess had taken over his head. In the loneliest hours of his solitary life her image was his sole companion. Still, he couldn't help but feel conflicted about spying on her at the behest of the Dumbarton bitch. The she-devil seemed determined to destroy the Aldwen's marriage and she was depending on him to help execute her evil plan. But unless he was prepared to lie, there was no way on earth he could manifest an extra-marital affair out of nowhere. A couple of times he had considered fabricating a few tawdry tales of bawdy misdeeds in the bushes. However, on reflection, he knew his hirer would insist on supporting evidence, such as details of places, times and dates.

Still, whatever happened, he was happy to continue watching the young wife. For weeks on end should that be necessary. And if the she-devil's suspicions proved to be correct, then the elusive Jack should shortly be showing his face. And Parker knew that as soon as he imparted the longed-for, much-needed news, she would waste not a single moment in informing the Major he was a cuckold. A cuckold trumped by some deprived willowy whelp of a lad. What happened after that was anyone's guess.

Chapter 57

Jack waved an arc, called out her name and ran to catch up with Isabella, who smiled with genuine delight when she saw him. He was making his way home from the farm where he sometimes found work on a casual basis. Mostly, he helped to muck out the cows and carry hay to the barn. It was tough work for low pay. As a rule, he kept to the perimeter of the Hall's grounds but, on that occasion, he made an exception to escort her home.

It occurred to Jack that many months had gone by since they last met, and he wondered how she was settling into her new life as the wife of a country gentleman. He needed no-one to remind him that now she was married they must conform to a strict code of conduct which insisted on no physical contact between them whatsoever.

Isabella thought Jack looked tired and thin, rather like his only coat, and in need of a hot bath. He smelled of hay, the soil and hard toil. Although she felt concerned about him, she knew to keep her counsel. Being acquainted with working-class culture and mindful of class differences, she was at pains to avoid appearing too pitying towards him and wounding his pride. She recalled helping Nora to carry home some baskets of foraged fruit and was shocked at her living conditions. The girl and her large extended family resided on a row of rotten houses on a street of despair named after some long-forgotten hero. The unsanitary slum dwellings had neither bathrooms nor inside toilets, and the only place to wash was at the kitchen sink. The family were cordial in a constrained sort of manner and offered her a cup of weak tea with watered-down milk. Isabella could not have returned the favour. In their affluent days the Actons had given alms to the poor, but those same people would not have been admitted to their reception rooms, except as servants or maintenance men.

As Isabella and Jack strolled the path together, they soon fell into reminiscing about their old exploits. After all, the Aldwen estate was their former playground and their escapades would forever remain in their mutual memories. They laughed with comical horror as they recalled their dangerous dares and daft forfeits. Jack reminded Isabella she was once something of a daredevil; a girl who never shied from a challenge no matter the risks involved; such as crossing the field with the bull in it.

Smiling, Isabella confessed she had only found the courage because she knew the beast was a yearling and mating season had ended. However, in hindsight, she admitted her actions were foolish and chortled at her own stupidity. And she could well imagine what Hereward would say if he knew, not that she would ever dare to tell him. She thought she would rather take her chance with the bull.

Despite Jack's determination to keep the topic of conversation neutral, he confided that their mutual friends had been shocked to hear she had gone ahead with the wedding. Somehow, they all felt sure she would shy at the last moment. However, the second he saw the disaffected look on her face, he regretted his comment. At the end of the day her marriage was none of his business. He knew he could never have married her anyway. They came from two distinct worlds. Wisely, she had returned to hers, he thought. Henceforth, their conversation became more circumspect.

When they reached the house, Jack requested a glass of water. In line with social convention, Isabella asked him to wait outside while she went inside to tell Tilly to fetch a glass of milk and a plate of biscuits. Although all classes had fought in the trenches together, class barriers were still, for the most part, deeply entrenched. Plus, she knew Boyle, being a snob of the worst sort, would have notified Hereward had she invited Jack inside.

Jack was heartened to see Isabella was still her old sweet self. Unlike many of her peers, she was neither conceited nor condescending. She looked even lovelier and more grown up than when he last saw her; but there was also a tinge of sadness behind her eyes. Then he dared to ask if she were happy; to which she replied she was fine and they left it at that.

Just as Jack was leaving, Hereward pulled up in his motor-car. After silencing the engine, he stared at him through the windscreen for longer than good manners allowed.

Out of social habit, Jack doffed his cap, nodded in his direction, then went on his way.

As he climbed out of the vehicle, Hereward noticed the empty plate and glass in his wife's hand. However, he withheld comment, although his facial expression betrayed his true emotions. Taking a deep breath, he watched Jack disappear down the road.

"Who was that?" he asked quietly.

"His name's Jack. He helps out at the farm sometimes when there's work available," she said, keeping her voice casual and light.

Although Hereward recognised him from the rushbearing festival, he was careful not to say so.

"What was he doing here?" he said, a suspicious edge to his voice.

Isabella resisted the temptation to make some sarcastic remark. "He was coming from the farm, and when he saw me on the path, he kindly offered to accompany me back." Then she paused before adding: "Awfully kind of him, don't you think?"

Hereward's jaw clenched and his neck tightened as he pictured them together, and he stated in a domineering manner: "Look here, my dear. Now you're married, it's most improper to be seen alone in the company of another man, more especially one who isn't a gentleman."

"Seen by whom?" she said with a short, tremulous laugh. "Who's there to see me? And for your information, Jack has always behaved like a true gentleman in my company. Your feudal attitudes really are verging on the ridiculous."

"Well, my dear, you never know who might be in the neighbourhood or the vicinity of the Hall," he said as his mind dwelled on their former friendship. He was yet to be convinced it had been purely platonic. "You looked very pally," he added accusingly.

"Well, I expect that's because we were once *pals*," she said saltily to his insinuation. She recognised that specific shade of green on her husband's face and what it denoted, having observed it on the rare occasions they went out together, even in church of all places.

"What was that you placed in his palm?"

"Money — from my allowance," she admitted.

"That's meant for your personal requirements," he snapped. "Not old pals."

"It's my money and I'll spend it as I see fit," she fired back with defiance. "His father's sick and can no longer work. The trouble with you, Hereward, is you've no idea what it's like to be poor. None whatsoever. You've never been poor. You've never felt the gnawing ache of an empty stomach. Never had to beg for credit at the corner shop. Never had to buy food in minute quantities because that's all you can afford. Whatever you want or need, you buy. Just like that!" she said clicking her thumb and long finger together for added effect. "Just like you bought me." Then she threw up her hands, stretched her jaw and emitted a strangled scream.

"I did *not* buy you and I resent the presumption," he said as he followed her up the Hall's well-scrubbed steps to the highly polished front door.

"I believe that's why my father forced me to marry you," she said half turning towards him. "My parents certainly appear to be better off since we tied the knot."

Mindful the servants might be listening, they hesitated on the threshold. Hereward lowered his voice to almost a whisper. "I would never have paid your father money to marry you. What the devil do you take me for? If you must know I agreed to give him a loan — at his request."

"A loan!" she snorted, "One he will never repay. I can promise you that. But then I expect you already know that." Isabella's brow furrowed and she looked askance as if something had only just occurred to her. "Pray tell me, *dear* husband, what sort of sum was involved in your financial dealings with my doting daddy?"

Hereward refused to be drawn. As far as he was concerned the subject was closed and he wished no further reference to it. Instead, his jaw tightened and he said: "In any case, I don't want to see that young good-for-nothing anywhere near you again, do you hear?"

Bile rose up in Isabella's throat and her eyes flashed in anger. "That's because you're a snob, Hereward, a horrible, horrible snob. Jack's worth a thousand of you because he's decent and sincere. He has never treated me with anything other than respect. I regret I cannot say the same about you."

Then she barged through the front door in boots, threw off her coat, stomped upstairs to her bedroom, and slammed the door with a vengeance.

As he dwelled on his wife's wounding words, the veins stood out on Hereward's temples and neck. To be compared in less than favourable terms to Jack hurt his pride more than he was willing to admit. Isabella knew where to aim her deadly arrows and, on this occasion, she had hit the mark with pinpoint accuracy.

Chapter 58

Once the duelling duo disappeared inside, Parker emerged from his hiding place and began walking home. Despite having finally seen the young lady with her alleged lover, he had nothing of substance to report to the devious Miss Dumbarton; definitely nothing to enable the vile virago to ruin the Major's marriage. Two young people chatting together on a path did not lovers make, he reasoned. One need not be a psychologist to note the absence of physical contact between the two acquaintances. Throughout the entire encounter, Jack kept his hands firmly in his threadbare pockets. Plus, there was no prolonged eye contact between the two. And definitely no romantic gestures to speak of. The source of their accuser's information, he decided, was either a mischief maker or very much mistaken.

They were so focussed on their conversation and oblivious to the surroundings that Parker had found spying on them unbelievably easy. He recalled seeing the young woman pointing at the cow field while laughing her head off. He liked her laugh, which had a playful ring to it that was very appealing. It made him want to laugh with her. He had never before seen her jolly, most probably because she was usually alone. And he felt glad she wasn't romantically involved with Jack, as it would have made him jealous and want to beat him up.

A day later, Parker arrived at the home of Miss Dumbarton to update her on his progress, or lack of it thereof. Except to tell her he had seen Mrs Aldwen and Jack in each other's company, he had nothing useful to report, not a farthing.

"Well, have you come across anything condemnatory?" she asked with great expectations and a blatant disregard for his polite salutation. It was plain to see the scorn on her thoroughbred face was habitual. Habitual, that is, to specific situations. It appeared whenever she found herself in the presence of the lower orders, no matter how brief or fleeting the contact. Automatically, her neck stiffened, her nostrils flared, and her eyes, which were like cold copper coins, looked straight down her long Roman nose. Had Parker been required to describe her facial expression, he would have said it was that of a person looking at the contents of a communal ash-pit privy.

Parker stuck out his thick lower lip and shook his head in slow motion. "Nothing of importance, I'm afraid to say, *Miss* Dumbarton," he replied with slight emphasis on the prefix. He derived a certain satisfaction from the sight of her despondent face when he alluded to her spinsterhood.

"Are you absolutely sure?" she said in a voice damp with desperation. It was becoming increasingly apparent that her scheme to retrieve her lost lover was looking evermore tenuous since Barbara's recent telephone misreport and subsequent correction.

"Yes, Ma'am," said Parker, giving his right ear a good poke. "I couldn't be more certain if I tried. And I've been most thorough, I can assure you of that. As a matter of fact, the young lady spends less time roaming the Aldwen estate than she used to. She takes herself off into town now too. I've seen her racing down the road on her bicycle, and I don't mind saying the little sprite can't half move."

"What about the lad? Have you seen much of him?"

Rosalyn asked, ignoring Parker's open admiration for Isabella's bicycling proficiency.

"You mean Jack?"

"Yes, whatever his name is," she said shortly with an irritated flick of her wrist.

"I've seen him just the once, and only then very briefly. He and Mrs Aldwen were walking together on the path that leads straight to the Hall. And they're hardly likely to get up to owt there now, are they? Also, the Major arrived just as Jack was leaving. The young lady looked quite relaxed about her husband seeing them together, not guilty at all. And certainly not like a girl who's been up to no good, if you get my meaning. Let's be honest, if she really is having a fling, she's hardly likely to do it within sight of the house or under her old man's nose is she? Especially since the Major's not a man to mess with."

"No, I suppose not," she agreed, albeit reluctantly. "Although anything's possible," she said with significance.

Feeling almost dizzy with disappointment, Rosalyn questioned the reliability of Parker's report in her head. Her success depended wholly on exposing Isabella's infidelity, of which she remained convinced. Once her mission was accomplished, she felt confident Hereward would divorce his adulterous spouse. She outright refused to accept that the girl roamed the estate unaccompanied. To her mind the afternoon walk was a subterfuge. A subterfuge for an unsavoury, scandalous and sordid assignation. No sane, sensible and respectable lady wandered the woods alone on a regular basis. More especially in wintertime. Rosalyn's brain-racking deliberations caused her temples to throb and she rubbed them to relieve the pain.

To convince Miss Dumbarton his investigations had been rigorous, Parker provided her with a detailed account in which he described at length tracking his target over meadow, farmland and through forest. He said he had seen nothing untoward in her conduct, no evidence of wrongdoing, and definitely no romantic tryst with a young casual farmhand. Isabella Aldwen's behaviour was without question above reproach. Deep down, Parker thought the innocent young thing had done nothing to deserve the scheming Medusa's unjust accusation. Added to which, the girl really did forage. He had seen her with his very own eyes filling her basket or trug with mushrooms and berries. He realised her behaviour might appear odd to a town toff like Miss Dumbarton, but to him it was perfectly normal. All the same, he shared some of the posh pedigree's despondency, since he would have taken a peculiar pleasure in observing the accused pair mating in the bushes, even if did make him rabid with envy.

"One thing I did see," volunteered Parker in an attempt to justify his fee, "was the Major and his missus arguing outside the house after the blond fellow took off."

"Yes, they're known to argue a lot," stated Rosalyn without revealing her source. She recalled Barbara saying as much. Which made her wonder if Hereward also harboured suspicions about his wife's behaviour.

"Do you want me to continue, Ma'am, and if so, for how long?" Parker enquired.

"Another couple of weeks I should think to be absolutely certain," said Rosalyn with part resignation, not yet ready to give up hope.

Had Parker not decided to go on watching the Major's wife off his own debauched bat, he would have felt bereft at the impending termination of his assignment. An assignment funded by a scorned woman's imprudent prodigality; or what his dearly departed mother called money for old rope. He patted the fat envelope in his inside pocket with a small smile of appreciation in the knowledge it would fund his proclivity for some weeks to come.

However, his mission had gone from being a straightforward surveillance operation to an all-consuming pathological compulsion. In addition to which the stealth factor, as always, made the activity infinitely more stimulating, since he found watching the subject of his voyeuristic yen without her knowledge intensely arousing. Not given to soul searching, solipsism or introspection, devoid of uprightness, lacking moral insight, and insensible to the concept of sexual deviancy, Parker did not consider for one single moment his peculiarities abnormal, extraordinary or perverted. What he did know without a doubt, however, was that every time he ogled the unattainable object of his desire, his fixation became further reinforced.

Nonetheless, Parker, somewhat paradoxically, was aware that spying on another man's wife ran counter to the male code of honour, as in the tenth commandment: thou must not covet thy neighbour's wife. He also knew that if Major Aldwen copped him hiding in the bushes, either within or without the grounds, he would become suspicious and most likely thrash the living daylights out of him.

Such was the nature of Parker's obsession, that despite the Dumbarton woman's insistence on keeping his distance, the young lady had almost caught him watching her on a few occasions. Let's be honest, he said to himself, warning him not to get too close to her was like telling a cat not to chase a mouse. His addiction, as with all addictions, was beyond his control. He felt compelled to watch her, compelled to invade her privacy, compelled to intrude on her innocent life, compelled to peep at her drawers drying on the clothesline. He knew not what drove his desire, except to say the sight of her thrilled him like nothing else. A thrill he needed to experience over and over again like a narcotic. It kept his private parts from rusting, so to speak. He was after all, or so he believed, a normal man with normal needs and he considered looking at young ladies perfectly natural.

Unfortunately, his inability to touch the young wife felt increasingly frustrating and stressful. Although self-indulgence relieved his innermost tension, it was a poor substitute for fornication with a well-endowed woman, or girl. And with each passing day the compulsion to grope her grew stronger and harder to resist.

Chapter 59

A couple of days after bumping into Jack, Isabella set off on her regular ramble around the estate. She had no specific distance in mind when she departed the house. She simply felt in need of a good dose of fresh air with which to oxygenate her lungs. Inside the Hall the air felt clogged and stagnant because Boyle insisted on keeping the windows closed when it was especially cold outside. And being winter, it often was. Concerned only with conserving heat, he seemed incapable of understanding that stale air was unhealthy. Old habits die hard, she supposed.

As she cut through the orchard, Isabella caught sight of a sudden flash of movement out of the corner of her right eye. She stopped and stared at a fixed point in the trees for a few seconds. However, after noting nothing of concern, she continued towards the main path.

Should she come upon Jack again, Isabella wondered what she should do. Say a simple hello? Chat to him as normal? Be honest and admit Hereward had forbidden her to associate with him? Gosh, marriage is so complicated and restrictive, she said to herself. But since Jack was working elsewhere that day, she need not have worried.

Upon reaching the lakeside, Isabella sat on her regular log, picked up a large round pebble and tossed it into the still water. As she went on sitting, she detected an unpleasant smell beneath her. Thinking an animal must have fouled the log, she transferred to another one nearby.

She loved to watch the dark ripples spread out on the lake's silvery surface. It felt so relaxing, hypnotically so. Therefore, she remained sitting for a good thirty minutes watching the birds fly over. But when a dark ominous shape appeared high in the sky overhead, they took instant flight in search of sanctuary. Who'd be a small bird? she thought, rising from the log.

Owing to her husband's repeated reminders, Isabella was well aware of the whims of the weather and had acquired the habit of checking the sky at regular intervals. That day the sky was a uniform dirty grey, insipid and sunless; typical for that time of year. Although the humidity felt high to her, she had no way of knowing whether it would rain later on. She preferred to avoid getting caught in a downpour because Hereward always kicked up an almighty fuss whenever she returned to the Hall looking like a drenched dog. She recalled a very recent conversation with him in which he admitted he feared she might catch pneumonia, which could prove fatal. And he advised her it was best to stay indoors when it looked as though it might rain.

Isabella reminded him she was young and healthy. "Gosh," she said, "I've a greater chance of dying from boredom inside the house than I have from catching a chill outside. The last thing on my mind when I'm out walking is sickness and death. You really are a cheerful Charlie, aren't you? I can't imagine what makes you so morbid."

Hereward paused at length to consider her comments. His words when they came were measured, propitious and efficacious.

"The other day in a roundabout way you asked me how much I paid your papa for your hand," he began. "So, I'll tell you, my love. I paid him nothing. Not a single penny. I agreed to extend him a loan on the basis that we would shortly be related through marriage. Part of which I then invested on his behalf. A loan he is still required to repay in full, by the way. I don't deny money was a motivating factor in his agreement to our union. However, since I can only speak for myself, that conversation is one you must have with him.

"You also asked me to disclose the figure involved in my financial arrangement with your father. That is to say the size of the loan. I assume by that you wish to know what I consider your worth in monetary terms. So please allow me to tell you." He paused a second time, took a deep breath, then went on. "To me you are beyond priceless and that's why I worry about you when you're out on the estate. I realise you think I'm being neurotic, but I know only too well how the weather can turn suddenly, and with such large tracts of forest, we see more than our fair share of showers in these parts."

"That's very sweet of you," she responded, "but I'll be fine, I promise."

Although she saw nothing to support her suspicions, Isabella's sense of an indefinable presence close at hand continued to plague her from time to time; waxing and waning for no apparent reason. She could never quite get a handle on it. Sometimes it felt strong, at other times weak. On occasions, she fancied she saw dissonant shapes shifting in the shadows. Then her insides shifted too and her heart rate trebled as foreboding's ice-cold fingers stroked her spine and shoulders.

Mindful that her strange perceptions were marring the pleasure of her walks, Isabella tried to convince herself the fleeting movements were simply mirages created by transitory tricks of the light; such as when clouds float across the sky or branches bend in the breeze. Each time she felt nervous she said to herself: I'm so ashamed of you, Isabella Acton, I mean Aldwen. Despite doing so, it did little to reduce her symptoms.

Anxiety, she decided, was a pernicious state, destroying one's confidence from within. In addition to which, no matter how much she analysed her fear, she found it impossible to identify its root cause. It defied explanation. It was without foundation. It lacked reason. It was a feeling not a fact. Yet every time she felt at risk of some vague unquantifiable threat, she kept a lookout for the phantom watcher until her eyes hurt and her head ached.

To her detriment, a lack of solid evidence prevented Isabella from sharing her unsettling experiences with Hereward. She feared he might think her insane. And who could blame him? she reflected. So instead, she told herself it was perfectly safe to wander the estate and that the problem would ultimately resolve itself. More than threats to her safety, she feared becoming the sort of limp female who wouldn't say boo to a blessed goose.

Now and then, Isabella even wondered if Hereward were spying on her. She believed his possessive nature combined with his military prowess made it a distinct possibility. After all, the estate's topography provided the perfect location for mounting a one-man military-style operation in reconnaissance. But then the very idea of her highbrow husband hiding in the bushes was risible and made her chuckle to herself. And besides, Hereward was too wrapped up in his own selfish interests to follow her around outdoors. She did recall his once saying that although legitimate hunters no longer stalked the estate, it still paid to be chary of poachers. People, he explained, had been crossing the land since time immemorial and, provided they caused no problems, there was no point in trying to prevent them. And anyway, their numbers had dwindled to almost nothing since the Great War.

As the day wore on, the weather became colder and the sky grew dimmer and mottled. Treading the paths, conscious of the slowly developing dusk and the air's heavy dankness, Isabella began to feel a trifle uneasy. Again, she felt a strong sense of a figure, a faceless figure, yet solid in form, walking the woods within range. An uninvited guest in her vicinity. The sensation felt similar to being in a supposedly empty house yet sensing a living presence inside. Friend or foe, their vibrations could be felt in the atmosphere.

Still, she reasoned, nothing bad had ever befallen her out on the estate, nothing evil had ever revealed itself, no axe-wielding madman had ever chased her through the trees, and no hungry wolves wandered the woods anymore. Throughout the entire afternoon, she had seen only small animals, birds and insects, none of them dangerous.

Sometime later, in the remote density of the forest, Isabella began to feel an odd energy in the atmosphere. During the same period, the trees gave the impression they were bearing down on her, rather like they had on her wedding day. Plus, now they also looked as though they were about to entangle her in their twisted limbs. They seemed restless and quivery too. The longer she stared at them, the more they seemed to grow wider and taller, making her feel even smaller.

Drops of dread dripping inside her head, Isabella's angst resurfaced. Seized by an acute attack of anxiety, she sensed something bad was about to happen. It made her feel lightheaded, weak-kneed and tachycardic. As the muscles in her throat contracted, she felt as if her vital organs were assailing her from within. Despite making a valiant effort to compose herself, the fear held fast. She no longer felt brave; only tiny, fragile and defenceless. The girl she once was had vanished inside herself, and was struggling to break free from her self-persecutory prison.

Walking quickly in the relative silence of the estate, Isabella became increasingly aware of her own footfalls on the forest floor. To her ears they seemed oddly loud. Louder than normal. Then to her dismay, she became aware of something moving around, something upright whose footsteps mirrored her own. Except the invisible steps sounded heavier than hers and, more worryingly, human rather than animal. As soon as she speeded up, the footsteps did too. Flee! flee! flee! urged her brain. In a frank state of alarm, her vulnerability laid bare, adrenaline pumping through her body, she surged forward into a run, even though she had no idea what exactly she was running from. Her face an agony of fear, her boots beating the path, she ran like a pickpocket pursued by the police. As she flew past the trees, every so often a brittle branch or a shrivelled leaf fell to earth, or a bird flapped its wings, or something squeaked in the undergrowth, causing her to convulse in terror.

Once the Hall came into view, Isabella drew up exhausted and drew in a battery of breaths. Then she quickly looked all around to make sure she was safe. Satisfied nothing and no-one lurked in her proximity and deciding it must have been a poacher she heard in the woods, she bent down to tighten her bootlaces. Hereward often warned her that one day she would trip over her ties, fall flat on her face and fracture her nose. What a fusspot, she thought. No-one had ever shown so much concern for her welfare. Her cold-hearted parents never had, believing that was one of the nanny's duties. To amuse herself, she once asked him whether he would divorce her if she ever did break her nose.

"That depends on how badly it's bashed and the resultant asymmetry," he had joked. But on reflection he looked a touch hurt and said: "You must think me rather shallow to even ask such a thing."

She admitted she considered him deep rather than shallow, which he said was almost equally hurtful.

Isabella was about to straighten up when her attention was

drawn to a discarded dog-end on the path. It seemed odd to her somehow considering no-one at the Hall smoked cigarettes. Boyle, it was reported, enjoyed a pipe after his supper, which he always puffed away on in his own room. And she doubted the maids could even afford cigarettes. It could be a poacher's, she thought. Except she doubted a poacher would dare to venture close to the house. Or else a pedlar might have dropped it there. But these days it was rare to see even pedlars on the path.

Having regained her calm, Isabella recalled how she used to like looking at pedlars' boxes of cheap wares whenever they visited the town in the summer months. She remembered a lady pedlar in a colourful headscarf, who claimed to be clairvoyant, gave her a tacky charm as an amulet and warned her to beware of a big scruffy man. However, as soon as Agatha Acton laid eyes on it, she binned it in abhorrence. Big scruffy man, thought Isabella. There was no shortage of big scruffy men in and around Oakwich. Or anywhere else for that matter.

Her nearness to the Hall gave Isabella a false sense of security and her strange experience soon began to fade from her mind. As she straightened up and went forward, she had no idea that behind her in the distance, peering around a tree trunk, his unblinking bloodshot eyes posted on her back, a sex-deprived predator watched her go.

Chapter 60

It took Martha a minute or so to place the woman in the well-cut camel coat adorned with a black-mink collar. It was the garrulous gorgon once seen ranting in voice-straining volume at Isabella outside the shop. The girl had looked tiny beside her; tiny but not intimidated. Martha wondered what the woman wanted, since she was clearly a *custom-made* and not a *ready-to-wear*, as they said in the business. She felt tempted to tell her to leave.

The woman edged closer as if inviting a confidence. Martha edged back and eyed her up in more detail. She put her in mind of the mannequins in the shop window. The bust was small; definitely an A-cup in a pointy bandeau brassiere; the body elongated with a high waist. Her unnaturally smooth silhouette indicated she was wearing some sort of foundation garment under her clothes.

Most of the shop's stock was too short for those of exceptional height. Martha often noticed the way some tall women stoop and round their shoulders in an unconscious effort to appear shorter. Not this one, however. The gorgon was far too high and mighty. To avoid suffering the inconvenience of lowering her chin, she simply looked down her snooty snout at her inferiors.

"Good afternoon," said the woman with a substantial plum in her mouth and a whiff of expensive brandy on her breath.

"I'd like to see the latest styles in lingerie please."

In complete silence the shopkeeper went to the back cabinet, slid open a drawer and picked out a few items. "These are from our newest collection," she said, laying them out on the glass countertop in a business-like, no-nonsense manner.

Rosalyn took a cursory look at Martha's merchandise and chose a pair of pink lace-edged, legless knickers with lace panels at the sides and bows on the front.

"Will that be all, Madam?" asked Martha, who wondered why a wealthy woman had purchased a pair of knickers without the matching brassiere.

"Yes, thank you," she replied, a hard edge to her voice.

Without speaking Martha wrapped the purchase in a thin sheet of tissue and slipped it inside a paper bag advertising the name of the shop on both sides. After which she handed the dragon her drawers, bid her a blunt goodbye, and bore a hole in her back as she departed the shop.

Soon after, Isabella turned up. Martha was relieved the ghastly gorgon had gone. She preferred to avoid a confrontation inside the shop. For one thing, it would be bad for her business's reputation. Although she felt sure she could rely on Isabella to conduct herself with dignity and decorum; unlike Miss High-and-Mighty.

Martha passed her young friend her tea in a porcelain cup with a picture of rose on the inside. They were sitting in a small room at the back of the shop where they met every Thursday afternoon after the shopkeeper bolted the door for half-day closing. Following which, they usually visited the cinema or attended a tea dance. Theirs was an unlikely association. Martha was older than Isabella and hailed from the lower-middle class. However, they had hit it off soon after they met. Initially, she had felt sorry for Isabella because she looked so lonely and lost. But their acquaintance had soon blossomed into a firm friendship.

"Would you like a biscuit?" Martha asked Isabella.

"Yes, thank you. Have you ever known me to decline a biscuit?"

"No, as it happens," replied Martha.

They both laughed.

Martha offered Isabella a plate of homemade macaroons.

Accepting one, Isabella said: "Martha do you mind if I ask you a question?"

"No. Provided I can ask you one back."

"Yes, of course," said Isabella before taking a bite of her biscuit. "That's only fair."

"Ask me anything you like, my dear, and I'll do my best to give you an honest answer."

"Did your husband object when you first opened the shop?"

"No, of course not. Why should he?"

"What I mean is did you have to take his permission?"

Martha tried not to laugh. "Absolutely not. He has his business and I have mine."

"You know you're awfully lucky, being able to work and be independent," said Isabella after a thoughtful pause.

"Luck has nothing to do with it," replied Martha. "I choose to work. It gives me financial freedom and I don't have to beg my husband for handouts, housekeeping money, or have him settle my bills." Martha closed her eyes at her own tactlessness. "I'm sorry that was thoughtless of me."

"That's alright," said Isabella, helping herself to another macaroon.

"Now it's my turn," said Martha. "What made you get married so young?"

"Well, I wasn't really given a choice, to be honest," Isabella confided to her friend. "My father insisted I marry. He said that if I refused, I would have to leave the house. And since I had no money, no qualifications, no training, and no experience of any sort, and nowhere to go, I had to obey him."

"That must have been very hard?"

"Yes, it was. Horrendously so. More than anyone could possibly imagine. But I'm gradually adjusting to married life. In my family no-one ever married for love. It wasn't the done thing. Nowadays it's rare for people from the upper classes to have arranged marriages. I'm sure mine must be one of the last. My parents' marriage was more of a business-type arrangement in many respects, a union between two old families with long lineages and the right social connections. Back then, the upperclass marriage system was based on forming advantageous monetary and societal alliances. There was no romance involved as such; well very little. It was assumed the couple would grow fond of each other in time. And even if they didn't, it wasn't considered a problem. They simply tolerated each other and led mostly separate lives. Mama blames the film industry, cheap magazines and lowbrow novels for giving young ladies unrealistic expectations about marriage. She said a woman should aspire to make a good marriage, not a romantic one. My fate was sealed the day Hereward contacted my father to ask for my hand."

The two friends sipped their tea simultaneously in a moment of companionable silence.

"Were you in love when you got married?" Isabella asked Martha.

"I suppose I must have been."

They both laughed again.

Isabella became reflective. "Somehow, I always expected to marry for love. Except I thought I would be much older than I am now. I had this fantasy that it would be terribly romantic. I assumed my future husband and I would have lots in common and share the same interests. Well, I suppose it just wasn't meant to be," she said fatalistically.

"It must have been very hard for you, being so young."

"It was. It was absolute torture. I can't even begin to describe my distress the day I married Hereward. All my dreams and ambitions down the drain, so to speak. What's more, no-one enlightened me as to what would happen on my wedding night. Well, not in sufficient detail, you understand. Still, as I said, one becomes accustomed to being a wife and what it entails," said Isabella, sighing with sad resignation.

"What were you planning to do with your life before you were obliged to marry?"

"Oh, I had ambitions to study. Attend university like Maud, you know Hereward's sister, whom you've met. She's frightfully clever and completely independent, and she does whatever she pleases. I must say she's inspirational. She drives a motorcar. Can you believe that? And she travels to all sorts of interesting places. Plus, during the war years, she was some sort of volunteer. Isn't that amazing? There are so many things I would love to do, but I must first seek Hereward's permission, not that I always do. I regret to say he's a dyed-in-the-wool conservative."

"I've heard he's very handsome, which I suppose is a huge consolation," offered Martha, whose increasingly rotund husband had a rapidly receding hairline, and who snored so loudly it rattled the bedroom door.

"That's what I remind myself," Isabella admitted. "But he's also terribly controlling. Although to be fair, he's very caring too. And he can be awfully witty if you catch him in the right mood. And he's extremely intelligent, of course. I mean it must be ghastly being married to a dullard. Plus, he's generous and thoughtful. He always brings me back a small gift whenever he pops into town. So, you see, I really mustn't complain. He's had to adjust to my presence in the house too, and according to Maud he doesn't respond well to change."

"Well, we really must be going," advised Martha. "We mustn't be late." Then she collected the teacups and plates and took them to the sink to be washed. Looking out through the window as she put the pots to drain, she caught sight of a fleeting movement through the open gate that gave onto the back alleyway behind the shop. That's odd, she said to herself, I could have sworn I closed it earlier.

Chapter 61

The note in the bright-blue envelope arrived during the afternoon. Hereward was busy typing at his desk, while Isabella was dancing with Martha at the church hall. Boyle had brought it in with the rest of the post on a silver tray.

Once the butler left the room, Hereward turned his attention to the post. It was the usual mixture of bills, invitations, catalogues, and business and personal correspondence, including a letter from his brother in India. Leaving the bright-blue letter till last, he opened them in his usual methodical manner, then placed them in the letter tray to be dealt with later in order of importance.

When he came to the bright-blue envelope, he noticed it was addressed to him in capital letters in a neat, childlike hand. Fashioned in a contrived way, he thought. As soon as he opened it, he checked for a signature. It was unsigned. Frowning he began to read:

YOUR WIFE IS HAVING A GALA TIME IN TOWN ATTENDING TEA DANCES WHERE SHE DOES THE FOXTROT AND OTHER MODERN DANCES WITH LOTS OF YOUNG UNMARRIED MEN

Almost immediately a red veil of wrath clouded Hereward's vision. It was Thursday and Isabella had simply told him she was meeting Martha and made no mention of a dance. Springing to his feet, he kicked the swivel chair out of his way and watched it spin out of control before hitting the wall. Then he stormed back and forth across the library floor with both his jaw and fists clenched. He felt sorely tempted to go and find his duplicitous little Jezebel and teach her a lesson to last a lifetime.

"Yes, that's partly correct," a red-faced Isabella admitted under close questioning as she shrank from her husband's judicious stare. Knowing full well her face would betray her if she lied, she had no choice but to tell the truth, the whole truth and nothing but the truth.

Hereward's dark brows coupled in a hostile scowl. "Partly correct?" he said in an interrogative tone. "I was hoping the accusation was completely *incorrect*."

Under a ruby-red rayon bolero, Isabella had on a matching dress with a panel waist and swinging hemline, and she looked all feminine and flustered. Her hands were knitted together so tight, the tops of her knuckles had turned white.

"I've attended a couple of tea dances at the church hall held to raise funds in aid of the orphanage," she began in a quiet voice. "There were no men in attendance; only ladies, and mostly middle-aged, middle-class ladies at that, with little else to do I expect. I don't see how you can object to such a worthy cause. I danced with Martha most of the time. She kindly offered to teach me because I'm rather a dunce at dancing. Father Flaherty was the only male there, but as a holy man I expect he doesn't count. In the interval some nuns from the nearby convent came in to serve tea and biscuits. You can ask the priest if you doubt my word." Then Isabella's lower lip trembled like a child's and she burst into tears.

In an instant, Hereward's frown fell from his face. "Why didn't you say where you were going?" he said in a placatory tone. He felt angry with himself for accepting without question the word of some anonymous muckraker. He, of all people, a staunch advocate of confirming one's facts and not jumping to conclusions. However, on this occasion the green-eyed grotesquery had prompted his precipitancy.

"Because you would have objected, that's why. You always do," said Isabella as she sobbed quietly.

Hereward stepped forward and placed two consoling arms around his weeping wife. She looked like a lost and lonely child and his heart went out to her.

"I'm desperately sorry, my darling. I know I'm a beast," he said, his voice and face full of remorse. "I deserve to be horsewhipped."

Snuggled against his broad chest, held tight in his strong muscular arms, comforted by the steady beat of his heart, Isabella was conscious for the very first time of a sense of solace and security. At one time she would have pulled away, but at that moment she was content to remain in his warm embrace.

Hereward kissed the crown of her head. "Of course, I wouldn't have objected, my loveliness. Not when you had the convent sisters present to ensure none of the housewives got carried away with the curate."

Isabella snorted a laugh through her tears. Then she peered up at him perplexed. "How did you know I was at a dance? Who told you?" she asked. "Someone must have."

Hereward released her and handed her his handkerchief. Then he removed the anonymous note from the top drawer of the desk and gave it to her without comment.

With a childlike look of bewilderment on her damp face, Isabella read the libellous missive twice over while shaking her head.

"Gosh, someone must really hate me," she sniffed and her eyes welled up again. "Have you any idea who might be behind this?"

"Who knows? said Hereward. "Whoever's responsible, it's certainly someone with malicious intent. It pays to remember that in Oakwich everyone's business ultimately becomes common knowledge. In future you must keep me informed of all your activities. That way it becomes impossible for someone, such as this poison pen, to cause mischief in our marriage." He had his suspicions, but declined to share them right then.

A few days after the dance ado and the anonymous missive, Isabella wandered into her future bedroom to see how the refurbishment was progressing. The combined odours of paint, sawdust and varnish overpowered the air. Despite several setbacks, everything was reported to be back on track. Nevertheless, there remained much to do, including repapering, repairing and reupholstering. And since the room adjoined Hereward's by a connecting door, a quick completion was in his best interests, since it would mean no longer having to cross the landing for his night visits.

Isabella had first learned from Tilly that her current bedroom was originally the main guest room. In innocence, the maid had also let slip that Miss Dumbarton always slept there during her overnight stays. A wave of disgust washed over Isabella at the thought of her husband and his former ladylove lying in her bed like two illicit lovers besmirching themselves in some seedy hotel. In the moral compass of her chaste mind, it had never occurred to her that Hereward was anything less than a monk in his bachelor days.

Banishing the sordid image of the pair from her head, Isabella refocused her attention on her new bedroom. With keen interest, her eyes swept over the walls, floor and ceiling. Taking care not to touch any sticky or wet surface, she went to the window and gazed out at the garden. Come summer, she was looking forward to waking up in her new room when all the trees were in leaf, the flowers in bloom and the migrant birds on their annual visit.

Sensing a presence behind her, Isabella half turned and glanced over her shoulder. From the communicating doorway she saw Hereward observing her. She had no idea how long he had been standing there. Without acknowledging him, she went back to looking at the garden.

Saying nothing, he walked up to her and stood at her back, his breath warming the nape of her exposed neck. Peering over her head, he looked at the lawn briefly. When he spoke, the deep timbre of his voice vibrated in the unfurnished room.

"As you can see, my dear, things are well underway now," he said, transferring his focus to the room. "This was my late mother's suite. Since her death it has remained unoccupied and has been rather neglected. Having said that, it's an excellent room with a great view of the garden."

"I see," said Isabella softly. "What was she like, your mother?"

"Typically Victorian," replied Hereward before changing the subject. "The floor requires a couple more coats of varnish and I expect the new bathroom will take a few weeks to install. Boyle assures me that despite the delays everything is on course for completion in accordance with the newly agreed timescales."

Isabella, however, did not share her husband's faith in the butler. The probability of Boyle taking an active interest in something of benefit to her was as likely as his bald crown sprouting a cornucopia of curls.

"How much longer do you think it will be before it's ready?" she asked, moving out of his reach and twisting around to face him.

"All being well, no more than a couple of months at most I

should think. Still at least the room you're in now is comfortable in the interim," he stated.

A cloud of consternation crossed Isabella's face as tasteless images of her unfeminine foe flooded her mind. All she could see was Rosalyn: Rosalyn's lofty frame in her bed; Rosalyn's bourgeois bottom on her stool, Rosalyn's big-boned body in her bathtub. Isabella suspected Boyle was behind the decision to allocate her Rosalyn's old room, since the Hall had several bedrooms from which to choose. Had she been given the option she would have chosen to sleep in one of the attic rooms rather than lie on the former lovers' immoral mattress. She wondered how many women in total Hereward had hosted in her bed.

"Is something wrong, Isabella?" he said, having noticed the sudden change in her facial expression.

"No nothing, nothing at all. Everything's fine," she assured him with a smile that went nowhere near her eyes. In truth, she felt far from fine.

That night Isabella entered her room later than usual. By which time Hereward was already sitting in the debased bed with his arms crossed and a fractious look on his face. The two plumped-up pillows supporting his back had clearly been given a good pounding. With an audible sigh, he uncrossed his arms, reached over and grabbed her book from the bedside cabinet.

"You're late," he said curtly, flipping through the book's pages with apparent indifference.

"I wasn't aware we had an appointment," returned Isabella tartly.

Hereward looked up from the page and regarded her as if she were a tasty dish about to be served up for supper. Then he replied in a smug-faced manner: "It's an appointment of sorts. Our regular appointment."

Isabella squirmed inside. After which she told herself that

henceforth she must be in bed before Hereward's arrival to avoid repeating her present predicament. The thought of removing her clothes under his intemperate gaze was beyond embarrassing. And since her room lacked a dressing screen, she grabbed her nightclothes and went to the bathroom to get changed. To her profound relief, the lock on the door had at last been replaced. Although Boyle had taken his own good time to organise it. No doubt on purpose, she suspected.

Hereward was propped up on four pillows looking to all the world like a Roman emperor when she returned. To express his annoyance, he banged shut her book and placed it on his lap, while with acquisitive eyes he followed her every move around the room.

Refusing to be pressured and knowing it would vex him further, Isabella sat at her dressing table and spent an age brushing her hair a hundred times in the mirror. Then she disrobed, discarded her slippers and tumbled into bed with a light bounce.

"Please may I have my pillows back?" she said shortly.

"The next time you keep me waiting, expect to be punished for your appalling bad manners," Hereward informed her as he relinquished the pillows.

Isabella looked at him aghast.

Lowering his voice, he said with a look of amused devilment: "Which means they'll be no puddings for you for an entire week."

Isabella laughed with a sort of nervous relief.

"This book is rather good," he said, picking it up again and putting it aside. "Nothing beats a good adventure," he whispered in her ear before adding: "Especially in bed."

Scandalised, her cheeks magenta with mortification, Isabella told him to turn off the light. And before the blush could fade from her face, Hereward was already busy unbuttoning her nightdress and hitching up its hem.

Chapter 62

"In case you've forgotten, dearest, we're expecting Maud and Cynthia this evening," Hereward reminded Isabella as she breezed through the front door in the manner of an insouciant cat returning from its daily round of the neighbourhood. He whipped off her hat, helped her out of her coat and hung them on the hall stand beside the door.

"Of course, I haven't forgotten," said Isabella airily. "I'm hardly likely to forget the rare occasions we entertain guests, even if they are always the same people. Now if you'll kindly excuse me, I'll go and have my bath. Tilly always keeps everything ready. The maid's a marvel, so please don't fret. And besides, I'm sure the girls won't mind if I'm a couple of minutes late."

"Perhaps not, but I most certainly will," he said. For most of his adult life Hereward had loathed lateness, and yet he had somehow managed to marry the world's worst timekeeper.

Purposely to annoy him, Isabella took her own good time to change her footwear, cross the hall and climb the staircase.

As he watched her go, Hereward fought the urge to grab hold of her, throw her over his shoulder and drop her fully clothed in the bathwater. Unlike all the previous women in his life, his wife had that unfortunate effect on him.

When she returned downstairs, more promptly than when she went up, Isabella quickly redeemed herself in her husband's eyes as he stood waiting in the hall. She smelled rose scented and looked radiant in a teal-coloured taffeta gown with a notched neckline, fitted waist and gathered shoulders.

"You look ravishing, my darling," he said, raising her hand to his lips. "Is that a new dress?"

"Yes, it is," she said brightly. "It's from Martha's. She said the colour's perfect for me."

"I have to agree one hundred percent," he replied. "Now come along before we all starve to death."

"Don't be silly," she said with a chuckle.

True to form, Boyle's attitude to Maud and Cynthia oozed deference. When he greeted the two women with a low obeisant bow, Isabella suspected the hinged manoeuvre was more for her benefit than for theirs. From the day she moved into the Hall he had made it a point to disregard her at the table. But what upset her even more than the butler's overbearing behaviour was Hereward's apparent indifference to it. She believed his silence sent out the wrong message, effectively condoning Boyle's conduct. As mistress she recognised the importance of asserting herself over the servants. She thought about how her mother would handle a cocksure manservant; forsooth with ice-cold condescension and magisterial disdain. But whatever Isabella did, it only created more conflict.

Notwithstanding, dinner was, as always, a pleasant affair. Hereward hosted his sister and Cynthia once a month. Other than that, he showed no interest in socialising or entertaining, not even for Isabella's sake. Which was one of the reasons being married to him often made her feel bored and miserable.

At the evening's end, Isabella felt inspired as she waved off the two women in Maud's shiny Wolseley saloon. The sight of a woman sitting at the wheel of a motorcar looked to her so exciting, so liberating, so convenient. Think of the freedom, she said to herself. There and then she decided she would learn to drive as soon as possible. It would mean no longer having to confine herself to the house in wet or extremely windy weather.

To Isabella's terrible disappointment, Hereward's response was not what she had been hoping for when she broached the subject of learning to drive. Her first mistake was waiting until after the ladies had left, forgetting Maud made a powerful ally regarding the issue of female independence. The second mistake was assuming the wine would have mellowed his mood and made him more amenable to suggestion. How wrong she was in that estimation. He was his usual hidebound, intransigent self. And when he looked at her with forbearance, laughed and shook his head, Isabella was staggered.

"I'm so glad the idea of my driving a motorcar amuses you," she replied as they returned to the sitting room.

Ignoring the obvious sarcasm, Hereward assured her: "There's absolutely no need for you to drive, my little poppet. None whatsoever."

Isabella pursed and twisted her lips in response to Hereward's use of another patronising pet epithet. Little poppet! she said to herself. Whatever next? He appeared to possess a limitless supply of sweet nothings with which to infantilise her. She wouldn't be at all surprised to find on his desk a volume of sickly endearments similar to one of those compilations of baby names.

"I don't see why not," she gainsaid. "Lots of women drive. It's considered the norm now. I see them in town all the time," she added with a dash of hyperbole to bolster her case. "It's an absolute must for those of us marooned in rural areas."

Hereward exhaled through his teeth in frustration. "Because dear child, I can take you wherever you wish to go," he said in the slow, patient voice he reserved specially for her.

"But why should I have to depend on you?" she argued.

"Because that's how it is. Now we'll say no more about it."

"But you have failed to provide a single indisputable reason and I believe that you should."

Hereward stared hard at Isabella. "Oh, you do, do you?" he said.

Ordinarily, Isabella would have walked away with the intention of revisiting the subject at a later date, but the alcohol, for which she had now acquired the taste, emboldened her.

"Yes, I do, as it happens."

Hereward looked at her with steadfast eyes. "Driving a vehicle isn't quite as simple as you think it…"

Isabella interjected: "Maud drives. Are you saying she's capable of driving and I'm incapable?"

"Maud is a good deal older than you are and has far greater experience of life. And in case it has escaped your notice, my dear wife, she is also unmarried and therefore, unlike you, hasn't a husband to rely on."

"Lucky lady," said Isabella under her breath.

"Excuse me!"

Isabella paused and drew in a deep breath while she reloaded her verbal revolver.

Meanwhile, an inflection of authority crept into Hereward's voice and he stated: "What's more, you are too young to drive and too immature to drive unsupervised. And I very much doubt your ability to deal with any adverse situation that may arise during the course of a road journey."

Isabella's mouth grew into a grimace as she unconsciously twiddled her wedding ring on her finger. "Not too young to get married though, am I?" she rejoined. "You're a hypocrite, Hereward, a horrid, horrid hypocrite and I hate you."

Stunned by her vehemence, Hereward gaped at his wife's face flushed fuchsia with the combined effects of anger and alcohol. Although her harsh words had wounded him, he remained resolute, ignored her outburst and maintained his composure. Weighing her words in his mind for several moments, he stood up and looked down at her like a teacher confronting an impudent, pig-headed pupil.

When he resumed speaking, Hereward's voice had a hard and uncompromising edge to it. "I will reconsider your request when you come of age and not a moment sooner," he said. Then with the expression of a man unaccustomed to pertinacity, he asserted: "Now I've said all I'm going to say on the subject and I suggest you take yourself off to bed forthwith before you vex me further."

The finality with which Hereward spoke made Isabella feel like a small child denied sweets or a new toy. The fact that his sister drove whenever and wherever the mood took her had no influence on his backward thinking. And since the motorcar belonged to him, Isabella could not override his decision. Well, she would put her plans on hold until she found a way to overcome his resistance. She was unwilling to wait four long years, tantamount to a lifetime in her estimation, for permission to drive. Plus, there was no guarantee he would even agree when she reached the age of majority.

The following day at luncheon, Isabella, disgruntled still by her disagreement with Hereward the previous evening, replied in monosyllables to his attempts to engage her in casual conversation. As far as she was concerned, it was not simply a case of sulking for sulking's sake. She felt seriously aggrieved by attitude towards her. What gave him the God-given right to dictate the suitability of her pursuits, pastimes and occupations? she asked herself. Besides which, sulking was not only safe, it was also preferable to having one of their acrimonious set-tos, the likes of which would have disturbed the dead had there been a graveyard in the Hall's vicinity. A pair of concert cymbals in a series of deafening acoustic clashes could not better describe their worst ding-dongs.

Desirous of escape from the Hall's enervating atmosphere, Isabella decided she needed a walk more than ever. After Hereward returned to the library looking less than happy, she rushed to the boot room and quickly got herself ready. And still buttoning her coat, she stepped out into the fresh air.

Outdoors, Isabella observed the grounds were beginning to look rather neglected. The lawn was overgrown and the beds and borders colonised by weeds. She knew Boyle had still to appoint a new gardener and he seemed to be taking forever. Unless there were no suitable applicants, she reflected. Currently, houses remote from the main community were struggling to employ reliable, hardworking staff, especially if the pay was paltry. And Boyle was reputed to be parsimonious with the Hall's expenses. According to Tilly, he behaved as if the staff's wages came out of his very own wallet. Thinking he could at least mow the lawn, weed the flowerbeds, and trim the hedge tops, Isabella considered suggesting Jack as a temporary substitute until the butler could employ an experienced gardener. But then she doubted Hereward would agree on account of his jealousy. She found his dominating behaviour tiresome and their ongoing quarrels debilitating. At such times only the secluded sanctuary of the estate, where she could pass the time in blessed solitude, gave her succour.

After trudging through the gateway and dropping the latch back into place, Isabella set off along the path. Everywhere she looked the vegetation appeared strangled and choked as numerous unchecked plants competed for control. Walking between junglelike hedges lined with tall willowherb along the way, she lamented the loss of the Hall's gardener. Until, that is, with sudden trepidation, she recalled the grotesque features of the person called Parker peering in at her through the library window. She shivered at the memory of the colourless, cold-blooded eyes in the sloping skull, the twist of the broad head in the rigid torso, and the pronounced leer that brought to her skin's surface a passel of goosepimples. Gosh, she thought, I hope he never requests his old job back. Were that to happen, I should be too afraid to enter the garden.

Chapter 63

As he reclined in a shallow hollow behind a tall hedge, Parker patted his paunch, belched like an old toad and wiped away a spot of spittle on his lips. Apart from a little lumbago and sore eyes, he felt up to scratch and ready to go. He was expecting her shortly, assuming she came at her regular time. He ardently hoped she would.

Feeling his nasal airways congested, Parker sat upright, pressed the side of each nostril in turn with his thumb, and cleared his nose of catarrh. Comfortable again, he began to crave tobacco. After searching his pockets, he found his fags, tapped one from the packet, struck a matchstick down the abrasive strip on a matchbox, lit up and infused his lungs. The first drag made him cough like a dog with distemper. The cough, however, served as no deterrent. As it was, there were few pleasures in life for a baseborn bloke stuck on society's lowest rung.

Periodically, Parker peered around to make sure he himself wasn't watched. The irony of one watcher observing another amused him. Not that he need worry, he told himself. Being a beefy bruiser, he felt confident he had little to fear from his fellow man. Except perhaps Major Aldwen. Now there was indeed a man to beware of: hard as flint, strong as steel and fit as a fiddle. Even so, the Hall's former gardener couldn't help but raise a smile at the thought of being paid to follow the gentleman's fine lady around the countryside, where he had the pocket-size pretty all to himself. The activity brought a welcome change to his laborious and boring life, making him feel more alive and animated than he had in a long time. And who would have thought there was money to be made from being a peeping Tom? he sniggered.

While sucking hard on his cigarette, Parker studied the sky as if it contained some hidden message. His red-veined eyes felt raw and inflamed. He rubbed his eyelids, scraped the crusted matter from his tear ducts with a dirty fingernail, then looked up once more at the grey expanse. Something in the quality of the light enabled him to estimate the time. He had never owned a timepiece, wrist or pocket. Even without the sun's guiding hand, in common with most rural folk, he depended on his internal clock. Thankfully, there was no sign of precipitation, which meant she would most likely come. He decried the days when she stayed indoors, or rode off into town, and he had to trudge all the way back home feeling as though he'd been robbed of his most-prized possession.

The second he heard her approach, Parker's face lit up with unseemly glee. Hurriedly, he doused his cigarette and popped it behind his ear. Then from his vantage point in the hedge, like a voyeur squinting through a keyhole, he watched her walk into view, looking charmingly cosy tucked into a woollen coat with buttons all the way down the front. Her feet were encased in well-polished black ankle boots, and her head protected by a cloche hat.

Using his hands, Parker pushed himself up from the ground, stretched fully and rubbed his lumbar region. Then he craned his neck as best he could above the hedge to check how far she had gone ahead of him. Mired in her comeliness, he started to stalk her dainty diaphanous steps on his thick stumpy legs, compensated for by a long, broad torso. His almost nonexistent neck gave the impression his head had been plonked directly on top of his shoulders like the head of a pig on a platter. He had the type of physique and physiognomy that made a man conspicuous in the town's upmarket quarter, whereas in the slum public houses and inns nobody gave him a second glance; while the animal inhabitants of the Aldwen estate eyed him with keen suspicion and kept their distance.

Speaking of suspicion, Parker continued to feel concerned about the way his quarry displayed periodic signs of wariness whenever she wandered the estate. Wariness in much the same way a deer lifts its head, pricks its ears and engages its eyes to check the coast is clear before it returns to grazing.

With the back of one cruddy sleeve, Parker rubbed his rheumy eyes. Despite constantly watering, they felt gritty and dry. To his botheration, since his fortieth year his vision had lost some of its sharpness. Bearing his disadvantage in mind, he recognised the importance of maintaining a tactical distance between himself and the girl. Too near risked revealing himself, too far risked losing sight of her. It had never occurred to Parker to bathe his eyes every day and buy himself a pair of glasses.

Moreover, in wintertime the leafless trees made concealment a greater challenge than in summertime, even when he was clad in camouflage. Fortunately, the plentiful shrubs, evergreens and long grasses throughout the estate provided him with adequate cover. However, to be on the safe side, Parker always made sure to smear himself in soil, silt and mud before rolling in rotted leaves, thereby enabling him to blend in better with the natural environment. All that remained, he repeatedly reminded himself, was to tread silently and not to whistle at all costs; for if she became aware of his presence, she might stop wandering the woods altogether.

Grimacing, Parker recalled his most-memorable mistake.

In an attempt to discover the lovely lady's eye colour, at a guess glass-green, he had ventured too close to her. In danger of being seen, he had dropped into the ground hole of an uprooted tree at the very last second. Stiff as a corpse, he had held his breath upon hearing her come to a brief standstill, as if she were listening out for something. Then to his relief, she set off none the wiser. And there he remained until she gained a good distance from him.

Sensitive to her moods now, Parker noticed her air of despondency and peculiar tension in her posture. His earthly angel was clearly out of sorts, and he wondered what ailed her. Her eyes were drawn to the ground and she ignored a huddle of cows as it raised its collective head to look at her when she mooched past the farm field. Quite often she stopped, steepled her hands in front of her mouth and called the herd over to her. It was a plangent call, resonant and haunting, which he loved to hear. And when the cattle responded and came close to the gate, she spoke to them as if they were pets and not livestock.

Later on, when she stopped at the lakeside, Parker, peering over a clump of tall grasses, studied her from behind with unflinching eyes. He liked the way her long coat clung to her trim waist as if hidden hands were pulling it tight from inside. Somehow, she looked chaste as a nun, yet sexy as a pinup, buxom as a barmaid, yet dainty as a damselfly.

When she faced about very suddenly, Parker bobbed down barely in time to avoid her notice. Sitting on his heavy haunches, he puffed out his cheeks, exhaled a draught of air, and said to himself: Bloody Nora, that was close. In many respects, watching her through primal eyes felt like a form of torture. It hurt the very base of his being to look at a thing forever denied him. He wondered why he continued to torment himself. It felt painful. Inexplicably painful and pleasurable all at the same time. And in a moment of enlightenment, he suddenly understood the painful pleasure of compulsive love.

During the same period, Isabella felt strange and unsettled, which she attributed to her low spirits. The bird chatter, such as it was in the winter months, sounded strident and strained. She missed the summer birdsong, full of good cheer and optimism. Feeling physically and mentally depleted by the malcontents in her marriage, she wished she could fly away to a different world. A world in which women lived free from the limitations imposed on them by their menfolk. That's if such a place existed. She doubted it did. Was it any wonder marriage was called wedlock? she mused half amusedly. However, as she went on walking, soothed by nature's charms, she soon shook off her sense of martyrdom.

As was her habit, Isabella lingered awhile at the lakeside. There the woody scents of alders and earthy odours of dank vegetation hung heavy about the air. Since the lichen-coated logs on the littoral looked damp, she remained standing to spare her coat, knowing only too well what Hereward would say if she marked it. Some days she found his fastidiousness insufferable.

After tossing a speckled pebble into the water, Isabella watched with wonderment the ripples spread out, dispersing the gold-flecked leaves languishing on the surface. As she observed the deciduous trees' skeletal limbs quiver in the lake's liquid mirror, a raven flew over and sliced the air with its shrill cry, provoking a chorus of clamorous responses from a variety of avian voices.

Turning aside, Isabella glanced at a strip of slippery, shiny grass over which fat melanic-brown slugs slid unimpeded. Repulsed at the sight of the rubbery beasts, she recoiled and half pivoted with sudden promptitude. In so doing, she caught sight of a fleeting movement in her peripheral vision. Standing stock still, she sucked in a sharp breath, turned her head and stared at the spot where the motion had manifested. Whatever it was had vanished. Still, she reassured herself, it was bound to be either a bird or small mammal, and so she set off again.

Leaving the lakeside for the woody wildness of the Aldwen estate, Isabella recalled the previous evening's contretemps with Hereward, whose words had left a bitter taste in her mouth. His arbitrary husbandly authority always infuriated her. After he had wished her goodnight, to which she had not replied, he kept to his own room; a rare occurrence. But then she expected he knew she would rebuff his caresses with a cruel coldness. Still, she decided, whatever happened between them, there was nothing to be gained from being angry. Even if an eruptive row did vent her pent-up rage. Arguing with Hereward was counterproductive. It only made him dig his heels in even deeper. The best strategy was to learn the art of gentle persuasion. Whatever he said, she refused to renounce her ambition to drive a motorcar.

Later on, when the weather began to change unexpectedly and mist patches started to circulate, Isabella thought it best to abandon her ramble and make a swift return to the Hall. In wintertime the weather was less predictable, which only added to her general nervousness. Despite being fairly familiar with the Aldwen demesne, she knew she would struggle to find her way back in thick fog, especially if it descended too rapidly. On the less-trodden tracks and trails it would be all too easy to wander off in the wrong direction. The very thought of being lost in a fog-filled forest, with the tree trunks standing like ghosts, gave her the willies, so she hastened to locate the path leading back to the Hall.

Thankfully, the grey wisps of mist soon bloated into discrete drops. Nevertheless, Isabella dashed onwards, shooting through the trees at top speed, anxious to be back in case the rain turned torrential. A few minutes hence, finding herself back at the lakeside, she breathed a little easier; until with an inner groan she thought of what Hereward would say if she returned to the Hall soaked to the skin. It didn't bear thinking about. Must hurry, she told herself. At one point she felt tempted to leave the path in favour of taking a shortcut through the long grass, but then decided against it. The grass would be wet and more black slimy slugs might reveal themselves.

Nearby, wearing the look of a peon deprived of a week's wages, Parker stopped and watched the Major's wife cut short her walk. Execrating the unexpected rain under his breath, he scratched his head and debated whether to go home himself. But since the power of his obsession proved stronger than the promise of food and fireside, he set off after her.

He could see her moving at speed. Distracted by her perfect proportions in motion, and in his eagerness to keep pace with her, Parker suffered a sudden lapse in concentration and trod on a thick brittle branch. In the eerie silence of the estate, the sound of the limb cracking beneath his weight rang out like a whip crack. He froze, contorted his face and cursed his stupidity and poor application as he watched her reel around like a startled cat. Despite being a seasoned hunter, his desperate infatuation had once more reduced him to a bumbling amateur.

When a sudden unexplained noise pulled her up in alarm, Isabella decided not to dwell on its cause. But the moment she set her feet in motion, an enormous rust-coloured rat scurried across her path, bringing her to another swift halt. In a convulsive recoil, she hung back in case its family and friends shortly followed in its tracks.

However, while she waited to establish the coast was clear,

a tense figure, dark as a dobermann, swung into focus, rushing towards her with dogged determination. Oh no, she thought, setting her teeth and clenching her hands, now I'm in major trouble.

Chapter 64

"You know, it might be a good idea to carry an umbrella with you on your walks. In the event of a sudden downpour, it'll save you from getting soaked," Hereward advised Isabella as they stood talking under a large black canopy.

Isabella, who was in a more-forgiving mood after her amble, suffered a sudden pang of guilt. Because he was hatless, she assumed Hereward had rushed out to meet her, having seen the rain through the library window. His thoughtfulness made her regret the ugly words she had used to injure him the night before, so she tried not to sound too ungrateful.

"Because umbrellas are heavy and cumbersome," she complained, "and I should find carrying one an awful burden. I would much rather risk getting wet. Also, if I lost it in the forest, you'd be terribly cross."

"Of course, I wouldn't be cross," he objected.

"But you would be. You always are," she said with a pout.

"Then I promise to be less cross."

"I would prefer you not to be cross at all."

"Very well then, if you insist, I shall *not be cross at all*. However, I must warn you that suppressing my spleen places me at greater risk of spontaneous self-combustion. And should that happen, don't be surprised to find me in a melted mess on the library floor."

The thought of her husband as a melted mess on the library

floor made Isabella laugh out loud, and she poked his arm with a playful finger and told him he was frightfully silly.

Hereward raised one eyebrow and looked down at her with affectionate frustration. "As I've told you a million times, my lambkin, I don't want you catching a chill and developing life-threatening complications. If that means sacrificing the odd umbrella, then so be it. It's a price worth paying. In fact, I don't care how many umbrellas we lose in the interests of keeping you safe and sound. We have a fair few of the things in the boot room anyway. It's foolish to be out on the estate in bad weather without proper protection. You know what it's like: first a drop, then a drizzle, and finally a deluge. I do wish you would listen to my advice. But then you have always been a stubborn little madam, more stubborn than a lady buffalo, I might add."

"Yes, and you are equally stubborn," Isabella hit back.

It did not take the mind of a genius to know to what she was referring. When he married Isabella Hereward had not expected her to be so difficult. He wondered from whom she had inherited her independent streak. To some extent he also blamed his sister for his wife's obstinacy. To his mind, Maud's modern views on the subject of female independence and women's rights made her a poor role model for Isabella, not to mention a negative influence. He suspected his sibling of filling her impressionable head with all sorts of subversive nonsense, of which he decidedly disapproved, and he had no idea how to counter it. What's more, he realised he had been naïve to think a teenage girl would respect his rules. Still, what was done was done, and he would have to live with the consequences. But no matter what, he would not permit Isabella to drive a motorcar. According to the newspapers, every year thousands of people were either killed or maimed on British roads, so the thought of his beloved wife behind the wheel of a potentially lethal machine unnerved him like nothing else. It was bad enough watching her ride down the road at full speed on the bicycle while standing up on the pedals. A position he considered most unladylike.

"Please, let's not quarrel," he said as he playfully tweaked her nose.

Simultaneously, slack-jawed, sad-eyed and dispirited, Parker watched the Aldwens converse on the path. From further back a few moments earlier he had observed the Major under an open umbrella hurrying towards his wife. Seeing them together made him feel painfully jealous. Yet although the scene hurt his heart, something inexplicable held him there, and he continued to spy on them as they chatted.

The umbrella's metal frame reminded Parker of batwings. He loved to observe the small mammals at dawn and dusk launch themselves from their roosts, fly freely, effortlessly, frenetically. He admired their swift swooping manoeuvrability. He decided that if he were blessed with a bat's capabilities, he would fly to the Hall every evening, peep through the bathroom window and ogle the beauty in her bathtub. Except in his excitement, he forgot the bathroom window was frosted glass.

As he went on watching the couple, it occurred to Parker he had never used an umbrella. A man like him had no truck with such fancy contrivances. In his experience only the better-off brigade carried umbrellas. White-collar workers needing to protect their smart clothes, he thought with an eye roll. The Major could undoubtedly afford as many umbrellas as he liked. Parker had no idea what the rain shields cost, but he doubted the poor could afford them.

Since there was nothing to be gained from following them, and feeling like an unshorn sheep marooned on a wet moor, as soon as the couple started making their way back to the Hall, Parker decided to withdraw. Plus, he was worried in case Major

Aldwen spotted him there, became suspicious and asked him why he was hanging around the estate. The man was nobody's fool. Without a convincing explanation on his tongue, the snoop knew it would be like walking straight into the lion's den. And the Major had every right to protect his wife, he told himself. After all, a wife was a man's property.

So, for the umpteenth time, Parker left his peeping paradise and set off for home, this time sidestepping puddles on the paths. Ravenous now, he was looking forward to lighting a fire, roasting a rabbit slain with ruthless efficiency, and wolfing it down with a large tin mug of boiling-hot tea, while all the while fantasising about the lovely lady's most-succulent parts. In the festering depths of his purulent mind, he imagined forcing his fetish face down over a log, rendered helpless as the rabbits he ensnared, and using her as nature intended; culminating in an audible moan of pleasure that would have made Isabella vomit had she heard it.

Chapter 65

At Christmastime Hereward surprised Isabella with several presents from him to her. They were placed under one of the trees Boyle had been instructed to put up early on Christmas Eve. Assisted by the maids, Isabella had decorated the tree with plaster ornaments purchased unashamedly from the new Woolworths on the high street, shiny bright-coloured baubles and a set of fairy lights new to the market, which Hereward had ordered at her request. He liked to spoil her and never denied her rare requests for material things. In fact, he had never known anyone as sensible and careful with money as his wife. Sometimes he couldn't help but compare her with Rosalyn, who constantly ordered new outfits, makeup and scent.

With irrepressible excitement, Isabella was looking forward to opening her parcels. In fact, she could hardly wait. Much to Hereward's amusement, she found it impossible to walk past the tree without picking up one of her gifts and giving it a gentle shake in order to guess its contents.

"If you continue to mishandle your presents in that manner, young lady, don't be at all surprised if you discover on Christmas morning Father Christmas has crept in overnight and removed them," warned a waggish Hereward.

Isabella chortled with good cheer. "I'm sure Father Christmas is far too kind and caring to do something so mean and horrid," she replied.

Hereward shook his head as if he were dealing with an incorrigible but adorable child. It was the first time he had seen her look truly happy, which made him feel happy too. If only it were Christmas every day, he thought wistfully.

When Christmas day dawned Hereward invited Isabella to join him for breakfast in the morning room prior to opening their presents. For the very first time since coming to live at the Hall, she had the privilege of choosing the size of her own breakfast portions. And she made sure to fill her plate. As she ate, she could barely contain her excitement and bolted down her food, earning her a strong look of disapproval from her husband.

Once breakfast was finished, they moved to the hall, where Isabella sat on her heels on the floor beside the tree. Meanwhile, Hereward occupied a nearby chair. She had not felt so joyous in years.

"Well now, let's see what good old Father Christmas has left for us," he said, rubbing his hands together. "What one receives does of course depend on one's conduct throughout the year," he added with mock solemnity. "And since, Isabella, you've been an impish miss on countless occasions, I'm not sure to what degree this has affected Saint Nicholas's generosity."

Isabella giggled girlishly and told Hereward he was perfectly potty. After which she looked up at him expectantly.

"Well, ladies first," he said, motioning with his open hand to the parcels.

"I don't know where to start," said she, cupping her face in her hands with childlike perplexity.

Decisively, Hereward picked up the smallest package and pressed it into her palms. "Happy Christmas, darling," he said.

Visibly excited, Isabella unwrapped a small black-velvet box, flipped up the lid and gasped audibly.

"Allow me," he said smoothly. Then he released the ruby

and white-diamond pendant from its hold, placed it around her throat and, with fingers as gentle as they were strong, fastened the gold clasp behind her neck.

"I bought this during my London trip," he explained. "I've been waiting for weeks to give it to you."

Isabella tilted her chin to her chest and stroked the sparkling pear-shaped jewel. "Gosh. I wasn't expecting something so stupendous. It must have cost a king's ransom," she said, voicing her thoughts.

"I'm pleased you like it," said Hereward.

"Who wouldn't?" she answered. "Thank you so much." And she rose up on her knees and lightly brushed his cheek with her lips.

"Only the finest things are worthy of you, my darling," he said smiling. "Anyway, onto the next one."

Isabella instantly recognised the cashmere shawl she had been admiring in Martha's window display for weeks. She had agonised over buying it for herself, but after much reflection decided the expense was unjustifiable.

"How on earth did you know about this?" she asked in astonishment. Suddenly all became clear. "Ah, now I know. You've been conspiring with Martha. It's funny but I noticed a week ago it had disappeared from the shop window, so naturally I assumed it was sold. Which of course, it was. Gosh, you're a dark horse."

"Yes, I admit to ringing her. She's quite the saleswoman. The shawl was her idea by the way, so I really can't take the credit. Naturally, I had to swear her to secrecy."

"I'm touched by how much trouble you've taken," said Isabella.

"Gift number three now," said Hereward, hoping to make a little more headway into her heart.

The Viennese snow globe put a huge smile on Isabella's

face. After giving it a good shake, she watched with delight the tiny white fragments swirl under the small glass dome.

"Wow! This is amazing," she squeaked. "You know I used to look at these things in the gift-shop window and promise myself that if ever I had some spare shillings, I would buy one for myself."

Next came a huge box of chocolates. Although tempted to open them there and then, Isabella managed to control herself for once.

However, it was Hereward's fifth and final gift that reduced her to tears. As he handed her a solid package in the shape of a cube, Isabella looked at it and said: "This just has to be books. One can never have too many books." After which she untied the ribbon and tore off the silver wrapping to reveal three leather-bound volumes with embossed lettering down their spines. They appeared strangely familiar. She stared at Hereward, then at the books, her eyes lighting up in recognition. Raising each of their front covers in turn to confirm her suspicions, she discovered the old dedications inside: *To Isabella on the occasion of your birthday. With love Mama and Papa xxx.*

"When did you buy them?" she asked, her hand on his arm, her eyes moist with emotion.

Half smiling, Hereward tapped the side of his nose with his finger, then gently wiped a tear from her cheek with his thumb.

Next it was his turn. Isabella, whose budget, unlike her husband's, was strictly limited, gave him a book, a monogrammed handkerchief, a silk necktie, and a photograph of herself in a silver frame. At Maud's suggestion, she had visited a professional photographer on the high street to have her picture taken.

The framed photograph was a huge success. Hereward loved it. "I think the best place for this is on my desk beside the typewriter," he said, a smile crinkling the corners of his eyes. "Then in future I shan't have to wait until luncheon to feast my eyes on that fabulous face."

Isabella blushed and grinned at the same time. She couldn't recall the last time she had enjoyed Christmas so much. Plus, the day had hardly begun. During their leanest years, the Actons had celebrated as best they could, but were dependent on the benevolence of relatives. At the mercy of her mother's cousin with the migrating hands, Isabella had hated every minute of it.

Later they joined Maud and Cynthia at late-morning Mass, after which the four of them drove back to the Hall for a huge Christmas dinner made by Mrs Jenkins and served by Boyle with the help of the maids. As usual, Isabella ate her fill. In fact, she ate so much she feared her stomach might burst.

During the afternoon, when they were all taking a much-needed respite in the sitting room, Isabella, feeling restless, got up from the sofa to stretch her legs. Glancing out of the window, she thought she saw the branch of a laurel bush move downwards. However, she blamed her overindulgence in port and wine for what she assumed was a simple misimpression.

On Christmas Day evening, Cynthia mixed them all cocktails from a collection of recipes featured for the first time in a national newspaper. A few hours later, Isabella, having imbibed one too many limb-inhibiting liquids, had to be carried upstairs by Hereward and, with Maud's assistance, put to bed. He laughed liberally as she serenaded him with unabashed gaiety while he tucked her in tight, fearing she might roll out during the night and hurt herself.

In the small hours, Hereward was awoken by the sound of vomiting in the bathroom. After going in to check, he found Isabella retching over the lavatory bowl while vowing never to touch another cocktail as long as she lived. He gently rubbed her back, fetched her a glass of water with which to rinse her mouth, wiped her face with a wet washcloth, and helped her back to bed. Then for the second time that night, he tucked her in tight and decided his lecture on intemperance could wait until morning.

On Boxing Day, the staff were given their bonuses, some small gifts, and the day off. Hereward and Isabella, her complexion a washed-out white, drove over to Maud's house for luncheon. He thought it best to keep his wife away from the Hall while the Boxing Day hunt charged across the estate, knowing full well the spectacle would upset her. Next year he planned to refuse permission, knowing full well it would make him a pariah in the hunters' eyes, but not being one to court popularity, he hardly cared.

After returning to the Hall in the evening, they ate cold-turkey sandwiches, fruitcake and mince pies in place of dinner, prepared in advance by Mrs Jenkins, who had gone to stay with her sister for one night.

Isabella was grateful they had the house to themselves for once, although Boyle was expected back later that evening. She welcomed the opportunity to speak freely without fear of being overheard by the butler or Barbara. She was half expecting to receive a sermon from Hereward on the perils of immoderation, but if he were cross with her, he showed no sign of it, for which she was grateful. Still feeling a touch woozy from the night before, she took herself off to bed early while her husband waited up for the butler's return.

Late on Boxing Day night Parker hung his jacket on a nail on the wall and got the fire started. The long trek home from the tavern had sobered him up and he felt cold and maudlin. Rubbing his hands together over the flames, he warmed them up until they tingled sharply. Although as rough as a tiger's tongue, they served him well enough.

That afternoon he had watched the Oakwich hunt hurtle past. The annual event included the usual collection of bellicose mad hatters on horseback, all of whom he hated. Desperate to return to his regular routine, Parker felt relieved the festive days were done and dusted. Christmas held little appeal for him now his mother was no longer alive. His mother, the woman he was brought up to believe was his sister. Aged fourteen, she had borne him out of wedlock, father unidentified on all documentation. Mother or sister, he still missed her. He recalled every Christmas they ate venison he shot without permission on the estate with the rifle he no longer possessed. Removing a crusty old rag from his pocket, he blew his nose, wiped his eyes, and blessed her poor soul.

As he spat on the fire, Parker's thoughts resettled on the hatchling and her husband. On Christmas Day, taking a calculated risk, he had covertly watched them enjoying a short walk accompanied by two stout ladies, one of whom he recognised as Miss Aldwen. He had heard them laughing, joking and chatting, which only compounded his sorrow and sense of loneliness. Worst of all, when he witnessed the Major put his arm around his wife's waist, Parker was consumed by murder-inducing jealousy. Had he been holding a gun he might just have shot him.

The lovely lady was in high spirits and giggled when the Major accused her of quaffing too much port. Parker found her fascinating in a way other females were not. He considered Major Aldwen far too sober and serious for the vivacious young woman, who moved with the flexibility of a fawn and laughed like a green woodpecker. For a substantial time, he had felt the need for a woman on whom to focus his attention and now he had found one. And he felt suddenly grateful to Miss Dumbarton for drawing his attention to her.

Later on, after the Aldwens had returned to base, like a burglar staking out a property, Parker had homed in on the Hall's windows, eager to steal a glimpse of the girl before taking off into town. And when she made a sudden brief appearance at the glass, he felt like a hungry dog hanging about outside the butcher's shop hoping for a few scraps. After swallowing hard, he chewed his fist in frustration. She looked good enough to eat. He imagined his mouth on her flesh and her intimate sweetness on his tongue. He understood why the Major had married the tiddler instead of the detestable Miss Dumbarton. No man worth his salt would touch mutton when there was tender young lamb on the menu, he said to himself with a squalid smirk.

Before leaving, Parker had opened his fly and sprayed a bush with frothy green fluid. He shook his member a couple of times, returned it to its cruddy enclosure, and began trekking to the slums' seediest tavern. While there, he drowned his lovesick sorrows in several tankards of warm bitter ale and bored all and sundry with the virtues of his newfound fetish, taking care not to name her.

Chapter 66

Come January, most of the conservatory's new plants had survived winter's worst. Even some of the originals had rallied thanks to Isabella's gentle devotion. Over the course of a few short months, she had transformed the forsaken space into an oasis of semi-tropical calm and tranquillity, inspired in part by her visit with Hereward to the Botanical Gardens. The glass gleamed, the glazed floor tiles shone and the tables boasted new linen napery. It was no longer a plant cemetery, but a delightful place to sit and admire the surroundings.

Despite his initial resistance, Hereward no longer discouraged her from revamping what he wryly described as Isabella's jungle. Sometimes he even showed some interest in her efforts. One afternoon when he was afflicted by a bad case of writer's block, he wandered into the conservatory in search of his wife's society, thinking a break and brief chat might help clear his head.

Isabella was tending to her plants when he entered. She looked across at him, smiled briefly, then returned to her tasks. Something about his cool, casual, confident manner and sure stride always made her feel bashful, although she could never quite work out why.

Hands on hips, Hereward surveyed the room. "I must say my green-fingered little fairy, with each passing day this place looks more like a rainforest than an English glasshouse," he said with a teasing grin. "But seriously, my sweet, in no time at all you've turned a dilapidated space that once stank of stale tobacco into a splendid indoor haven."

Isabella's lips curved into a shy smile and she thanked him for his kind comments. Although she never sought his approval, she nevertheless felt pleased. The conservatory gave her much pleasure and provided her with a refuge when it rained. Plus, there was less chance of bumping into Boyle in there, who kept out on account of his seething resentment of the way she had made the place her own.

Hereward adored his wife's shy smile, which made a welcome change from her truculent chin. After inserting himself in one of the new cane chairs, he patiently waited for her to pass by. Then when she did, he grabbed hold of her, pulled her onto his lap and planted several kisses on her face and neck.

"This place is perfect for you," he said, a touch of humour in his tone.

"Why is that?" asked Isabella with a puzzled frown as she tried her best to prize herself from his lap.

"Because it's a hothouse for a hot-tempered little hussy," he said holding her tight while recalling the time she threw the pail of dirty water all over him. He could make light of it now. Then he began to tickle her and threatened to continue until she promised to be good.

Meantime, Boyle was pretending to potter about in the adjoining room so he could eavesdrop on the couple in case they started arguing. Since he still hoped their marriage would end in divorce, he loved to hear them at loggerheads. But when he heard Isabella shrieking with laughter while begging Hereward to stop tickling her, he was visibly overcome with a vehemence more virulent than a vile of green venom. To his offended ears she sounded more like a common market girl than a true-blue lady.

Unable to tolerate their good humour, Boyle slid away like a slug in the night. Having grown to love the earnest young gentleman, it hurt the butler to hear him giving way to his baser instincts. He regretted more than anything the Major's marriage and he wished he had it in his power to end it.

With great difficulty, Isabella extricated herself from Hereward's hold. Then from a safe distance she studied him with interest. She had never known anyone as fastidious as her husband. His close-cropped beard was always trimmed to perfection like the top of a topiary hedge. She sometimes wondered how he would look clean shaven. But what most intrigued her was the hairline scar on his upper lip. And since he was in a good mood, she drew in a quick breath to steady her voice, motioned to his lip and enquired outright how he had managed to injure it.

"The tip of a sword was the culprit," he said. "I regret I can't boast it was due to some heroic action on my part. At least not on that occasion," he added after a pause. "I was fooling around with some fellow officers during a heavy drinking session and unfortunately one of the blighters got a bit carried away." As he laughed at the memory, his teeth gleamed and his eyes shone. "Because the lips are quite vascular, it bled like the devil," he explained. After which, he stroked his chin in contemplation and said: "So, you've been studying me closely, I see."

Isabella's face flushed fluorescent red.

Sharp as a scalpel, Hereward regarded his wife with interest. He liked her attention. He liked her curious liquid-green eyes looking at him instead of away. It meant she wasn't indifferent to him. Indifference was death to a relationship.

Then he stood up as if to leave. "While we're on the subject, is there anything else you'd like to know about me?" he said, thrusting his hands deep inside his trouser pockets, stretching the fabric tight across his hard, flat stomach.

"Yes, as it happens, there is one thing," she said with renewed boldness. "During your time in India did you ever shoot a tiger?"

The answer was a firm no. "I've never desired to kill such a magnificent beast," he declared. "Unlike many of my compatriots, I have never felt the need to prove my manhood other than in battle or on the sports field."

Isabella felt a mixture of admiration and relief. She detested the brutality of big-game hunting and the wholesale, bloodthirsty slaughter of God's creatures for human gratification. She saw nothing heroic in such endeavours.

"Tiger shoots can only be considered sporting when both sides have guns," added Hereward with a facetious grin.

"Quite so," agreed Isabella. "All the same, as a landowner you're unlikely to endear yourself to the local hunting fraternity with such views."

"I expect not. Anyhow, when did you first notice the scar as it's not that obvious?" he said, changing the subject.

"The first time I saw you at my parents' house." Then when her face blundered a third time, Isabella excused herself and returned to her tasks.

"We can have a wager if you wish," suggested Hereward the following day. "How about a pound? Or ten shillings if you consider a pound prodigal?"

"Certainly not," said Isabella. "Gambling's a sin in the eyes of the Lord."

"So is stealing apples," he reminded her.

"That's different, I was hungry," she said sadly.

"I'm sorry I mentioned it. Forgive me. It was a poor attempt at humour on my part."

"Yes, it was. But since I'm not one to bear a grudge, I forgive you," she said tongue firmly in cheek.

"That's a relief, thank goodness," he said, giving her a gamesome look.

"Anyhow, I plan to get up extra early to watch you. That way I'll know for sure if you've been telling me fibs."

"Fibs, me?!" he joked with his hand on his chest.

"Well, you do rather like to amuse yourself at my expense."

"I do?" said Hereward with mock incredulity.

"You know perfectly well you do. In my experience, country gentlemen, or any gentlemen for that matter, don't chop wood. They employ woodsmen, or get the gardener to do it. And in town the stuff's delivered ready cut."

"I've no doubt they do," agreed Hereward. "But, my dubious little darling, as I've already said, I need the exercise and I enjoy working my muscles. I don't understand why you're unwilling to accept my word."

"Because I prefer to see for myself if you pass muster."

"Ah, *pass muster* you say! I thought by now you would be fully acquainted with my mastery," he exclaimed with a wicked glint in his eye."

Aware he was toying with her again, Isabella clammed up, mumbled an excuse and escaped the room.

When the time came to chop the logs, Isabella hurried down to the boot room, grabbed an old shawl and threw it around her shoulders. Having risen early, she hadn't had time to dress, so she was glad the morning was mild and dry with only a light breeze.

Hereward was already outside warming up for his morning exercise when she arrived. He had on old khaki trousers held up with brown-leather braces, the sleeves of his combinations were gathered above his elbows, revealing strong muscular forearms, while the unbuttoned top displayed a triangle of pale-bronze flesh.

Except for a little light gardening, Isabella had never seen a gentleman performing manual work. Although Hereward was strong, she could hardly imagine him doing anything arduous, and suspected him of pulling her leg still. Work-wise, her idle father had lifted nothing heavier than a pen. He considered having a regular job beneath him. Not that he would have found one. Hence when their money disappeared in some high-risk ventures, he made no effort to find gainful employment. Heirlooms and whatever they possessed of value were either pawned or sold, with Isabella appointed pawnshop patron to spare her parents' humiliation.

From the boot-room step Isabella watched with interest as Hereward prepared to swing the axe in his black-gloved hands. With his feet flat on the ground, his legs shoulder-width apart and his face muscles tight with concentration, he straightened up, rose onto his toes, raised the blade above his head and, with a mighty downswing, split a huge block of hardwood into several sections.

Set-faced and serious, Boyle gathered up the logs in a basket and transferred them to the woodshed to dry out. As a rule, he enjoyed the joint enterprise enormously. The woodcutting process enabled him to work directly alongside his beloved master. Therefore, he resented the mistress's presence and considered it none of her business. In fact, he thought her indecent and indecorous standing there in her nightwear watching her husband chop firewood.

With relief, Isabella gave herself a huge pat on the back. Had she accepted Hereward's wager, she would now be poorer by at least ten shillings. And knowing him, for pure devilment he would have insisted on her discharging her debt. She could almost picture the smug satisfaction on his face as she handed over his ill-gotten gains.

Meanwhile, Hereward wiped his brow with the back of his hand, then removed his handkerchief to mop the moisture from his face and neck. After grabbing a thick branch from the ground, he snapped it over his knee as if it were a mere twig and threw it aside. Somewhat surprised that Isabella had risen early to watch him, he gave her a lingering look as the breeze parted the split of her robe, revealing a glimpse of white-cotton nightgown beneath, and tousled her cascading curls still on bedtime release. The enticing flow of her form made him want to dump the axe, shoulder her upstairs and exercise his muscles in her bed instead. And who could blame him? She looked utterly divine; to be savoured on the palate like a fine wine.

The evidence before his eyes, Hereward surmised that unlike Rosalyn, Isabella had a lackadaisical attitude to her appearance. She gave the impression she cared little for her face or figure. Nor did she coat her face in slick cosmetics, he was pleased to say. But then she had no need to. Her complexion was as smooth and flawless as the inner flesh of a fresh coconut. There was nothing affected or fake about Isabella. Her unadulterated face was the perfect match for her unadulterated nature.

Chapter 67

During the woodchopping operation, panting and sweating like onions in a frying pan, his lips leaking spittle, one greasy hand inside his age-stained long johns, Parker peeped through a crack in the door of the empty stable stall, where he had spent the night on the straw-strewn floor. The place still retained a faint odour of horse manure and urine from the time before the horses were sold off.

Parker regretted giving up his gardening job at the Hall for one closer to his village. On reflection, he deemed it a monumental mistake. Had he known a wonderful young woman would be coming to live there, he would have stayed on. Several times he had considered asking Boyle for his old job back. From what he could gather they had still to appoint his successor. Yet something told him the snobby butler was glad to be rid of him, and Parker wasn't about to beg.

Like a starving stray eyeing up a beefsteak at a butcher's stall, Parker licked his leprous lips. The Major's missus in her night robe was a sight to behold. He was surprised to see her up and about so early, more especially before she was dressed. A fortuitous treat, nevertheless, he thought. He was also surprised Major Aldwen permitted his wife to stand on the boot-room step inappropriately attired; even if she did resemble a chaste medieval maiden. And a very alluring medieval maiden at that.

Inch by inch, his eyes displaying an unnatural glaze, Parker's gaze travelled up and down her body before finally settling on her bosom. Blimey, she looks fresh and flavoursome, he said to himself with an unsavoury smile; as fresh and flavoursome as the first squeeze of milk in the morning, and tastier than the cream at the top of the bottle. Which reminded him, since waking he'd had nothing to eat or drink. Once the coast was clear, he planned to stop by the Hall's kitchen on the pretext of passing by and beg a billycan of sweet milky tea and a biscuit from the chunky cantankerous cook. As he was already known to the staff, he felt sure they wouldn't begrudge him a little sustenance. But the moment he remembered he was meant to be in disguise, he quickly abandoned the idea.

A little later, when he witnessed the Major's wife toss her hair aside, Parker forgot all about food and drink. With his tongue poking through the gap in his lips, he leered at her like a gluttonous amphibian. It was the first time he'd seen her hair hanging loose and he admired the way it flowed over her shoulders and back like a cataract. In his opinion, it looked a hundred times more fetching than the Dumbarton hag's helmet-style hairdo. Parker detested the Major's old flame and despised her ice-cold superiority. A cartload of tan-coloured slap couldn't warm up that wintry face, he decided. Nothing would give him greater pleasure than to knock her off her self-important pedestal with a well-aimed punch. No wonder the Major had ditched her. The woman might be a toff, but she was a tart all the same, he said to himself with untypical pietistic sentiment, the irony of which was lost on him.

Often when Parker paraded through the woods, he pictured himself as his hero, Robin Hood. In his boyhood he had loved listening to tales of the outlaw and his band of merry men, told to him by his mother. He now also indulged himself by imagining the Major's missus as Maid Marian. Besides the present Mrs Aldwen, no woman had ever had such a powerful effect on him. Not even Mrs Parker in her first flush of womanhood; before, that is, she ran off with a ratcatcher.

As he went on watching the action, Parker grew worried about his situation. He feared Boyle might enter the stable block with any surplus firewood and find him hiding there, blowing his precarious cover as a result. Normally, the risk of exposure somehow added to his excitement, but seeing the Major wielding a large axe had a subduing effect on him. In need of a convincing excuse for his presence in the event of discovery, he planned to say he was taken ill on his way home the previous night and sought shelter in the stable. And if he were lucky, they might take pity on him and offer him a little nourishment.

After scratching his scrotum Parker withdrew a penknife from his breast pocket. To check its sharpness, he ran his thumb along the blade's edge to its point. Satisfied with its razor-sharp quality, he put it back and returned to spying. As he did so, a falcon screeched a warning cry above the stable block. That instant he observed Mrs Aldwen shudder, tighten her robe and return inside. Disappointed by her sudden departure, Parker lay down, put one hand behind his head and waited for the Major to finish his task.

Back inside, Isabella wondered why the falcon's cry had caused her to shiver with such violence. She hoped Hereward hadn't noticed. Had he done so, she knew to expect a scolding later on for standing on the step in her nightwear. Recently, he had grown more tolerant of her wearing her hair down, provided she tied it up when she left the house. For the sake of convenience, she sometimes considered having it cut short at one of the fancy salons in town. But then she knew he was certain to disapprove. For if she were to appear in his presence in the guise of a blonde Joan of Arc, and a curly Joan at that, she giggled to herself, he would probably burst a blood vessel.

Later that same day at luncheon, once Boyle had vacated the room, Hereward gently admonished Isabella for standing at the open door in her nightwear.

"Whilst I must admit you looked deliciously indecent this morning, my darling," he said. "Or should that be indecently delicious? You also seemed rather cold. I noticed you shiver."

"I was perfectly warm, I promise," Isabella assured him. "I simply suffered that odd sensation of a sudden unaccountable shudder. There's that popular phrase, isn't there? You know the one. Someone just walked over my grave. Which I think describes it rather well."

"Well, whatever the reason, it's not warm enough at this time of year to stand on the threshold in your nightclothes," he advised her. "Especially so early in the morning. You seem determined to catch a chill."

Isabella smiled and changed the subject. "Well now you've confirmed you really do chop the wood by yourself, I must apologise for doubting you. It's just that most, if not all, of my male relatives rarely lift a finger. Papa was forced to start dressing himself when he could no longer afford to employ a valet. I remember we were down to just one maid, and that was only because she had nowhere else to go, and my parents expected the poor woman to do everything. Since I felt desperately sorry for her, I used to assist her in the kitchen. And make my own bed too. I don't ever want to become too dependent on others. It's all very well having servants and suchlike, but one must also be capable of taking care of oneself should circumstances demand."

"You are wise indeed for one so young, my dear," said Hereward. "But I suspect your insecurity stems from your family's financial troubles. However, you mustn't fret about money. My ancestors weren't strictly country people. Some of them worked in the City too and invested substantial sums of money in land, property and safe concerns. I learned from them, which is why I've remained relatively unscathed by the Depression."

"And I have the privilege and pleasure of exploring this beautiful land at my leisure," rejoined Isabella.

"And long may you continue to do so, my darling," he said in conclusion.

Chapter 68

Her small fingers clinging to the handle of a basket of berries, Isabella hared headlong over the misty meadow in the fading light of a dismal day. Glancing back over her shoulder, she saw a fox the size of a deerhound coursing after her; its thick brush suspended in a horizontal plane. It was the largest fox she had ever set eyes on. A fiendish fox with yellowish flesh-stripping fangs and evil eyes. Never in her life had she expected to be chased by a rabid animal. Never had something so vicious looked so elegant in the way it covered the ground with effortless, limb-stretching strides.

Stricken with panic, Isabella tripped over a thick grassy hassock and went down with a thud. Too terrified to look back, she hurled herself up from the ground and valiantly forged ahead. But before long her limbs grew heavy and her muscles became tight. She felt as though she was wading through wet clay. To increase her momentum, she swung her arms in a quadrant, but the movement made little impact on her pace.

The mad canine continued to chase her with alarming speed. Isabella knew she could not go on much longer with the crazed creature snapping at her heels. She feared that once it caught hold of her, it would carry her off to its den to be devoured alive like a hen.

Since the Hall was still far away, Isabella decided a tree offered the best protection. So, she looked for one with low-growing branches strong enough to take her weight. Fortunately, there was one close by. Despite her exhaustion, with a mighty effort she managed to climb the trunk. But then to her horror, the fox snarled, flexed its feet and clambered up after her with squirrel-like ease, forcing her to go higher than she originally intended.

Taking in a panoramic view from high up in the tree, Isabella spotted Hereward in the distance. He seemed to be searching for her. She screamed his name with such force she feared she might rupture her larynx. However, he failed to hear her. Hoping to catch his attention through different means, she waved wildly, but to no avail.

As darkness began to descend over the estate, it dawned on Isabella that she was trapped; trapped by a predatory fox intent on having her for supper. Growing evermore desperate, afraid she might soon lose her balance and hurtle to the ground, she again attempted to scream, but the sound only stuck in her throat.

Then with its razor-sharp teeth, the fox grabbed the hem of her dress and tugged…

Isabella's eyes flew open and her heart hammered in her chest like a metronome gone mad. Her nightdress, damp with perspiration, clung to her skin. Momentarily, time, sense and space lost all meaning. Then her disorientation dissipated, her adrenaline rush receded and she regained her mental faculties. Once she knew she was safe in her own bed, her breathing slowed and her panic subsided.

It was the fourth time in as many days that Isabella had dreamt of being chased by a fox. She tried to make sense of the recurring nightmare by meditating on its possible significance. Was it symbolic? A warning? An omen? She knew not what to make of it. It seemed to her such an odd thing when, in her own funny way, she liked foxes. The red-furred creatures fascinated her and she loved to observe them in and around the Hall's grounds.

Isabella checked the time on the small clock on the bedside cabinet. There was still an hour to go before breakfast. Feeling spent, she considered going back to sleep. After all, without a useful occupation she had no compelling reason to get up and dressed. However, as she was about to roll onto her side, the bedroom door swung open and Hereward stepped into the room.

With a show of concern, he said he had heard her cry out and had come to make sure everything was all right. Not long out of the shower, he wore a small white towel draped around his neck, his hair was damp, his skin was moist, and he smelled of ivory soap and mint toothpaste. After sitting beside Isabella on the bed, his thigh touching hers, he noticed her clammy clothing and tiny beads of perspiration on her brow.

"What is it, darling, are you unwell?" he said placing his palm on her forehead to check for signs of a fever.

Where his towelling robe gaped Isabella could see part of Hereward's naked thigh. Despite trying her best not to look, to her eternal shame, the sight of his firm flesh drew her eyes like a magnet, and a rosy red flash rolled over her chest, neck and cheeks. Discomposed by a sensation new to her, she lowered her eyes, looked at her hands and hoped he hadn't seen her gawping at the gap in his robe. Then as soon as she felt she had sufficient mastery over herself, Isabella met Hereward's solicitous eyes and replied in a quivery voice: "I'm fine. Really. It was just a silly old nightmare. Nothing to worry about. Honestly."

"Are you sure?" he said, gazing deep into her brilliant-green eyes, fraught with tension.

"Yes, of course I'm sure," she answered rather quickly.

Too quickly, thought Hereward.

Then, after a short pause, she added: "You know I read somewhere that dreams are simply reservoirs of random thoughts that get all mixed up in one's mind, so there's no need to be alarmed by them."

"Mm," he murmured dubiously. He noticed she was wringing her hands as she spoke. And her cheeks were pale and blotchy. "Well let's hope you haven't caught a chill. I think to be on the safe side it might be wise for you to stay in bed for the rest of today and keep yourself warm. I'll arrange to have extra logs brought up to your room."

Meeting her husband's concerned gaze, Isabella felt tempted. But then what would she do? "No really, Herry," she said placing her small hand over his in an unconscious placatory gesture. "I'd much rather get up as soon as I've had breakfast."

A strange look passed over Hereward's face. It was the first time she had used a diminutive of his name. She had done so unknowingly. Never in his life had anyone shortened his name. Nor had he ever had a nickname, not even at school. And no-one had ever given him a pet name, not even his sister. Being addressed by Isabella as *Herry* felt special somehow. Special in an intimate way. Perhaps his wife was a little fond of him after all, he said to himself. Well, he could only hope.

"Very well then if you're absolutely sure," he said giving her thigh an affectionate tap. Then he leaned over her, brushed her brow with his lips and tucked a curl behind her small cute ear. And before he could succumb to temptation, he forced himself up from the bed and returned to his room to get dressed.

Feeling drowsy all of a sudden, Isabella yawned, rolled onto her side, closed her eyes, and drifted off to sleep.

However, when she awakened an hour later, she was overawed by a sense of foreboding. No matter how hard she tried, she couldn't shake off the feeling that something bad was about to happen. Thinking her recurring nightmare might be some kind of portent, she thought she would check to see if the Hall's library held a book on the subject of dreams. But then she thought it unlikely. She could hardly imagine Hereward having an interest in symbolism, the occult, or for that matter anything based on abstract reasoning. To him her nightmare was nothing more than a plain and simple bad dream, and a nonsensical one at that.

"There you are," said Hereward upon entering the conservatory. "I thought I might find you here. You didn't come to listen to the wireless and your cocoa has gone cold."

"Oh, has it? I'm awfully sorry," said Isabella. "I forgot all about the cocoa and I wasn't in much of a mood for the wireless. Sometimes I just like to listen to silence, if you know what I mean?"

Neither spoke for a few moments.

Passing his hands over his crown, Hereward smoothed his hair down. "Is there something wrong, Isabella? You seem very quiet, if not a little on edge. You're not still dwelling on your bad dream I hope."

"No, everything's fine," she assured him with a weak smile.

"Come then, it's time for bed," he said holding out his hand. "Boyle's waiting to lock up and rewind the clocks."

The blessed clocks, she thought. How their lives were ruled by the clocks; marking every second, every minute and every hour of every day.

"Just a few minutes more and I'll be along," she promised, ignoring his outstretched hand.

Thank heaven there isn't a clock in the conservatory, she said to herself. And I shall resist all attempts to include one in here too.

After Hereward left the room, Isabella rose from the chair and gazed at the garden bathed in the moon's luminescence. The lunar light cast the grounds in a cold, blue-white, almost metallic glow, long shadows, dark as damson, lined the lawn, and unblinking bark-embedded pareidolia stared out from the trees.

Feeling shattered yet stirred, in slow motion Isabella moved close to the window. She realised she was still adjusting to life in the country, and life in the country was taking some adjusting to. I do believe living in this secluded place is affecting my nerves, she told herself. During the times she had roamed the estate with her friends, she had never felt nervous. Not even once. But then they always made sure to leave before nightfall. Nightfall was different: different sounds, different sights, different guises.

As she continued observing the scene, the bushes bordering the lawn began to rustle and swish like a long silk-taffeta skirt. From the corner of her eye, Isabella caught sight of a barely perceptible movement. Pressing her palms and face flat to the cold glass, she squinted in an effort to make out its form.

With hesitancy, in a tense rectilinear movement, an elongated, slender shape stole out from behind the bushes. But without warning it turned tail and departed, quick as a flash. As Isabella stood spellbound at the glass, a cloud drifted over the moon, creating a brief blackout. Then during the moon's re-emergence, a young fox limbered out from between two plump laurels on the hunt for creatures brave enough to leave their hideouts. Adopting a low crouch, it crept across to one of the flowerbeds and, like a pig hunting for truffles, swept the cloddy earth with its nose. Startled by another sound, it retreated into the bushes, only to reappear when it spotted something of interest. Then it pounced, grabbed its provender and sped off.

Unable to tear herself away, Isabella gasped in horror and covered her mouth with her hand.

Over successive nights the fox made numerous appearances around the Hall's grounds. Every night before climbing into bed, Isabella looked out of the window in the hope of catching a glimpse of the stealthy creature. Although she was captivated by foxes, she understood most countryfolk loathed them. Some even derived a peculiar pleasure from killing them. Sometimes on Sunday mornings she observed the local hunting fraternity clad in pink jackets riding through Oakwich town centre, most of them arrogant and full of themselves. She could hardly begin to imagine how it must feel to be pursued for miles before being ripped apart in a frenzy of violence. She knew Hereward classed foxes as vermin, but, in their defence, he also said they reduced the nuisance rabbit population.

With each consecutive visit the young fox ventured closer to the house. Once upon entering the bedroom, Hereward caught Isabella in her nightclothes standing at the window. When he ordered her straight to bed, she affected not to hear him. So, he strode over, picked her up like a disobedient puppy and put her to bed himself. She had giggled, bucked and flailed, but to no avail; his prodigious strength making resistance futile.

"I do believe the fox is looking a bit straggly," said Isabella in all seriousness. "I think it mightn't be getting enough to eat."

It was Hereward's turn to laugh and he did so heartily. "Foxes, my darling girl, are excellent hunters," he said in a professorial tone, "cunning, stealthy and sly. They stalk their prey with infinite patience through the use of their highly developed senses. So, if I were you, I shouldn't worry too much about their welfare. In fact, there are so many cursed rabbits on the estate, I'm surprised the foxes aren't obese."

"There might be a den nearby in the undergrowth,"

suggested Isabella brightly. "There may even be some cubs there. Wouldn't it be wonderful if there were? I think I might take a look on my next walk."

"It's called an earth," he said with a flat scholarly air. "And for your information the cubs aren't born until spring. Now I think that's enough about foxes for one day. It's time to turn your attention to a more thrilling creature."

"Which creature is that?" she asked, blinking in innocence.

Gazing deep into her eyes, Hereward grinned and said: "That, my dearest darling, is what you're about to discover.

As realisation dawned, a flush spread over Isabella's face like red dye on a white-linen cloth.

Chapter 69

Hiding in a dry dyke beside a hedge, Parker drew a deep drag on his fag and infused his tarred lungs with tobacco vapour. Since financial reward had ceased to be his primary motivation, he took greater pleasure from observing the Major's wife. It was worth braving the cold weather to trail her around the sprawling estate for the pure delight of ogling her beautiful body. And he wondered whether her breasts would grow any bigger. He certainly hoped so.

Parker well understood why Major Aldwen had fallen for the girly lady instead of the manly Miss Dumbarton. Or 'Duchess' Dumbarton as she was commonly known in the town; the ironic honorific having been bestowed on her by the good people of Oakwich who had the misfortune to come into contact with her. Although not a single soul had the courage to say it to her hifalutin face. A face that wouldn't look out of place in a waxwork museum.

Despite a lifetime of hardship and deprivation, not to mention the years engaged in bloody battles abroad, Parker felt fortunate to be alive still at forty plus years. Hardy as he was handy. Having spent a good part of his life exposed to wintry weather conditions, he knew the cold climate wouldn't kill him. If anything, he was more likely to die from loneliness and lack of female companionship.

Shoving an exploratory finger up one large round nostril,

he recalled his youth spent hunting game illicitly under the nose of Gordon Grimes, the gormless gamekeeper. Grimes was long gone. So much had changed since the war. Country folk, including women, were migrating in droves to work in the new urban industries as manufacturing increased its output, despite high levels of unemployment in the economic downturn. None of which made sense to Parker, who preferred to be as self-sufficient as was humanly possible. To his regret, long-established customs and practices were dying out at a rapid pace in rural areas.

Parker removed his faded olive-green cap and ran a hand over his low-sloping brow, the skin of which was mottled like a diseased leaf. He needed no-one to tell him he was nought to look at. Not so much a sight for sore eyes; more a sight to make the eyes sore, he said to himself. Brown warts studded his skin, deep lines textured his cheeks and broken veins and capillaries striated his nose. Even his ears hadn't escaped the ugly wand thanks to his wallop-happy grandad who turned violent in drink.

The longer Parker sat there, the more he could feel the cold, damp earth seeping through his trusty old sack. At that point in his wait, he could kill for a tin mug of strong, sugary, steaming-hot tea; strong enough to stand the spoon up in. And the moment his belly rumbled, he produced from his pocket a fresh meat sandwich spread thick with dripping and wrapped in a sheet of yellowing newspaper. The sandwich smelled good, and he knew it would taste good too. Loudly smacking his lips, he unpacked his meal and gobbled it up in his open mouth with gusto. His missing molars and incisors made chewing a challenge, but he just about managed with his remaining teeth.

After finishing his food, Parker sucked clean his fingers with a loud slurp, wiped his greasy hands down his front, tipped back his head, and glugged a large volume of water from a battered enamel bottle. His hunger and thirst fully quenched, he emitted a mighty burp, refolded the newspaper and popped it back in his pocket to be reused. Then with one eye closed, he watched a flock of noisy starlings fly in formation overhead until they disappeared from view.

Fishing a well-honed knife and chisel from his inside pocket, Parker began carving an effigy from a small block of softwood. His first attempt at a human figure. Working mostly from memory, but occasionally from studying creature corpses on his cottage floor, he created tiny figures of small mammals and birds. No-one could deny his natural talent for turning his observations into impressive three-dimensional forms, most of which he undersold to a man on the market for a few coins when he needed money.

Since the rain clouds were in the habit of sneaking up on the land, Parker sniffed the air and checked the sky at regular intervals. He knew only too well that unless she was already out and about, the Major's missus remained indoors whenever it rained. On those dreary days, crushed by the weight of his disappointment, he hunkered down in his hamlet hovel and listened to the rain drip rhythmically into a rusty old tin bucket through a hole in the thatch.

To his dismay, Parker had begun to notice she now roamed the estate less often. Every Thursday she took herself off into town on her bicycle. He feared she might soon cease exploring the countryside altogether. For him, there was no better place to observe her than in the fields and forest, nowhere as isolated and secluded, where the loneliest trails lay mantled by monumental trees, and where he had already scouted out the best places to hide.

Parker couldn't bear the thought of never seeing her again. Her absence always made him feel mournful; so mournful, he increasingly risked breaking cover to catch a glimpse of her through the glass of the Hall's curtainless conservatory. Never before had he pined for a posh piece of womanhood. His previous crushes, all of them incomparable to the lovely lady, had hailed from the lowest lines. Lower even than that, he sniggered. Every one of them a mucky mare with lax morals.

In the wild weald of the Aldwen estate, he could stalk her for hours on end without growing tired or bored. The place benefitted from her appreciative presence, which always lifted his spirits, more especially on the most-miserable days when the sky looked as heavy and grey as asbestos. He thought about her unendingly. To him she was a thing of great mystery; little more than a girl, but a girl in a woman's body. And to his mind, too young to be mistress of Aldwen Hall.

With his thick-lidded, soulless eyes fixed in atavistic attention below yard-brush eyebrows, Parker ran his tongue over his squamous lips as he fantasised about what he would do to her to gratify his needs. He imagined being acquainted with her on an intimate basis, imagined fiddling with her in all the same special spaces the Major accessed, imagined his mouth on her young flesh. And while the pain of sexual starvation pulsated in his groin, he grew sick with envy and sick with desire.

When his fetish finally strolled past the hedge, Parker put away his occupation and pulled himself up onto his haunches in preparation to follow her at a discreet distance. Unless the heavens opened up, he expected her to remain outdoors for two hours at minimum. As a rule, her general predictability made pursuing her easy; however, what made him uneasy was her increasingly apparent guardedness. A number of times he had noticed her posture and gait were tight with tension and her face wore a worried watchfulness whenever she wheeled around at any sudden unexpected sound. It gave the impression she could sense his presence in much the same way an animal perceives the hunter when he gets too close.

To his own irritation, Parker continued to forget how far noise travelled in the winter woods without summer's sound-absorbing foliage. Fortunately, he knew the land like the back of his hand, knew where all the ditches and dykes ran and the locations of many hollowed-out trees large enough for an adult man to hide in, and sleep should that be necessary.

However, with each passing day, as he trained his predatory eyes on his appetising prey, he found controlling his primitive impulses increasingly problematic. And as the impetus to grope the girl grew stronger, he felt a powerful urge to grab hold of her and make her his own, especially when she was far from home and far from her formidable husband. After all, which normal man wouldn't? he asked himself. It was only natural when temptation was placed in his way. Just like Adam in the Garden of Eden, he reflected, recalling his Sunday School classes, from which he had been banned for beating up a boy who had called him an inbred bastard and his mother a spread-legged bawd.

Despite her ongoing disquiet, Isabella continued to walk the woods at will, albeit a little less often than she used to. Walking was a compulsion, a necessity, an activity vital to her physical and mental wellbeing, not to mention a refuge from domestic obtrusions. Although the Aldwen estate sometimes unnerved her, it was nevertheless her own special Eden, an extraordinary demesne quite literally on her doorstep.

Except for the agricultural tenant farmers and seasonal workers on the farthest side of the estate, and the occasional passer-by, few people were seen in the area. Alone in the secluded location, Isabella's imagination soared, overloading her senses and filling her head with mendacious mental images. The nagging sensation that some secretive being, some invisible visitant, some disembodied soul, shadowed her on her walks persisted in her mind. Sometimes the presence was strong, other times weak, sometimes still, other times moving. At its strongest, the sensation crawled over her body like a black ten-legged spider and pricked her nerves with a thousand needles. But since there was never anything there, she questioned the validity of her own judgment.

Determined to conquer her unfounded fears, Isabella continued to dismiss the idea that taking solo walks compromised her safety, even when the forest felt more frightening than friendly. She preferred to see it as a romantic realm, infrangible and flawless; not a place where danger lurked behind every tree and bush. The land, if it were dangerous at all, would be dangerous only after dark. During the daytime the place was safe, she assured herself, as safe as the nursery with nanny in charge.

For no matter where she ventured, or how far, except for a single cigarette stub on the path, Isabella had seen nothing to support her suspicions. She struggled to articulate her fear, except to say it was a funny feeling, or, more aptly, a formless figment of her foolish imagination. And, as such, she refused to give it credence. For should she succumb to her mental maladies and rampant irrationalities, what little freedom she enjoyed would be curtailed and her married reclusion complete.

Isabella often reminded herself she was an import, a rural novice, an urban-bred girl acclimatising to country life. Nevertheless, as time went on, shadows grew more menacing and shapes shifted whenever she stared at them for long enough. Determined to soldier on, alternating between spells of neuroticism and stoicism, she told herself that paranoia is a psychological sickness that poisons the mind and soul.

As she emerged from the woods that day, the icy breeze wafting off the lake made Isabella shiver. In the late afternoon, the odours of damp soil and composting vegetation hung heavy about the air. After fastening her coat's top button, she tightened her scarf around her neck and pulled her hat down over her ears. Her hands felt cold and she regretted forgetting her gloves, so she shoved them deep into her pockets to warm them up.

Halfway between the lake and the Hall, Isabella heard the faint sound of footsteps. In one swift motion, she pulled up and swirled around like a spinning top. But all she could see was an empty path behind her. Still, barely perceptible unexplained sounds always made her nervous, and she had a sense of some undefinable, unpredictable presence amongst the reticent trees, which also gave the impression they quietly observed her. Moreover, she noticed a transient niff of something nasty in the air. With anxious eyes, she scoured the trees for anything that stood out. But it was like looking at a jigsaw puzzle with one piece that didn't quite fit, except she was unable to identify the misfit.

None the wiser, as always, Isabella resumed walking, but at a faster speed. As daylight faded the sky began to change face, adopting a dark sepulchral expression. Then with a sudden sense of urgency in every step, trying her best not to panic, her scarf fluttering in the light wind, she hastened towards the Hall. She knew that repeatedly glancing back slowed her down, but instinct told her to remain alert at all times.

Once the Hall's tall chimney stacks came into view, Isabella breathed a little easier. Even so, treading the path, tense with trepidation, hemmed between high hedges, higher than her head in some places, she kept her eyes peeled for any sudden movements and her ears pricked for unfamiliar sounds. As she cut through the orchard, the creaking trees triggered memories of the night she heard strange noises on the landing outside her room while Hereward was away in London.

When she reached the side gate, Isabella noticed it was swinging with a slight wheeze, as though someone had only just passed through it. Thinking it must have been one of the maids, she looked around, but there was no-one present nearby. How odd, she thought, as her attention was drawn to something small, grey and furry on one of the gateposts. Intrigued, she stepped forward to take a look at the oddity.

For several seconds, Isabella could only stare at the dull object. On closer inspection, she realised it was a rabbit's foot, severed clean at the ankle and with a spot of dried blood on one toe. How it came to be there she had no idea. With sudden repulsion, she pulled a face, tweezed the amputation between the extreme tips of her left thumb and forefinger, flung it as far as she could over the hedge, then rushed inside to wash her hands.

Chapter 70

Having dwelt at length on the rabbit's foot and her fluctuating sense of uneasiness while roaming the estate, Isabella decided to remain indoors for a few days to allow her nerves to settle. In truth, she admitted herself fatigued; not so much physically as mentally. Despite her best efforts, she couldn't dislodge from her mind the idea of some hideous hellhound or heinous heel waiting to pounce; or the notion of the estate as some kind of tyrannical territory fraught with hidden dangers. And tired of her insecurities marring the pleasures of her walks, she spent many an hour in quiet contemplation attempting to rationalise her strange sensations.

Isabella disliked being confined to the house, even when the confinement was self-imposed. When she married Hereward, she had no idea he was practically a recluse who rarely left the estate and avoided most forms of social contact. Not that her heartless parents would have cared had they known. Had Martha not befriended her and invited her out once a week, she felt sure she would now be insane, certifiably so.

The chime from the hall clock reminded Isabella she had still to dress, even if doing so made little difference to her dull domestic life. With languid steps, she moved over to the window and gazed at the grass strip and bush belt beyond the gravel. Except for a few manic bark-stripping squirrels and industrious birds hopping about, everywhere was quiet and still. And since she remained rattled by the rabbit's foot, she reasoned that a thieving raven had inadvertently dropped it on the gate post. Or possibly a magpie or a crow.

During Isabella's pre-dinner preparations the previous evening, Tilly had explained that a rabbit's foot was considered by some people to be a lucky charm. More especially countryfolk. However, to be truly lucky, she said the rabbit to whom the foot belonged must be smote on a grave. Isabella believed butchering some poor bunny on a person's final resting place was not only gruesome, but also an act of gross disrespect.

As she stood in her underclothes ruminating on the rabbit's foot, the door unexpectedly opened and Hereward, wearing his most-decadent smile, ambushed her in the bedroom. Shocked at his infringement of her privacy yet again, she insisted he leave the room forthwith. Lacking the layer of protection normally provided by her dress made her feel vulnerable and exposed, not to mention decidedly indecent. Come what may, she was glad she had on her decent drawers and not a pair many times mended. They hugged the hemisphere of her curvaceous rear like the skin on a peach. And beneath the thin satin fabric of her chemise, her nipples stood out like small nuggets, while her unbrushed hair hung loose in a tangle of twists and twirls.

Like a puma preparing to pounce, Hereward inched closer.

Alarmed at his audacity, Isabella stepped back and raised her hands in a blocking gesture. "No. Absolutely not!" she said in the most-forceful tone she could muster. "Get away from me and remove yourself from my room this instant!"

"Why aren't you wearing a brassiere?" he said, faking a frown. "You're quite the little tease aren't you, you naughty girl?"

"Excuse me?" she replied with a heavy helping of indignation. "Why is that any business of yours? What I choose to wear or not to wear under my clothing need not concern you."

"Why ever not? You're my wife," said Hereward with an impish grin. "Of course what you wear concerns me. It must meet with my approval."

"Poppycock," she snorted. "Now please leave and allow me to finish dressing. I'm sure you must have something to be getting on with."

"I can think of something I'd like to be getting on with," he said with a dazzling display of dentition as he continued inching towards her.

Again, Isabella backed away. "Please stop being such a pest," she begged. But her plea fell on deaf ears. Moreover, she knew she had no means of escape. "Tilly's due at any moment," she informed him in a desperate attempt to subdue his ardour.

But Hereward reminded her that she always got dressed unassisted in the mornings. However, to be on the safe side, he barricaded the door with a chair in case of unbidden entry.

"There, that should take care of Tilly. Now get into bed," he commanded. "I'm not going to tell you again."

Isabella glared at him with glacial-green eyes. "Stop right there!" she demanded in her deepest, strongest, most-assertive voice.

Disregarding her order, Hereward stepped in close, took hold of her tiny wrist and began pulling her towards the bed as he said: "Come along now my lovely, time to submit to your husband's wishes, wicked though they are I must admit."

In fury, Isabella anchored her feet to the floor and pummelled him like a punchbag with her small fists.

A guffaw emanating from deep within his throat, Hereward deflected the blows as if he were batting away a bee. He often forgot how little his wife weighed despite her womanly proportions.

"Get your hands off me you disgusting barnyard beast," she bawled. "I said get your hands off me."

His eyes glowing dark with indecorous intent, he stared at her. "Come, you have whetted my appetite standing there in your clingy white underwear," he said, lust lighting up his face. "You look so mouth-wateringly delicious I must simply devour you, my gorgeous girl."

Isabella's cheeks gave the impression of having been painted pink and she began to perspire a little. Although she knew there was no contest between Hereward and herself, she wasn't willing to concede defeat quite so easily. Hence, she attempted, without success, to grab hold of a hardback book with which to hit him. But he only tightened his powerful grip, half raised one eyebrow and smirked infuriatingly.

"It's not funny. Get off me!" she cried as she continued to struggle.

With next to no effort, Hereward hauled her up into his arms, carried her across the room, dropped her onto the bed, and deftly flipped her onto her front.

As her face pressed into the fluffy feather pillow, Isabella wondered if all husbands behaved so outrageously with their wives. And when he slid his hands up the legs of her spotless drawers and fondled her illustrious bottom, she sank into the mattress knowing she had no choice but to surrender to his wanton will.

Chapter 71

"Martha, how does it feel to be in love?"

Martha considered her young friend's virtuous face for a moment. "Since love means different things to different people, I can only speak for myself," she replied. Then pausing to arrange her thoughts, she took a deep breath and began to deliberate on what to her was a sensitive subject. "It's difficult to explain, but I'll give it a go, so bear with me."

"Of course," said Isabella.

"The first time I fell in love it was so instantaneous it took my breath away," said Martha looking into some distant space. "Hard to believe, I admit. Yet I recognised it for what it was as a matter of instinct. Love at first sight is the strangest sensation. It's overwhelming. Having said that, it's also incredibly special. I lost complete control of my emotions. I couldn't sleep, I couldn't eat, I couldn't concentrate. I had butterflies in my stomach every time I arranged to meet my young man. I loved to look at his face, listen to his voice and watch him walk up the street towards me. I read his letters over and over again until the paper split along the folds. I felt all warm and fuzzy inside. But what I remember above all else was being so blissfully happy."

Martha became suddenly silent and a tear rolled down her rouged cheek, leaving in its wake a thin white vertical line.

"Forgive me," she said in a choked voice, her baby-blue

eyes as wet as a waterhole. "It still upsets me. Poor Stanley was killed fighting at the front in the final months of the war. Such a terrible waste of a young man's life. And hardly any thanks for it either from the powers that be," she added bitterly.

"I'm so terribly sorry, Martha," said Isabella. "I had no idea." And she took hold of her friend's hand in a gesture of sororal comfort.

Martha quickly recovered her composure and considered Isabella with a quizzical eye. This poor thing has been forced to grow up far too fast, she thought. It was plain to see she was struggling with something.

"Why do you ask?" enquired Martha.

"I'm not quite sure," Isabella replied.

"What is it you're not quite sure about?" prodded Martha after she blew her nose with a clean cotton handkerchief and tucked it up her sleeve.

"Well, you see it's like this," began Isabella in a hesitant voice. "I've been given to understand that a lady should always discourage her husband from being uhm…, you know, i-intimate," she stammered. Then after a polite cough, she added. "I suppose what I'm trying to say is that I've been led to believe that what takes place in the privacy of the bedroom is distasteful and should be performed for the sole purpose of procreation."

Martha understood only too well her friend's meaning. "Well, I expect they did say such things during Victoria's reign," she chuckled. "Why on earth I can't think. After all, the Queen was herself reputed to be a passionate lady who was madly in love with Prince Albert. It was the great love affair of its time. Remember how many children they had too. I doubt their bedchamber activities were purely in the interests of propagating the Royal race, if you'll pardon my parlance."

Isabella smiled coyly, as if she had a secret she was bursting to share. She was also attempting to get to grips with the complexities of sexual relations.

"It's just that when we were first married, Hereward and I were practically strangers. I barely knew him at all. So, I'm sure you can imagine how nervous I felt when he visited my bed for the very first time," she confided in a half whisper. "Especially when I considered him more an adversary than a comrade. Sometimes I still do," she added with a light laugh after a pause. "It's my understanding that according to certain religious and legal rulings, one's husband is entitled to demand certain favours and one mustn't refuse him without a solid reason."

Martha gave Isabella a look of encouragement to continue.

"Well, to be perfectly candid, I wasn't quite sure what to expect on my wedding night. My knowledge of the birds and the bees was strictly limited to seeing what cattle got up to occasionally in the fields. Oh, and some lurid details my friends divulged in order to tease me. I hadn't a clue if their claims were true; especially since it all sounded so messy and abhorrent. Initially, I detested lovemaking to the extent that every night I dreaded going up to bed. Then, after a time, I grew accustomed to Hereward's devotions and even began to find them quite tolerable. In fact, once I learned to relax and began to feel less resentful about my situation, I didn't mind them so very much.

Isabella paused to take a long, deep breath. "Well, you see, now I no longer find intimacy unpleasant and sometimes I even look forward to his visits. Especially when he gives me a big manly cuddle. He doesn't know that of course, otherwise he might think me a harlot. So that's why I feel all confused."

"Confused?" asked Martha. "What is it you're confused about?"

"Well because Mama's generation still hold the view that a demure wife must remain perfectly still and not take pleasure from her husband's ardent attentions."

Martha resisted the temptation to laugh at her young friend's naivety, since she didn't want to discourage her from expressing herself freely.

"It's perfectly acceptable for a woman to enjoy what goes on in the marital bed, my dear," she assured her. "And your husband won't think any less of you for doing so. It may even surprise you to know that a man prefers his wife to respond positively to his lovemaking."

"I hope you don't mind my telling you this, Martha, but Hereward has an insatiable appetite."

"Well, you can hardly blame him for that. I'm sure he must find you irresistible."

"Yes, I suppose he must. Except on Sundays, when for some reason or other he keeps to his own room. I have no idea why that is, but in the beginning, I very much welcomed the respite."

"Perhaps it's for religious reasons," suggested Martha, who was still trying her best not to laugh. "Sunday is after all a day of rest," she added in half jest.

"It's impossible to say," said Isabella. Hereward's not especially religious. Sometimes I suspect he doesn't believe in a supreme being at all, even though he insists on attending Sunday Mass, which means I must go too. He also insists on saying grace before every meal and I mustn't laugh or he becomes terribly cross."

"Have you never thought to ask him about Sundays?"

"Gosh no, Martha! I'd rather die. I do like Sundays though," said Isabella to change the subject, suddenly regretting her indiscretions. "We have luncheon at Maud's place. His sister and I get on awfully well despite our age difference. She's very supportive of me. In fact, I really don't know what I'd do without you both."

"Is Maud a spinster by choice?" enquired Martha.

"Yes, she is. Hereward said she's never shown the slightest interest in getting married. Or for that matter in men. She prefers spending time with her female friends, especially Cynthia, to whom she's very close."

"Wise woman," joked Martha.

"The contrast between the two siblings is striking," Isabella went on. "As you know, Maud is comparatively small and plain in appearance, but larger than life in personality. She's also less conventional and conservative than Hereward, and has strong views on social and political reform, which she expresses without fear of condemnation or censure. She's especially scathing of those who insist men are superior to women. Her house is bright and cheerful, full of fun and frivolity, and she and Cynthia sometimes get a bit giddy on the port. Much to Hereward's obvious displeasure. After Sunday luncheon we always play boardgames from a large compendium kept to hand in the sideboard. Or sing popular songs around the piano. I must say I enjoy the diversion. Life at the Hall is so dreadfully dull during the daytime and the evenings are only slightly better because of dinner and the wireless. Maud makes it a rule that everyone must join in. There are no exceptions allowed, not even for Hereward. He's more sociable when we're at his sister's house. There's also a younger brother, whom I've yet to meet because he's abroad in the Indian Civil Service. Maud has his photograph on her sideboard and he looks as handsome as Hereward, only less grave and more agreeable."

Martha smiled.

"Anyhow, I must be going. I'll be glad when it's summer and the days are longer. Then I needn't worry about being back at the Hall before dark."

"The dark never used to bother you. Has something changed?"

"Oh, I don't know. Sometimes I get these strange feelings

and I really don't know what to make of them."

"Strange feelings?" queried Martha in a quiet voice.

"Yes. Every so often when I'm out walking, I feel as though I'm being watched. Which I know is highly unlikely. I mean who'd be interested in watching me, for heaven's sake? And to be perfectly honest, what with work and all that, who has the time? I've never seen anyone hanging about the woods, not once. I do meet people on the main path now and then, and if it's a man, which it often is, he usually raises his hat if he's wearing one, comments on the weather and continues on his way. I've never seen anyone loitering around the estate, and yet I find myself increasingly on my guard."

"Have you mentioned your suspicions to your husband?" asked Martha.

"Good grief, Martha, are you mad? Hereward would stop me going out altogether. Well not without an escort. And I'm not willing to run the risk of his insisting Boyle chauffeurs me everywhere. Gosh, perish the thought."

"Trust your instincts, my dear," advised Martha. "That's what they're there for. They're the brain's way of warning you to beware and pay close attention to what's going on around you. And that means wherever you happen to be. Believe me, there are some serious oddballs about. Only recently, I had some bearded freak hanging about outside the shop. Kept peering in through the glass in the door, he did. I suspect he was trying to catch a glimpse of one of my ladies in a state of partial undress. I chased him off with the yard brush. Told him if I saw him anywhere near the shop again, I'd call the constabulary and have him arrested. If something feels wrong, then nine times out of ten it usually is. If you have the slightest doubt don't hang about. That's my motto and it has always stood me in good stead. Better to be safe than sorry."

"Yes, I suppose so," said Isabella softly.

Chapter 72

Against Hereward's better judgment, or so he thought in hindsight, Isabella persuaded him to accompany her to a luncheon party at the house of a former childhood friend, Lucinda. He had ultimately consented, or caved in under pressure, as he preferred to say, to his wife's relentless but endearing entreaties. However, the overriding reason for his acquiescence was her threat to go alone if he declined the invitation. Moreover, compared with dinner, he considered luncheon the lesser evil, since it was shorter and, with luck, they should be back at the Hall by teatime.

Lucinda, who was slightly older than Isabella, lived with Randolph, her husband of one year, in Oakwich's most-exclusive district. When she heard of the upturn in her friend's fortunes, she decided to renew their acquaintance. She felt confident Isabella would understand that their original friendship had inevitably faltered because Archibald and Agatha Acton could no long afford to reciprocate social invitations.

Isabella was given to understand that the occasion was meant to be a small intimate gathering. However, unbeknown to her, after she accepted the invitation the guest list had grown exponentially. Not that she would have minded had Lucinda informed her. Hereward, however, would have taken a markedly different view.

For the occasion she wore a dress purchased from Martha's most-exclusive contemporary collection; having decided to make an effort to look elegant and stylish in order to put Hereward in the best mood possible. Martha, who said there was no point in having a neck like a flamingo and not flaunt it, had persuaded her to wear a lower neckline. Isabella, however, refused to reveal so much as a hint of cleavage and insisted on buying a dress with a full bodice. The manner in which men of all ages stared at her chest made her want to hide behind the sofa.

The Hollywood-inspired blue-chiffon dress with its cinched waist, full skirt and fluted hem showed off her figure to perfection. To complete the look, she wore a cute pair of curved-heel shoes with pointed toes. At Martha's insistence, she had yielded and agreed to wear a pair of silk stockings. However, instead of the insufferable suspender belt, she opted to hold them up with lacy elastic garters. Given the choice, she would have preferred to wear plain woollen socks inside her beloved black boots; or failing that, her sensible brown brogues. Tilly, a genius with a hair brush, comb and a couple of clips, had fashioned her recalcitrant curls into a foxy chignon.

With the maid standing behind her, Isabella considered herself in the mirror. "Well, Tills, how do I look?"

"You look amazing, Ma'am. I'm sure the master will be proper impressed when he sees you looking so lovely."

"Let's hope so," said Isabella, who was unaccustomed to the gilded glamour of her peers, most of whom were now debutantes. And for once she felt more like a woman and less like a teenage girl.

Hereward, who was pacing the hall with his usual impatience, looked up at his wife and smiled with adulation as she stood at the stairhead in her new outfit. She appeared to him taller, more grown up, more sophisticated, and more alluring than ever.

Isabella was too focussed on her precarious feet to notice her husband's beaming admiration. Having never worn heels before, she feared she might lose her footing and tumble downstairs in ignominious fashion. With her left hand gripping the banister, and her right hand holding her pochette, she descended one careful step at a time.

As she landed on the lowest tread, Hereward stepped forward, took hold of her hand and raised it to his lips. "Upon my word, you look so utterly ravishing my darling, I'm tempted to lock you up," he said looking her over with absolute approval.

"Thank you kindly, said Isabella.

However, as she walked across the hall's hardwood floor, her heels clacked like a handloom, making her feel silly and self-conscious.

Upon hearing the uncommon sound, although strictly speaking it wasn't uncommon to him, Hereward was reminded of Rosalyn, who always looked ridiculous in the tottering heels she insisted on wearing whenever they attended some function or social event. Once at a party in Paris, he had overheard an observant guest jest that the Eiffel Tower had an English competitor besides the Blackpool version. But rather than defend her honour, Hereward, secretly amused, had turned a deaf ear to the sardonic incivility.

The luncheon party also provided Isabella with an opportunity to show off her sparkling new necklace. However, instead of relying on Tilly, she asked her husband to do the honours and fasten the clasp at the back of her neck. And Hereward was more than happy to oblige, following up the action with a courtly kiss.

When the Aldwens arrived at the residence of their hosts, a

suitably accoutred and respectful butler took their coats. With a playful grin animating her face, Isabella whispered they should poach him and offer Lucinda and Randolph Boyle in his place.

Hereward's face contorted with a mixture of mirth and demurral. Looking straight ahead, he said out of the side of his mouth in a muted voice: "Now, now, Isabella, please behave."

Isabella smiled mischievously and linked her arm through his as they were shown into a large reception hall where the hosts were awaiting their guests' arrival. A brace of servants stood by bearing glasses of sherry and lemonade on silver salvers, while another pair circulated with trays of colourful canapés.

Following the customary polite preambles between themselves and their gushing hosts, Hereward handed Isabella a sherry in a slim diminutive glass and collected one for himself. Then after taking his first sip of the smooth aperitif, he warned her under his breath to take things steady.

Isabella cringed inside at the memory of the intoxicating effects of Cynthia's Christmas cocktails. And to her mild annoyance, lest she forget, her husband was ready to remind her whenever she came within sniffing distance of alcohol. Fortunately for them both, she found fortified wines too heavy and rich, even those of excellent quality.

Since the Aldwens were the last to arrive, a throng was already assembled inside. Many more than Hereward had anticipated based on Isabella's information. Most of them were rich, glamorous and sophisticated types whose alcohol-fuelled, effusive chatter enlivened the atmosphere enormously, contrasting sharply with the Hall's hushed solemnity. And while he had no objection to a little boisterousness now and again, he nevertheless detested the way the men's eyes travelled over his wife.

While Isabella welcomed the opportunity to socialise with other young people, the gaiety brought home to her what a circumscribed life she led at the Hall. Hereward showed no interest in Oakwich's elite social scene or consorting in the right circles. Still, to her profound relief, he was charming and regaled the company with tales of his Indian exploits. It was a facet of his character with which she was unfamiliar and it surprised her. Ordinarily, he spoke little of his army days, unless she asked him a direct question about them. The gentlemen all listened to him with open admiration while the ladies swooned at his audacious good looks. And Isabella had to admit he looked dashing and debonair in a well-cut suit, ivory silk shirt and purple paisley necktie.

When the butler entered to announce luncheon was served, the loquacious crowd filed into the large dining room in twos. After which they began checking the gold-bordered place cards on the long, extended table draped in a white-damask tablecloth and adorned with short-stemmed floral centrepieces flanked by brass candelabras. The room was enriched with Persian rugs, gold-brocade curtains, and silk-papered walls on which hung realistic still-lifes of flowers and fruit, while from the ceiling's centre dangled an extravagant lead-crystal chandelier.

Randy, as Randolph was known to family and friends, escorted Isabella to the table and seated her on a high-back mahogany chair upholstered in the same fabric as the curtains. After which he seated himself beside her and immediately struck up a conversation. And soon enough they were sharing jokes, brief anecdotes and mutual interests.

From the opposite side of the table Hereward kept a close eye on his wife while he conversed with Lucinda and the guest seated to his right: some wide-hipped, weasel-faced woman in a brazenly low-cut dress. So low-cut, she appeared to have a pair of plump buttocks growing out of her chest. To give further emphasis to the prodigious pair, the point of a heart-shaped gold pendant drew the eye to her chasmic cleavage. As to the seating arrangement, Hereward decided with distaste that he had definitely drawn the short straw.

To maintain the conversation, the weasel woman informed him she was engaged to the chinless chappie across the table whose toucan-like nose and mole-like moustache made him doubly conspicuous. At regular intervals, to rally Hereward's flagging attention, she placed her bejewelled fingers on his arm, leaned in close and treated him to a front-row view of the voluptuous duo. To avoid yawning at her droning tone, he kept his mouth shut tight, causing his nostrils to flare. Not an attractive look, he knew. In an attempt to cope with the situation, he pictured himself swatting her with a rolled-up newspaper as one would a persistent wasp.

The awfulness of his predicament was further compounded by the close attention Randolph was paying to Isabella. And because of the clatter of silverware and clamour of lively chatter around the table, he struggled to decipher their topic of conversation. All the same, he consoled himself with the thought that her bounteous assets were thankfully ensconced within a full bodice; assets he had himself yet to see in the actual flesh. Lord she's beautiful, he said to himself, wishing he was seated beside her instead of the weasel woman. Yet despite his spousal pride, he would have preferred his wife to be concealed behind a purdah screen at that precise moment. Female segregation has much to recommend it, he reflected with fallacious sentiment.

After luncheon, Isabella, having observed the house had a rather splendid conservatory, asked Randy, with whom she got on well, for his advice on plant propagation. And when he offered to show her his prize orchids she gladly accepted, and away they went without telling anyone.

Having grown bored with small talk, and always the first to leave a function, or for that matter any social engagement, Hereward went in search of Isabella to inform her it was time to head back to the Hall. However, since she was nowhere to be seen, he assumed she must be in the cloakroom powdering her nose. But after waiting out in the hall for what felt like an eternity, he grew restive, realised she must be elsewhere and began looking for her.

Alerted to the sounds of voices in the conservatory during his search, he stepped into the room and came upon Isabella alone with Randolph, who was proudly showing her his exotic plants. He was standing so near to her that Hereward was convinced she could feel his breath on her face. No woman should remain in such close proximity to a man other than her spouse, father or brother, he thought angrily.

In a reflexive response, Isabella stepped back from Randolph as soon as she caught sight of her husband in the room.

Hereward, inserting himself between his wife and the host, consulted his wristwatch and said with an inflexion of authority in his voice: "It's time we were going, my dear."

"By jove, is that the time? Goodness me. Sorry old chap," said Randolph. "My fault entirely for detaining your good lady. According to my wife, once I get started on my plants there's no stopping me and I lose all sense of time."

Hereward, throwing Randolph a ruthless look, replied: "It appears you aren't the only one."

Isabella reddened and cringed inwardly when she noticed the prominent veins on her husband's neck and the tight set of his jaw. Never a good sign.

Begrudgingly, Hereward thanked Randolph for luncheon, took Isabella by the arm, escorted her from the conservatory, helped her into her coat in the hall and hurried her out to the motorcar. Blaspheming under his breath, he turned on the engine, engaged the gearstick and drove off at speed.

They then bickered all the way back to the Hall.

"What the Dickens did you think you were doing alone with that leering Lothario?" he said. "Whom I might add you barely know."

"I doubt very much Randy's a Lothario," Isabella replied with a churlish chuckle. "He and Luce got married only a year ago and they're still desperately in love."

An unpleasant smile formed on Hereward's lips and he replied: "Oh so it's Randy now, is it? Very chummy, I must say. Well, allow me to remind you, my dear, that it's most improper for a married lady to be alone with a man who isn't a close relative. What if any of the other guests had seen you? Tongues would soon start wagging and before we know it you and Romeo would stand accused of making love in the conservatory. And your reputation would be in ruins because you allowed yourself to be alone with that buck-toothed runt."

"You belong in the last century," said Isabella with a hollow laugh. "I was almost expecting you to challenge poor Rand... Randolph to a duel at forty paces. I can't think what came over you. Your rudeness was excruciating. You behave more like a warder than a husband. It's downright ridiculous. You should have married a mature woman. Someone of my mother's generation would make you the perfect companion."

"Don't be absurd," Hereward retorted, but her words stung him nonetheless.

"Well forgive me for forgetting my crinolines," added Isabella. "You're the one who's being absurd. Men no longer govern every aspect of a woman's behaviour and you'd do well to remember it. And for your information, we were doing nothing wrong. He was showing me a plant. A silly old plant, for pity's sake. That was the extent of it. It was certainly nothing to get all hot under the collar about. Next thing you'll be insisting I wear a veil and a chastity belt," she said, before colouring at her own unwitting reference to the intimate female device.

Damnation, thought Hereward. It was as though she could read his mind. He realised where his wife was concerned, he would forever be afflicted by a pathological sense of possessiveness. Isabella emanated an irresistible sensual energy that he had himself succumbed to. He recognised how easy it was to become mired in a state of jealousy and obsession. Maud once said that everyone was a little bit in love with Isabella and he should rejoice in the fact that he had someone so special, and mustn't let anyone or anything come between them. Wise words, he knew, but easier said than done.

"I don't know what my father was thinking getting me married to you," she went on. "An insecure recluse who's well and truly stuck in the Middle Ages."

"Well, allow me to tell you," Hereward said with a scathing smile. "Your dear papa couldn't offload you fast enough to the first bidder. Of course, the sly dog waited until after we were married before informing me that you were more than a handful. And I have to agree the old blighter was right. He also advised me you would need a firm hand and not to tolerate any nonsense from you." Feeling the need to be cruel, Hereward was about to say more when Isabella's tears checked him.

"I'm sorry," he said. "I shouldn't have said that."

"Perhaps not," she sniffed, "but as regards my father marrying me off to the first suitor that came along, you're not far wrong."

"Be that as it may, I should learn to hold my tongue."

"Please, let's just forget it," said Isabella. "I'm tired of arguing."

That night Hereward tried not to appear too sheepish when he entered Isabella's bedroom. He still regretted starting the argument about Randolph and wished he could better control his emotions. Being married to Isabella felt like owning a priceless diamond at constant risk of theft. Remembering the way men looked at her at the luncheon party made her even more desirable, if that were possible. And he decided it would be wise to apologise for his behaviour, especially since he didn't want her to go running off to the bathroom again.

"I'm truly sorry about this afternoon, Isabella," he said. "My behaviour was unforgivable. All I can say by way of explanation is that I was insanely jealous, and I'm afraid I took it out on you, which you most definitely didn't deserve. The problem is that when I see you enjoying yourself in male company, and laughing at their jokes and funny anecdotes, I become unreasonable, irrational and senseless. I can't seem to help it when I watch them making love to you with their eyes. Today the whole damned lot of them were circling around you like vultures. And I have to say you looked so utterly divine in your new blue dress that I felt like the luckiest chap on the planet."

There followed a tense silence, broken by Isabella when she spoke in a voice soft and cool. "There was no need for you to feel jealous. I was simply being polite and sociable. What do you expect me to do in such circumstances? Snub them all? Tell them I'm forbidden to speak to the entire male species? Pretend I'm deaf and mute? Run for the hills? You know perfectly well you're the only man I've ever known. When I made my marriage vows, albeit under some duress, I promised always to honour you. I have never dishonoured you with another man and I never shall. Yet you made me feel like a whore for chatting to Randolph, who I must remind you was our host. Why should I be made to feel ashamed of speaking to someone of the opposite sex? And for your information, it was all perfectly innocent."

Hereward could see how unconscious Isabella was of her own beauty and magnetism. But he also considered his own conduct unacceptable. It was unfair to hold her responsible for a situation over which she had no control. However, he also knew that where men were concerned, she was too naïve and trusting.

"It's not you I distrust, darling, I swear. It's that damned devil of a man. The bounder was all over you. In fact, I don't trust a single man to behave themselves around you."

"Heaven's above, Hereward, do you seriously believe I was going to stand there and allow a fellow I barely know, or any fellow for that matter, to make love to me in a glass room visible to all and sundry? You're being ridiculous as always. Please have some faith in me."

"I will, I promise. I'm sorry."

Although Isabella didn't doubt Hereward's sincerity at that specific moment, she also felt his jealous behaviour was ingrained. However, since she saw no point in prolonging the discussion, she rolled onto her back and reminded him to switch off the light.

At breakfast the next day Hereward would have eaten a large piece of humble pie had one been available. He grimaced when he recalled his unwarranted rudeness to Randolph and his unjust and spiteful remarks to Isabella. You're nothing but a damnable rotter, he told himself. Time to make amends and send out for another palatable peace offering. At this rate, he would soon be the confectioner's best customer, he thought.

Later when Hereward joined Isabella for luncheon, she seemed to have forgotten all about the previous day's contretemps and was actually quite civil to him.

"Something smells good," she said wrinkling her nose.

Unfortunately for Hereward, her civility made him feel even worse. He realised he must learn to control his temper. But then he hadn't met the green-eyed grudge before he married Isabella. Much as he would prefer to, he knew he could hardly keep her locked up. At the party she had looked so happy, like a vibrant blue butterfly blazoning around a buddleia on a warm sunny day. And instead of being glad for her, he had caused a row and reduced her to tears.

"Herry, you're looking right through me. Is something wrong?"

"Sorry, my dear," said Hereward, coming to. "I was in a trance and I just happened to be looking in your direction."

Boyle came in with a tureen of steaming-hot soup and set it down on the table. "Mulligatawny today, Major. Thick, meaty and smooth, just as you like it."

Hereward ignored him. He was too busy worrying about Maud. What if Isabella complained to her about his appalling behaviour at Randolph and Lucinda's luncheon party? His sister would be sure to blast him. And not without justification, he thought.

Boyle ladled the mulligatawny into their soup plates. "Will that be all, Major?" he asked as a matter of course.

Hereward ignored him, so Isabella answered on his behalf. "No, this is fine, thank you," she said in a sedate voice.

Thoroughly befuddled, Boyle cast a look back at his master a couple of times as he left the room.

Unknown to the butler, Hereward was still mulling over Maud's possible reaction. A while back she had not only denounced his chauvinistic mindset, but also made reference to Boyle's appalling attitude towards Isabella.

"My dear boy, I do appreciate the problem of employing servants in the countryside," she had said in earnest. "However, you really must address the butler's behaviour, more especially at the table, where he treats Isabella with open disdain. It's totally unacceptable. Instead of watching men feasting their eyes on your wife, and don't deny it because I've seen you in church of all places, focus your eyes on what's happening right under your nose. Far be it from me to venture an opinion on staff that aren't mine, but his attitude towards her is jolly bad form. And the problem won't go away by itself if you fail to take action. It's disrespectful to her and, by extension, disrespectful to you too as her husband and his employer."

"I'm aware of it," admitted Hereward. "I've been meaning to tackle him for some time now. It's not that I'm afraid to lose him. If he goes, he goes. I shan't be blackmailed no matter how efficient or loyal he is. I know I've let Isabella down. The truth is I was hoping things would improve without the need for my intervention. I genuinely believed he would see the error of his ways first. I mean it's impossible not to like her. Especially since she places few demands on the servants and is respectful of their time. Tilly simply adores her, I can tell. But I suspect the situation has more to do with the fact that Isabella has her own way of doing things, which makes him feel threatened and undermined."

"What's wrong with you today?" asked Isabella interrupting her husband's ruminations. "You just completely ignored Boyle. I answered on your behalf, although I don't know why I bothered."

"I'm sorry, darling. My mind's not my own today."

"You don't say. I hope you're not still brooding over Randolph."

"No, of course not. In fact, I rang him earlier to apologise about yesterday and to thank him again for a most-enjoyable afternoon."

"Did you really? I'm so relieved. What did he say?"

"He was fine about it."

Once the meal was over Isabella rose from the table and gave Hereward a light peck on the cheek. "Thank you for putting things right with Randolph," she said before passing out of the room.

He put his hand to his face and smiled. Well, it was a start.

Chapter 73

Boyle was surprised to be summoned by Major Aldwen to the library that afternoon. When he entered, the Major was occupied at his desk, head bent, scribbling away on a notepad. Linking his hands behind his back, the butler waited for him to look up. Why, he couldn't quite say, but he felt worried, rather like a schoolboy in the headmaster's study praying he wasn't in for a good caning. As he stood poised in expectation, the pen's nib scratching across the paper began to fray his nerves.

"Sir, you wish to see me," said Boyle breaking the silence with an inquisitive intonation.

No reply.

Boyle shifted uneasily on his feet.

Then, after what felt like forever, Hereward finally looked up, stared at him coldly, then said in an equally cold voice: "Why do you insist on referring to my wife, who in case it has escaped your notice, happens to be mistress here, in the third person instead of addressing her directly?" he demanded to know.

Except for the purple dome of his podgy nose, Boyle's face was bone pale. "Forgive me, Major, I'm not quite sure what you mean?" he squeaked, scratching his head and frowning in bogus bafflement.

Hereward took no time at all to enlighten him. "At dinner,

for instance, you ask me if she's having wine, as if she requires my permission, or as though she's a small child unable to speak for herself."

"Sir, I m-must apologise. I genuinely hadn't realised. I c-can assure you it was quite unintentional," he stuttered.

"Perhaps, Boyle, you should be apologising to her."

"Yes of course, Sir," he said with a small solemn head bow.

"And I've also noticed," Hereward went on, "that her breakfast portions are child size. Barely enough to satisfy a mouse. Who the devil's responsible for filling her plate, for heaven's sake? It can't be Mrs Jenkins. Of that, I'm sure. One could be forgiven for thinking there's a bloody war on with strict rationing. You must be aware by now my wife has a hearty appetite."

Boyle opened his mouth to respond, then thought better of it.

"And there are never enough logs in her bedroom basket, so that when she rises first thing in the morning the room is invariably cold and she has to wait for Tilly to light the fire. You seem to forget how draughty that room is. I also happen to know that she sometimes lights the fire herself. Only the other day I came across her collecting spare logs from my room."

"Sir, she had only to inform the maids," whined Boyle. "The girls would have dealt with it in a trice."

Hereward withdrew his handkerchief and wiped his brow. Controlled though it was, his anger was causing him to perspire.

"Because she, as you so respectfully referred to her just now, avoids complaining in case it creates more problems. And God knows we've had our share of those in this house. But don't think I don't notice what goes on around here, because I can assure you, I do." And before the butler could further defend himself, Hereward dismissed him from the room. "That will be all, Boyle."

"Yes, Sir."

"And Boyle."

"Yes, Sir?"

"I expect my observations to be acted on with without delay."

"Yes of course, Sir."

With nothing else to add, Hereward returned to his work and left Boyle to see himself out.

It was the first time in many years of steadfast service that Boyle had fallen foul of his emperor, as he often thought of him in intimate moments. Beside himself with angry grief at what he considered a gross injustice, the embattled butler closed his eyes and shook his head, taking care not to disturb his counterfeit coiffure. Learning the Major had been observing him quietly for months left him feeling shocked and upset. And it dawned on him with alarming clarity that he was no longer as powerful and abiding as he once imagined himself to be.

Deluded by his false sense of infallibility and influence, Boyle also believed that prior to Isabella's arrival he had effectively been his own boss. He was convinced she had turned his beloved master against him in an act of calculated cunning. He blamed her one hundred per cent for his humiliating downfall. Added to which, he held the view that in common with all wives she knew full well how to manipulate her husband. And the fact that her most-powerful weapon lay between her legs made her invincible.

Boyle felt certain that as long as the mistress remained at the Hall her dogged determination to usurp his power and position would continue unchecked, making his life unbearable. What might she do next? he asked himself. Demand to see the Hall's accounts? The ledgers he had kept for years, with every detail recorded in his best handwriting. Even the Major had never asked to see them. In his mind's eye, Boyle pictured himself storming the gun cabinet, grabbing a pistol and shooting his antagonist point blank in the head. However, when he also imagined himself on the scaffold with the hangman's noose tightening around his neck, he thought better of it.

Furthermore, not only did he feel it was too late to start anew at another house, Boyle was also too attached to his master to resign his post. Feeling bilious all of a sudden, bitter fluid burning the back of his throat, he rushed downstairs to his room, removed a liquorice root stick from his box of medicinal remedies and chewed it like a twig. Following which, he went to the bathroom sink, removed his ill-fitting false teeth, rinsed them under the tap and examined them in detail. It was plain to see they were worn down in several places, presumably from repeatedly grinding them in suppressed rage. At a loss to decide what to do for the best, he nevertheless felt the need to do something to regain control. Otherwise, he would never know peace and happiness again.

Chapter 74

Isabella surveyed the sky's headstone-grey reflection in the lake. The atmosphere felt as heavy as a headstone too; as did the stodgy pudding in the pit of her stomach. The mucid odours emanating off the water evoked memories of damp mackintoshes and muddy wellington boots.

After ten minutes spent watching the ducks and coots sailing across the lake like miniature boats, Isabella left the littoral and joined the path leading into the forest. She continued walking until the path diverged into two distinct trails. On impulse, she opted for the right-hand route that ribboned into a more remote section of the estate, where many of the most-ancient trees grew.

As she walked on the solid soil, Isabella was soon enamoured by the natural beauty all around her. Even in winter the woods were magnificent. The enormous crowns of the congregated evergreen holm oaks compensated for their deciduous cousins' nakedness. And she wished she had a brownie camera to record her impressions.

With a step as soft and as light as a child's, Isabella delved further into the forest. In she went as if lured by some powerful magnetic force impossible to resist. The deeper she went the darker and cooler the atmosphere. Trancelike she ventured forth, soothed by a soft soporific voice in her head that said: Go now, it is safe here, nothing will harm you. And with every step she grew calmer and more relaxed.

Even in the company of her friends, Isabella had never delved so deep into the woods. There was something truly magical about the crowded commune of trees around and through which multiple tracks and trails insinuated themselves. In the arcadian seclusion she absorbed herself in mindful musings while breathing the pure clean air and inhaling the recent rain's residual scents.

An hour into her ramble, Isabella came upon a ghostly glade; as ghostly as the greenish glow of gaslight in the town's streets after dark. Placing herself at the centre of the open space, she imbibed the bosky ambience. The air, seasoned with flora, herbage and resins, together with the background sound of a rivulet running over rocky ground, soon revived her depleted spirits.

Then all at once Isabella was beset by the strangest sensation. She felt herself floating into a different dimension. A dimension in which wild and savage beasts roamed the land. A dimension in which prehistoric battles were fought and won, fought and lost. War cries of warriors and screams of dying men rang out in her head. But just as soon, the figment faded and she moved on in a haze of bemused amazement.

Floating from glade to glade in the arboreal resplendence, imagining herself an adventuress in the wilderness, Isabella failed to notice the trail vanish under layers of leaves, sphagnum and algae. Eager to soak up the rich atmosphere, she searched for somewhere to sit and spotted a suitably sized boulder matted in bright-green moss. To protect her coat, she produced from her pocket a white-linen handkerchief and laid it over the rock's rutted top. Then she sat, hugged her knees, inhaled deeply, and filled her lungs to capacity.

Soon enough, Isabella grew restless and cast an uncertain eye at the surround of trees and scrub, dense as a winter eiderdown. Why, she couldn't quite say, but she felt a sudden strange sensation come over the atmosphere. Something seemed off. Afflicted by an unexpected pang of anxiety, she sprang from the boulder, stamped her feet and straightened her coat. And after tearing a leaf off a nearby shrub, she tore it into tiny pieces and watched them float to the ground like green confetti.

Undeterred, Isabella continued to be seduced by the wiles of the Aldwen woods. And once her anxiety waned, as it always did, she decided it might be fun to venture a little further inside the unmapped territory, where few set foot and where deer and other secretive creatures maintained many of the trails. However, after roaming for another half hour or so, she feared she might have gone too far. Feeling too remote from civilisation all of a sudden, she resolved to make an immediate return to the Hall.

Believing it would lead her back, Isabella turned east and forged ahead. But after tramping for several minutes without locating the main path, it dawned on her she must have become disorientated and taken a wrong turn. In an attempt to establish her bearings, she paused and leaned against the green-tinged trunk of an elderly oak, mindful of the rough bark against the smooth fabric of her coat. Standing in shade, overawed by the sheer scale of the tremendous trees, she felt like a tiny scrap of insignificance. The part of the woods in which she stood contained some of the oldest specimens on the estate, their mighty girths as thick as lighthouses. Owing to their advanced ages, they gave off a sickly gaseous odour that made her want to sneeze.

None the wiser as to her position relative to the Hall, Isabella set off again, trespassing on twigs, leaves, old acorns, insects dead and alive, bark flakes and other detritus. As her disorientation led her off even further in the wrong direction, the terrain grew increasingly inhospitable, and the crooked, twisted tree limbs soon resembled a mangled mess of dusky sinuous snakes and writhing brown rainworms.

As she continued trying to find her way back, Isabella's attention was drawn to some sort of solid structure tucked into the trees. Overcome by curiosity, she stopped and squinted through a snarled mass of vegetation, withered branches and tall weeds. With the branches snagging her clothes and hair, she stole towards it. Then ducking under a low muscular bough barring the way, intrigued by the mysterious construction, she nosed closer.

In the midst of the strangled overgrowth stood a tumble-down two-room dwelling she assumed was once the old gamekeeper's cottage. Like the gamekeeper himself, the building was beyond rescue: a recumbent beech blocked the doorless doorway, lichen and mould blighted the exposed walls, and a sapling sprouted through the gaping roof. Outside in front, broken flowerpots, mossy stones and charred animal bones littered the ground. Little by little a resurgent nature was reclaiming its territory.

While she fixated on the ruin amongst the snarled chaos, Isabella became aware of an alien sound in the pressing silence. Then something made her look up. Directly above her, perched on a high branch, a murder of crows, their eyes more sinister than mortal sin, regarded her with mute interest. Abruptly, the black assembly took off, hacking the air with brisk flapping and harsh cawing.

Assailed by another anxiety attack as a skittish squirrel fled up a tree, fear boring into her bones, quivering like a tiny leaf in a querulous wind, Isabella regretted venturing too deep. To calm herself, she closed her eyes and drew in a prolonged breath. Acutely conscious the afternoon was wearing away she also noted the light was starting to fade. Hence with a sudden sense of urgency, she resumed trying to find her way back.

However, after plodding for a good fifteen minutes or more over a sprawling mattress of spongy moss, Isabella feared she was hopelessly lost. In whichever direction she turned streets of trees stretched as far as the eye could see. In that particular area the regimented lines of more recently planted pines put her in mind of the gridded graves of a war cemetery. Try as she might, she could not for the life of her locate the required path. As a rindle of polar-cold perspiration ran down her back, she felt trapped, trapped in a fortress of trees; a fortress without walls. How could something so commodious feel so confining? she thought.

Not knowing what else to do, Isabella stopped, looked and listened with close concentration in an attempt to reorientate herself. Significantly, the sound of running water in the background was now absent. Trails, where they once existed, lay buried beneath millions of leaves, debris and duff. She wanted to kick herself. Why in God's name had she not carried a compass?

Having no choice but to resume walking, Isabella navigated her way over and around decaying timbers whose cavities quivered with ants, grubs and larva. Roots resembling giant reptilian feet protruded from the bases of trees, gripping the ground with their scabrous claws. How could something so innocuous look so unnerving? she wondered. Why had she stupidly strayed so far from the major path without marking her way in a place with no obvious points of reference, landmarks or signposts?

As her concerns continued to mount, Isabella heard a short inconsonant sound float towards her. Her brain buffeted by fear, she slowed her tired feet and cocked a concerned ear. Yet the forest seemed strangely silent: as silent as the barn owl before the hunt. Once more, and perhaps unwisely, she stopped, looked around and listened intently.

To her dismay, she detected a current of creepiness in the atmosphere, as if the place were possessed by some malign spirit wandering through the trees. Trembling inside and out, hands clenched, fingernails piercing palms, tongue dry as desert dust, heart beating like a big bass drum, Isabella scanned the trees. Yet again, she sensed something watching her, assessing her, sizing her up with a glassy gaze. Then to her distress, she heard a stifled splutter cut through the silence, as though someone was trying to suppress a chronic cough. Sick to her stomach, she spun around like a shot putter on a circular slab. And as her protuberant eyes probed the trees, it dawned on her she had company.

Chapter 75

A spasm of shock rocked Isabella's frame as she caught a split-second sight of two palish, close-set eyes beneath cumbrous brows observing her from the trees. The eyes, set in a hirsute visage, had a hideous ophidian immobility to them. And although they had a disturbing familiarity, she couldn't quite place them in her muddled mind.

Lost in the ligneous labyrinth, nothing to see but trees, scared witless, eyes agape in a face whiter than her teeth, heart jumping like a gymnast behind her ribs, Isabella heard a hysterical voice in her head scream: Go! Run! Get away from here however you can! The situation felt surreal, the fear indescribable. It was the worst fear she had ever felt in her entire life. Yet instinctively it fuelled her muscles, powered her feet and propelled her forward, enabling her to run like a hare attempting to dodge the hunter's bullet.

Soon after, startled by an equally surprised rabbit that appeared out of nowhere, Isabella's soles lost purchase and she landed on her back with a splat on a patch of waterlogged ground. Caked in black mud, twisted twigs and dead leaves, she scrambled to her feet and resumed running. And although her warm coat hindered her progress, she didn't dare stop to remove it.

A few minutes later, to her absolute horror, Isabella heard a sound not far behind her. Not the sound of a four-footed animal, but that of a top-heavy, two-legged, large-footed creature, almost like a bear walking on its hind legs. Pressure building within her, panting with panic, blood pounding in her head, she ran at random through the trees. But she soon found moving at speed impossible with so many obstacles in her path: raised tree roots, hidden holes, stumps, logs and countless other impediments.

Overcome by a chest-squeezing sense of impending catastrophe, her fear at its highest level ever, her intestines contracting with an almost incontrollable intensity, feeling she was about to burst every blood vessel in her body, Isabella saw a gap open up in the trees to reveal the main path. Spurred on by fresh hope, straining every ligament, tendon and muscle in her legs, she pelted past the lake and kept going until she reached the Hall's grounds. Febrile, sweat beads blistering her brow, gasping for air, and close to collapse, she barged through the side gate, crashed through the boot-room door and crumpled in a heap on the seat of an old oak chest. And there she remained trembling like a leaf in a force-ten gale until she recovered.

Isabella had only just revived and risen to her feet, though her body still ached and her head felt fuzzy, when Hereward, his face crabby as a crustacean, marched into the room. As always, he looked pristine, which by comparison made her appear even scruffier. Clearly unimpressed, he scowled at her mud-spattered hair, clothing and footwear.

"I see you are back from another one of your little expeditions in the estate's bowery boulevards," he said mordantly. "You look an absolute mess. How the devil did you get yourself into such a dreadful state?"

"Slipped in some mud," she said sheepishly, shoulders hunched, eyes averted.

"And whereabouts was this particular mud patch?" Hereward asked with a suspicious frown.

"Near some trees," she replied.

"And which trees were these?"

"I'm n-not quite sure," she stammered. "Somewhere over near the lake."

"I see," he said in a tone cold as steel. "Normal people usually return in the same condition as when they go out."

Bracing herself for a thorough upbraiding, Isabella cringed inside like a cowed dog.

Hereward did not disappoint. "But not you. Oh no," he seethed through his teeth. "You must insist on returning looking like a guttersnipe." Then he paused as if for thought. "And how far into the forest did you actually go? There's certainly no mud on the periphery."

Feeling both defensive and defiant, Isabella declined to answer.

"What would you have done had your fall caused you to injure yourself? You could easily have sprained an ankle or broken a bone. Then what would you have done?"

Still, she did not answer.

"Cat got your tongue, has it? You are a foolish child, Isabella," he stressed. "A foolish, foolish child. It's about time you grew up and started behaving like a responsible adult."

"If you'll excuse me, I'll just see to this," said Isabella meekly as she removed her coat.

"Leave the coat!" he snapped. "Tilly can deal with it. Now go and clean yourself up right this minute."

Isabella felt tempted to tell Hereward to tone down his temper. However, she was so relieved to be back safe and sound, his bad mood was a mere trifle. What she really needed was a big husbandly hug, but she felt too shy to request one.

Then after leaving the room, she decided that never again

would she venture so deep into the woods. The psychological stress was too much to deal with and she felt it just wasn't worth the risk. Until, that is, she remembered she had left her new linen handkerchief on the boulder.

Chapter 76

Tilly entered the bedroom.

Isabella smiled at her maid. Unlike Barbara, the girl had the kindest face and the sweetest nature.

"Would you like some help with your hair, Ma'am?"

"Yes, thank you. I'm afraid I returned in an awful mess this afternoon, and it has taken me some time to wash the mud out of my hair. Thank goodness there's lots of hot water in the house. Makes life so much easier."

"That's the advantage of having a big boiler, Ma'am. Well, your hair certainly looks nice and clean again."

"I'm so sorry, Tills, you got lumbered with cleaning my coat."

"Don't worry yourself, Ma'am. It's simply a matter of letting the mud dry, removing it with a stiff brush and dabbing it with a damp cloth. How did you manage to get yourself covered in mud anyway?"

"Please, Tilly, promise me you won't breathe a word to anyone. I lost my way in the woods, which is where I slipped. My husband has no idea how far in I went. If he were to find out he'd be perfectly livid. He wasn't in the best of moods when I arrived back."

"Funny you should say that, because Mr Boyle has also been in a bad mood. He's hardly said a word all afternoon."

"Why is that?"

"No idea, Ma'am. It's hard to say what's going on in that mind of his. He's not one to share confidences."

"I expect not," said Isabella.

"You're very brave you know. I'm too big a coward to wander around the woods, even with my young man to accompany me." Tilly visibly quivered. "I just find them far too creepy."

"Too creepy?"

"Yes, because anyone could be hiding in the trees or the bushes. So many terrible things go through my mind when I'm alone in a secluded place. Not that I ever am. I make sure of it."

"Yes, well today I was afraid when I heard what sounded suspiciously like a — I'm really not quite sure how to describe it. Some things simply defy description. All I can say is that it sounded something like a sort of throaty grunt or a stifled bronchitic cough. And I just couldn't find my way back. Believe me, I ran as fast as a hare from a hungry fox. In fact, I must have run faster. The problem was I hadn't a clue in which direction I was running. I simply had to follow my nose. I don't mind saying I felt perfectly sick."

Tilly ran the comb through Isabella's gleaming locks. "You've managed to remove every single mud splodge from your hair, Ma'am," she chuckled. Her mistress often made her laugh without actually meaning to. "I dread to think what Master would say if you sat down to dinner with your curls caked in mud."

"I'm sure he'd be perfectly cross," admitted Isabella with a light laugh. "I can imagine what a sight I must have looked when I arrived back this afternoon. I was literally covered in the stuff."

After a pause she grew serious again. "Tilly, do you by any chance believe in the existence of ghosts?"

But before the maid could respond Isabella began to

ramble. "Only every time I'm out on the estate I hear the strangest sounds. Yet when I look around there's nothing there. Nothing visible at least. I know that trees move and creak, and that animal noises can sometimes sound almost human. Like bird whistles, for instance. Still, it's really very unnerving to feel something is out there watching one without actually knowing what it is. So many things go through one's mind at such moments, such as terrifying thoughts of devils and demons and half-human creatures. I mean I know the forest is a hive of activity and animals make all sorts of odd noises, such as deer snacking on tree bark. Except today I'm almost certain I saw a face in the trees. It looked exactly like something out of the stone age, yet its eyes had a strange familiarity. I could swear I've seen them somewhere before. Probably in one of my nightmares." Isabella shivered as she recalled the savage image. "It was only for a fraction of a second. It looked all hairy and horrid and I feared it might be some sort of werewolf. Some people claim they really do exist. However, I've yet to hear any howling on nights when there's a full moon. I happen to be reading a novel about a werewolf at the moment and it's awfully scary, I can tell you. So, I can't help wondering if the story is having an adverse effect on my imagination. You know the way horror stories make one fear things that don't actually exist, like vampires for instance. Then they begin believing in them and even imagine seeing them, especially after dark.

"I do sometimes bump into people passing through on the main path. A few days back I met Mrs Heathcote, you know the farmer's wife. She was returning from the direction of the river. She appeared to be in a hurry and went on her way with just a quick hello instead of stopping to exchange a few words. But she looked happy enough, not at all nervous or frightened. If there was something out there, something dangerous, she wouldn't be out on her own, would she? Not only that, but she would also have warned me about it. So, I know the estate must be safe. And if one thinks about it sensibly, the woods are too secluded for a person to simply hang around in them all day long, and I can't imagine anyone living in them, can you? Unless perhaps it's a deserter who fears being shot and has no idea the army has stopped doing that sort of thing."

"Why wander the estate at all, Ma'am?" said Tilly, who did believe in ghosts, ghouls and goblins and considered all deep woods dangerous after reading *Hansel and Gretel* and other scary tales during childhood.

"Because I can't bear being cooped up in the house all day long, and I do so love the forest and the lakeside. It's so refreshing to immerse oneself in nature. And how else would I forage? And I must tell you something more. Today I came across the old gamekeeper's derelict cottage. The place is completely overgrown now and unimaginably spooky," said Isabella in a vibratory voice.

"Perhaps it was the gamekeeper's ghost you saw," suggested Tilly with a sudden shiver. "Come to think of it, grizzly Grimes did have a big hairy beard."

"Uhm, I wonder. Gosh, let not my husband hear me speak of such things. First of all, he'd call me a perfect crackpot, then he'd subject me to a long lecture on my silliness, which is guaranteed to give me a fit of the giggles."

"Whatever it is, Ma'am, always trust your instincts. If something feels wrong, then it almost always is. That's what my mam says and she's usually right."

"That's what everyone advises," agreed Isabella.

Tilly put down the comb, pulled her mistress's hair into a bunch, twisted it into a chignon, and secured it with hairpins and a ribbon.

"There now, you look right as rain again, Ma'am, and I must say very pretty."

"Let's hope my husband thinks so after my mud bath," laughed Isabella.

"Just smile sweetly and don't say a word, Ma'am. According to my mam it never fails with the menfolk."

"I think you're quite right. I shall try that. Thank you, Tilly," said Isabella, who was still to be convinced. Where men were concerned, Hereward was altogether a different breed.

Chapter 77

Frowning, Isabella studied her hands and thought about booking a manicure. Her nails were rough and ragged from foraging and potting plants without the benefit of protective gloves. I really must buy some gardening gauntlets, she said to herself, especially since Hereward had commented on the poor condition of her nails more than once.

Despite the dirty disadvantages, Isabella considered the art of foraging civilised and feminine. Unlike hunting. Hunting she associated overwhelmingly with men. She had no desire to chase or ensnare an animal, slaughter it and deal with death's gory aftermath.

After checking her nails again, and reminding herself she could now afford a few of life's little luxuries, Isabella considered finding a beauty parlour. It would need to be an establishment not patronised by Rosalyn Dumbarton; a woman she imagined would enjoy hunting on horseback in a pack of baying humans, and whom she preferred to avoid at all costs. Should the two of them happen to meet in any public place, she could well imagine the scene. The woman not only bore a grudge, she also behaved like a madwoman.

Isabella dabbed a little scent sparingly behind her ears and on the insides of her wrists from a bottle of Chanel No 5 Maud had given her for Christmas. Bringing the inside of her wrist up to her nose, she inhaled the mingled molecules of rose, orchid and vanilla. It smelled delightful and she wondered how much it cost.

The buzz of a bluebottle going berserk and repeatedly striking the windowpane began to grate on Isabella's nerves, so she rose from the dressing-table stool, raised the sash and released the droning beast. Outside it was slightly windy and her nose detected a whiff of something obnoxious in the air which competed with the Chanel's sweet notes. Except for the odd hoot and distant screech, it was comparatively quiet outside now the diurnal birds were abed for the night and the scavenging squirrels asleep in their shelters.

As Isabella fastened her gaze on the trees opposite the house, she observed an indiscernible dark shape shift very slightly in the shadows. Wondering what it might be, she tried squinting. But her visual limitations combined with the overgrown grass and verbiage bordering the grounds made the shape difficult to decipher. No doubt another secretive creature of the night, she told herself. Suddenly, alone in the house except for the staff, who were all below, she experienced a distinct twinge of unease.

However, before she could investigate further, Isabella's attention was diverted to the sound of a vehicle pulling onto the drive and a beam of light beaconing the bushes. But when she returned to perusing the trees, the unidentified shape had completely vanished. How curious, she thought. Still at least Hereward's back now and I can't see a single dragon or werewolf or vampire for him to slay, she mused self-mockingly.

At the same time as the vehicle's headlamps flicked off and its engine shut down, Isabella lowered the sash, closed the curtains and returned to the dressing-table stool. Facing the mirror, she unpinned her hair and placed the clips in a small receptacle. Then she leaned forward, studied her face for a moment, and decided she looked a little more mature than when she was first married.

Isabella was rubbing her scalp with her fingers when Hereward strode in, crossed the room in the manner of a sleek, confident jungle cat, stood at her back and looked at her in a quizzical manner.

Shyly, she raised her eyes and gazed at the handsome hunk of humanity reflected back at her in the mirror. There was no denying his rampant masculinity. He gave the impression of being oblivious to his own good looks and cared not a jot if people liked him or not. She wondered how many women in total had forfeited their virginity to sample his spicy virility.

"Why were you standing there with the sash up?" he enquired. "You'll catch a cold."

"Evicting a bluebottle. Infuriating little things. It kept hitting the glass like a lunatic and I got fed up."

"Why didn't you just swat it with something?"

"I would have done, only the wretched creatures are masters of evasion. Anyhow, it's gone now, thank goodness. How was the club?"

"So-so," replied Hereward. "Oswald's an old friend, as you know, and since he's off to India soon I thought it only right to attend his farewell and wish him bon voyage."

"I remember him from the wedding. I overheard him saying he was returning to India to escape the claws of some Delilah intent on taming his excesses." Reference to their nuptials always made her feel a little uncomfortable, so to disguise her discomfort, she picked up the hairbrush from the tray on the dressing-table top.

Hereward looked at Isabella with an undeniably dark-eyed intensity, put his hand to his neck and loosened his tie. Then he said suavely: "Allow me," before gently removing the hairbrush from her hand. After which, with slow diligence, he began working the brush through her hair from front to back, repeatedly elongating her curls and allowing them to rebound.

"You require a hundred strokes of the hairbrush. Is that correct?" he enquired.

"Apparently, but I rarely reach a hundred," she admitted.

"Except when you keep me waiting deliberately. And don't even try to deny it," he said with a glint of amusement behind his eyes.

Suppressing a smile, Isabella looked up at him under her long eyelashes, then blinked rapidly with feigned innocence.

"So, my giddy goddess, what are you and your partners in crime doing tomorrow?"

"Tomorrow's the cinema. Maud and Cynthia can't make it unfortunately. They're attending some sort of society meeting in town. I can't recall what the society's called, but I believe it has something to do with the women's movement and the issue of women's rights."

Hereward pulled a face and groaned. "Women's rights! It gets worse. That sister of mine's insufferable."

"Why, don't you think women should have rights?"

"Of course I think they should have rights," he replied shortly. "But to Maud this damned business of female emancipation is nothing more than a form of recreation, a sort of hobby if you like. She never could get the hang of needlework or horse-riding. And she was always too bulky for ballet lessons."

"Now you're being fatuous," said Isabella reprovingly. "Speaking of recreation, why don't you visit the club more often? I remember my father spent more time at his club than anywhere else. Until that is he could no longer afford the fees."

"At one time I did. But it soon lost its appeal. I'm not really that sociable a fellow, as you must have gathered by now. Too many members are dreadful old bores. Most of them seem to congregate in the smoking room, which is a place I prefer to avoid. It's like floating fog in there when it's crowded. I have to say it smells ghastly. I've never understood why I'm one of the few people on this planet to find smoking perfectly detestable. I deplore the stench of stale tobacco on my clothes. It quite literally gets up my nose."

"I must agree. I dislike it too. Yet surprisingly smoking's incredibly popular at present. All the magazines carry advertisements featuring beautiful models with long cigarettes in holders. They make it look so terribly glamorous and sophisticated. I've noticed it's promoted in all the films now too. All the big stars are rarely seen without a cigarette between their fingers."

"And not a rattling cough between the whole damned lot of them, I expect," said Hereward dryly.

"Only recently I came across an article in one of the newspapers which quoted a German doctor as saying smoking harms the lungs," said Isabella. "It was right next to a tobacco advertisement of all things."

"Interesting juxtaposition," declared Hereward as he stopped brushing to consider her for a moment. He could never have had a similar discussion with Rosalyn, who read only rubbish and made no attempt to increase her knowledge or broaden her mind. Placing the brush back on the tray, he stretched out his fingers, ran them through her hair and massaged her scalp using firm but gentle circular strokes.

Hereward's fingers felt divine. Soothed and sedated, Isabella stretched her neck, closed her eyes, parted her lips a little, and emitted a soft, muted moan. Then as soon as he stopped, she slowly opened her eyes and gazed at his reflection in the glass.

"Where on earth did you learn to do that?" she asked, eyes agog.

"India. Where else?" After which, he squeezed her shoulders

and whispered in her ear: "I'll just go and get changed while you hop into bed my beautiful bunny."

Having seen it so often, Isabella recognised the hot glint of excitement in Hereward's eyes. Although his amatory attentions always abashed her, she had nevertheless begun to appreciate the seductive power she held over him. If anything, it was revelation. And she enjoyed being desired the way he desired her.

Chapter 78

When Hereward returned to the bedroom, to his surprise Isabella was still on the stool. She was shaking with rage while clutching a small colourful silk bag.

"I found this ghastly garish thing in one of the dressing-table drawers," she said rising and turning to face him. Although she felt tempted to swear for the first time in her life, she didn't dare do so. "What I wish to know is what it's doing in there? This keeps happening and I'm getting sick and tired of it."

Hereward recognised the small coin purse straight away. Its bright interwoven gold and red threads and its ornate clasp made it memorably distinctive.

"It was hidden under my handkerchiefs," Isabella explained, her eyes nailed to his face.

"It must have got mixed up with the laundry," said Hereward.

"What nonsense. Please don't take me for a fool," she asserted.

"Don't get all worked up now over nothing, my dear. I'm sure there's a perfectly plausible explanation. The maids must have assumed it was yours by mistake."

"I very much doubt that. Tilly knows very well which items are mine and which ones aren't. She's too experienced to make that error. And if she has the slightest doubt, she asks me directly. No, I'm thoroughly convinced someone is trying to torment me for whatever reason. It's vindictive and plain harassment."

"Oh, come on now. You can't be certain of that."

Isabella emitted a derisive snort. "It may surprise you to know that I happen to have in a box in my closet a collection of what I presume are your old flame's personal effects." Then she began counting on her fingers as she ran through a list: "There's a handkerchief, a lipstick, a jar of face cream, a pair of silk stockings, a bookmark, a glass bangle, and a few other bits and bobs, some of which are Indian in origin, and now there's this fancy purse to add to the harlot's hotchpotch of used goods." Owing to extreme embarrassment, Isabella omitted to mention the fancy bright-pink knickers in the bathroom, not her style at all. "And who might I wonder is placing these things here? It's definitely not Tilly. Of that I'm a hundred percent certain. Which leaves only Boyle and Barbara. Oh, and the new girl. But then it couldn't be her because the problem began long before she was taken on."

"Well, I expect it'll take some time to rid the house entirely of Rosalyn's things," said Hereward. "She was in the habit of leaving her stuff here. I always had the impression she was moving in a piece at a time, until I made her permanent, so to speak. Anyhow, I'll get Boyle onto the problem first thing. He can check all the cupboards and drawers, have a good rummage around to see what's remaining. Then hopefully that's the last we'll ever see of Rosalyn's belongings."

"Why didn't you marry Rosalyn?" Isabella blurted out, slipping out of her dressing gown and under the bedcovers.

Caught off guard by the abruptness of her question, Hereward hesitated before he answered. "I didn't love her, that's why. It's as simple as that."

"Why not?"

"What sort of question is that?" he said, sliding in beside her.

"It's a question that tells you I'm interested to know."

Isabella had a unique way of looking askance that was intensely alluring, making it impossible for Hereward to take his eyes off her.

"Well, if you must know," he said with infinite patience, "Rosalyn's not a very lovable person. In fact, she's the least-lovable person I've ever known. Arrogant, pompous and conceited. More peacock than peahen, I'm afraid. She considers herself lovable, of course, but in reality, she's self-obsessed, deluded and lacks insight. Her hide's harder than a rhinoceros and her tongue's sharper than a machete. She's cold, calculating and duplicitous. And finally, she reeks of cigarette smoke." He then paused for effect. "Other than that, she's quite nice," he joked.

Isabella half smiled.

"Unfortunately, she set her sights on me the second she clapped eyes on me at a party in India I'd just popped into. Then when she thought she had me in her talons, she clung on tight. I suppose she was fun to begin with, until she began making increasing demands on my time. Not only did she expect complete commitment from me, she was also under the erroneous impression I would one day marry her. Then you came along, my darling girl, and the rest is history. Anyway, why do you wish to know about Rosalyn?"

"No reason. Just thought I'd ask."

"Are you jealous of her?" said Hereward in a teasing tone, giving her a playful prod in her side.

Isabella opened her indignant mouth to deny it, then hesitated. "Why ever would I be jealous of Rosalyn?" she eventually said in defence of herself.

"You, tell me. Anyway, my little bookworm, what are you

reading now?" he asked, desperate to change the subject.

"Your very first book."

"What?"

"Your first book," she repeated. "The one about the Indian British Army. Or should that be the British Indian Army? It was on the bookshelf so I helped myself to it. I hope you don't mind."

"To help you nod off, presumably," he said with a self-deprecating smile.

"As it happens, it's actually very interesting. And I have to say you write awfully well." Then she paused. "Oh, I *see*. You think that because I'm a girl I want to read sickly, sentimental pigswill featuring silly females with names like Fanny and Jemima and Daphne, and goodness knows what else. I don't believe in all that boys' books and girls' books rubbish. It's a complete nonsense. I read what appeals to me. Male or female, I don't care who it's written for. As it happens, I enjoy reading historical stuff, especially more-recent history. And I'm not referring to medieval romances with dark knights charging around on white horses rescuing helpless maidens while fighting off dragons with swords. So there!"

"Oh dear. Sounds like you've been listening to my radical sister again," said Hereward.

"No. And I resent the assumption. I have a mind of my own and I can think for myself, thank you very much."

"Yes, I know you can. Forgive me, I was just being flippant. Another awful fault of mine, I'm afraid," he said with an apologetic smile.

There followed a brief silence.

"I wouldn't read something I found boring unless I was obliged to," she said when she resumed speaking.

"Then you might like to help me with the project I'm working on at present," suggested Hereward. "Check for typing errors, repetition, tautology, spelling mistakes, that sort of thing. To be honest with you I could use a helping hand. I've been mulling over the idea of employing an assistant, some sort of secretary, but in the meantime, you can help me out. That's if you're game."

"Gosh, I would love to," she said with a beaming smile. "Do you mean it or are you just being flippant again?"

"Except when I'm joking or being facetious, I never say anything I don't mean. Of that I can assure you," he stated without revealing the method in his madness. Having his wife assist him in his work was one way of keeping her close and safe from harm, he thought. Knowing Rosalyn was forgotten and he was back in Isabella's good books, he snuggled up to her and nuzzled her neck. As always, she looked as tempting as a caramel custard and smelled as fragrant as frangipani. The heat of her body radiating through her bedgown raised his raw passion and, like a glutton at a banquet, he found it impossible to resist dining at the table of her toothsomeness.

Chapter 79

Rosalyn stood at the window staring another bleak day in the face, a brandy in one hand and a Sobranie between the fingers of the other, wishing she was back in the sun-filled Indian subcontinent with Hereward by her side. They were wonderful days as she remembered them. And she felt her life was hardly worth living unless she could win him back.

As she was about to take another drag on her cigarette, Rosalyn's hand stilled in front of her open mouth as a familiar motorcar pulled up outside her house. Following which, her former beau climbed out and bounded up the path to the front door, looking as handsome as ever in a dark wool blazer, pale-blue shirt and beige flannels.

"Jeepers!" she cried, frantically stubbing out the Sobranie and banging her glass down on the mahogany coffee table. Conscious of the smell of tobacco and alcohol on her breath, she grabbed a mint from a cut-glass bowl on an occasional table, popped it into her mouth and ran to the mirror to check her face was in order. Her lipstick had worn off and there was no time to reapply it to her pale lips. Speeding to the drawing-room door, she almost collided with the butler on his way in to inform her Major Aldwen was out in the hall and insisted on seeing her immediately.

But without waiting to be shown in, Hereward barged past the butler, who wisely and politely removed himself from the room forthwith and waited in the hall in case his services were called upon. However, the look on Miss Dumbarton's visitor's face told him refreshments would not be required.

When Hereward spoke, his words were the opposite of what Rosalyn was hoping to hear. Nor was she expecting him to sound so angry and irate. She tried to think of a way to defuse his fury, but her mind was devoid of ideas. And there was no point in offering him a tipple, since she knew he never touched a drop before dinner.

"I don't know what the devil you think you're playing at, Rosalyn, but it has to stop right now, do you hear?" he bellowed in her face. The mingled odours of brandy, tobacco and peppermint on her breath combined with a generous application of expensive French eau-de-cologne on her skin made him nauseous.

Astonished by the violence in his voice and facial expression, Rosalyn took a quick step back. Having never experienced that level of Hereward's anger before, she felt a little afraid. And to her surprise, tears began to form in her eyes.

"Why do your personal belongings keep turning up in my wife's rooms, including the bathroom of all places, when you were meant to have removed them months ago?" he asked. Close up, he noticed her skin was beginning to crimp from too many days spent sunning herself in the candescent kiln of the Indian climate.

"I have absolutely no idea what you're talking about," lied Rosalyn as the mint slowly dissolved in her mouth. Even though her lips were bare, she was glad she had made up her eyes that morning with mascara, eye shadow and black liner. Fortuitously, her hair had been coloured the previous day, so there were no aging silver strands on display.

"Oh, but I think you do," he said in a slight singsong voice, staring at the wall behind her on which hung her portrait painted in oil on canvas. The artist had softened her angularity and made her appear more feminine. All the same, Hereward was sorely tempted to smash his fist through the render of her vain visage.

"I'm sorry but I don't," she repeated, this time less convincingly.

"Please don't take me for a fool Rosalyn," he snapped. "What I need from you is the name of the person at the Hall performing your dirty deeds. I have a fair idea who the conniving little culprit is anyway, and as soon as it's confirmed there'll be hell to pay. I can promise you that."

Rosalyn offered no response. She was too busy thinking about all her wasted efforts. From the very beginning her devious plan, born of desperation, had been ill considered and poorly executed. Instead of widening the rift between Hereward and his wife, she realised she had only succeeded in angering him, pushing him further away, and no doubt costing the moronic maid her job.

Speaking of her accomplice, Rosalyn cared little about the girl's fate. The little fool had willingly collaborated in her scheme because it suited her to do so and not out of any sense of loyalty, sympathy or compassion. Not being the brightest bloom in the flowerbed, Barbara had been easy to exploit. Her hatred of Isabella and the promise of a return to her former role had provided her with sufficient incentive. Now she would be forced to find work in a hellish factory or some seedy establishment. Without proper references she was finished in domestic service; for no respectable household would employ her, even at the lowest level.

Despite the depressing finality of Hereward's words, Rosalyn was not yet ready to give up the ghost. And since she had nothing left to lose, she decided she may as well have one last shot at undermining his marriage.

"I have it on excellent authority," she began in a high-pitched, supercilious voice, "that your cute little virgin bride has been liaising with one of her old boyfriends deep inside the Aldwen woods. Some illiterate, low-class lout without a penny to his name. Just think, if she's preggers you'll have no idea who the father is."

A momentary spasm afflicted Hereward's face. However, he soon recovered his aplomb. "Which friend might that be?" he asked, even though he could easily guess.

"His name's Jack. He's a young blond boy, similar in age to your wife, and they go a long way back. They're similar in appearance too. The lad's good looking in an ignoble sort of way. I suppose that's the reason they're attracted to one another. Isn't it said that people are most-attracted to those bearing the closest resemblance to themselves? Your wife and Jack were teenage sweethearts. Said to be inseparable until you came along quite literally out of the blue. Apparently, they were planning to elope. In fact, they were together the day before you got married. Why do you think she was weeping like a waterfall at the wedding? Any fool could see they were hardly tears of joy. I bet she managed to fool you on your wedding night too. We women know all the tricks. We've been at it for centuries. A quick trip to the butcher's shop for a vial of blood and viola, sorted!"

Their eyes were almost level as Hereward stared hard at her for several seconds with undisguised hatred. Had she been a man, he would have happily punched her on the nose for slandering Isabella.

"From where exactly do you derive your information, Miss Dumbarton?" he asked with a sneer.

Although the matronymic made her wince inside, Rosalyn retained her self-possession. "I have my sources," she said, her top lip thinning in a contrived smile. "And very reliable sources they are too, I have to say in all honesty."

Hereward guffawed. "Honesty, you! Please spare me. Would they by any chance be connected to cowardly anonymous libellers who write in upper case letters on bright-blue paper?" he said in an accusatory tone. "To be expertly devious, old girl, one requires brains."

The icy coldness in Hereward's countenance and tone of voice made Rosalyn shrink inside. The way he loured at her, as if she were a lower life-form, felt like a knife twisting deep in her core. How could the man she loved with all her heart look at her with such homicidal hatred? Feeling crushed, she sank into the nearest armchair and closed her eyes momentarily.

"Won't you sit down?" she said, looking up at him and crossing her smooth stockinged legs. She desperately needed a cigarette, but she knew how much he detested the smell of tobacco.

Hereward, however, remained standing as his facial expression grew evermore disparaging. "Nice try, Rosalyn, but it may surprise you to learn that I trust my wife. She's pure in heart, mind, body, and soul. Unlike you, she isn't a conniving and venomous witch intent on wrecking someone's marriage."

Rosalyn stood up, drew near to him and lowered her voice to almost a whisper. "How can you be so sure?" she said, her eyes searching his. "Let's not be naïve. As it's so often said, there's no smoke without fire. I mean be honest with yourself, Hereward, she's not quite the saint you profess her to be. It's no secret she associated with some very dubious and unsavoury characters before you rescued her from penury. As I've already made clear, my source of information is most reliable. It came from a friend of hers who has absolutely no reason to lie."

Enraged, Hereward thrust his face in Rosalyn's and roared: "No smoke without fire! Oh, for heaven's sake, woman, not that old chestnut. Show me the evidence. By that I mean verifiable evidence and not hearsay and gossip from some former acquaintance of my wife's. And let me tell you right now, there's not a chance in hell of my seeking a divorce, so put that possibility out of your mind this instant and stop wasting your time and energy making unsubstantiated accusations. Only a fool would be persuaded by your grievous falsehoods. Your tongue's toxic, woman, your mind's warped and you're rotten to the very core."

Despite his terrible insults, Rosalyn was still not prepared to concede defeat quite so easily. "It's common knowledge that you and your wife are always arguing," she asserted.

"Oh really, is that so?" said Hereward as he stared at her mean, mirthless mouth with distaste. "I very much doubt most people are interested in the minutia of my private life, unless they've taken leave of their senses, or they themselves live such sad and empty lives they have nothing better to do than gossip. All married couples have disagreements from time to time. It's par for the course, human nature, a simple fact of life. Furthermore, my marriage is none of anyone's damned business. And certainly not yours. Now I'm warning you, Rosalyn, keep your accursed possessions out of my house and stop wasting your time trying to undermine my marriage, because it's not going to work. No matter what happens, I will never give up Isabella. Not ever. Now good day to you," he said before the temptation to muzzle her mawkish mouth on a permanent basis proved irresistible. "Oh, and thank you all the same," he added, "but I'll see myself out."

After he left, Rosalyn, who was trembling for the first time in her adult life, poured herself a large brandy and lit her tenth cigarette of the day. Forced to face the fact there was no hope of a reconciliation, she realised there was only one course of action left open to her. Taking a drag on her cigarette, she picked up the telephone and prepared to dial. It was time to start making arrangements for a return trip to India. With a heavy heart she sighed and said to herself there would never be another Hereward.

As Hereward drove back to the Hall doubts began to sprout in his mind. Was Isabella's prudishness, her coyness, her shyness between the sheets, a ruse to throw him off the scent of her duplicity with Jack? Perhaps that was why she visited the woods several times a week and remained out for hours. Recalling her promise never to dishonour him, he wondered whether he was naïve to take her at her word.

Chapter 80

In late March spring slipped into winter's slot, bluebells swathed the forest floor, and the sweet fragrances of a replenished earth perfumed the air. In the meadows the tips of the long grass twinkled like a zillion stars under the lemony sunshine in a lucent pale-blue sky, delicate as a watercolour wash. Throughout the estate the deciduous trees, sprouting new buds, were preparing to make their summer debut.

It was Isabella's first springtime at Aldwen Hall. With a skip in her step and gladness in her heart she was soon lulled into the land's loving embrace. Content in her own company, singing softly to herself, she capered along the paths and trails like a lively child. However, owing to her unnerving experiences, she no longer ventured too deep into the woods; just far enough to forage for wild herbs, spring greens and elderflowers.

For the very first time in her young and difficult life, Isabella felt grateful. The land she so loved also belonged to her now by virtue of her marriage. Although she felt sure she would never forgive her father for forcing her to wed, she was slowly adjusting to married life, despite its ongoing challenges. In many respects Hereward was a caring, considerate and affectionate husband when she allowed, and she was slowly becoming accustomed to his volatility. She also derived great satisfaction from assisting him in his work a couple of mornings a week, sitting at her own small desk in the library overlooking the garden. The biggest hurdle she had still to clear, however, was his mulishness regarding her ambition to drive a motorcar. And the hurdle remained a high one. Notwithstanding, she intended to keep up the pressure on him until he capitulated. Whether Hereward liked it or not, times were changing and, ultimately, he would have to change with them.

Returning from foraging at the forest's edge, Isabella heard faint footsteps falling in with her own, matching them stride for stride. She stopped, looked around at the leafy greenery and feathery undergrowth, and listened closely. There was nothing there. Nothing visible at least. Why do I spend my life looking over my shoulder for something with no basis in reality? she asked herself. This has been going on for far too long? Please let it stop.

Isabella set off again. But as a passing cloud concealed the sun and dimmed the landscape, a sudden wave of cold fear washed over her. And when another odd noise, rather like the snapping of a celery stick, attracted her notice, she wheeled around and viewed the scene. As usual the path behind her was deserted. Still, she had a strong sense of something lurking in the locality. What form the something took she could only imagine until she recalled the pallid eyes staring at her through the foliage like a picklock peering through a letterbox. Unfortunately, she still struggled to decide if the peculiar eyes were real or not, especially since the sighting had been so brief.

Once, during childhood, Isabella had awoken in the small hours to see a tall figure bathed in bright light standing over her. The figure took the form of a huge stag with human eyes. She could still remember her sense of terror at the time. With a weary sigh she castigated herself for her whimsicality and reminded herself that in all the time she had roamed the estate nothing bad had ever befallen her. And with a roll of her eyes in a show of stubborn bravado, she sallied forth.

However, still afflicted by the long spiny hands of fear, a fear difficult to define, the failure of Isabella's internal reasoning soon became clear as disturbing images of murderous lunatics, runaway convicts and escaped circus cats came to life in her imagination. She pictured them lying in wait for her in the trees, preparing to pounce at any moment. Stop it, for heaven's sake! she cried inside. You're being ridiculous. After which she continued walking, stopping every so often to check nothing was creeping up on her.

As she orbited the lake, where the pale sun shone through the trees, and the ground looked slippery in some places, Isabella breathed in the dewy air with a significant sigh. Although everywhere smelled fresh and fructuous, for reasons she couldn't explain there remained something definite but unquantifiable in the atmosphere. So, with her hand shielding her eyes, she twirled around and surveyed the surround. Right then she was forced to admit that being female gave her a fearsome sense of her own fallibility. And it seemed to her unfair that when a man hears strange noises, observes dubious shadows or perceives odd vibrations, he pays them no heed unless they present an overt threat to his safety.

Halting briefly by a single hunky hazelnut tree, Isabella reflected on Hereward's story of a married couple, Ram and Sita, featured in one of the Hindu holy books he had brought back from India. In the ancient legend Sita steps outside the circle of safety imposed on her in the forest and is kidnapped by a demon king. Isabella loved to listen to her husband's stories. Occasionally, when he was in the right mood, he would narrate them in his rich, mellow voice while gently stroking her head as she drifted off to sleep. Sometimes she questioned his motivations. Were his tales meant as warnings to be wary when she wandered the woods? After all, no-one could say with complete certainty there was nothing to fear.

Far off in the distance the farm dogs could be heard yapping in a call-and-response routine. A large dog like a mastiff or Irish wolfhound would make a worthy companion and protector, thought Isabella suddenly. A sort of canine bodyguard with an inbuilt detection and early warning system activated by its superior senses. Unfortunately, Hereward's health condition made having a guard dog, or any pet for that matter, impossible. And Isabella cursed her poor husband, even though she knew it was unfair to blame him for something outside of his control. Then for the first time in her life she considered carrying a weapon in case she ever needed to defend herself. But what sort of a weapon? And a weapon against what exactly? And was she even capable of wielding one? she asked herself as she glanced at a fallen bough on the grass. Without picking it up, she resumed walking.

Satisfied his camouflage blended in well with the new season, Parker swept aside a branch and peered at his compulsion through a pair of borrowed binoculars his mate had confiscated from an enemy soldier. Or so he claimed. A goatish gurn animated his features, turning his face into a grotesque caricature. Then he set off after her.

After months spent tracking the Major's wife, it had finally dawned on Parker that whenever he came within a stone's throw of her, she seemed to sense his presence. There was something in her bearing that reminded him of a highly strung roe deer. Thus, with that in mind, he resisted the temptation to get in close to her. Which is where the binoculars proved invaluable, enabling him to home in on her most-salient attributes at close range.

To further reduce the risk of being heard, Parker removed

his boots, emptied his pockets of any noisy objects and concealed them below a bush. Then walking on the external blades of his bare feet, he began to parallel her pace, making sure to stay below her sightline in case she pivoted with sudden abruptness. Within the thick of the shrubs and trees, eyeing her with raptorial greed, his rigid raised organ prodding the inner fabric of his flies in readiness to discharge its imbecilic seed, Parker fought his most-primal mammalian impulse, unsure of how much longer he could postpone claiming his prize.

After leaving the lakeside Isabella decided she wasn't yet ready to return to the Hall. Instead, she decided to see if any cute calves were with their mothers in the cow field. Although she admitted herself slightly anxious, she felt that to succumb to her fear would mean forfeiting her precious freedom to wander the Aldwen estate at will. And she told herself that had there been anything out there it would surely have shown itself by now.

As she went on walking, shuffling through old leaves and treading on large pebbles periodically to feel them under her feet, Isabella detected vague vibrations in the slumbering earth. Perturbed, she stopped and scanned the area a section at a time in slow motion, taking in as much detail as she could. Seeing nothing to cause her concern, she resumed walking, but at an escalated speed while staying alert.

Hemmed in by hedges higher than her head in some places, Isabella felt as though she was walking through a long leafy tunnel. However, as soon as she saw the Hall's tall chimney stacks, she felt a large measure of relief. And it suddenly seemed to her ironic that the place she once considered a prison now felt more like a sanctuary. Even more so since all traces of Rosalyn Dumbarton had been removed, Barbara had bolted and Boyle had been brought into line.

Feeling more relaxed, Isabella settled into a steady trot. Far behind her in the deepest part of the woods could be heard a dead tree crashing to earth. In her head she pictured the scene: split, shattered and fractured limbs strewn over the ground like the aftermath of an exploded bomb. Throughout the estate she often observed trees ripped from the ground as if by some giant hand, some of them fully uprooted, their root balls waving in the wind like the legs of a recumbent beetle engaged in a desperate battle to upright itself. Numerous times, Hereward had advised her to watch out for falling trees. Except for a sudden short creak, he said they gave little warning before keeling over like drunken tars on shore leave.

"Remember," he once said, "the woods are not as innocuous as they look. Still, at least we no longer need worry about dangerous beasts roaming around in them such as vicious wolves, wild boars and brown bears."

A sudden breeze stroked Isabella's skin, tickled the leaves and swished the daffodils. Up ahead, a conspiracy of crows was taking a break on the branch of an old oak, reinforcing her fears of what she knew not. Despite telling herself over and over again that except for falling branches and unstable trees there was nothing dangerous on the Aldwen estate, she continued to suffer spates of intense anxiety during which phantom figures came to life in her head.

Recalling both Martha and Tilly's advice to trust her instincts, Isabella presumed they were referring to one's sixth sense. However, she had no way of knowing if instincts were reliable. Not only that, she also questioned the wisdom of modifying her behaviour based on some vague, undefinable sense of threat which might easily be wrong. After all, she reasoned, it was possible to dislike someone on first sight, yet come to like them on closer acquaintance. Or vice versa. Furthermore, she was unsure to what degree instincts and common sense were in any way connected. And as she went on with her internal ramblings, Isabella reckoned that one required the benefit of hindsight to determine if one's instincts were correct. Added to which, there was no point in saying one should have trusted one's feelings after the fact, she went on, tying herself up in cognitive knots. Come what may, it was impossible to predict the future. Well not without a crystal ball. And she preferred not to spend life constantly looking over her shoulder.

As Isabella continued to dwell at length on the subject of instincts, she heard an inner voice whisper her name. Weirdly, at the same moment, her brain registered an oddity at the outer edge of her visual field. Slowly turning her head to home in on it, she did a double take. Above her eye level on the trunk of a tree she had never before noticed featured an assemblage of carved marks with an uncanny familiarity.

Thoroughly intrigued, holding her arms close to her sides, treading down spiky grass and flowering weeds beneath the balls of her feet, Isabella picked her way towards the tree. Flabbergasted, her chin tilted upwards, she stared at the marks. There within a heart-shaped outline she read her name scored deep in the dark pachyderm bark. But instead of saying Isabella Acton, like the one she had carved herself, it stated in misspelled words: *Isabella Aldwen. The luvliest fairry in all the forist.*

And as she stood rooted to the spot, her throat tighter than a reef knot, her face fossilised in shock, a rivulet of ice-cold fear rolled down Isabella's back. There was something deeply disturbing about the uncredited homage. Moreover, the air had begun to smell bad, as if contaminated by some noxious substance. Contracting like a daisy in the rain, all her pores perspiring panic, her limbs tingling with trepidation, she stepped back from the mutilated tree. Then sensing a menacing presence behind her, cagily she turned around.

Chapter 81

Fully expecting to find some shifty satanic figure standing in the shadows, Isabella was relieved to see nothing stood behind her. Certainly nothing poised to pounce. Nevertheless, everywhere the air bristled with negativity. Cautiously reassured, she placed her trug on the ground and turned her attention back to the tree. Fear competed with fascination as she studied the rough rutted text.

Her skin crawling with the creeps, in an unconscious gesture of self-protection, Isabella pulled together the lapels of her jacket. And when a dark wide-winged bird soared high in the sky overhead, her old misgivings re-emerged. A myriad of explanations ran through her mind, none of which made the slightest sense. Also, the inscription gave the impression it had been produced only recently, and that its mystery scribe must be local to Oakwich, since he or she knew her new surname.

Meanwhile, as the sun took a short siesta behind a cloud, Isabella was assailed by an indescribable sense of danger. Fear spread rapidly through her body like a gushing subterranean stream. As the hairs on her neck stood up, she felt two bulging bestial eyes boring into her back like big black anchor bolts. Grabbing her trog, she turned rapidly on her heels and plunged through the grass towards the path. And although her legs felt as heavy as logs, she galloped all the way back to the Hall.

Close by, but hidden behind a holly bush, his face puffy and ketchup red, his savage, insentient eyes popping from their sockets, his skin wet with the sweat of excitement, feeling his pintle might shortly rupture, Parker let the binoculars dangle down his front. Then he struck his chest with his fist and coughed like an old bullfrog.

"Bugger," he bleated under his breath, dismayed at seeing the girl dash off after reading his romantic tribute. Parker had somehow expected his pretty compulsion to be pleased, not panicked. Her face, illuminated by the sun's reappearance, had looked frantic and confused, reminding him of a rabbit about to be put to death.

Thrusting his head forward and staring in the direction of the Hall until her treads ceased to sound on the path, Parker sucked in a draught of air through his nose and swallowed a thick blob of phlegm lodged in his throat. Then he turned and headed homeward, all the while thinking about the young wife's tantalising torso. Even though she appeared taller than when he first started spying on her, comparing their respective strengths and sizes, Parker knew he could still overpower her with minimal effort. It would be like a heavyweight wrestling a featherweight in the ring. Or a bird battling a butterfly — no contest. Earlier that afternoon he had almost lost control when he saw her bend over to yank some rhubarb stalks from out of the ground and place them in her trug. Seeing her superb rounded rear upended in the grass put him in mind of a juicy steak on a bed of fresh greens. Spawning a seedy smile, his mouth watering, Parker imagined himself inside her and the taste of her intimate sweetness on his tongue.

Never before had he seen a more magnificent body than the one on the Major's wife. Without question he loved her; loved the nimble-footed, fine-limbed little lady with all his heart. Her existence gave meaning to his pedestrian life, reawakened his manhood, turning his flaccid worm into a mighty mamba. He only hoped she stopped growing, since her small stature held special appeal for him.

However, at that moment, and for no apparent reason, an image of Miss Dumbarton became manifest in Parker's mind. She had the legs of a giraffe, the head of a horse and the fixed stare of a sparrowhawk. Intrusive thoughts were funny like that, he mused, appearing unbidden at unexpected moments. And as he patted her highness's wasted pounds in his pocket, he thought he would like to punish her by hunting her down and giving her highbred hams a good humping.

Through a process of word association, Parker's mind turned to the subject of hunting. He knew only too well that hunting required not only skilled stealth but also infinite patience. Something he once had in abundance, especially before he was forced to sell his rifle. He remembered how thoroughly he enjoyed taking revenge on the mangy foxes that caused carnage in the henhouse.

One time, Parker had also aspired to ride to hounds. However, he soon discovered riding to hounds was not for the hoi polloi like himself, who had anyway long been priced out of hunting on horseback. Riding to hounds was almost exclusively the preserve of toffs. Tory toffs to be precise, who called each other old boy and old chap and old fellow, and shouted tallyho and holloa and other toffee-nosed terms.

As he went on with his introspections, Parker was suddenly reminded the morrow was Thursday. He detested Thursdays, although he always made sure to reach the Hall's grounds in time to see the Major's wife ride off on her bicycle, so he could ogle her perfect behind perched high on the saddle as her leg muscles pumped the pedals. A number of times he had noticed the Major also watched her from the dining-room window. However, Parker presumed she mustn't have known, for she never waved to him before setting off.

Parker's roving thoughts then turned to his tea. Seeing fear on the faces of his intended food had an aphrodisiacal effect on him, stimulating an intense desire deep within himself. Drilled in violence from an early age, he took pleasure in the theatre of butchery, in seeing rabbit parts spread out on the floor like soldiers' dismembered bodies on a blood-soaked battlefield. He thoroughly enjoyed snapping the animals' necks, stripping their fur and gutting their innards before roasting or braising them. Passing his tongue over his lips, Parker smiled to himself and returned to fantasising about the Major's wife.

Chapter 82

Hereward was still at his desk when Isabella arrived back from her walk looking tired and pale. He checked the time on his wristwatch against that on the carriage clock. She was earlier than usual and appeared a little breathless and troubled, as though something had ruffled her feathers. Even though he considered the estate to be overall safe, he still worried about her when she was out alone and at the mercy of the weather, not to mention falling trees and branches. He also feared she might fall and injure herself.

"Are you alright, my little skylark?" he asked as she slumped into one of the hearth chairs and closed her eyes.

Isabella's eyes sprung open. "Yes, of course I'm alright. Why shouldn't I be?" she said with a note of defensiveness in her voice.

"No special reason. It's only that you look as though you've just run a race. Don't tell me you've taken up cross-country training to keep fit," he teased.

"No. Walking a reasonable distance at a brisk pace is all that's required to maintain one's fitness," she replied.

"Then why do you look as though you've been running?"

But before Isabella could answer, Boyle came in with the tea things and acknowledged her, albeit with reluctance. His appearance always produced a peculiar aversion in her.

Shifting her bottom backwards on the seat to pull herself

upright, she waited for him to exit the room, then resumed speaking.

"Well, it looked as though it might rain, and had I got soaked then you would've bawled at me like you usually do about my getting pneumonia or some other deadly disease. I have to say you're obsessed with pneumonia, even in spring, and probably in summer too, I expect. So, I ran just to be on the safe side."

Hereward lowered his brows and twisted around in his seat to look through the window. "The sky's almost as clear as a blank canvas," he said turning back again. "There's barely a cloud in sight. Well certainly no rainclouds." Then he paused and puckered his forehead. "And besides, I never shout," he said with feigned indignation. "I might raise my voice a touch so as to emphasise a point."

Isabella guffawed. "Gosh, Herry, you seriously need to have your hearing tested if you think you don't shout. The townspeople must be able to hear you when you're in one of your frightful tempers."

Hereward loved Isabella calling him Herry. "Very well, just this once I'll concede the point. Now be a good girl and pour the tea. I shan't be long. In fact, I'll be with you as soon as I've finished typing this sentence. In the meantime, don't forget to save a sandwich for me."

Isabella's lips parted fully as she laughed. Sometimes she just couldn't help herself.

As she nibbled a crumpet, she felt tempted to tell Hereward about the inscription on the tree trunk. However, after a moment's reflection, she decided against it. Out of pure jealousy he might blame poor Jack and prohibit her from going out alone ever again. Not that she would take any notice. Still, she preferred to avoid another quarrel about her old friend, especially since she rarely saw him nowadays. For a brief moment she wondered whether he was responsible for inscribing her name on the tree trunk, but quickly dismissed the notion, knowing it wasn't his style. Ultimately, she decided it was probably a prank. A prank made by someone known to her who happened to be passing through the estate. And knowing it would most likely forever remain a mystery, she advised herself to forget all about the message.

Chapter 83

Aldwen Hall slowly diminishing in size behind her, Isabella strolled in the direction of the woods. Following a few days' respite, and having decided to develop a tougher backbone and stop seeing the woods as the type of place described in scary fairy tales and common folklore, she resumed roaming the estate. For reassurance, she also reminded herself that sudden odd noises were a normal feature of forest life, caused mostly by branches, fruits and nuts hitting the ground, or roots shifting underground, making the trees groan, grind and creak.

For some strange reason that day, Isabella felt like the only person on the planet as she passed through an ancient grove of flowering yew trees whose trunks were twisted, deformed and split, and whose toxic leaves Hereward had warned her never to chew when she was foraging. Thinking him unnecessarily neurotic as she trampled on the yews' discarded needles, she heard a green-winged woodpecker laugh as it tapped the bark of a nearby tree, then removed creepy crawlies from its crevices.

Isabella was looking forward to visiting the estate at the height of summer when it was dressed at its best. It then occurred to her that come August she would have been married for a whole year. Thankfully, things had turned out better than expected. Smiling with excitement, she realised she would soon be eighteen. She hoped Mrs Jenkins would bake a special birthday cake with candles on top, and Hereward would take her out to dinner at some plush hotel. Preferably one with a dance floor and a lively band playing. Then, thinking of possible presents, she imagined he would give her something frightfully expensive. But having already received from him a diamond necklace and gold wristwatch, she had no idea what he might give her.

Still smiling to herself, Isabella raised her sleeve to check the time and the smile died on her lips. Puzzled, she stared at her left wrist for several horrifying seconds. She could hardly believe her eyes. Her wrist was bare. Completely bare. As bare as the day she was born. Thinking she must have fastened her wristwatch on the wrong arm, she checked her right wrist. But her right wrist was also bare.

"Oh cripes!" she cried out loud when it occurred to her it must be lying on the ground somewhere. But where? It could be anywhere between there and the Hall. Assuming she had failed to fasten the catch properly, Isabella began to cry like a small child. Apart from her new necklace, the wristwatch was her most-valuable possession. Her very first gift from Hereward. Oh no, Hereward! she thought. And she couldn't bear to think of his reaction when he discovered she had lost his gift.

In desperation, she considered keeping the loss of the watch a secret, but sooner or later he was bound to notice it missing and, knowing her husband, it would be sooner rather than later. Thinking it wise to attempt to find it, Isabella started retracing her steps. However, the process of sweeping the ground with her eyes while walking was painstakingly laborious and difficult in the dim light and she despaired of ever locating it. Nevertheless, she continued, too afraid to return without it.

Some thirty minutes later, Isabella finally accepted defeat. Unless she got lucky there was little chance of spotting the timepiece on the paths and grassy tracks in the gloom. She decided, therefore, that it made sense to abandon her search and resume it early the next morning when the light was bright. All the same, she was forced to face the fact that if she still couldn't find her wristwatch come noon, then she would have to own up.

Isabella groaned inside at the thought of confessing her irresponsible crime to Hereward. She wondered how she was ever going to face him. Perhaps he was right to call her a foolish child, because that's exactly what she was. In desperation, she considered buying herself a replacement, but quickly dismissed the idea. For not only did she lack the funds, but he also paid for all her major purchases.

With a heavy heart, Isabella continued making her way back to the Hall. Then shortly after, she came to a sudden stop. "Gosh! Silly me," she said audibly when she remembered removing the wristwatch before applying a drop of bergamot oil to her hands. And unless Tilly had put it safely away, it must still be lying on the dressing table.

Ecstatic with relief, Isabella felt like jumping for joy. Then, recalling her promise to Hereward to be on time, she set off again at a dash. However, by increasing her speed too rapidly, she was stalled by a stitch in her side. Doubling up and wincing in pain, she felt as though she had been stabbed with a knitting needle. Unable to move, she pressed her fingers to the spasm and hoped the agony would soon subside.

Once it did, Isabella straightened up a vertebra at a time and got going. But as a collection of smouldering clouds coursed across the sky, she encountered the strangest sensation: that of something dark and sinister hovering within range. Her body reeled with an involuntary shudder, then stiffened up. She noticed the air smelled like a damp cellar and wondered whether rain was imminent. Turning up soaked to the skin in addition to being late was bound to anger Hereward, and

Hereward's anger was best avoided.

However, to avoid suffering another agonising stitch, Isabella walked at a slower rate than before, thinking it wise to increase her speed in increments. Then as soon as she felt able to, she picked up her pace and pushed on past the cattle field. At that time of day, the cows were confined to the byre, from where they could be heard lowing with hunger, along with the horny bull corralled for the night. Up ahead of her agitated squirrels scooted out of harm's way, while the birds beat their wings in brief bouts of frenzy.

Then as the wind changed course very suddenly, Isabella caught a flash of something in her peripheral vision. She froze as a feral farm cat flew across her path and disappeared into the tangled undergrowth.

"Gosh! I'm awfully nervous this afternoon," she whispered, staring after the flying feline, thankful it wasn't another big ugly rat.

Upon reaching the point at which the path bore back to the house through the orchard, Isabella slowed and screwed up her nose. Feeling as if a giant gnat had invaded her right nostril, she rubbed her columella with the knuckle of her forefinger to relieve the irritation. Thereafter, the reek of something truly rotten, strong enough to repulse a belligerent bull, stung her delicate nasal mucosa. Experiencing a sudden build-up of pressure inside her chest, she closed her eyes and discharged a powerful sneeze into the air before she could withdraw her handkerchief.

Despite her mounting unease and sense of something unseen observing her from the shadows, Isabella tried her best to remain calm and prevent her vivid imagination carrying her off to faraway places of phantoms and freaks. Not much further to go now, nearly there, she told herself. Stay strong and you'll be fine. Whatever happens, don't panic. Although panic, she decided, was like a weed, once planted it was impossible to fully uproot.

Presently, there came the sound of a whistle cut short with sudden abruptness. Skidding to a stop, Isabella looked around. "Whatever was that?" she whispered, her stomach sinking to her knees as the air throbbed with a tangible threat. But there was nothing visible within her limited visual scope.

With haste, half satisfied nothing was trailing her, she got going again, hoping Hereward was the as yet unidentified whistler on his way to meet her in case it rained. What a relief it would be to see him heading towards her on the path. Except it couldn't be him, she reckoned, because he never whistled. Whistling wasn't his thing. Now and again, he sang in his booming baritone when he felt especially buoyant. A rare occurrence. Usually something from Gilbert and Sullivan, which she quite liked to hear. And she had never known him to smell other than scrupulously clean. Denying reality, she reassured herself it must have been a blackbird whistling, having heard they sound remarkably similar to humans when they sing. Not that she had ever before noticed.

While the landscape continued to leech colour, the cold wind strengthened, chafing Isabella's cheeks. Yet in spite of the chill, her skin felt clammy under her clothes. And she flinched when a withered leaf skimmed her face before floating to her feet.

Under an emerging pale moon, Isabella, moving between tall hedges lined with rampant weeds and lofty waving willowherb, made sure to remain in the centre of the path, which somehow felt less intimidating. At the same time, she cursed herself, for had she not tarried she would already be back at the Hall, safe and sound; not in fear of some insane psychopath pursuing her to satisfy his bloodlust. Admitting herself fatigued, she longed to be sitting in the library, having her tea in front of a brisk fire in the company of her husband.

As her worried eyes came to rest on the corpse of a tree snapped at its base by a hurricane wind, Isabella's ears pricked up at a barely audible scuffling sound. There simply has to be an animal nearby, she said to herself without conviction. But then to her horror, the louder rasping rattle of a phlegmy cough registered in the air.

Coming to a startled stop, her heart pulsating at a hundred plus beats a minute, terror tingling her limbs, Isabella prayed the noise was made by nothing more dangerous than a small deer, having heard their coughs also sound strangely human. And besides, she asked herself, still hoping the noise was innocuous, what else could it be? But then deer, she knew, were skittish creatures determined to keep their distance from mankind with good reason. Moreover, its superior sense of smell enabled it to detect its enemies from hundreds of feet away. Yet this deer seemed daringly close. Too close for its own comfort. And hers. What's more, she told herself, deer don't smell like tobacco. All alone, feeling small, fragile and extremely vulnerable, with a sickening sense of presentiment impossible to suppress, her eyes huge opalescent orbs, Isabella repeatedly glanced around.

Not to her relief, it turned silent again. As silent as a Victorian schoolroom with a sadistic cane-wielding master in charge. The absence of sound seemed loaded with significance. It made her feel especially fearful in the dim light. In the unnatural noiselessness, nothing stirred now: no birds called, no frogs croaked, no squirrels chattered. Having quickly died down, even the wind had ceased to whistle, whimper and whine.

To add to her problems, Isabella's boots were beginning to rub a little. Despite telling herself otherwise, she knew intuitively that something was wrong. Everything felt off key and out of kilter. And although her brain urged her to run, she didn't dare risk incurring another painful stitch in case it proved perilous. Then as another brief noise attracted her attention, Hereward's warning returned to haunt her: *If you were to meet with an accident, or for that matter any misfortune, I would have no idea. If I have no idea that you're in trouble, then I cannot come to your rescue, should that be necessary.*

Since her heels felt increasingly sore, Isabella was forced to slow down. In a gesture of self-protection, she wrapped her arms tightly around her trembling torso, then withdrew them in case she might need to defend herself. Naively, she once believed she could look after herself. But as her fear continued to grow, she recognised only too well her physical deficiencies. Feeling weak and assailable, and thinking a weapon might prove useful, she looked around on the ground for a branch big enough use as a cudgel, but there was nothing of a suitable size. Her thoughts returned to Hereward. If only her strong, brave, fearless spouse would appear on the path, even in one of his tyrannical tempers, she would be eternally grateful.

As it continued to grow dark, Isabella felt like a soldier passing through enemy territory. The Hall seemed too far away to be of comfort. To hasten her return she considered quitting the path and taking a shortcut instead of cutting through the orchard. However, that would involve forcing her way through the garden hedge and there was a good chance she would get stuck and become a sitting duck for whatever was out there. Therefore, she remained on the path.

Again, she stopped when the sinister laugh of an owl sent a flock of birds into orbit. Isabella, her heart now racing at a reckless speed, her irises white-ringed with terror, pressed her cold hand to her chest as foreboding's long creepy fingers climbed her spinal column a notch at a time. If fear had a colour, hers would be scarab black.

Chapter 84

Holding his hand-engraved slide pencil in his fingers, Hereward swivelled around, looked through the library window and wondered, as he so often did, whether his wife would be late again. As usual she had left the house before she had digested her lunch. Still, he mused, she seemed happier of late, which improved his mood too. He hoped he had seen and heard the last of Rosalyn Dumbarton. A few days previous, Maud had happened to mention that according to someone from her women's group, his old flame was in the process of returning to India. Good riddance, he thought. Even if she were the only woman on earth, he still wouldn't marry her.

Hereward consulted his wristwatch and thoughtfully stroked his chin. He hoped Isabella had remembered to wear hers; which made him think of her slim wrists, slender arms and smooth shoulders. Following which his mind meandered over the rest of her body. A body with which he was now fully acquainted by touch, but not by sight, to his ongoing disappointment. And he wondered whether he ever would ever have the privilege of seeing her naked.

For some unknown reason, Jack sprang to mind. Disconcerted, Hereward mulled over how much of Isabella's body the youth had seen when they swam as part of a group in the lake. Had she had gone into the water fully clothed, wearing a bathing costume, only her drawers, or completely starkers? he pondered. Leaning back in his chair, he threw back his head, spread his legs and frowned with frustration. The thought of other males gazing at Isabella's bare body tormented him. However, he smiled when he recalled tapping her bottom with the newspaper as she was leaving and reminding her not to be late. And in response she had laughed at him in her typical cheeky way.

Desire burning within him all of a sudden, and wishing bedtime wasn't still hours away, Hereward pictured himself divesting Isabella of her drawers, raising her nightdress and fondling her flesh. Back to work pronto, old boy, he advised himself, or you'll soon require a cold shower.

However, as the clock chimed on the chimneypiece shelf, Hereward put down his pencil, got up from his seat, moved to the french window, and gazed at the garden without taking in any specific detail. Standing tall and statuesque, his eyes fixed on a line of distant trees, he thought of Isabella somewhere out on the estate. God only knows what she does with herself all afternoon, he said to himself. He felt tempted to go and meet her. She never seemed to mind when he did. But that was usually because it was pouring down. And since there was no sign of rain, he returned to his work.

As Hereward picked up his pencil, the telephone trilled at the same time as a timid triple tap sounded on the library door. The shuffle of feet could also be heard in the hall. Whoever that is can jolly well wait, he thought as he took the call. Must be one of the damned maids wanting to enter the room for some obscure reason. The new girl presumably. Silly Milly, as Boyle referred to her, since Tilly knew better than to disturb him at his desk.

"I'm afraid you have the wrong number," Hereward barked into the receiver before banging it down. "Blasted idiot," he muttered with a shake of his head. Without knowing why, he felt a sense of unease, on edge, unable to concentrate. Call it a soldier's instinct, but he couldn't help feeling something catastrophic was about to happen.

The knock repeated. A little louder and more pronounced.

"Come," he called with a curt locution as he stared at the door and suspired.

Chapter 85

"What is it Tilly?" asked Hereward, looking at his watch for the umpteenth time.

Tilly was hesitant in manner and hesitant to speak. After all, he was the master and she was only the maid.

"Well, spit it out girl," he said in his usual impatient, short-tempered fashion.

Under his compelling gaze, Tilly shifted uneasily on her feet, clasped her hands in front of her apron and squeezed them tight. No matter how many times she stood before him, the Major always made her feel nervous.

"Sir, it's s-something Jack said last night," she stammered. It's been preying on my mind all afternoon. I should have spoken sooner, but because I was busy helping Mr Boyle with some additional tasks it slipped my memory."

"Jack! What has that young scoundrel got to do with anything?"

"Sir, with respect, he's not a scoundrel."

"And how would you know what he is?"

Tilly reddened, picked her thumbnails, but stood her ground. "Because he's my young man, Sir, and I'd have nowt to do with a scoundrel."

"Well, I'll have to take your word for that."

"Sir, with respect…"

"Get on with it, girl, I haven't got all day," he said as he checked his wristwatch again before picking up a stack of papers and banging them down hard on the desk.

"Sir, Jack told me to warn the mistress to be careful when she was out on the estate."

"Careful?" queried Hereward with quiet alacrity.

"Yes, Sir. He said the farmer's wife happened to mention she'd seen a scruffy man in army-style clothes hanging around the farm. Said he had the look of the barn about him. She also said her husband suspected he was the same person sleeping rough in one of the byres now and again. She said there's something odd about his behaviour and she doesn't like the look of him one bit."

For exactly four seconds Hereward stared at Tilly, then he sprang from his chair and ran like he had never run before.

Chapter 86

His face expressionless as a bear's, his eyes trained on his quarry, Parker inhaled the irriguous air. He could detect a tinge of her refined fragrance in the atmosphere. Using his fingers, he scraped his long, matted beard. Rough as the husk of a dry coconut, it fanned his upper chest, neck and chin. Pulling in his neck, he looked down at his old battered boots; boots so decrepit, their fronts turned up like the toes on a pair of Turkish slippers. Plus, whenever they got wet, they squeaked like mouse pinkies in a tin pail.

Since bare feet made less noise, Parker removed his boots. The sprung odours sailed into the air and wafted through his nasal passages. Long immune to his own personal pong, he remained unaffected and unperturbed.

It was plain to see his fetish was nervous and on edge as she made her way home. Home to her neglectful, uncaring spouse. Puffing out his cheeks in frank disapproval, Parker thought Major Aldwen stupid for permitting his wife to wander the estate unaccompanied. All alone in the wilds, with no-one to watch over her or spring to her defence, a woman like her became fair game. Should something happen to her, the Major had no-one but himself to blame. A woman's place was in the home, safe and sound, not roaming the countryside like some homeless cur. Speaking of which, he felt like a starving mongrel staring at a beefsteak in the butcher's window as he measured her up like a piece of fresh, juicy meat. He thought it a shame her inner seal had already been split. Presumably by her husband. He would have relished the privilege of being the first.

In his anticipatory state of excitement, Parker detached the head of a daisy from its stem and began absently tearing apart its tiny petals. A hot spark shot through his lower torso as his deprived appendage dilated. He ran his thick tongue over his lips as his eyes burned with a yearning for that long denied him. He liked what he saw. Liked everything about her. She was special. Too special to pass up the perfect opportunity. After all, he persuaded himself, impervious to all possible repercussions, woman was put on earth for man's pleasure and to service his needs. The Major was a lucky man. And he was about to be a lucky man too.

Chapter 87

In the vast space of the estate even a shrew sounds like an elephant when it rustles the leaves, Isabella reminded herself. And pine cones and acorns and other fruits make a resounding thud when they fall from the tree. All the same, she found the atmosphere inauspicious and charged with negative energy. To her myopic eyes everything in the distance appeared blurred, indistinct, out of focus. Small trees and saplings resembled freakish figures, boulders and low bushes crouching forms, fortifying her sense of insecurity and uncertainty. At that moment she recalled the pale eyes in the neanderthal face staring at her like some carnivorous monster from its cavernous lair. Racking her brains, she tried to remember where she had seen them before. Perhaps it was at the Friday cattle market in Oakwich.

On seeing Isabella approach, a raven gorging on the gruesome remains of a rabbit emitted a deep croak, became airborne and circled above her. Close by, a small lizard in dire need of cover scurried under a rock, a skittish squirrel swiftly scaled a tree trunk and an unseen bird screeched.

With the shrill, raucous sound ringing in her ears, Isabella visibly quivered as her anxiety level peaked. Drawing in a deep breath through her nose, she forced the dank air into her lungs, then tried valiantly to convince herself her fears were unfounded. But she failed. Miserably.

To take stock of her situation, Isabella took refuge beneath a tall weeping willow with scabby, bulbous growths dotted about its bark. Its long-fringed limbs dangled like pendulous serpents suspended by their tails. As a hush fell again, something light and creepy touched her cheek. With a squeaky shriek, she frantically pawed her face and dispatched a corpulent, thick-legged black spider to the ground.

Fearing more fat-bodied, large-limbed arachnids were about to land on her, Isabella quickly emerged from beneath the tree and continued making her way back to the Hall. In the sickening silence she could hear her heart thumping inside her chest and blood gushing around the inner space of her head. To avoid being crept up on from behind, she turned and began treading backwards, all the while keeping her wide-sprung eyes alert to signs of movement. To help maintain her balance, she kept her arms free from her sides. Moving in reverse, however, she soon discovered, proved to be a painstaking manoeuvre on the unmade path, placing her at risk of tripping up, and hampering her progress.

Meanwhile, darkness continued sneaking up on the land, bruising the sky and further reducing translucence and clarity. Isabella knew it was vital to reach the Hall before nightfall made its final descent. Believing every step took her closer to safety, but unable to see behind her, she stumbled over a depression in the path and twisted her ankle.

Gosh, I've been so utterly stupid, she told herself, hobbling in pain. She sorely regretting not making a run for it when she was still able to. As she turned, still limping on her injured limb, she was overcome by an unspeakable sense of impending peril; as if she were about to stumble into a horror movie at a critical moment. Then a warning voice in her head whispered: Beware: not all silences are the same. Some silences are soothing, others sinister. At that point she could no longer discount the significance of that specific silence. It was the silence that ensues when a predator prowls the forest.

It was then she remembered the sparrowhawk and the hover before the dive.

Chapter 88

The sheer strength, power and determination of a creature craving copulation can never be overstated. As with any ambush situation the element of surprise is crucial. With a deep-throated rumble, he tore through a gap in the hedge like a taunted bull, drove himself into her body and tackled her to the ground.

Although thunderstruck, she grasped the intruder's intention immediately. With a lightning flash a tempest of terror exploded in her head. Thus began Isabella's battle to save herself from one of man's most-brutal and degrading crimes. A battle she instinctively knew she was unequal to. Nevertheless, in a desperate attempt to resist him, she rocked, rolled and twisted, thrashed her limbs, begged him to stop, screamed for help, invoked God's name. All to no avail.

The creature's crushing bulk pinned her to the compacted soil like an elephant's foot on a fawn. Bile burned her throat as his hot, putrid, vomit-inducing breath sopped her face and neck. Blood filled her mouth as her teeth clamped her tongue. Then hope began to die in her breast.

Deranged as a rabid dog, soaked with sweat, lips retracted in a leer, eyes bloodshot and demonic, the rapacious stranger compressed her mouth with his unholy hand, muting her cries for help.

A current of adrenaline cascaded through Isabella's bruised

and abused body, spurring her on to fight. Writhing convulsively beneath him, like a crazed cat she scratched and clawed, scraping her fingernails down the monstrous mad-eyed face. She knew he was too strong for her but bravely she fought on. She would not, could not, must not let him have her. She was not his to have.

Raring to take her, to feel his bulging beast inside her, to shoot his sordid seed up her pubescent slot, he tore off her modest white drawers and removed his hand from her mouth in order to open his fly.

Exhausted, bloodied, battered, lungs fit to burst, her nose and throat clogged with his stench, convinced she was about to die, Isabella seized the last chance to save herself and screamed into the air, hoping beyond hope that someone would hear her plea and not mistake it for the mating cry of a fox.

Fearing help was beyond her, depleted to the point of paralysis, on the verge of accepting her fate, Isabella felt the debaucher's burdensome body lifted off her as if by an invisible hand. Then a familiar voice roaring with rage reached her ears and, besieged by a battery of punches, the attacker crashed back to the ground.

And as the action continued to unfold before her eyes, Isabella scrambled onto her knees with an almighty effort. Never before had she seen Hereward so fired up, so fearsome, so formidable. Witnessing the attack on his wife had detonated inside him a deadly need to avenge the evil atrocity. With his face fixed in fury and his eyes glowing ominously black, he appeared unreal: a preternatural, unassailable, animalistic force of nature. Breathing hard and fast, he squeezed the maniac's neck in his tungsten grip like a big cat's fangs on the throat of an ungulate.

Parker fumbled for the hunting knife in his inside pocket without success. In the interest of self-preservation, realising the tables had turned on him, fearing his lungs would pop, recognising the folly of fighting a superior force, he surrendered.

The moment he felt the depraved deviant go limp Hereward released his grip. Then like a rugby player taking a penalty, he kicked him where it he knew from experience it would cause him the maximum pain.

Writhing in agony, the peccable coward curled up, emitted a groan like that of a wounded buffalo and cupped his detumescent member in his unsanitary hands.

As he sized him up, Hereward suddenly recognised the beast beneath the beard. He could barely believe his eyes. It was Parker. Parker of all people. Then as the Hall's former gardener attempted to rise with the aim of making good his escape, he kicked him back down with a whomp, then placed his foot on his chest.

Fearing what her husband might do next, Isabella cried out in a croak: "Hereward, please, stop now before you kill him!"

Diverted from his merciless campaign by her desperate plea, Hereward turned to look at her. Suddenly, the wind shifted and lifted his hair, putting her in mind of the black-maned lion standing on a mound while surveying its territory. Unlike the barbarian beneath his boot, her husband was without doubt a noble warrior with the soul, heart and courage of the African big cat.

Thereafter Hereward rushed over to his wounded wife, tenderly raised her from the ground, and bore her back to the Hall cradled in his arms.

Parker, meanwhile, crawled a few yards through the grass and collapsed face down.

Chapter 89

"Well, I have to say I'm very much relieved the brute has decided to plead guilty after all," remarked Maud. "Parker. Who would have thought it? But then he always did strike me as being a bit creepy. Had that look about him. Anyhow, I'm sure it must be a load off Isabella's mind. And yours too, my dear."

Agitated, Hereward stood up and walked to the window. It was sunny outside and the front garden was looking its best.

"So am I," he replied, staring at nothing in particular. "I doubt very much she could have coped with attending court. Can you imagine having to look at that demon in the dock and being reminded of what he'd done?"

Maud grimaced at the image it brought to her mind.

"Nowadays it's impossible to persuade her to leave the house," said Hereward. "The trauma's still fresh in her mind. She's on the mend physically. The evil ape broke three of her ribs. But the psychological effects will take much longer to heal, I've been advised."

"That's only to be expected," said Maud sympathetically. "It must have been absolutely terrifying for her, poor child. That kind of experience is bound to have a lasting effect on even the most resilient amongst us. Thank the Lord you got there in time," she added with a shudder. "The alternative doesn't bear thinking about."

Still burning inside with rage, Hereward turned and paced the room clenching and unclenching his fists. Then he sat on the sofa with a deep sigh and stared out at the sky.

"I can't bear to think of what might have happened had Tilly not warned me in time. He could easily have killed Isabella. Then I would most definitely have killed him," said Hereward, his voice cracking. "The beast's a cesspit. Smells like one too. I recall Boyle complaining about Parker's body odour. Said it became unbearable when he was due to pay his annual visit to the bathhouse. I wasn't too bothered provided he remained outside and his work was satisfactory. I don't know why he allowed himself to get into such a disgusting state."

"Nor do I," agreed Maud.

"I think he lost all motivation after his poor mother died. He was devoted to her apparently. Still, there was nothing to stop him filling a tin tub with a few buckets of boiling water and giving himself a good old scrub in front of the fire. It's not as though there's a shortage of firewood around the place."

Maud grimaced at the mental image of Parker scrubbing himself in an old tin bathtub.

"In India even the poor take a bucket bath every morning," Hereward said after a lapse in the conversation. "I tried it myself. It's not difficult. A bit inconvenient perhaps. Anyhow, the doctor's diagnosed Isabella with agoraphobia," he revealed.

"That's understandable," said Maud, giving him a sympathetic look.

"He thinks it's a temporary reaction to shock, but it can develop into a chronic condition requiring long-term treatment. She's going to need heaps of support. I'm praying she makes a full recovery. The doctor's advised lots of patience and encouragement. Said to take things a day at a time. Small steps, as they say. Allow her to build up her confidence gradually."

"She's strong. I'm sure she'll be fine given time. I'll do whatever I can to help, of course," volunteered Maud.

Hereward stood up, returned to the window, looked out at the bright-blue sky and shook his head. But as he tried to speak, a sob caught in his throat. After which he stood silent for several moments while he struggled with his emotions.

"Look, it's a beautiful day outside and Isabella's cooped up inside the Hall. She even refuses to step into the garden unless I'm there to accompany her. And then she holds onto me as though she's standing at the edge of a precipice. I suggested replacing the hedge around the garden with a wall to make her feel safer. It's my understanding that agoraphobics prefer walls to open spaces. But she rejected the idea out of hand. Said it would be even harder to see what was on the other side. It hurts when I recall how confident she was before Parker attacked her. She loved roaming the estate and she's been robbed of the pleasure. If it were up to me, I'd have the coward castrated. You know, I seriously regret not dashing out his brains."

"That would have been a foolish act of self-destruction, my dear. Why subject yourself to a possible manslaughter charge? Or worse, murder. Furthermore, that would have trebled Isabella's trauma when she needs every ounce of your love and support."

"My wife doesn't love me," said Hereward bitterly, "and would be perfectly happy without me, I'm sure. I knew that when I married her, but I hoped she would come to love me in time."

"It's plain to see the girl's awfully fond of you. Be patient, my dear."

"There's a huge difference between love and fondness, Maud, as well you know. I was fond of the horses, but I wouldn't go so far as to say I loved them."

"You've barely been married five minutes," said Maud.

"Isabella did tell me she couldn't have coped had you been imprisoned. Or worse. When she saw you thrashing the hell out of that monster, she feared you would end up on a murder charge. That's why she screamed at you to stop. It wasn't for his sake, but for yours, and hers. Can't you see she cares for you?"

Hereward said nothing.

"Human wickedness never fails to shock," Maud went on. Especially when it hurts the people we love. And who would have believed Rosalyn had a hand in it too? Well, they do say hell hath no fury like a woman scorned. If I'm honest, I never did like her. She's an insult to womanhood. A betrayer of her own sex. You know, she used to invite herself here and drop huge hints about marriage to you. I had the distinct impression she expected me to pressurise you into legitimising your relationship. She even hinted she would do me the honour of making me a bridesmaid. At my age indeed. Said it in such a way as though I should be grateful. I told her I wasn't partial to carrots. She never mentioned marriage again after that, not to me anyway, thank goodness."

"For a while I stupidly took her allegations about Isabella having an affair to heart, admitted Hereward. "I'm glad you reassured me on that score when I confided in you. What was I thinking? You were quite right to reprimand me for allowing Rosalyn to poison my mind. I have to admit I've felt remorseful ever since."

"She's back in India now, or so I hear, presumably on another quest to find some poor unsuspecting chap foolish enough to get involved with her. Heaven, help him, whoever he is. And Barbara's gone to God knows where. Without a reference she's finished in service. I suspect she was also responsible for damaging Isabella's snowman and removing its scarf, although we'll never know. I didn't see the act's significance at the time. Well, I had no reason to.

"I forgot to mention, a few weeks ago Barbara's mother turned up unannounced at the Hall to apologise for her daughter's behaviour. Boyle was about to send her away but, in the end, I decided to hear what she had to say. She explained Rosalyn had exploited the girl's gullibility. Promised she would become her lady's maid on a permanent basis as soon as Isabella was deported to the land of the disgraced divorcee. I told the poor woman that although it explained her daughter's behaviour, it most certainly didn't excuse it, thanked her for her apology and sent her on her way. Barbara bore Isabella a grudge because she preferred Tilly as her personal maid. According to Boyle, she works long days in some giant factory now. I hear that it's hard graft, gruelling and repetitive, and there's no free food, gallons of hot water, and warm, comfortable accommodation provided."

"At least Boyle's had his wings clipped," said Maud.

"Indeed, he has," confirmed Hereward. "Although I do believe for all his faults he was genuinely upset when he saw the state of Isabella after the attack on her. The first thing he did was to grab a blanket to protect her dignity. And he's been fussing over her ever since. Making sure all her favourite dishes are on the menu. Strange, isn't it? The other day I even saw her smile at him. No, I can't fault him. He's been a huge support."

"Well, that's one less problem, I'm sure."

"You know if I'd taught her to drive, which was all she asked, she might have spent less time wandering the woods and would probably have been elsewhere on the day Parker was prowling the estate. If I'd spent more time taking an interest in her and less time admonishing her for trying to entertain herself..."

"Too many ifs and buts, my dear," Maud interjected. "I expect it would still have happened, except on a different day.

So, you mustn't go blaming yourself. In an ideal world a woman would be free to go where she pleases without fear of assault. The reality I'm afraid to say is somewhat different."

"In an ideal world, yes," agreed Hereward with a heavy sigh. "Isabella was naïve. Imprudence prevailed over reason. She has admitted to ignoring her gut feelings. Blamed her suspicions on her state of mind. She truly believed she was suffering from some sort of psychosis. After reading an old book on psychiatry she unearthed, she diagnosed herself as suffering from some kind of delusional state. Plus, being town-raised and unacquainted with the pitfalls of country life, and its relative remoteness, placed her at a distinct disadvantage."

"Do you think Rosalyn secretly hoped Parker would be tempted by Isabella's beauty? You know, find her irresistible? Be unable to control himself, if you take my point. She must have known he was an odd character and that she was putting Isabella at risk by employing him to spy on her."

"I have often wondered about that myself. As you know, after questioning him, the police learned that Parker became obsessed with Isabella after being paid to track her. Rosalyn managed somehow to convince herself that she was having an affair based on some dubious information she had overheard. So, she engaged him to gather the evidence on her behalf. The idea being that once I knew, I would throw Isabella out and demand a divorce, paving the way for Rosalyn's rapid return.

"Apparently, he carved an effigy of her which he keeps with him like some sort of comfort doll. At one point during his interrogation, he accused Isabella of leading him on. He said she used to sashay and sway her hips when she passed by him on the path. Gave him the come-on with her eyes as she walked into the woods as an invitation to follow her. He also said she knew he was watching her and played up to him. As if she would."

"Unbelievable."

"Yes, I know. To imply she was immoral, he also accused her of meeting a blond lad in the woods. The blond lad of course being Jack. Except Jack was already courting Tilly by then, not meeting Isabella as was claimed. In fact, it was Isabella who introduced them when Tilly served him refreshments one day. And it was Jack who told Tilly to warn Isabella. Therefore, I'm forever grateful to him.

"Nobody would believe Parker's despicable slurs," scoffed Maud, appalled. "The man's a louse on the scalp of the earth. You know I wouldn't be surprised if Isabella's not his only victim. He's probably been at it for years. Many women don't bother to report sexual assaults, especially working-class women. Mostly because they know they'll be accused of being whores and sluts, women of easy virtue. Can you imagine having to endure being interrogated by some sceptical detective when you've already been through hell? Hence men like Parker continue to abuse women with impunity. What's more, the obligation to relive the ordeal in court must be a major deterrent to those seeking justice. And to compound it all, there are women like Rosalyn who care nothing about the oppression of their own sex. In fact, they're agents of it."

"Rosalyn once stood beside me in the mirror," revealed Hereward. "As you know, she's distinctly tall. She said we made the perfect pair — like two bookends. Bookends indeed, I said to myself. Yes, with a great big gap in between."

Maud shook her head. "We can't say for certain if she hoped Parker would attack Isabella. But she must have known she was running the risk. It wouldn't surprise me at all. I mean she must have realised there was a good chance a beautiful and vulnerable young woman wandering the woods alone would tempt a depraved goat like him, who I assume has to pay for his pleasures. As I said, when he worked at the Hall, he always struck me as being perverted. His eyes lingered on certain parts, if you take my meaning. It made me feel rather uncomfortable. I know Jenkins couldn't bear to have him anywhere near her, although she never explained why. Perhaps it was down to some kind of feminine intuition. But I never imagined he was capable of perpetrating such an atrocity. Perhaps Rosalyn truly hoped he would. As she saw it, that way you would no longer want to touch your wife because he had soiled her. Still, we can analyse the situation till the cows come home, but we'll never know for certain what was in her twisted mind."

"I expect not," he concurred. "Anyway, Rosalyn's gone now, good riddance, and let's hope she never returns. I shan't ever forget she tried to destroy my marriage."

"Well, she failed, fortunately."

"You know," said Hereward, going off at a tangent, "I knew Isabella was mine the second I set eyes on her at the summer parade. Some things are just meant to be. What's the word? Oh yes, preordained. The way everything just fell into place. Obviously, the Acton's unfortunate circumstances helped. Had Archibald Acton not been in dire straits, I'm not sure he would have so readily agreed to my proposition. But I've no regrets. And even had I not met Isabella, there's no way on earth I would have married Rosalyn. You can be sure of that."

"You're definitely a man who knows his own mind," said Maud with a smile.

Hereward stood up and straightened his tie. "I must be getting back. I don't like leaving Isabella for too long. Martha's with her at the moment. She visits once a week, which is a great help. My mother-in-law came once. Can you believe she called Isabella a foolish girl? Said she'd been stupid to wander the estate on her own. Said men succumb to their weaknesses far too easily and therefore it's incumbent on women not to put temptation their way. I was sorely tempted to tell her to get out.

I have to say she's rather a cold fish. Stayed overnight unfortunately, so we had to suffer her at dinner. Archibald hasn't been near, thank goodness. Can't abide the devil."

"That kind of attitude is all too typical of Agatha Acton's generation, I regret to say," said Maud. "Women should be free to go where they please without fear of harm."

"Quite so. Anyway, I've promised to teach Isabella to drive when she's ready," revealed Hereward. "I intend to teach her to shoot too, although we shan't be using live rabbits and her favourite pheasants for practice. I can set up a target in the garden. I must tell you that once Jenkins served pheasant for dinner and Isabella downright refused to eat it. I told her there's no room for sentimentality in the countryside and she should acquaint herself with the reality of rural life. But she wouldn't have it. You know how stubborn she can be sometimes. Anyway, I digress. When she's ready to go walking again she can take a pistol with her."

Maud sighed. "It's regrettable how women are forced to live under such constraints, but then on balance one must remember such incidents are indeed rare. Most men are decent types. Isabella was unlucky. Had Rosalyn not hired Parker it would never have happened and Isabella mustn't allow it to ruin her life or dictate her behaviour."

"Well, we'll have to see how things pan out."

As he was about to leave, Hereward hesitated in the doorway. "You know I haven't visited Isabella's bedroom since the attack. I've decided to wait until she's ready. After much reflection, I've come to believe a woman is entitled to have complete autonomy over her own body, even in marriage. I don't give a damn what the law says, or the Church."

Wholeheartedly, Maud agreed. Pleased her brother's conscience had been pricked at last.

By the time Hereward arrived back at the Hall Martha had

left and Isabella was alone in the sitting room staring into space, a languid look on her face.

"How was your afternoon?" he said bending down to give her a customary kiss on the cheek.

"Fine, thank you," she replied, flinching ever so slightly.

She looked down in the dumps and dispirited. Her unbrushed hair hung loose, there was a small tea stain on her blouse, and her over-scrubbed skin looked pale from lack of sunshine and fresh air.

"I thought we might take a short ride out tomorrow on our bicycles," said Hereward. "Or in the motorcar if you prefer. It's a shame not to take full advantage of this wonderful weather, assuming it lasts. If you're not happy, we can easily turn back. Let's at least give it a try and see how you get on. Make it a challenge. You used to enjoy a challenge. Mostly challenging me, as I recall. You'll be perfectly safe, I promise. Naturally, I'm not going to force you to do something you find uncomfortable or distressing."

"We'll see," she said barely above a whisper. "Tomorrow's another day."

"Just promise me one thing," he said with a wicked grin.

"Yes, what's that?"

"If, as I've suggested, you allow me to teach you to fire a gun, and since I have no wish to hasten my demise, you must promise not to turn it on me when you're having one of your strops."

For the first time since the attack, Isabella smiled on the brink of a laugh.

Epilogue

A wood owl hooted from on top of one of the Hall's chimney pots. Ever fearful, Isabella trembled, unaware the bird was not considered a bad omen in rural parts. She removed her slippers, folded back the bedclothes and climbed into bed in her lovely new bedroom. It was a splendid space full of luxurious furnishings. The big comfortable mattress was new too, and happily Rosalyn Dumbarton's sapid malodour had never pervaded its depths. Fit for a princess, Hereward said of the room, with whose assistance she had chosen the silk wallpaper embellished with pink fuchsias on a dark-navy background, the sumptuous damask fabrics and the ivory thick-pile carpet. Having her bedroom adjoining his made her feel a whole lot safer too.

After reading for a while Isabella's eyes grew heavy. Putting aside her book, she switched off the lamp, slid down under the covers and closed her eyes. Then for the umpteenth time she told herself to put the horrific incident behind her. It was over. And she reminded herself she had suffered no lasting harm, at least not physically.

Aside from coming to her rescue in the nick of time, Hereward had been an absolute brick since the attack: sensitive, supportive and infinitely patient with her. An altogether different man from the one she thought she had married. She had seen him at his most lethal and most loving.

In his presence, she felt protected, confident no evil fiend would ever dare to assail her.

The memory arose in Isabella's mind of the first time she set eyes on Hereward. It was in the Aldwen orchard, from where she had launched her shameful attack on his unsuspecting back. She hadn't known his name then, but correctly assumed he was from the Hall. It was impossible to forget his face bloated with anger, the surprising speed of his recovery, his steely determination to catch her, and the aftermath of his success. Had she known then he was her future husband, she would have fainted with fright.

Now he no longer visited her bed, Isabella missed him. She ached for his strong physical presence and his loving caresses beneath the bedcovers. She missed their sleepy postcoital conversations before he returned to his room. She longed to tell him how much she craved his company at bedtimes, but lacked the courage and, still being shy with him, struggled to express her needs. Worst of all, she feared he no longer desired her because he considered her despoiled by Parker's pernicious paws.

As Isabella began to doze, slipping into another fitful sleep haunted by nightmares and disturbing dreams, a sudden sound jolted her upright. Wide awake, she sat motionless in the darkness and attempted to attune her ears to the nocturnal dimension. Upon hearing the shrub outside the window below her bedroom rustle a couple of times, she thought of Parker and began to panic. Suddenly, a reel of terrifying images unrolled across the screen inside her head as multiple questions arose in her mind: had Parker escaped from prison? Had he broken into the Hall? Was he about to sneak into her bedroom? Carry her off in the night to claim that denied him? Was Hereward already deep asleep and dead to the world? If only she had something with which to defend herself. Frantic with fright, she tried to figure out the best place to hide, but couldn't decide on under the bed or inside the wardrobe.

No longer able to contain herself, Isabella flicked the light switch, leapt out of bed, flew across the floor, and burst like an overinflated balloon into her husband's bedroom through the communicating door. Then in sudden confusion, she halted and stared at his empty bed. At the same time, she observed on the carved oak bedside cabinet a copy of *The Rubaiyat of Omar Khayyam*, a black-leather tasselled strap peeping out from between its pages. Slowly, she looked around, then started. Hereward was standing in front of the fire looking surprised to see her. Barefooted and tousle haired, his pyjama bottoms hanging loose just below his navel, he appeared poised and imperturbable, as if equipped for all eventualities.

"What is it, my love?" he said, his facial expression showing concern. "You're shaking. Come here and tell me what troubles you."

Forgetting the recent outside disturbance, Isabella stared at the man in her midst with awe, as if seeing him for the very first time. In her heightened state, the way he looked down at her felt almost intimidating. He seemed taller, broader, more muscular, and more powerful than ever before. Standing tall, stately and picturesque, his torso tight and erect, his thighs hard and thickset, he was a classical Italian sculpture brought to life. She found his spicy primal aroma, dark gleaming eyes and grave dignity intensely arousing. So much so, that her face glowed like a golden aureole.

And then it happened. As if a sudden spark had ignited inside her. The precise moment Isabella knew without a doubt she was madly, wildly and passionately in love with her husband.

For a short period neither moved nor spoke. Unblinking, they beheld each other at length, their bold, beautiful eyes locked in mutual magnetism, glistening like dew drops on the summer grass.

Isabella, her body enfolded in the generous flounces of her nightgown, her lips curved in a sultry smile, stole forward with tentative steps. Still gazing into his eyes, she reached up, caressed Hereward's cheek, then walked her soft pink finger pads down his steel-hard sternum and toyed with the tiny tufts of hair that ran a trail down his torso. Standing on tiptoes, she kissed him full on the mouth for the very first time; a long lingering kiss with lips moist, plump and tumescent. Drawing back from him a little, she gently touched the tiny scar on his upper lip before planting a small kiss there.

After pulling her towards him, Hereward pressed himself hard against Isabella's breasts. Then he released her, hoisted her into his arms, carried her like a virgin bride to his kingly bed, and laid her down gently on the soft eiderdown. To his delight, she raised no objection when he stripped off her nightdress and gazed with edacious desire at her unadorned loveliness. Then he kissed her brow, her eyelids, her nose, her lips, her throat, continuing all the way down to her toes. Intoxicated by her seductive intimate scent, he caressed and fondled every inch of her celestial flesh. Sensing his passion might overspill at any moment, he discarded his pyjama bottoms, eased apart her thighs and slipped expertly inside her.

Driven wild by the intense and subtle sensations he excited in her, every nerve fibre quivering on her skin, Isabella threw back her head, arched her spine, curled her toes, and abandoned herself to utter unashamed bliss.

And finally, as the moon rose high in the sky above the Hall and a star burst in some distant galaxy, Isabella and Hereward reached the zenith of their perfect confluence safe in the knowledge that this was only the beginning.

Printed in Great Britain
by Amazon